The Unseen Force

BOOK TWO OF THE *SISTERS OF CHAOS* TRILOGY

CATHERINE FITZSIMMONS

Milton, Ontario
http://www.brain-lag.com/

Brain Lag Publishing
Milton, Ontario
http://www.brain-lag.com/

Cover artwork by Catherine Fitzsimmons

ISBN: 978-1-928011-33-0

Library and Archives Canada Cataloguing in Publication

Title: The unseen force / Catherine Fitzsimmons.
Names: Fitzsimmons, Catherine, 1981- author.
Description: Series statement: Book two of the Sisters of chaos trilogy
Identifiers: Canadiana (print) 20200187589 | Canadiana (ebook) 20200187597 | ISBN 9781928011330
  (softcover) | ISBN 9781928011347 (EPUB)
Classification: LCC PS8611.I8973 U57 2020 | DDC C813/.6—dc23

The Sisters of Chaos trilogy

Enduring Chaos
The Unseen Force
Elderra's Champion (forthcoming)

Other tales from Elderra

Ruins of Change
by J. R. Dwornik

Also by Catherine Fitzsimmons

Aurius
Halcyon
A Jewel on Sapphire

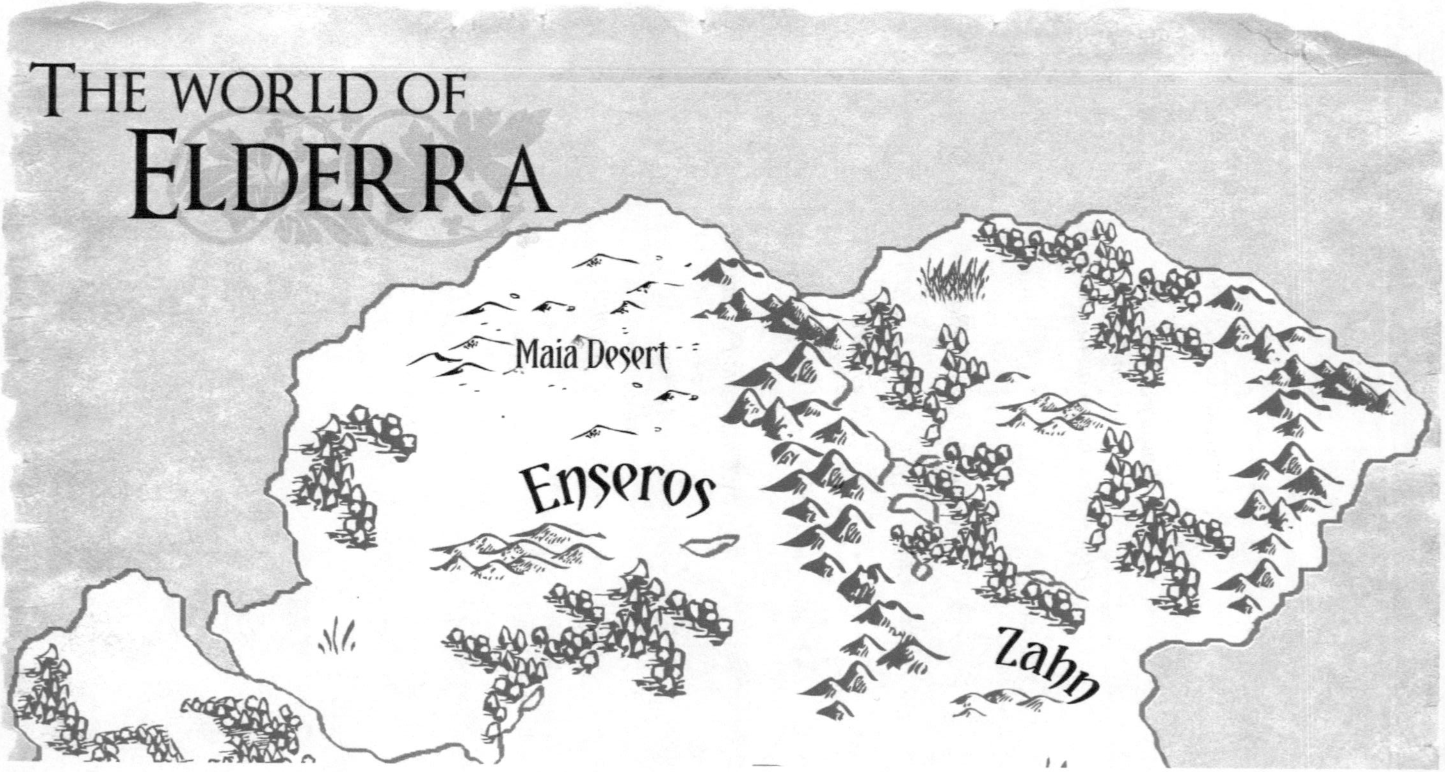

THE WORLD OF ELDERRA

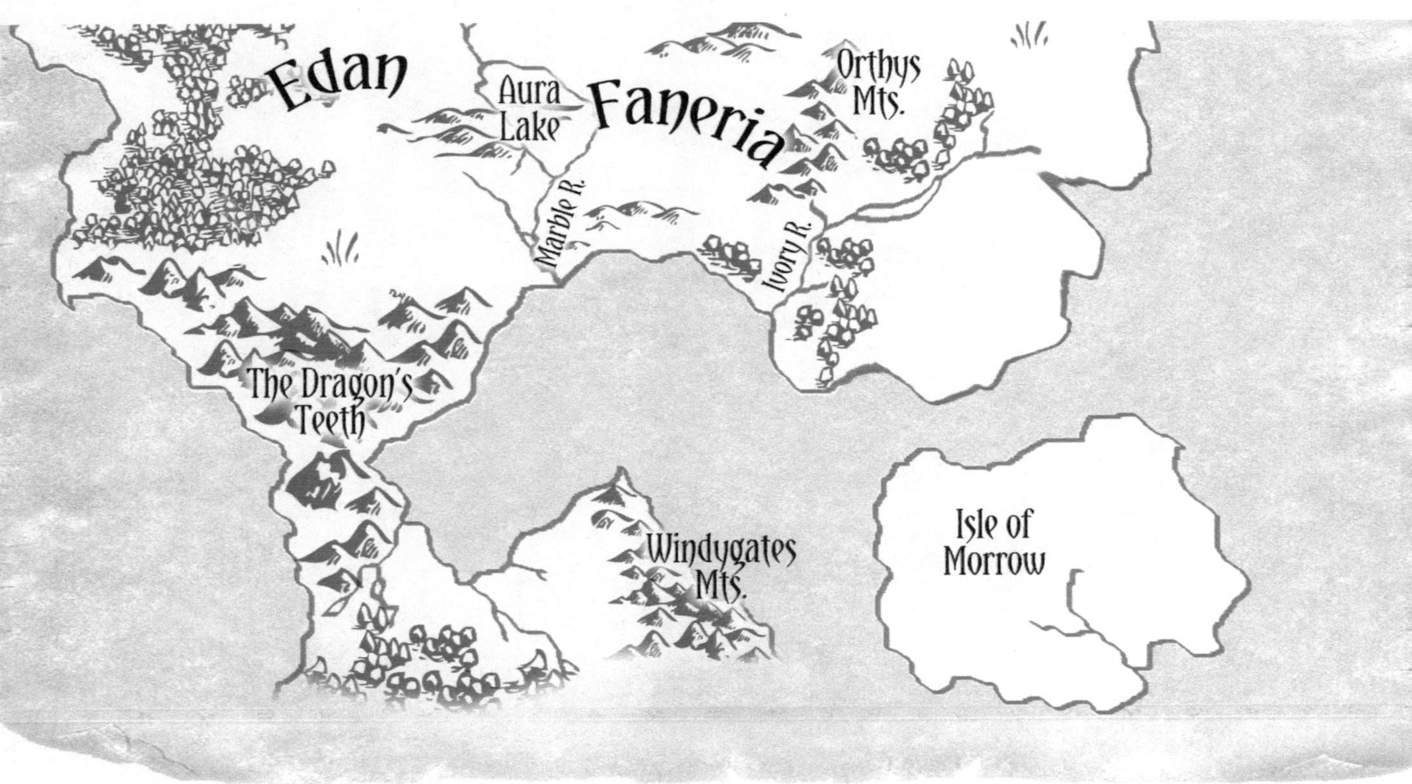

Edan
Faneria
Aura Lake
Marble R.
Ivory R.
Orthys Mts.
The Dragon's Teeth
Windygates Mts.
Isle of Morrow

CHAPTER 1
ECHOES

REDGE AWOKE TO the room lit by the glow of sunlight against the drapes, during that short period of the year when the sun rose before he did. He sat on the edge of the bed and rubbed his face, the stone floor cool against his feet. His wide room was silent, the thick walls of the tower muffling all sound.

Redge rose from the bed, gently so as not to disturb his wife. He scratched at his close-trimmed beard and ran a hand through his medium length dirty blond hair, seeing silver from the corner of his eye. Slipping on his boots, he strolled to the window and pulled back the drapes.

A private training yard lay four stories below, secluded from the rest of the castle. Half a dozen men sparred or ran through their exercises in the shadows of the walls surrounding the yard. Most of them wore battered training armour or coats of mail. Only one, standing apart from the others as he followed the trainer's drills, wore his full suit of armour. Like the rest of the men, he wore no helmet. Redge didn't need to see the glint of red in the man's hair to know it was Sir Magni.

In a far corner, a handful of women tended their small garden while children ran about playing nearby or watching the knights at their drills. Seemingly happy, despite that this was the only glimpse of the outside world they ever saw. Redge's face fell and he let out a sigh.

He turned from the window to take in the stand in the corner holding his own suit of armour. Meticulously polished, intricately detailed, stylized like all Agaesi armour into modern blacksmiths' imitation of dragon scales, his standard suit of plate was finer than most knights' parade armour. And long unused, from the layer of dust on the neck and base of the stand.

Redge crossed the room, but left the plate where it hung, donning only a long mail tunic and strapping an arming sword over it.

Opening the door to the common room of his suite, he found his own children up and playing as well. Most of them, anyway. He bid good morning to the boys and younger girl, but his eyes remained on the closed door to his eldest daughter's room.

Redge continued out of his suite. The corridor outside, like all the floors in this secluded tower, was narrow and unadorned, barely wider than his spread arms. Unlike the other floors, the door to Redge's suite was the only one along this hall before it turned a corner. Turning away from the bend in the hall, he moved to the spiral stairs along the inner wall and climbed down.

He stepped off the stairs on the second floor and crossed the mostly empty dining hall. Only a handful of women, children, and elders ate at the long tables. Redge greeted them as he passed and continued toward the far side of the tower, exiting onto the stairs leading down to the training yard.

Until the sun rose over the wall surrounding the yard, Redge supervised the training and ran through his own drills. His aging body protested the exercise at first, but his movements swiftly eased and grew faster as the power of Agasis coursed through his body. The ancient dragon's strength filled Redge's muscles and seemed to lift his own weight away. He wasn't quite as fast, nor could he last quite as long, as in his prime, but his abilities were still greater than an ordinary knight half his age.

The mail pressed heavily against him and he was drenched in sweat by the time he finished. His assistant Brannik waited near the stairs, holding a handful of folded cloth.

Redge smiled at the young, thin, pale boy as he dried himself off. Redge tried to ignore the guilt that rose as his thoughts turned again to his daughter.

I can give Brannik something better for his life, Redge thought, *but even as the captain of the Agaesi, I can do nothing for my own daughters.* He moved behind a screen to change into clean clothes.

"Anything new this morning, Brannik?" Redge asked, fully expecting the answer to be the same as every day. Correspondence about requisitions, maintenance of weapons and armour, updates on the whereabouts of the few Agaesi knights on assignments, general news and gossip in the province and the kingdom.

"Actually, Sir," Brannik said, the wheeze in his breath a little softer in summer, "there was a note from the duke this morning requesting your presence."

Redge paused as he pulled his trousers up. "What?"

"It's for later this morning, Sir. That's all it says."

Frowning, Redge hurried to finish dressing and handed off the sweaty garments and mail to Brannik. Redge ate swiftly and retreated to his office on the ground floor to address what correspondence he could, but his thoughts were on the summons from the duke.

When the time came and he crossed the castle to a drawing room, however, he found several others waiting inside the room as well. Other nobles and high-ranking knights, field marshals for Hesperia's large standing army, had also been summoned, though the curious and concerned looks on their faces told Redge that they knew no more than he did about this meeting.

The Duke of Hesperia turned to acknowledge Redge's entrance. Osmarus Valikov was broad of shoulder, chest, and girth, a bear of a man who commanded, rather than demanded, attention. His curly, dark hair was pulled back from a widow's peak and tied at the nape of his neck, and his thick, full beard, without a moustache, tumbled over his chest.

"My Lord Duke," Redge said as he bowed.

"Sir Warwick," the duke's booming voice replied. "Please come in. We are waiting on just a few others."

Redge nodded as he crossed the room to stand among the others gathered. Two more people soon arrived and the duke stepped forward to address them, everyone falling silent.

"Thank you all for coming on such short notice. I know how quickly stories travel, so I wanted to brief each of you personally on this newest development as soon as possible.

"I assume you have all heard the rumours about an army gathering in Edan."

Murmurs of assent rippled among those gathered. Redge nodded along with a few others. He was uncertain how to feel about a meeting regarding the so-called Army of Light in the kingdom to the west.

The duke reached into his coat and pulled out a folded letter. "I gathered you all here to tell you that those rumours have been confirmed."

A flurry of murmurs, surprised looks, and shuffling rose.

"I received this message last night from a trusted source."

"Spies?" asked one of the others.

"Allies," the duke answered. "Friends of Faneria who wrote to inform us that the King of Edan has announced his joining forces with the malakh Niabi."

Greater murmuring rippled as some turned to speak to others. Redge frowned. He perhaps knew more than many in the room about Niabi, the malakh, servant of the Gods of Light, who was responsible for no small amount of damage done during the Battle of Albrith several weeks ago. His personal beliefs aside, Redge didn't like the idea of her gathering an army in Edan, or of their king joining her.

"What does this mean for us?" another knight asked.

"For now, nothing," the duke replied. "But we must all be watchful of what transpires from this alliance."

"Is it true, then," said someone else, "that their goal is to convert unbelievers and snuff out all trace of the old gods?"

"The king has not officially claimed her supposed cause as Edan's," the duke said.

"Then why join with her?"

"He had to," answered another of the nobles. "The stories say one in every five men within fifty leagues of Brighton has joined the Army of Light. Their king's position is still tenuous. If he did not officially join with her, he would quickly lose power."

"But why?" pressed another. "Why assemble an army so large if not for a specific campaign? What is that malakh planning to do?"

"I've heard that she's already moved south to recruit more men," said one. "Mark my words, we'll be their next target."

"That," the duke said before anyone else could respond, "remains unconfirmed. Speculate outside this room, gentlemen." He held up the letter. "We are here to discuss facts." With that, he tossed the letter onto a table before him. Redge moved forward to read the letter as the others continued discussing the news. The note said little more than the duke did, and only mentioned Niabi as she related to the King of Edan.

"What do you require of us?" Redge asked.

"Keep your eyes and ears open for any news on this front," the duke answered. "Nothing else has been confirmed at this point, but I think that some of you are right that this could prove troublesome for us. I have a strong feeling this will not be the last we hear of the Army of Light."

*   *   *

The ballroom was a sea of brocade and lace that reflected upon the polished marble floor. Sunlight gleamed through the high windows and glinted off gold, silver, and gemstones adorning the soft-spoken crowd that filled the room. Elaborate gilded chandeliers hung high overhead, set with perfectly even candles that remained unlit, daylight filling the room on the long summer day. The tender notes of a harp issued from the gallery as the aromas of fruit and flaky pastries rose from the tables along one wall.

Garrick took it all in at a glance as he stepped through the door. Half a year ago, this sight had been a beacon of hope to him, but now, all he wanted to do was turn around and leave.

Funny, he couldn't help thinking with a sardonic grin, *after going out in the dirt and hard labour of the real world, these silks and jewels have lost their lustre.*

He had, however, cultivated his reputation here too much before he had left Misengrad to abandon it entirely. There were already enough whispers circling about his extended absence from court. His excuses ran dry, and if he hadn't come, he would have to address those rumours. These lords and ladies wouldn't appreciate him admitting he'd rather spend his time with brewers and cobblers.

Arriving fashionably late, he and the resplendent middle-aged woman on his arm managed to avoid overt attention as they entered the hall. Garrick's brown hair, slightly curled and with a hint of red in the light, was tied back in a tail that fell between his shoulder blades. His embroidered coat was perfectly tailored to hint at the chiseled muscles beneath, while outwardly displaying only grace and poise. As usual, he was one of few knights of high enough standing to attend this ball. As always, he was the only Agaesi.

Catching movement from the corner of his eye, he turned to the woman whose arm was linked in his. Lady Estrina Valikov smiled at him. Dressed in scarlet, the fainter details of her fine gown seemed only to make her stand out more. Rather than hiding the lines in her face and grey in her immaculate dark hair, it complemented them, giving her a radiant, mature beauty.

The smile she gave him seemed perfectly benign, but he knew her well enough to see the hints of something else in her eyes. Equal parts confidence and caution.

He smiled his assurance and approached a knot of nobles congregating near the dance floor. They were deep in conversation.

A woman with elaborately coiffed white hair, but standing with back straight and eyes sharp, spoke with an air of disdain. "Those Albrithites so love their stories, it sounds the more outrageous with each telling. I still refuse to believe that a malakh was seen after so many years and centuries, let alone a god." With a sigh, her features smoothed. "Though the scars from the attack were clear. Much of the rubble had been cleared away, but the damage… well, let me say that I have given thanks each night since that those villains did not decide to unleash their wrath closer to home."

A gentleman of large stature but little hair sneered. "Vile mages." He spoke the word as though a bitter taste filled his mouth.

A young lady shuddered, dark ringlets bouncing over her pale shoulders. "It gives me chills to think of one of the old gods leading an army of mages through Albrith."

Garrick spoke up then. "Would it ease your mind, then, to learn that it was the other way around?"

All eyes turned to him. The young lady and her timid-looking escort straightened and caught their breath, though the white-haired lady and the large gentleman merely inclined their heads in greeting. However, Garrick didn't miss the flicker of interest in the old woman's eyes.

"Lady Estrina Valikov."

"Lady Petrochenko," Lady Estrina replied with a smile and nod, greeting each of the others by name. They smiled, bowed, and greeted her in return.

Lowering a hand, Lady Petrochenko placed it on her hip as she turned to Garrick. "And Sir Magni."

Garrick smiled radiantly, large green eyes glinting. "My Lady, it's a pleasure and an honour to see you again."

Lady Petrochenko stared at him, looking unimpressed, but with curiosity clear in her eyes. "Well, now that you have finally made an appearance at court, perhaps you would care to elaborate."

The gentleman carefully watched Garrick. "Yes, we have all heard that you were pivotal in turning the tide of the Battle of Albrith."

"And you with a Sword of Annas!" the dark-haired young lady said excitedly.

Garrick kept himself from fingering the medallion around his neck. Although the heavy gold chain sat wide around his shoulders and the palm-sized emblem with its embossed swords hung in the middle of his chest, the medal for bravery felt more like a noose, and like the only thing he wore.

"It has certainly taken you long enough to show your face at court again, after disappearing for over a season without telling a soul," Lady Petrochenko added.

Immediately, Garrick wondered if they savoured the suspense, but for once, he hesitated to speak the thought. Instead, he simply said, "I do apologize if I have caused any inconvenience. I was unaware that—"

"Please, Sir Magni," Lady Petrochenko cut across him. Garrick watched her carefully, but the look of annoyance on her face was genuine. "False modesty suits you ill."

That wasn't who I was here, he realized too late. *These people loved the proud and dashing knight, the one whose armour and blade had never been dirtied by battle.*

From the corner of his eye, Garrick saw Lady Estrina turn to him. The look was casual, but the action was full of meaning. A warning. He reflected on her lessons on handling court politics.

Never show any sign of weakness.

"We have been dying to hear your story," the young lady added, cheeks colouring. "You have kept us waiting far too long."

Garrick sent the nobles a sly smile. "Do forgive me, my ladies and gentlemen, but I am sure you must understand that a hero's work is never done."

The young lady tittered and her escort's awe and envy were unmistakable, though the gentleman and Lady Petrochenko each gave Garrick dubious looks. The latter, however, couldn't entirely hide the amusement she obviously tried not to show.

"And what 'hero's duty' has kept you so occupied that it took you weeks to finally appear in the duke's court?" Lady Petrochenko asked.

"Why, the most taxing work of all," Garrick answered with a grin. "Reports. I had to relay the entire story to my captain, the captain of Hesperia's forces, advisors, enquirers, and His Grace himself. A threat of this magnitude demands that all my reports must be made firsthand." He glanced askance at Lady Estrina, her arm still linked in his as she silently listened to the conversation. He smiled at her as he recalled another of her lessons.

Nothing draws more interest than a mystery.

Garrick slid a suggestion that he was hiding something into his voice and lowered his chin faintly as he faced the nobles again. "Scheduling such time alone has been a nightmare."

Lady Petrochenko scoffed as she picked up on the cues, though her smile began to break through. "Fine, keep your secrets. I see that fame and recognition have done nothing to change you into a respectable gentleman."

The young lady giggled. "Oh, but how boring would he be if he were?"

Her escort joined in chuckling along with the ladies. More eyes turned toward them from nearby as other nobles stepped forward.

"Enough about our peculiar dragon knight," said another lord. "You were about to tell us of the battle."

Everyone has their own agenda.

Smiling over his feelings, Garrick told the gathering crowd the tale of the Battle of Albrith. His retellings to his various superiors had all been the same, but he knew the nobles didn't want a dry or even factual account of events. Knowing that he would have to repeat this story several times before the night was over, he forced himself to tell it once again, engaging his audience with appropriate pauses and emphasis and manipulating the events to make him sound more the hero they thought he was.

What he didn't have to embellish was the scale of the damage or the power of the attackers. "I saw it with my own eyes," he said again as a new listener expressed her doubts. "The Goddess of Chaos looked exactly like what depictions remain in the temples, and few others could wield such power as she. And I promise you that she battled a malakh in the streets of Albrith. She was seven feet tall if she was an inch, with the head of a fox, and shining brilliantly from the power bestowed upon her by the Gods of Light."

"Thank the gods for that!" the young lady exclaimed.

Garrick didn't need to ask which gods she was referring to. Even as she believed every word he spoke about the Goddess of Chaos being reborn, to her only the Gods of Light existed. Strength, Justice, Wisdom, Love, and Life. There was no place among these nobles for the old Gods of Time, or any others.

"I fear to imagine what would have happened had that malakh not been there," spoke another new listener.

It took all Garrick's self-control to keep his smile from faltering. Yes, these nobles were not interested in the truth. They didn't want to know that the servant of their deities levelled as many buildings and took as many lives as Nephrita, or that the Goddess of Chaos showed more compassion toward humans than the malakh had, or that the Gods of Light had been the ones to open a chasm that swallowed up a village.

Much as Garrick had believed in the virtues of the Gods of Light, the thought of any devotion to the figures themselves left a bitter taste in his mouth. Fortunately, that was easy to remedy.

The nobles who had so raptly listened to his tale now spoke

excitedly to each other, so none objected when he bowed to the crowd and said, "If you will excuse me, My Lords and Ladies, I have been deprived of the fine work of the duke's kitchen staff for far too long." As several in the crowd waved their approval, he nodded and smiled at Lady Estrina, who had stepped to the edges of the circle as he spoke. "My Lady."

She returned a knowing smile. "Sir Magni."

With that, Garrick slipped away from the crowd and strolled to the velvet-draped tables, laden with overflowing silver dishes, behind the marble pillars ringing the dance floor. Other nobles nodded as he passed, but he made his way uninterrupted. Most of those on this side of the ballroom had heard at least some of his tale.

Garrick had just slipped the last bite of a delicate cinnamon pastry into his mouth when someone spoke beside him, "That was quite the compelling story."

Garrick took in a breath as he recognized the low, powerful voice, but averted any other reaction. Turning, he bowed low. "My Lord Duke."

Osmarus Valikov nodded in greeting. "Sir Magni." He approached the table and picked up a miniature meat pie. "I dare say that tale was far more interesting than the one you told me."

Garrick grinned. "I shall remember that you prefer the dramatic rendition the next time I have to tell you that I saved the kingdom, Your Grace."

The wryness in the duke's smile made it clear that he heard the sarcasm Garrick kept out of his voice. "Indeed. Though I do hope you will not gloss over the contribution of the other heroes of the day, as you did just now. What was the name of that fellow you mentioned who slayed the rebel mage leader?"

"Sir Lyle Hitchcliffe, Your Grace."

The duke nodded thoughtfully. "Yes, that was it. The man who formerly commanded the city guard here. I still have not had the opportunity to meet him."

"A grievous oversight, Your Grace." *Or an intentional evasion,* Garrick added silently. It had been clear from their briefing with the king and his advisors that Sir Hitchcliffe held many secrets and knew far more about what had happened with the rebel mages than he let on. However, despite being trapped on the same ship on the return journey to Misengrad, Garrick had been unable to learn anything from the reticent Lyle. Blunt as the man was, Lyle was very good at avoiding topics he was determined not to discuss.

"One that will be corrected before long." The duke turned toward the outer edges of the ballroom, moving just deliberately enough to make it clear that he wished for Garrick to follow. The duke may not have cared to play the courtly games that his sister excelled at, but he had been raised with the same training to understand them. The subtle concern in his eyes, peppered with distaste, made Garrick realize that was precisely what was on the duke's mind.

Politics at the fore of the duke's thoughts. The rarity of such a discussion alone was enough to make Garrick uncomfortable. For a brief moment, Garrick considered acting as though he had missed the cue and instead wander off into the crowd. Of course, Lady Estrina would have some choice words to say about that idea.

Never alienate the most powerful person in the room.

Without missing a beat, Garrick fell into step beside the duke.

"In truth," the duke continued, "I am more interested in hearing more of what you have to say about Albrith. Factual reports are the more necessary, but I need not speculate that those who deal in rumours must be falling over themselves with glee to discover that the rebel mages marched out of Hesperia."

The duke stopped as he reached the wall, methodically turning his goblet around in his hand as he planted a firm look upon the knight.

"So tell me honestly, Garrick. What is our standing at the king's court?"

This is the only thing I'm good for. The thought crossed Garrick's mind before he became aware of it. He quickly shook that off as he reflected upon the whispers he had picked up on during his brief stay in the king's castle. Whether this was his destiny or not, the duke was looking to him.

"The king is true to you, Your Grace." That much had been clear from the regard the king and queen had shown Garrick, though despite his embellishments, he had contributed little enough to the victory. Garrick lowered his voice, carefully eyeing the crowd nearby for eavesdroppers. "I did not have an opportunity to attend court while I was in Albrith. I only heard some secondhand rumours. I will not pretend that no one wishes to use this against you, Your Grace. However, the impression I received was as fodder to move against the king, rather than against Hesperia." Garrick thought back to the mood in the castle the day and even the hours after the final reports of the battle had been given.

"The wolves are circling," he added, watching the nobles mingling and dancing across the room. "There is instability in the king's court. I think there are some who would go to great lengths to undermine his authority." Garrick returned his gaze to the duke. "His Majesty will need all the allies he can get, Your Grace."

The duke looked sombre. "I see." He let out a breath. "Dark days are coming. I think we shall all be in need of allies. Speaking of which…" The duke turned to look into the ballroom. "How is your mother?"

Garrick followed the duke's eyes. On the dance floor, Lady Estrina swayed gracefully with an older man. A seemingly carefree and uncomplicated smile lit her face. Had Garrick not been raised by her and lived his entire life with her, he would never have suspected any cunning thoughts hid behind that look. He couldn't help smiling as he watched her, completely at home amongst the nobility.

"She is well, Your Grace," Garrick answered.

The duke nodded slowly, his eyes fixed on her. "She always is when she is here." A smile creased his face. "She took to the court like a bird to the sky. Even when we were children, she always knew exactly how to handle people."

Garrick's smile faded slightly as he and his uncle watched Lady Estrina dance.

She could have been queen, Garrick thought, *and instead, she spends her days locked in the Agaesi tower.*

His throat tightened. He couldn't help feeling like a shackle around her leg. The only thing still holding her to her lonely life among the Agaesi.

Garrick was about to excuse himself from the duke's company when he noticed someone walking toward him from the corner of his eye. As he looked at the new figure, some of the tightness in his chest eased and his smile grew warmer.

The Markiese of Gredsk was a square-jawed youth with a shock of flowing ebony hair. Though thinner about the shoulders than the duke, Cedryck Valikov seemed to have filled out in the chest and arms since Garrick last saw him half a year ago. He had also begun growing a beard, dark but still thin.

As he approached, Cedryck spread his arms, covered in a ruby coat that reached his knees. His face split in a broad smile. "Garrick. I was beginning to fear you would never return to court."

"Fighting to save the kingdom takes a lot out of a man, Lord Gredsk," Garrick replied with a wry grin, not bothering to completely hide the sarcasm this time. It was already getting exhausting to maintain the appearance he had so easily worn at court before.

Cedryck rolled his eyes. "Come on, Garrick, we aren't going to start with the titles now, are we?"

Garrick grinned and gestured at the ballroom around them. "We are all under the obligations of social structure, My Lord."

Cedryck matched the look. "Then let us go somewhere they can rot in darkness. It's been too long since I've seen you." Planting a hand on Garrick's shoulder, he strode swiftly along the edge of the ballroom.

Garrick looked over his shoulder as they passed the duke. He bowed his head. "Your Grace, it was an honour, as always."

The duke smiled wryly, watching as Cedryck and Garrick retreated. "Sir Magni. Do not wait so long before returning next time."

Garrick could only smile and nod as Cedryck pulled him out of earshot of the duke. A few heads turned as they passed, but soon, they slipped behind a tapestry and escaped into a narrow, dark corridor hidden behind it. Slinking through the back passages of the castle after Cedryck, the years slipped away and a genuine smile lit Garrick's face. As they emerged into a public hall, he grinned and winked at a servant who started and bowed at their appearance. They continued jogging down the hall toward the entrance to a secluded tower.

As they turned a corner, Cedryck and Garrick both drew up short. A fair-haired woman in a gown of ivory and gold leaned back in surprise.

"Oh, Lord Gredsk…" She curtseyed, then her eyes shone as she saw Garrick. "Sir Magni! I did not realize you would be here tonight. It has been entirely too long."

A couple of the ladies-in-waiting accompanying her whispered and giggled.

Garrick kept his smile and posture even, though inside he wilted. He knew what Lady Sarkova wanted, and talking usually didn't happen until after. Cedryck had paused as they faced the lady, but behind his back, Garrick nudged Cedryck toward the entrance to the tower.

"My deepest apologies, Lady Sarkova," Garrick said, "but Lord Gredsk has requested my attention personally. You understand, I do hope?"

Lady Sarkova nodded. "Of course. But don't leave me waiting."

Turning, Garrick caught a glimpse of the surprised look on Cedryck's face before the markiese led the way to the door and inside the tower.

The heavy wooden door shut behind Garrick, locking him and Cedryck into the silence of the spiraling staircase. Only the crackling of the torches mounted along the walls broke the stillness.

Cedryck glanced over his shoulder as he began climbing the stairs, a curious look still marking his face. "I'm surprised, Garrick. I've never known you to dismiss Lady Sarkova's attention."

Garrick sniffed. "I don't really need that kind of attention right now."

Cedryck stopped in his tracks, his eyes wide as he stared down at the knight. "Garrick, what happened to you?"

Garrick paused as he saw the shock on Cedryck's face. Had he said something he shouldn't have? Garrick didn't think he had, but something clearly didn't portray right to Cedryck. The instincts ingrained into Garrick from his mother screamed his next course of action. He had to deflect attention to another topic.

But this wasn't a rival or some court schemer. This was Cedryck. If there was anyone Garrick could speak honestly with, it was him. His cousin, and the closest friend Garrick had.

…and the future duke.

I've made enough bad judgment calls lately.

Garrick let out a sigh, putting all his effort into making his words sound earnest. "I'm sorry. It was the battle. It was exactly what I trained for, but…" Raising his head, he met Cedryck's eyes. "I couldn't do a thing against them. I might as well have not been there at all." It wasn't a lie. That had bothered Garrick, and saying so brought back the helplessness he felt when the malakh and the Goddess of Chaos battled in the streets of Albrith. At least it worked to deflect Cedryck's attention.

The stunned look on Cedryck's face faded to one of understanding. He shook his head. "I can't even imagine what it must have been like." He fixed his gaze on Garrick. "I want to hear about it. The real story."

Garrick nodded as the markiese turned to continue climbing the winding staircase. Cedryck didn't want to hear the embellished version told to the nobles, nor the bland, factual version he had heard when Garrick reported to the duke. Cedryck was the one person who wanted to know the truth about the gods and the other players in the battle.

At least Garrick could give him that.

Chapter 2
A Dark Guide

WIND HOWLED THROUGH the Orthys Mountains, an early winter storm battering the higher peaks. Snow lanced through the air, eddying into crevices and veiling distant peaks and passes behind a wall of grey-white.

Ashik strode along a well-trodden path in the lee of a mountain, holding the lead of a mountain goat with long, thick, curving horns. Leather straps cinched the goat's shaggy fur to its thick body, holding a pair of saddle bags to its flank, along with Ashik's fur cloak. Though his breath misted on the air and ice crusted in his thin moustache and beard and in his topknot, he wore only a thick wool shirt, vest, and trousers. The cold breeze gradually wicked away the sweat of his climb. Like the goat, Ashik was stout and muscular, his face flat and cheekbones wide. His village was just over the next rise and he was eager to return.

The goat hesitated, the lead pulling taut as it stuck its cloven hooves fast and grunted.

"Come on," Ashik said, tugging at the rope. He made a face as the goat's head turned toward the lead, but its body stayed put. "Don't do this to me now, Urda."

The goat bleated loudly and lashed backward, tossing its head nearly enough to impale itself with its own horns. Ashik planted his feet and fought against the goat, but then he heard the rumbling. He looked up as a pebble bounced past and saw rocks tumbling down the mountainside.

He lunged back down the path, Urda eagerly leading the way. The ground shook beneath Ashik's feet as the crackles and thumps of the rock slide tumbled across the trail where he had just stood. It was past nearly as soon as he stopped fleeing it. Looking back, he found boulders strewn across the path.

His brows knitted. "This pass was safe."

Bad enough that the rest of the mountains were getting too treacherous to traverse. If even the comfortable trails that had been faithful for centuries were growing dangerous, his people could be in serious trouble.

He laid a hand on the goat's neck and continued down the path, weaving around the boulders. This time, Urda followed obediently.

Ashik had just rounded another bend when he heard a call through the whistling wind.

"Ashik! Ashik!"

Peering through the wet snow, he found a woman with ropy muscles standing on the next rise, dark braid blowing in the wind. He raised his arm as high as he could and swung it wide back and forth. Her face turned toward him.

"Ashik! There you are." She skidded down the hill toward him.

"What is it, Chakha?" Ashik asked as she came close, slowing her descent.

Chakha leaned to the side to examine the goat's saddle bags, a smirk on her face. "So, what did you catch?"

"Weasels and shrews, and one buzzard." He threw the goat's lead at her and she stumbled to catch it. "At least I found that laurel Grandmother told me about." They began climbing the rise.

"My brother, the fierce hunter of small rodents."

He shoved a fist against her shoulder.

Chakha grinned. "I can see you're taking my archery lessons to heart."

Ashik tilted his chin up and shook his head. "Well, it's not like there's any trading to be done these days."

"Then I guess it's a good thing I'm here to tell you that the Uniter has already arrived."

He snapped his gaze to her. "What?"

Her grin widened.

Leaning forward, Ashik sprinted up the rise, the cold air biting his lungs as he climbed. He soon reached the top and looked down.

The familiar valley opened up below. A huge lake curved around to the right and continued out of sight, the water rippling from the wind but still reflecting a crystal clear, sapphire blue. To the left, mostly harvested fields lay dark with turned soil, ready to sit out the long winter. Everywhere he looked, sheep, goats, and huge, woolly murok cattle grazed, heedless of the snow drifting over the valley and collecting on their backs.

Straight ahead lay the village of Khaladon, a collection of flat, stone buildings along the lake shore. From this height, Ashik could just see several people standing in the courtyard at the centre of the village, watching the wide path coming through the mountains from the far side. Down that path, Ashik saw a stream of people, many on horseback, moving toward the village.

Chakha reached the top of the rise beside Ashik and he punched her arm again. "You made me think I was late!"

She snickered. "Well, you wouldn't want to be, would you?"

"You're insufferable."

"Come on, let's go see!" She skipped down the steep path, the goat nimbly trotting behind her. Ashik followed her with a smile and a shake of his head.

They both kept up a light jog across the open grass toward the village. Weaving between the many animals scattered over the valley, they occasionally caught glimpses of the group reaching Khaladon. Several minutes later, they came to a short, rocky rise just outside the village with a clear view of the courtyard.

"There he is," Chakha remarked giddily.

Qualeth, the Uniter, now stood in the courtyard, speaking with the chief of their village. That was obvious from his height, taller than nearly everyone there, and his thin frame, though he was so bundled against the cold that Ashik couldn't make out much more at this distance.

"Oh, I would love to get into his bed," Chakha murmured.

Ashik snorted a chuckle, though the casual confidence of the Uniter made him understand how she felt.

His sister sighed. "If only he wasn't already committed to that one."

A woman stood behind the Uniter, tall and lithe and full of leonine grace. Her raven hair cascaded down her back and over one eye in waves and thin braids woven with feathers and glass beads. She was adorned with hematite jewellery and a circlet of antlers and bones. Like the Uniter, she wore layers of wool and hide, though where he wore a sabre on his hip, she had a pair of gourds hanging from her belt.

Ashik gave his sister an odd look. "She's his spirit singer, goat-brain."

"Well, obviously. But she has always been all but attached to his arm."

"Weren't you paying attention the last time he was here?"

She looked put out. "I was eleven."

"It's a wonder you had enough patience to learn the bow. She was his guide when he came to unite the southern peoples."

"Oh." Chakha returned her attention to the group in the courtyard. "I wonder how a spirit singer is in bed."

Ashik shook his head. "Just get Urda back to the stable. I have real work to do."

"Go speak tongues to them, fierce rodent-slayer!"

Ashik stepped off the edge of the outcropping, hopping and climbing from narrow ledge to small pocket as he made his way into the village.

As he jogged toward the courtyard, he glanced at the group of people gathering behind the Uniter. All were bundled thickly in furs and leather, but glimpses of unusual features showed the surprising array of people from across the free territories that accompanied him. Eyes lined with kohl, brightly coloured feathers peeking out of wrappings, hide ponchos dyed with bold patterns and fringed with beads. A man with the thick, black beard and round, turbaned head of the desert empire of Enseros stood near the Uniter and his spirit singer, his red-brown cheeks even ruddier in the crisp mountain air. To Ashik's surprise, he also found some pale-skinned people with angular features, sharp blue eyes, dark clothes and armour, and dark hair.

Rturans, he thought with surprise.

"Ah," the village chief said in accented Trade, holding a hand out to Ashik as he drew near. "This is Ashik, our village's best trader."

Ashik bowed before the Uniter, his Trade clearer than the chief's. "It is an honour to be of service."

A derisive snort came from off to the side. Ashik saw a Rturan woman with short hair and scuffed leather armour muttering to a man with a scar on his chin beside her. "Trader," she remarked in the guttural language of the Rturans. Ashik couldn't make out precisely what she said, but he caught the words for 'profit,' 'work,' and 'other people'.

Ashik bristled, though he half expected that reaction, so he didn't show his annoyance. He turned to the woman with his shoulders back and an unconcerned look on his face. "Among my people, it is an honour," he said as best he could in Rturan.

She snapped her gaze to him, eyes narrowing suspiciously.

"For without trade, we could not prosper." Ashik waved a hand around the village, the gesture encompassing the longhouse, the forge, and the bales of hay and barrels visible from the courtyard. "And my work allows the makers to focus on theirs."

The woman continued to sneer at him, though the scarred man she had been speaking to smirked in amusement.

By now, most of the party that accompanied the Uniter, some five dozen men and women, crowded the courtyard. The other side of the courtyard was packed with the villagers, nearly the entire population come away from their tasks to meet the group. Ashik's heart hastened and not from the chill that began to seep through his wool.

A message alerting them to the Uniter's approach had come over a moon-turn ago. It didn't say why he was coming, but looking at the people he led, Ashik was sure that he could guess their purpose. He recognized each of these peoples and had lived among many of them.

They were warriors. The most dangerous that called the free lands home. Their appearances said that to Ashik more than the glimpses he saw of spears, swords, cudgels, and unstrung bows.

There weren't many reasons the Uniter would need to travel all the way to Khaladon with such a force. Ashik knew the next moments would change his life forever.

"People of Khaladon," the Uniter announced in clear, barely accented Trade. "I come to you today with grave news." He held his hand out to the man from Enseros. "This is Ayyat al'Hashid of the desert empire. He fled his home for sanctuary within the free lands, but when I heard his tale, I knew we had to act immediately."

He nodded to Ayyat and the turbaned man stepped forward.

"My home was attacked," Ayyat announced in deep, rolling Trade, "by a huge force out of Edan, far to the west, that calls itself the Army of Light. I faced one of their knights as they ran through my town, and he was eager to tell me of their 'crusade.' They fight for their Gods of Light and mean to wipe out all traces of other gods, and the people who worship them."

Murmurs began among the villagers, standing behind Ashik and the chief, though the warriors stood still as Ayyat spoke.

"They call us heathens and you all worse. Leading them is a creature out of their fables, a servant of their gods with the body of a woman and the head of a fox with golden hair."

Ashik drew in a breath. "The malakh."

The chief turned to him. "Ashik?"

"I heard of this creature when last I ventured over the mountains. The stories say she has great power over living things, and single-handedly assaulted the capital of Faneria, levelling many buildings and killing many." He faced the chief. "He speaks true. She is cruel, yet has inspired great adoration for their burning gods. She could do this."

"Did you see her?" one of the villagers called out.

"No," answered Ayyat. "But the forces that outnumbered us fought in her name. They showed no mercy. My brothers and I, we were lucky to flee, but not before we saw those who surrendered being killed where they knelt, even the women and children."

An uproar rose among the villagers, and the chief raised a hand for silence.

"The Army of Light grows larger every day," Ayyat continued. "It promises nothing but death and destruction." His gaze darkened. "Their knight told me they vow to 'rend the earth beneath the feet of those who give false idolatry to any but the True Gods.'"

Gasps, murmurs, and exclamations rang out through the villagers. Ashik's eyes widened.

"You can see," said the Uniter, "why we took Ayyat's tale to heart."

"All the upheaval in the mountains over the last years," Ashik uttered.

"Are you saying that this fox-headed creature is behind it?" Chakha shouted behind him.

"That her sorcery has made our mountains impassable?" cried another voice.

The Uniter glanced at his spirit singer. Ashik was close enough to see her one visible eye fixing on the Uniter as she nodded.

"Not just your mountains," answered the Uniter. "The northern jungles are drying out. The herds the peoples of the plains hunt suffer plague and starvation. Other peoples have been fighting famine for years. The very earth beneath our feet seems to have turned against us, and now," he said, his voice growing more animated as he gestured at the spirit singer, "the spirits say it has all been the work of this creature. She has been waging war upon us for years already, this is merely the final blow meant to eradicate us forever."

The villagers murmured, whispered, and grumbled behind Ashik. Some muttered uncertainly, but Ashik couldn't imagine how they could be unmoved by such an impassioned speech.

"She will not stop at Enseros," the Uniter went on, his voice rising. Ayyat and several of the warriors nodded along with his words. "She will come for us, every last one of us. We have done nothing to her and her people, yet she has decided that we must be destroyed. Well, if she wants to march on the free lands, then we will show her just how well we can make war."

Several of the warriors shouted their answer. Now, a few of the villagers echoed them, including Chakha.

The Uniter spread his arms, encompassing both the villagers and the warriors. "Free peoples, you have honoured me for letting me bring peace and guide you these last ten years. We have become good neighbours, but now, we must come together for more. For our protection. For our survival!"

He faced the villagers directly. "We need you. The Army of Light is massive, the force that assaulted Ayyat's town only a small fraction of its strength. We need every spare hand we can get to drive them back. It is time to show the westerners that we will not bow to them!"

Ashik joined the cheer that rose from both sides of the courtyard.

"Time to fight for our freedom!"

The villagers and the warriors alike screamed their defiance.

"To take back our lands!"

The courtyard roared with shouts of support, the ground vibrating under Ashik's feet as many of the villagers jumped up and down. Fervor radiated through the air like heat, almost visibly making the air ripple with excitement. Ashik felt his heart thrum with the power of the Uniter's words, his blood pounding so heatedly he entirely forgot his lack of skill with arms.

The Uniter shouted at the top of his voice, "We will end them!"

This was followed by a roar of assent. The spirit singer swept her gaze around the courtyard, a smile upon her face as she watched the reactions to the Uniter's words.

Ashik caught her attention as she looked straight at him. Surprisingly, her eyes weren't dark, as they should be, but grey. As the wind tossed her hair to the side, he saw a spot of brown at the bottom of her right eye.

The villagers joined the warriors in a chant.

"Uniter! Uniter! Uniter!"

The chief, brawny and a handspan taller than Ashik, pumped a fist into the sky as he chanted along with the others. Ashik screamed along at the top of his voice.

I will make you proud, Ashik thought, reflecting both on the Uniter and on the village chief. *I will do what I can to save our people.*

*   *   *

A fire crackled in the large hearth, filling the parlour with light and warmth. Garrick sat a few chairs away from the popping flames in a darker corner of the room. Much as he appreciated how the fire dried out the air inside the tower, he found the added heat stifling. He shifted in his upholstered chair, missing the breeze and open spaces of the plains he rode through a season before. He wished the open air coming through the windows on one side of the room was fresher.

Blinking, he refocused on the page of the book open across his lap, realizing that once again his eyes had passed over the words without having any idea what they said. It was a futile effort. Spurned by others his age in his youth, he had spent many hours scouring the Agaesi library. There was nothing in this tome he did not know already and no further information to suggest what had happened to Nephrita. As far as he could tell, she had simply disappeared at the end of the Battle of Albrith.

He flipped another page with a sigh, the walls of the tower seeming too confining after his long journey across Faneria. With the one known band of mages left in the kingdom now executed or in hiding, it was likely he would never see another mission involving magic again. He had all the limitations of being an Agaesi without any of the camaraderie an order of knights should provide, or any of the assignments that made the dragon knights special.

Garrick frowned as he turned another page without having absorbed a word of the previous. Perhaps he could convince the captain to allow him to exercise Brenadier. The stallion had been nearly as cooped up as Garrick after the long journey back to Misengrad weeks previous, and he had not seen the horse since his return.

Garrick sat with his cheek leaning on his fist, staring at the same word as thoughts rushed through his head. His eyes felt heavy against the dry, hot air in the parlour. Then, voices and footsteps thrummed up the stairs beside him. It was the knights who had been summoned to the captain's office shortly before. Garrick blinked, instantly alert, but let his eyes scan the lines of script in the book as he tried to listen to the conversation. Sir Warwick had tried to act casual when he summoned the knights to his office, but it was rare that any mission required four dragon knights. Garrick picked up pieces of their conversation as they climbed the stairs.

"…knowing her intentions could help…"

"…really think she can be reasoned…"

"…why she would gather this force…"

"…going to need all the speed we can muster…"

Garrick kept his expression neutral and his gaze focused on the book. His heart quickened as they continued up the stairs toward the apartments, knowing that his suspicions about their mission had been confirmed.

They were going after Niabi.

Determination and frustration rushed through Garrick in equal measure at the thought of the fox woman, and he couldn't help rubbing his neck. The bruise from the vine Niabi wound around him like a noose had faded weeks earlier, but his throat still sometimes felt tight. Garrick breathed slowly until the frustration vanished, leaving behind only resolve.

He waited the agonizing seconds as the sounds of the knights faded away up the stairs. As soon as the last voice drifted into silence, he closed the book he had been reading and rose, climbing down the stairs.

Garrick put his shoulders back as he crossed the ground floor common room and entered the anteroom to Sir Warwick's office. The records keepers barely glanced at him as he strode through the room to the door to the captain's office. Young Brannik sprang to his feet with a wheeze.

"Ah, S-Sir Magni…"

Garrick softened his expression and voice as he faced the pale, thin youth. "I would like to speak to Sir Warwick. I won't be long."

Brannik nodded and turned to open the door. Nodding in return, Garrick stepped through, stopping just inside the door. The captain sat at his desk, scratching a crow quill across a piece of parchment, and didn't look up as the door shut behind Garrick.

Garrick saluted. "Sir Warwick."

The captain remained focused on his letter. "Sir Magni."

"Sir, I request to join the mission going after Niabi."

"I suspected you would, though I didn't think you would find out about it quite so quickly. I suppose discretion is only mandatory outside this tower."

Garrick stepped forward a pace. "Sir, whatever they are doing, I can help."

"They're only going to observe and try to learn more about her plans." Sir Warwick emptied his quill in the pot of ink on his desk and replaced the quill on a stand beside it, then finally looked up at Garrick. "And if I was going to assign you to the mission, I would have called you in with the other knights." The mild look on his face and his relaxed posture eased any sting the words might otherwise have incited.

Garrick moved closer to the desk. "I can blend in with the people of Edan and I have faced her before. My experience would be a valuable asset."

"Are you that eager to be so close to the most powerful creature to wander the land in the past century or more?"

A faint lump formed in Garrick's throat as he thought of Nephrita, but he didn't show any reaction. "The most dangerous, Sir. Not the most powerful."

Sir Warwick nodded thoughtfully, his eyes never straying from Garrick's. "I suppose that's true, but it doesn't answer my question." Sir Warwick stared at Garrick for a long moment, then shook his head. "With most of the men, I can at least guess at their feelings, but your mother taught you too well. From the day you started training, you've been a wall." Leaning forward, he rested his arms on the desk. "So tell me, is this about revenge?"

"I want revenge, but if the mission is not to stop her, then I won't."

"And why do you wish to go? Even if this isn't about revenge, this must be personal for you. You know better than anyone that she can sense us as much as we can sense her, and that those men may be marching to their deaths. You also know that most or all of the men on that mission distrust or at least dislike you." Sir Warwick's gaze bored into Garrick. "Is this about proving yourself?"

Garrick hesitated. "Yes," he answered. "But it is more about Niabi. I do know what she is capable of and I don't want to let her hurt any more innocent people."

Although he didn't smile, Sir Warwick looked satisfied. "I believe you. And I believe that you would give everything you had, without hesitation, to obtain the information we need, even if it meant walking away from her. I would like little more than for you to accompany the mission." Before Garrick could respond, Sir Warwick sighed and sat back, a weary look crossing his face. "Unfortunately, it wasn't my decision to keep you from it."

Garrick blinked. "What?"

"I'm sorry, Garrick. The Scion specifically forbade you from accompanying the mission."

Garrick's chest tightened, but he swept all emotion from his face. He bowed. "I understand, Sir. I apologize for wasting your time."

Sir Warwick frowned as Garrick turned and strode out of the office without another word.

Garrick tried to steady his breathing as he climbed the winding staircase to the fifth floor. Down the short corridor, he turned to the right, away from Sir Warwick's suite. A warm glow shone against the walls ahead.

Garrick stopped short of the corner, shutting his eyes and inhaling deeply.

We are all scions of Agasis, even me.

The tightness in his chest didn't ease. Setting his shoulders back, he turned the corner and walked through the open doors into the room beyond.

Though most of the public rooms in the castle were larger and more opulent than this one, the Den never failed to send a ripple up Garrick's spine. The room spread across half of the tower's width, the floor empty aside from support columns carved into organic shapes. The ceiling was no higher than any other in the tower. Incense and warm light filled the room, along with a crackling energy that made it feel alive. Lanterns lined the wall to one side with a row of windows admitting light on the other. The far wall was covered in an elaborate, high relief sculpture of a dragon.

The sculpted dragon crouched against its wall, wings pressing against the ceiling, tail coiling about its legs from where its flank and heel touched one wall, and long neck curving around so that the head hung free. Barely contained, it pressed out in all directions, the figure looking a hair's breadth from breaking free of the stone. Flickering firelight played over the carved scales and sinews, lending it a constant feel of movement. Although Garrick knew that this depiction of the source of the Agaesis' power was based no more in fact or observation than if he had designed it, the relief felt like the true face of Agasis.

Garrick stared at the carved eyes of the dragon, letting the energy of the room seep into him. It helped to ease his discomfort. The last time he stood in the Den was three years ago, when he felt the presence of Agasis fill him for the first time, and the sensation of being forever changed returned to him. He could no longer remember what it had felt like to be an ordinary man. The closest he came to remembering it was when he turned his eyes to the lone figure in the room.

In name, the dragon knights not only owed their power to Agasis, but worshipped him. However, Garrick knew he wasn't the only Agaesi who had not entered this room in years. No one outside the tower knew of the existence of the Scion of Agasis, and most of the knights and their families actively followed the Gods of Light. However, the Scion remained the closest link to Agasis, the conduit through which all dragon knights attained their power. Without him, there were no Agaesi.

The Scion sat cross-legged before the relief of Agasis, clad in an elegant robe cut like dragon scales and more expensive than anything worn by the ladies of the court. His hairless head gleamed in the firelight, ears sagging and deep wrinkles etched into the skin below his skull.

Garrick flexed his fingers, fighting the urge to turn and walk out before the Scion noticed him. He shut his eyes and inhaled deeply.

You're a wall.

I would like little more than for you to accompany the mission.

Opening his eyes, Garrick straightened and strode down the centre of the room.

"Sir Magni."

Garrick pushed on until he stood a few paces from the Scion. "Your Reverence." Crouching, Garrick bent over until his forehead touched the stone floor.

"I am surprised you remember tradition, considering you never step foot in the house of He who made you." The Scion's voice rasped like a knife stripping flesh from a hide.

Garrick didn't move. It was easier to stare at the floor. "Sir Warwick informed me that you forbade me from joining the mission to observe the malakh, Your Reverence."

"That I did."

Garrick swallowed. "With utmost respect, Your Reverence, I humbly request to know why."

"Do you question my judgment, Sir Magni?"

You know damn well the answer to that question, you high-and-mighty old badger. The Scion wasn't going to rile him up that easily. "Of course not, Your Reverence. Your word is the light that brings Agasis into our lives. I am only curious, for Sir Warwick did not divulge the reasoning for your decision."

"Hmph."

A rustle of swaths of silk sounded. Garrick lifted his head off the floor as the Scion stood. The Scion's pasty flesh hung off him, wrinkles disappearing into the collar of that elaborate robe. The Scion stared down at Garrick through milky blue eyes full of disdain.

"I refused to allow you on that mission because you are a failure."

Garrick focused on breathing evenly as he rose. The top of the Scion's head just reached Garrick's nose when he stood straight.

"With respect, Your Reverence, everything I have done followed the captain's orders and the tenets of the Agaesi."

"Do you deny that you failed?" The Scion strode in a slow circle around Garrick. "It is the duty of the Agaesi to protect the realm against magical threats. You were in the midst of the greatest to threaten Faneria in centuries, yet they managed to storm Albrith and nearly reached the king."

Like you give one scale of that ridiculous robe about the king, Garrick thought, but a lump formed in his throat. The smoke from the incense in the unventilated chamber stung his eyes. "No one Agaesi could have—"

"Not to mention your gross mismanagement of that girl who held a god inside her," the Scion spoke over him.

"I…"

"You could have prevented so much disaster with one simple solution, but you failed to do that, and now, hundreds of people are dead because of it. Because of you."

It felt as though Niabi's noose wound around Garrick's neck again. All the arguments he had made to himself for not killing Damian, or trying to kill Nephrita, died on his lips. He stared at the dragon's shoulder before him. "I helped lead the band of soldiers that defeated the mages, and the people in the village—"

"Do you think that excuses your failures?" snapped the Scion.

It took every moment of training Garrick's mother had instilled in him to keep his composure.

The Scion moved in front of him, stepping so close that Garrick couldn't avoid looking in his eyes. "Well? Do you?"

Bile rose at the back of Garrick's throat. "No."

The Scion smiled at him in a way that would have curdled milk. "No. It does not." He turned away and Garrick shut his eyes, watering and itchy from the smoky air. He fought the impulse to rub them.

"But I am not unreasonable. You may yet prove yourself."

Opening his eyes, Garrick found the Scion facing him with the same smile.

"After all, the threat remains. If you can bring in the rest of the rebel mages, including the one you were assigned to find in the first place, perhaps you may be redeemed."

The room pressed in on Garrick. The mages who had abandoned Yanuk could be anywhere between Misengrad and Albrith, or they might have fled even farther from reach. Some of the attackers at Albrith had escaped. The trail of the mage he had originally been assigned to track down had grown cold on the far side of the kingdom nearly half a year ago. All of them could use a spell to allow them to move in plain sight without being seen or sensed with his magic.

It was as good as exile. Yet if he refused, he would never be assigned another mission again. Garrick would be lucky if the Scion allowed him guard duty on the tower for the remainder of his days.

It was exactly the excuse the Scion had been looking for throughout Garrick's life. His stomach and the back of his throat burned as he stared at the Scion, and Garrick considered telling the old man what he really thought.

What more can he do to me?

The glee that thought brought consumed Garrick, until he realized nothing he could say, no threat he could pose, would wipe that smug smile off the old man's face.

Garrick bowed, keeping his composure but not moving his eyes from the Scion's. "It will be done, Your Reverence." Turning, he strode toward the exit.

"We shall see."

Out in the hall, rage flooded Garrick and he curled his hands into fists. Around the corner away from the Den, he punched the wall until his knuckles bled before storming down the hall toward the stairs. Closing his eyes, he summoned the lessons his mother had taught him and tried to collect his thoughts, to distance himself from the anger. As the fury faded, his throat grew thick, the Scion's words eating away at him.

Everything he said was true.

With a sigh, Garrick slid down the wall until he sat on the spiraling stairs, his limbs feeling heavy. For a long moment, he listened to himself breathe as he struggled with his thoughts.

I was given a mission.

He raised his head as that thought turned over in his mind. A smile crawled onto his face. He was leaving the tower. Opening his eyes, he inhaled the stale, musty air in the staircase, his memories drifting back to the rolling breeze, open plains, and rich forests of the world outside.

Better luck next time, old man.

Garrick stood, his shoulders back as he climbed the rest of the stairs to the next floor. His chance of success was slim, but this mission was an opportunity.

I am an Agaesi.

When he opened the door to his apartment, Garrick found his

mother sitting on an upholstered chair, embroidering one of her gowns. She looked up as he stepped inside, giving him a casual glance that he knew was taking in every aspect of his bearing.

"Is everything all right?"

Maybe some of his turmoil was showing, or maybe she was just guessing. Garrick's smile remained steady as he strode to the window, looking out over the endless sheet of Aura Lake.

"Yes. Everything will be fine."

The sounds of the forest rippled through the air. The rustling of leaves in the wind. Birds chirping. Squirrels climbing and leaping from tree to tree. Branches creaking as they swayed.

Niabi sat on her haunches in her fox form. The form was tiring to hold, but it was the easiest way to keep both her hands and her feet against the moss-coated earth. Her large ears took in the noises. Her eyes were shut. The breeze rippled across her golden fur.

Where her paws touched the earth, she could feel the flow of life energy all around her. It spread outward, reaching into the ground and above it, where the birds flitted through the air. There was even a thread of energy connecting her to the sprites that hovered in the air around her. She drew from that energy, filling her body with its strength.

She tried not to notice the mass of humans so near by, but the pulse of their energy permeated her being like a stench she couldn't wash off. Her muzzle twitched as their presence ate into her concentration, impossible to ignore.

She checked her irritation. Much as she would rather have nothing to do with the humans, they were her mission now, and the only way she could redeem herself.

A bitter taste filled her long mouth as she recalled the weeks after her battle against Nephrita. Desperation as she approached the gateway to the realm eternal, where her masters lived, only to be dismissed. The loss of the power of the True Gods. The madness that overcame her that almost made her topple the ancient ruin on top of her.

And then Ganodu, her dear, forgiving master, giving her another chance.

The humans here, in their kingdom of Edan, adored Niabi. A few words of the benevolence of her masters and they gave her their devotion unto the end of their own lives. Her Army of Light had grown quickly and had already begun its campaign against the heathens in the northern desert. Now this new force to the south swelled in numbers. Their desire to wipe out all trace of the old gods was nearly as keenly honed as Niabi's own.

She opened her eyes.

It was time.

Niabi rose onto two legs, the silken gown she conjured flowing over her body. Turning, she strode back toward the encampment. Too soon, she left the forest behind, the land opening into a wide field filled with the army encampment, spreading over a league back from the border wall. Her eyes, easily able to see over the heads of nearly everyone there, took in the rows of tents, the carefully erected paddocks for horses and other animals, the temporary kitchens, the forges, the tailors, portable mills, and more. It was like a new city that sprang up nearly overnight on the border with Faneria. Niabi couldn't help being mildly impressed, though she wished they could simply push through the border to continue their mission. Alas, their foolish human politics would turn even the devout across the border against them. Soon, she had been assured, they would be allowed passage. She tamped down her annoyance and hoped that was true.

As she passed into the encampment, humans bowed and greeted her with reverence. Holding her muzzle high, she set her features into a dignified look and nodded solemnly at those she passed.

She walked through about a third of the encampment before she came upon the largest, most extravagant tent there. Lord Ulfrich, balding already but still young, stood outside the entrance, chatting with a handful of his captains. He stopped, smiling widely as he noticed her approach.

"Lady Niabi," he greeted with a low bow. "Welcome back."

"Everything is under control?" she asked.

He craned his neck to look up into her eyes. "No problems to speak of, My Lady. You need not worry about a thing."

She nodded. "Very well. I have a task I must complete. I leave the force in your hands until I return."

He blinked, his smile vanishing. "You… you're leaving, My Lady?"

"You can handle things while I am away, can you not?"

"Of course, My Lady. But, what task must you complete?"

She gazed toward the border wall. "I seek information."

Lord Ulfrich followed her gaze and his eyes widened. "You cannot mean to go alone, Lady Niabi! If something should happen to you…"

She couldn't help her muzzle quirking in a wry grin. This small creature of flesh and blood and so few years worrying about her, a servant of the gods.

"Please, allow some men to accompany you, for your own safety," Lord Ulfrich went on.

It was unnecessary, of course, but this army proved that humans had their uses. She could placate Lord Ulfrich, and perhaps find some use for a guard set to her.

"Very well. But I mean to slip through the border, so I will accept no more than two."

Lord Ulfrich nodded. "I will find our two best men to accompany you, Lady Niabi. May Wisdom guide you to the information you seek."

She nodded, but didn't bother mentioning that the God of Wisdom could offer her no assistance in this task.

She needed to find the old gods themselves.

CHAPTER 3
A PATH ILLUMINATED

A BREEZE SWEPT over the town, bringing a chill as it rustled golden leaves. Many windows remained open, but smoke curled thickly out of chimneys into the crisp blue sky. The village wasn't large, but the town square bustled with the weekly market, the melons and berries of summer replaced with squash, apples, and corn.

Damian Sires strolled through the town, Liam at her side and another figure following at a greater distance. Slender and average in height, Damian's most distinguishing feature at first glance was her fashionable and well-made gown of mustard yellow and forest green. Her long, auburn hair was styled into a half chignon. To the people of Aether, her most remarkable trait was the one that was missing: her veil.

Damian turned her yellow eyes, a shade so pale it was difficult to distinguish the iris from the white, across the town square as she approached it. She smiled and nodded at the friendly waves and greetings directed her way. She tried to keep her attention on them, but many more other people simply averted their gazes or stepped aside as she approached. As she glanced around, she couldn't help noticing a few who scowled, hissed, or gestured for the Gods of Light as she passed.

Most of those sent the same looks toward Liam. The tall, broad-shouldered mercenary kept pace with her, most of his body covered by his black cloak. Liam Henricksson, the mercenary and murderer known as Domino or the Crow, glanced impassively back at her. The sight of that stoic visage with his broad face, copper skin, and shoulder-length brown hair never failed to cheer Damian. She had known him since the year began in mid-spring and had yet to see him smile. Although, she had never seen him frown, either.

They made their way across the square as Damian sought a specific stall, but soon found her progress blocked.

The farmer behind the stall glanced around furtively as she spoke, not meeting Damian's eyes. "I don't want no trouble, miss."

"You sold them to me last week," Damian pleaded.

"I'm sorry, but they put their foot down. I can't lose business from all of them." Her eyes flicked to the side and Damian followed the woman's gaze. Several people scattered around the square had stopped what they were doing to stare at her, some looking angry, some smug.

Damian faced the farmer again. "I'll pay you more for them."

She shuffled her feet, clearly uncomfortable but still refusing to look Damian in the eye. "I can't. Not no more. Please just go." She pointedly moved away to help another customer, who also kept her distance from Damian.

With a sigh, Damian spun around and strode quickly back across the town square, Liam following and her other shadow trailing a few paces after. Her hand moved to adjust the veil she no longer wore, though it would have made no difference if she had worn it. Her reputation had preceded her return to the village of her birth.

The stories that came from Albrith were muddled, exaggerated and twisted for dramatic flair as stories get, but enough pieces remained constant to ring of truth to even the most cynical. The unprecedented assault of a force of magic users, hiding in exile for years, that nearly cost the city and the king. A malakh, servant of the deities, wielding the power of the Gods of Light and hunting a dark figure out of forgotten history inside the city.

Damian Sires, linked to the Goddess of Chaos.

It didn't matter that Damian had not used magic since, or that many believed Nephrita had died in that battle. The taint of her magic was enough to mark Damian for life.

Frustratingly, she felt tears gathering as she hurried through the town toward her home. She rubbed her eyes roughly with her sleeve, unsure if she was angry or upset.

She soon returned to the house she had left so recently. It was a modest house along a street lined with similar ones separated by narrow alleys where refuse was piled before being carted away. The starkly crisp and clean exterior of her youngest years had given way to the same comfortable weathering as any other building in Aether. It hardly looked any different from the houses surrounding it, but Damian's stomach tightened in anticipation of escape within its sanctuary.

However, she paused a few strides before the front door, forcing her mind to calm and spreading a smile across her face. Straightening her shoulders, she stepped inside.

The sight that greeted her sent a pang of relief and guilt through her at once. Claude Sires, her father, sat on the sofa in the common room. The right side of his face was scarred from his cheekbone to a finger's length above his mangled ear. Much of the hair on that side of his head was gone, the rest greyer than it had been in the spring. He walked with a limp now and she could see constant pain in his eyes. Every time she looked at him, her stomach twisted. He had survived the fire she accidentally caused on their trade ship and escaped to the safety of a tiny hamlet along the river. While she thought him dead, he thought the same of her. The weeks had worn away the joy of returning to Aether to find him alive, leaving only the shame of causing him such lasting pain.

"Hi, Papa," she said as she stepped over the threshold, followed by Liam.

Her father glanced up with a smile, but it soon faded. "What happened?"

She allowed her smile to vanish at his easy reading of her mood. She sighed. "I didn't get any squash. She won't sell them to me anymore."

Sadness touched his eyes for a moment, then he smiled, his moustache turning up at the corners. "She's not the only one who grows squash in this town."

Damian's shoulders sagged. "It seems like more people are refusing to do business with me every week."

"Now, Damian, you know that's not true. There are lots of people here who still love and support you."

"People who have known me all my life." She opened her hands to either side. "Papa, what am I going to do?"

It was the same old argument. Her father's suppliers had started making more cloth and preparing for next year's trade journey, but a number of them, not to mention the local guild leader, wanted nothing to do with Damian.

"You could wear a veil again," her father suggested gently.

It was his same response. Damian looked away, the words pressing on her with a tangible force, like she was under water. The thought of wearing the veil again brought hope mixed with cynicism, relief, and sadness. She never had been able to put into words why the idea of wearing the veil again bothered her so much.

"It wouldn't make a difference," she answered softly.

"You never—" he attempted.

"I'm going to start on supper," she cut in, sweeping across the room toward the kitchen as a lump formed in her throat.

Supper was a quiet affair. Damian's father tried to engage her on various topics, though she had little enough to say. Instead, he asked Liam about his efforts learning to read. The mercenary clearly attempted to converse more with her father, leaving them with the startling result that Liam seemed to speak more than Damian during the meal.

"Damian," her father asked as they finished eating, "is there anything I can do for you?"

She glanced through the open shutters of the windows along the front of the house. "I think I'm just going to go for a walk." She looked at Liam, half hopeful and half concerned he would refuse. "Would you like to join me?"

His topaz blue eyes softened faintly and he nodded once. Rising, he helped her clear away the dishes from the table.

The sky had grown golden and the shadows long when Damian stepped out of the house again, wrapped in a cloak that was warmer than she needed. Liam silently followed her as she raised the hood.

Few people remained outside and the voices that had filled the streets now drifted out of windows, along with the clanking of dishes and aromas of a hundred meals. Damian stared down the street, her vision narrowed by the sides of the hood, and saw scarce few people, most of whom hurried toward their destinations. She caught a glimpse of one man just down the street who merely watched her. In or out of armour, that man had become a very common sight.

She let her feet carry her down the streets without much thought about where she was going. Lost in her own thoughts, her attention drifted down as she kicked a rock along in front of her.

Eventually, her eyes moved to Liam, striding silently alongside her. He had been a rock to her on the long journey home from Albrith over a season ago, a beacon of light among the surly and distrustful city guards who escorted her, along with the villagers who immediately recognized the yellow-eyed witch from the Battle of Albrith. She had clung to that support even after returning to Aether and had rarely left her house without Liam by her side.

Yet she knew who he really was. The cold-blooded murderer he had clearly left behind but who still haunted his steps, and the isolated wanderer who lived like a creature of the forest.

Will being here prove too much for him, she wondered not for the first time, *and I'll wake up one morning to find him gone?*

Or worse, was he only staying because she wanted him to?

"How are you feeling about," she asked hesitantly, waving her hand vaguely at the town around them, "all this?" Her voice trembled, equally guilty that she had not asked him before and afraid of his answer.

He frowned faintly, and she was surprised at the amount of uncertainty showing in his eyes. "It is… strange." He glanced at her, never showing any discomfort or reaction at all to her yellow eyes. His gaze softened. "But it's nice to feel welcomed." His smooth, low voice rolled over her as he spoke in his slow, measured way. Suddenly, he looked away, almost as if embarrassed. "Change often brings meaning to someone's life, even if it isn't entirely welcome."

Damian gave him a wan smile. "I think I know what you mean." Memories washed over her. The Battle of Albrith and her journey leading to it felt like a lifetime ago and like it was just last week at the same time. The words spilled out as they walked. "After all that we went through—we helped save Albrith! Facing a malakh, dealing with the Goddess of Chaos… After all that, trying to pick up my normal life again feels like I'm forgetting to do something important. I *want* to focus on those normal things, to sew clothes and cook meals and help my father. But it's not enough. It doesn't… it doesn't satisfy me." She shook her head. "It doesn't make any sense."

"It does to me."

Liam's response was soft but shockingly earnest. Damian turned to him and his eyes met hers, without flinching, as with every time he had looked at them. The corner of her mouth quirked almost into a smile, and his features softened in response.

She faced forward. "I don't know what to do."

Damian had been walking without purpose, but she wasn't surprised to find she had ended up across from an open green space arranged with stone markers inside the village. She turned and strode between the headstones on the trodden grass path, Liam silently following. Her eyes rose toward the statue at the centre of the field, but when she saw the marble likeness of the Goddess of Life, Damian's steps faltered. She turned to give the statue a wide berth as she made her way to one of the back rows of markers. One other person stood within the graveyard, but Damian didn't bother looking. The other should hurry away soon enough.

Near the back corner of the graveyard, Damian stopped before an old plot. It felt strange to be standing before the headstone without an offering to place before it, but the thought of leaving anything for the Goddess of Life made her stomach clench. It seemed that all the gods did was demand things of their followers. Damian glanced toward the statue at the centre of the graveyard from the corner of her eye, then shivered. The thought of the Goddess of Life, Ganodu, used to comfort her.

Damian returned her attention to the headstone. Her father had taught her to read. He could have supplied more information on the marker, but he had left it as simple as the headstones around it. Only a name was carved into its face.

Aithne Sires.

"I used to wonder what she would have thought of me."

Liam said nothing, nor did Damian expect him to. However, she never doubted that he was listening.

"I don't know anything about her. I mean, people have told me I look like her, and occasionally I would do something that made my father or someone say that was her influence. But, no one likes to speak ill of the dead. The way my father speaks of her, she was a paragon.

"Maybe she was. I'll never know. The only way I know her is through stories. Other people's memories. I can only guess."

Damian lifted a hand, staring at her palm and remembering the energy that surged out of it what seemed so long ago now. She let out a sigh.

"Sometimes I think I'm better off not knowing what she thought."

Lowering her hand, she stared at the carved words on the headstone, the only true definition and knowledge she had of her mother.

A noise of wry mirth drifted over the cemetary grounds.

"Would that any of us could speak with the dead."

Damian turned her head. The lone person she had seen when she entered the graveyard stood three plots down, a wizened figure wrapped in a dark cloak with the hood over her head. The old woman reached a hand out to a headstone before her, engraved with four names.

"But Justice is too fickle and Life not nearly enough."

Damian's gaze drifted away, an uncomfortable look crossing her face as she rubbed her arm.

The crone's dry, gravelly voice continued, "Sometimes I wonder if the gods watch over us at all."

A shiver passed through Damian as she thought of her experiences with gods both familiar and not. Niabi, endowed with the power of the Gods of Light. The voice of Nephrita that had whispered through Damian's mind. A fragment of a talisman in Trent blessed by one of the Gods of Time.

"You might be surprised," Damian replied quietly.

The crone gave a dry chuckle. Damian found a grin on the old woman's wrinkled face.

"I have lived a long time and seen much. Little would surprise me now."

She turned to face Damian as she spoke. The old woman's eyes were faded and rheumy, smoky grey with a large fleck of brown at the bottom of her right eye.

Damian cleared her throat. "I haven't seen you in Aether before."

"Nobody speaks of what I do." The old woman spoke without bitterness. "I am just an old woman who helped her small family herd sheep outside town. It is my lot in life. Some people will ever be merely spokes in the wheel of fate. Some people are born different."

Damian's eyes drifted to her mother's name on her headstone.

"Had I been touched with greatness," the crone went on, "perhaps my life would have been different."

Damian glanced at Liam, reading nothing in his expression. She felt simultaneously larger and smaller, a shiver rippling over the back of her neck. She tried to think of something to say in response to the old woman.

"Miss Sires!"

Damian spun at the call. A man she recognized as a warehouse worker entered the graveyard grounds, holding his side and panting. He paused to bow to the statue of Ganodu and held his hands and face up toward the sky before continuing toward Damian, something small and light in his hand.

"Letter came for you on the ship came in this afternoon, right?" He held up the folded page. "Would'a left it with your pa, only we were told it was s'posed to go straight to you." He paused to heave a breath, handing her the letter. "Took some time to find someone to read it, and then you weren't home, right."

She blinked, taking the note. "Thank you." As he turned to leave, she added, "Oh, wait." She reached into a pocket secreted within her sleeve and handed him a small, silver coin. "For all your trouble."

He grinned as he took it, standing a little straighter. "You take care, miss, right?" With that, he turned and jogged away through the graveyard. Damian watched him go, faintly realizing that the crone had left during the exchange.

Damian looked down at the folded note, staring at her name written in clean script. The seal on the reverse was marked with a fancy 'M'. Breaking the seal, she opened the letter, though she looked first at the end to read the signature.

"It's from Garrick," she uttered in surprise. Unfolding the page, she read the note.

Damian,

I hope this message reaches you safely. Dark clouds are gathering and I need your help. Niabi has emerged in Edan and she's gathering an army to help reclaim the Gods of Light's grip over Elderra.

I know this is wrong. After what she did to you, and me, and during the Battle of Albrith, I have no doubt that this will end in blood... a lot of it. She has to be stopped, but the Agaesis' hands are tied. We can't march into Edan without risking war. I can't just sit here and do nothing, but I can't do anything alone.

This is a dangerous gambit. I know that you're aware of the sympathy people have for her and the Gods of Light. I can't speak to anyone about this and I don't think I need to tell you that neither can you. Even my fellow knights don't believe that she is so dangerous. However, you know better than anyone what she's capable of and how far she will go to achieve her goals.

If you don't want to get involved, I'll understand. I won't expect a response. If you're willing to help me, however, come to Misengrad. I will find a way to meet you here.

Sincerely,
Sir Garrick Magni

A swell of emotion rocked through Damian as she read the letter. The last time she saw Garrick, he gave her a cryptic farewell after throwing her to the wolves at the meeting with the king in Albrith. When she read that he was asking for her help without so much as an apology, anger surged through her.

That rage faded quickly with the thought of Niabi leading an army through Edan and possibly into Faneria. Garrick faded from her mind as she became lost in memories of Niabi.

Liam shifting brought her mind back to the present. Clearing her throat, Damian refolded the letter and hid it in her sleeve. "It's about Niabi."

Liam's gaze intensified. "What did he say?"

"She's building an army. She wants to reclaim Edan and Faneria… everywhere for the Gods of Light." Merely speaking the words left a bitter taste in her mouth. As she looked at her mercenary companion, she saw that he looked ready.

And she realized that she felt the same way.

The village of Khaladon quickly became a maelstrom of activity, more frenetic even than that during the short planting and harvesting seasons. It took most of the afternoon for the villagers to get their guests set up wherever they could, their animals tended and supplies stored, and to begin preparing a feast in their honour.

Ashik moved back and forth, helping to translate as well as carry things as their visitors were organized. He smiled as he watched such different people work together to designate sleeping arrangements, cook unfamiliar dishes or share time-honoured recipes, and safely stow supplies. More than ten years had passed since the Uniter brought together the free peoples for the first time in known history, but it still struck Ashik as a joyous change. When he was a child, trade was minimal and each of these peoples tended to keep to themselves. Some had regularly warred with each other.

In fact, since Ashik was called to trading, he had helped to forge stronger alliances between some of these peoples. He couldn't claim much direct credit, but a spark of pride ignited to think that he had contributed to this unprecedented camaraderie.

He was still hard at work when the chief of Khaladon found him crossing the courtyard and called to him, "Ashik, the Uniter would like to speak with you."

Ashik could only stare wide-eyed at the chief for a moment before hurrying to follow. He stepped through the doors of the longhouse to find it sweltering to his senses. The Uniter had brought the village a gift of two wagon loads of wood, and real wood fires burned in the hearths that had lain unused for most of the year. The smoky fragrance of it filled the hall, at once strange and familiar to Ashik. People of all colours bustled back and forth as tables were set up, along with a stage, all coordinated by a handful of villagers. The air was thick with the aroma of heavily spiced foods wafting through the open doors at the far end of the longhouse, leading to the kitchens.

The chief pointed toward a quiet corner at the front of the building. Ashik turned to find a small table set up out of the way, where the Uniter sat. Ashik approached the table, the chief at his side.

In the warmth of the longhouse, the Uniter had shed his heavy wrappings to show the layers of his vibrant Tobrati garb, as well as his skin, close to the dusky tone of Ashik's people. He was as much at ease sitting on the floor as Ashik, and neglected to even use a cushion. He smiled as Ashik looked at him, and Ashik was struck once again by how ordinary the Uniter looked. He was quite tall, though he probably weighed little more than Ashik with his gangly, thin frame. His casual bearing and the quiet watchfulness in his eyes were like any Tobrati. Yet, he looked precisely the same as he had the last time Ashik had seen him, years ago. In fact, Ashik thought he himself now looked about the same age as the Uniter.

"Ashik," the Uniter greeted, gesturing to the floor on the other side of the table. He looked at the chief as Ashik lowered to the floor. "You may stay, if you like. None of this is private, I merely needed to speak to Ashik directly."

The chief glanced at Ashik. It was clear he knew that he should be out coordinating things, but curiosity burned in his eyes. Ashik held a hand out beside him and the chief sat.

The Uniter poured a cup of butter tea from a pot on the table and offered it to Ashik. "We have met before, haven't we?"

Ashik nodded in both thanks and answer. "Once, when I was living in Ithulikor. I met you briefly at the Festival of Lights."

The Uniter straightened, waving a finger toward him and smiling. "Yes, I remember now. You weren't so much taking part in the celebration as studying it."

"It was part of my training as a trader."

"Perhaps, but you seemed to be enjoying it even more. I take it your training went well, then?"

"I learned as best I could."

The Uniter grinned. "And modest, too. The way I heard it, you have helped set up regular trade for peoples across the free lands. How many languages do you speak?"

"Six fluently. Four others to varying degrees."

"I notice your Trade is impeccable. You have much knowledge and experience with Faneria?"

"I have been there many times, up until the last year."

The Uniter grinned. "As I thought, you're just the man I need."

Ashik blinked. "I beg your pardon?"

The Uniter sobered, setting down his cup. "You know about this fox-headed woman."

Ashik straightened. "I know some."

"She presents a grave threat to the free peoples. Not only because she is powerful in her own right, but because she inspires fanatical devotion by her followers."

Ashik nodded slowly. Even before rumours of the Army of Light began to build, his last foray into Faneria showed the support she had gained from the people. They had never even seen her, but they would already lay down their lives for her.

"She endows them with her own malice for the free peoples," the Uniter continued, "and for anyone who does not worship her burning gods. She is a symbol to them and the heart of the Army of Light. If we are to stand any chance of defeating them, she must be eliminated.

"But she is cunning, and she has great powers that… well, you heard how she laid waste to the king's city in Faneria. To defeat her, we must be equally cunning, powerful, and unexpected.

"She is too strong for any one force to overcome, nor do I think we would have any greater success sending an army of our own against her. Instead, I have assembled a strike force of fierce warriors of different backgrounds. Eight Makil warrior queens, eight Kathec eagle warriors, and eight Rturan assassins. Together, they have the greatest range of experience and strategies to bring to bear against the fox-headed woman. It is a small enough group that they can all attack her at once, but large enough to overwhelm her.

"And we must strike her now. My spirit singer has consulted with the spirits, and they told her that the fox-headed woman is travelling through Faneria alone. I don't know her purpose, but this is our best chance to put an end to her.

"Ashik, I want you to accompany this strike force and serve as their translator and guide."

Ashik drew in a sharp breath, and beside him, the chief straightened and turned to him. *Translator and guide for a band of warriors!* For a brief moment, he wasn't sure if he was excited or uneasy by the prospect. It was unlike anything he had done before. Of course, he could translate and guide them if he had no eyes and one leg, though he knew nothing of battle.

The more he considered it, however, the more the idea filled him with an electric energy. He would accompany the band of warriors that would hunt down and kill the malakh, the heart of the Army of

Light. It was the type of deed that was commemorated in song. And for the warriors that made up that strike force, battle meant honour. It meant respect. He wouldn't be only the voice in the centre of the bargaining table, he would be a part of what would become legend.

Ashik straightened, inhaling deeply. "I would be honoured, Uniter."

The Uniter beamed. "I am delighted to hear it." He held out a hand to shake, and when Ashik took it, he gripped Ashik's hand in both of his.

The chief clasped Ashik's shoulder, a wistful smile on his face. "You make us proud, Ashik, though it seems you are taken away from us once more before you can settle down."

Before Ashik could think of a response, the Uniter said, "I apologize for taking him from you." He smiled again at Ashik. "But I have the greatest respect for your decision to leave your home to help defend us all. Your success will pave the way for the rest of us to stop the Army of Light and keep the free lands free."

The Uniter spent a few more minutes telling Ashik of his mission, and impressing upon Ashik his desire for the force to leave the next morning. The suddenness shocked Ashik, but he knew the Uniter wouldn't ask it of him if their need wasn't urgent, so he agreed.

Soon, the sun set and the entire village, citizens and visitors alike, gathered for the feast. Voices rang off the low, flat ceiling of the longhouse as the sounds of singing and dancing filled the room. The air quickly grew warm and heavy with moisture and the aromas of a dozen cuisines from across the free lands.

Ashik briefly became the centre of attention when the chief of the village announced that he would be accompanying the force to hunt down and slay the fox-headed woman. The villagers let out a cheer, though Ashik noticed a few wistful, if not disappointed, looks at the announcement of him leaving.

A few people began trickling out, but the celebration continued well into darkness. Ashik eventually managed to leave while the feast and dancing continued with fervent energy. The temperature had dropped considerably since night fell, but after the fires and closeness of the longhouse, he was drenched in sweat and relished the cold air on his bare arms. He had slipped out through the kitchen and now clutched a small, tied bundle of mint and laurel. He paused a moment, breathing in the cool, dry air and allowing his eyes to adjust to the starlit darkness.

Voices, laughter, and light drifted out of the longhouse behind him as he walked through the central courtyard of his village. The lake gleamed glossy and still to his left like a vast pool of ink. In the distance, the lowing of the muroks and snorts of the goats rang across the open fields of the valley.

Silence gradually enveloped Ashik as he crossed the empty village. Soon, he came to a shrine that stood about chest high to him. It lay in the shadow of a building, barely a silhouette in the darkness, but he knew it so well that it seemed clear as daylight to him. He bowed before the altar.

"Ko," he said in a low voice, "please guide me well on this mission. I know I should have settled down and started a family since I returned home, but I have been adrift. I have missed trading so, even as much as I love the mountains. But this… this is a chance for renown, like I have never had before. I know I shouldn't wish for that, but I do. I know I cannot ask this of you, but I desperately want us to succeed. I want to be helpful, to be respected. I want to be *remembered*."

He hesitated, thinking that he heard distant threads of laughter from the feast, but only the chirp of crickets and occasional bleat of a goat challenged the deep silence. He laid the bundle of herbs on the altar.

"Show me my destiny, and open my eyes so that I may see it clearly."

Taking out flint and iron, he flicked a spark onto the herbs and blew on it to feed the flame that caught quickly on the dried bundle. The small fire illuminated the weathered statue above. Ko, her body indistinct and bundled in flowing fabric, spread her arms, a knowing look on her face and her cloak of stars billowing around her. Ashik stood and stared at her as the herbs burned.

"You worship a goddess of night?"

Ashik started and spun at the sound of the voice standing only a few paces away. In the faint light of the burning herbs, he could just make out the pale face and thin, darkly clothed form of the scarred Rturan man Ashik had seen that afternoon. Ashik's cheeks heated up with the thought that this man had heard his prayers, but the Rturan's curiosity seemed focused only on the statue of Ko.

Ashik let out a breath, glancing back at the altar. "Yes. Ko shows us that everything is ephemeral, and teaches us humility. Without night, there cannot be day. Without chaos, there cannot be order. That is why we must take comfort in sorrow, for it is necessary. Night comes too soon, so we must enjoy our time while we have it." He faced the Rturan. "That is why we celebrate loss, instead of mourn."

The Rturan cocked his head aside. "Interesting." The man had the lean, hard look of all Rturans, his dark clothes nearly making him invisible in the night, despite skin as pale as the westerners. Yet, there was an openness about his narrow face that was uncommon among his people.

Ashik cleared his throat. "I am afraid I don't know much of the customs of Rturans. Can I ask what it is you believe in?"

The Rturan waved a hand dismissively. "It isn't important. Our beliefs are from a bygone era."

"Your comrade this afternoon does not seem so inclined."

The Rturan huffed out a smile. "Ais Ainlan is from clan Atsura. They are staunch traditionalists who believe unfailingly that our people are destined to rise to power once more."

Ashik tilted his head to the side. "You have no such hopes?"

"I am a realist. Our emperor has no real power. Each clan rules its own land like a little kingdom of its own. There are so few of us left that we would not survive a real invasion. This mercenary work, this is our legacy."

The man was probably right, but the fatalism in his voice made Ashik's heart sink. He glanced at the statue of Ko, dismayed, despite her own teachings, to think that she would one day be forgotten. "You know, there are parts of Faneria where people still hold to cultures from the Time of Gods and Magic."

The man gave him a strange look. "Truly? In that Light-blasted kingdom?"

Ashik nodded. "Even conquered and controlled by a king, they follow ancient traditions, continue celebrating centuries-old festivals. In some small pockets, they even worship older gods."

"Are you saying there might be some out there who follow the Rturan way even now?"

"I am saying there is always hope. A king might claim sovereignty, but people remain themselves."

The man murmured skeptically, but Ashik could see a glint of hope in his eyes. "What about you?" he asked Ashik. "My people might be clinging to old ways, but yours seem to have benefited from interaction with the westerners."

"We have profited from trade, but we are not their people." He fixed the Rturan with his gaze. "And if they think they can cow us into following their burning gods, they are sorely mistaken."

The Rturan eyed him critically. "A fine sentiment, if you have the fight to back it up. The Army of Light does not come here to conquer. They come to annihilate. They will come to these mountains eventually."

Ashik frowned. He glanced over his shoulder at the carving of Ko. Was this his destiny? Was war sweeping toward the free lands like the tide coming in? Was it time for him to take up arms?

Everything is ephemeral, Ko's eyes seemed to remind him. It was difficult to accept, despite how it was ingrained into his culture. His people counted on the mountains to be stable and steady, even as they told stories about how they constantly changed. Even the peace and solace of Khaladon must eventually come to an end. Perhaps he couldn't stop it. But he could resist it.

"Then I suppose it's time for me to learn to fight." Ashik looked cautiously toward the Rturan. "Would you teach me?"

The Rturan cocked an eyebrow. "It is rare to find one who wishes to learn the Rturan way."

Ashik shrugged. "I definitely don't have the temperament for an eagle warrior, and the Makils wouldn't have me. Besides, our cultures are worth preserving, don't you think? After all, that's why you are here."

The Rturan tilted his head aside. "I suppose so." He stared at Ashik for a long moment. "You have a way with words, *korvesh-*Ashik." Unlike Ais Ainlan, the word he used for 'trader' made it into a title, much like the kind used among the Rturans. "I am beginning to suspect the Uniter was indeed wise to choose you to accompany our mission." He held out his hand. "I am Tir Kerstet of clan Onkaal, and you have my support."

Ashik clasped Tir Kerstet's hand. "Thank you."

Tir Kerstet grinned. "Even if your Rturan grammar is atrocious."

Ashik paused uncertainly, but the smile remained on Tir Kerstet's face. Ashik nodded in apology. "Forgive me. It's difficult to find someone to teach proper Rturan. I would appreciate any instruction you can give."

"It seems I have much to teach you on this journey."

Ashik bowed his head. "I don't mean to ask so much of you."

Tir Kerstet shrugged. "Well, we're meant to work together. It does none of us any favours if I refuse."

The light on the Rturan's face shifted to blue as the herbs smouldered and the fire died, while the moon rose over the peaks and bathed the valley in a pale glow.

"We have a long journey ahead of us," Ashik said. "We should get to sleep."

"Yes," Tir Kerstet replied. "We've a malakh to hunt."

Chapter 4
Into the Wild

GARRICK ENTERED THE main hall of Misengrad castle, the echo of his footfalls drifting down the cavernous corridor that bustled with its usual crowd of servants, clerks, and commoners come to plead cases before the duke. Heads turned as he passed through the crowd, eyeing the distinctive, elegant, serpentine plate armour of blued steel over polished mail that marked him as a dragon knight. His voulge, a glaive-like polearm, hung over his shoulder in a harness, the large, curved blade with its razor-sharp edge sheathed in leather behind his left calf. His grey-blue cloak, forked from his waist to his knees, drifted behind him. As ever, his head was bare, his reddish-brown hair hanging over the collar of his armour in a tail.

Garrick kept his eyes ahead as he walked, aside from an occasional grin or wink to someone staring intently. He hoisted the bulging leather bag he carried higher on his shoulder, food stores and other supplies straining the strap.

As he stepped out the immense open doors of the castle, he inhaled deeply. His whole body felt like it stretched out as he descended the stairs to the castle grounds, open air surrounding him for a hundred paces in every direction.

Garrick's steps lightened as he crossed the castle grounds, people passing in every direction around him. He soon spotted a lanky stable hand standing near the gates into the city, holding the reins of a huge chestnut horse.

Garrick spread his free hand as he approached the stable hand, his smile broadening. "Brenadier. It's so good to see you again."

The horse turned its head to regard Garrick with one dark eye at the sound of his voice. The stallion was as large and thick of muscle as any plough horse, yet with the narrow hooves of a riding horse. Brenadier was a destrier, a warhorse of the finest calibre. With his long, curly mane and tail, tufts of hair hanging off the backs of his hooves, and fine leather saddle and bridle, the stallion looked regal. He couldn't have looked more elegant if he was black, as his breed was supposed to be.

He looked exactly the same as he had a season ago, when Garrick left him with the survivors of a destroyed village in central Faneria so the knight could take a series of faster mounts to the Battle of Albrith. Garrick had never given up hope that he would recover the stallion, but part of him had worried that he might have lost Brenadier for good. Enough coin in the hands of a trustworthy messenger had gotten the horse back to Misengrad, but the weeks of second-hand assurances from the stables didn't compare to seeing the magnificent animal now.

Yet, when Garrick reached out a hand to the stallion's forelock, Brenadier snorted and moved his head away.

Garrick lowered the hand to his hip. "Oh, come on. Don't tell me you're mad at me, too."

The horse didn't move. The stable hand tried to suppress a smile.

"All right, fine." Opening the bag over his shoulder, Garrick pulled out a carrot chopped into rough pieces. Brenadier's ears pricked up and he turned his head toward the knight. Smiling, Garrick held out the carrot chunks and the stallion greedily ate them up.

"Do you forgive me now?" Garrick stroked Brenadier's head while the stallion chewed. He patted the horse between the eyes. "Next time I need to ride hard enough to kill a horse, I'll make sure it's you."

Pulling the sack off his shoulder, Garrick transferred some of its contents to Brenadier's saddle bags. Securing the sack behind the saddle, he mounted the horse and took the reins from the stable hand.

Garrick paused a moment, glancing around the courtyard from his vantage point atop the huge horse. The castle loomed behind, the ballrooms and splendour, the duke and nobles, and somewhere behind what Garrick could see, the Agaesi tower rose in its isolated corner, walled off from the outside and guarded from within.

Turning around, Garrick tossed the reins and rode out of the courtyard into the city. The mid-morning streets bustled as he made his way through the throng, greeting those who turned in interest or awe. Here at the heart of Hesperia, he didn't turn as many heads as he did elsewhere, but he still attracted plenty of attention as he passed. It was refreshing to finally be out of the castle and its grounds, yet with the buildings and people cluttering the streets of Misengrad, Garrick found himself hurrying when he could.

Finally, he reached the western gate out of the city and eagerly pushed through, the gate guards saluting as he passed. The handful of people in line to get into the city turned and watched as he veered away from the huts and shops outside the walls and rode toward the open fields stretching west.

"All right, Bren," Garrick said with a pat to the stallion's neck. "We need to make up for lost time." He lashed the reins. The horse took off at a gallop. Garrick leaned over Brenadier's bobbing neck and let out a whoop as the horse's hooves flew across the ground. The wind tossed his hair as his smile spread. The stallion's sinewy muscles rippled beneath him, Garrick's legs pulsing in time with the movement as he held himself above the saddle.

The powerful warhorse tired before long, and Garrick allowed Brenadier's gait to slow to a walk as he rode up the incline of a short hill. Garrick twisted around to look behind him. Misengrad lay less than half a league behind them, the towers of the castle rising over the walls in the distance. Houses scattered across the mixed cultivated fields between him and the city.

Facing forward again, Garrick patted Brenadier's neck and said, "Well, let's get to it." He nudged the stallion's flanks and turned toward the forest west of Misengrad.

Hesperian soldiers had tracked down Yanuk's old base after the Battle of Albrith, though the duke was assured there wasn't much left to find. It was as good a place as any to start searching for Yanuk's missing mages. Perhaps they had returned there, or Garrick could follow the same trail they had taken from the base toward Albrith and find them that way.

It was a slim chance. But slim chances were all Garrick ever had.

Soon, he reached the forest and a narrow trail running through it. For the following day, he picked his way through the forest, searching carefully for signs of the path leading to the abandoned base. He spent a damp night camping out in the wood with his cloak over his head to fend off biting insects.

Then, shortly after lunch the next day, Brenadier forded a sedate creek and Garrick spotted a faint gap in the trees that led northwest. The path was too narrow to be likely to lead to a village, yet too well defined to be a mere game trail. Aura Lake lay only an hour or two to the north, and the location seemed to match the directions

Garrick had been given to Yanuk's base.

Garrick pushed his way down the path, though it wasn't long until it curved toward a steep hill. Dismounting, Garrick led Brenadier up a winding trail slick with mud, overgrown, and littered with deadfall. To the north, the forest thinned considerably, showing only overcast sky beyond. Near the top of the hundred and fifty foot rise, he could look over the remaining hills and see the vast lake stretching into the distance.

The hill rose to a plateau, and Garrick slowed as the forest ended abruptly, a stretch of clear ground across the top. The grass on the plateau was overgrown and spotted with seedlings of trees eagerly attempting to reclaim the meadow for the forest.

As Garrick drew closer to the edge of the trees, he stopped. Across the top of the plateau, near the cliff edge towering over the rolling hills of forest beyond, he saw the old border fort. The stones were crumbling, the building outwardly in clear disrepair.

He gazed through the gaping doorway. The middle of the fort was illuminated nearly as brightly as the grounds outside.

As he watched, he saw movement within.

Garrick drew in a breath. *Someone's here.*

Staying well within cover of the trees, Garrick watched for a long time. He could see only one figure within. What the person did was difficult to determine at this distance.

Garrick watched a minute longer, then tethered Brenadier to a tree and crept his way through the forest until he was out of sight of the corridor through the entrance. He moved carefully across the open ground to keep his mail or plate armour from rattling. Coming up to the wall, he stepped alongside it until he stood beside the entrance. He peered around the doorway.

The entrance hall was ten paces long, opening into a large courtyard that seemed to make up about half of the interior of the fort. A young man with scraggly, dark brown hair and an unkempt, fuzzy beard moved about within. He knelt and picked at a plot of vegetables, pulling some to put in a basket beside him. He worked primarily with one hand. His other arm, hidden beneath his sleeve, looked unnaturally thin and seemed to end abruptly just below his elbow.

Garrick watched the man for a few minutes. He looked up at the cry of a hawk, but his attention never wavered from his task otherwise. While Garrick couldn't be certain no one else was there, it did suggest the man was alone.

Garrick's heart sped. It had to be one of Yanuk's missing

apprentices. There was no reason for anyone else to be out here, and certainly no way a one-armed man could survive on his own without knowing of the resources here. If only he would cast some spell, Garrick would have all the proof he needed, but he supposed the kind of magic Yanuk taught him would be of little use here. The spell likeliest to be of use to the man, the unseeing spell, would be the least helpful to Garrick.

Garrick glanced around the grounds, considering his strategy. He might be able to take the young man by surprise, but then, the youth might still be able to cast the unseeing spell before Garrick could catch him. Even if not, there was no way Garrick could take him all the way back to Misengrad under duress. Not unless Garrick thought he could make the journey without sleeping or eating.

Then I'll just have to convince him to come with me, Garrick thought.

He took one more look inside, focusing on the youth's face. It was difficult to make out the mage's expression at this distance, but the slump of his shoulders was of a man defeated.

Garrick's own shoulders sank. *Why am I doing this? He's not bothering anyone out here. In fact, he turned on his surrogate family because he* didn't *want to cause the trouble Yanuk was planning.*

Faneria wouldn't be any safer with this man locked away.

But he did willfully break the law by practicing magic, he rebutted silently, *and he may have stolen supplies from Misengrad as well. I can't just let a known crime go unpunished, especially after Yanuk felt emboldened enough to assault Albrith.*

Discomfort still nagged at him, much as he tried to avoid letting those thoughts coalesce. As he watched, the man finished tending the garden and picked up his basket, disappearing out of view.

Garrick let out a sigh as he slumped against the wall. As a knight, he had the power not only to apprehend criminals, but to pass judgment upon them as well. He was well within his rights to simply leave this mage alone.

But I have my orders.

Small consolation that was.

Finally, Garrick pushed away from the wall and stepped carefully over the grass again. As he reached Brenadier, he paused, glancing back toward the fort.

Do it, he told himself. *This is the only way to redeem myself. Just imagine the look on that smug bastard's face when I return and rub his nose in this victory.*

Thoughts of showing up the Scion made Garrick straighten, and he began unstrapping his armour. He would have to keep it packed away while he dealt with the mage, wearing only his mail. Even if he had a helmet, the style of his armour made it too obvious he was an Agaesi. If he was to have any chance of earning the mage's confidence, Garrick had to convince him that he stumbled upon him completely by accident and had no motives toward him.

What the mage really needed was a friend. Garrick could provide him that.

A lump formed in his throat at the thought, but he forcefully cast the distaste from his mind. He could always ask for mercy when he brought the mage to the duke.

Steeling himself, he inhaled deeply and untied Brenadier, turning toward the fort.

He perked up as he stepped out of the trees, in case the mage was watching. "Hey, look at that, Bren. We did find that shelter."

Garrick turned and moved straight toward the fort's entrance. He made no pretense at stealth and examined the fort as he approached as though for the first time. His boots stepped over the cracked stone walkway as he strode through the short passage, looking out at the courtyard.

He whistled. "We really lucked out, Bren. This place barely even looks abandoned. In fact…"

He let his voice trail off and his smile drop as his attention lowered to the ashes of a fire at the centre of the courtyard. His eyes darted around. A wide bucket lay near the remains of the fire, collecting rain water. Chickens pecked at the ground in a far corner. A couple of tools leaned against a wall near the garden.

A door creaked at the edge of the courtyard.

Garrick spun, drawing his voulge. "Who's there?" he called out, keeping his voice confident, but leaving out some of the force he would give it were he really trying to draw out a potential adversary.

A small yelp answered him, and he caught a glimpse of a figure darting away from the door to hide behind a pillar.

"Hello?" Garrick asked, quietly approaching the pillar. He cautiously peered around the edge of the pillar from several paces away.

The mage, trembling against the pillar, gasped as Garrick came into his view. Garrick straightened in surprise, lowering his voulge as he saw the mage fully.

"I'm sorry, Sir," the mage said in a rush of words. "I didn't mean to surprise you."

Garrick opened his mouth to begin weaving his story, yet as he stared at the mage, the words caught in his throat.

The mage breathed quickly and shallowly, worry clear in his eyes. Yet, he stood his ground. It should be easy for him to reach ingredients to cast the unseeing spell, or at least hide, but he let himself be seen by Garrick. His posture was guarded, but not hostile or completely closed off. As nervous as he was about this intruder, part of him did long for human company.

And Garrick was about to lie to him about being a friend.

Garrick let out a heavy sigh, the blade of his voulge lowering straight to the stone floor. He couldn't make himself do it. He couldn't condemn this man who had done nothing wrong, who desperately sought relief in the lies Garrick was going to tell him, to a lifetime of imprisonment, if not death, for believing them.

There was still no sense in scaring him off with the knowledge that Garrick was an Agaesi and knew he was a mage, so instead Garrick simply said, "You're hiding from something, aren't you?"

The mage's shoulders tightened and his eyes narrowed faintly. "What would make you think that?"

Garrick held a hand out at the weed-choked courtyard. "You're living out here in the middle of nowhere, alone." He watched the mage carefully, but there was no reaction to the claim that the mage was alone. "No one to help you if you need something or anything goes wrong. Seems to me like you're hiding. Maybe hiding from something you did?"

The mage shuffled slightly backward, his eyes narrowing a little more, but there was no surprise or denial in his expression.

Garrick looked away and found himself examining the evidence of this man's struggle for existence. The fort was crumbling and clearly drafty, the clothes hanging up to dry on a line strung across the courtyard were torn and threadbare, and likely he spent much of his day tending the garden and animals or preparing food, the same meals day after day. He had no company, no assistance, and likely no leisure time, either.

Garrick shut his eyes. This man had suffered enough, and for a crime that Yanuk committed more than him.

"Let me help you."

Garrick was giving up his entire future as an Agaesi, but he felt his heart lighten as he spoke the words and knew he could make no other choice.

He opened his eyes and faced the mage again, allowing his true face to show. "There's a village a few days west of here, off the beaten path, rarely gets any travellers. I can take you there and help you start up a new life."

The mage looked more wary, but not outright rejecting the idea. "What would I do there?"

Garrick shrugged. "Whatever you could. I'm a knight, I'm sure I could get someone to apprentice you, at the least."

"And why would you help me do that, if you think I've done something wrong?"

Weariness touched Garrick's eyes. He gestured at the fort around them. "Because you clearly don't mean anyone any harm."

The mage frowned, obviously wanting Garrick's offer to be genuine. "Why should I trust you?"

Garrick sighed, and he found himself being far more honest with the mage than he intended. "You probably shouldn't. About all I'm good at is lying and manipulating people." He slipped his voulge into its harness over his shoulder. "All I can do is swear to you that I'll help you reach this village, and if you don't want to accept, I'll leave and never tell anyone where you are."

The mage stared at him for a long time. His eyes twitched as he processed what Garrick said. Finally, he remarked, "You're… very strange."

Garrick smiled wryly. "That's far from the worst thing I've been called, or deserve."

"I'll think about it," the mage said hesitantly.

Garrick nodded. "I'm Garrick Magni."

The mage gave him a curious look. "I thought you were a knight."

Garrick grinned. "Not much of one if I really thought you had committed a crime, but was willing to help you escape it instead of arresting you. Just call me Garrick."

The mage looked uncertain, but answered, "Artra. Artra Langsdowne."

Garrick smiled and bowed to him, then looked toward the yellowing sky above the courtyard. "Can I just stay here the night? We can be gone in the morning. Me and Brenadier." He pointed toward the stallion grazing quietly several paces away.

"All right. I don't have much extra food, though."

"I won't impose. I'm happy to share any of mine, if you wanted something different."

Artra perked up, but was reluctant to follow up on the offer.

Garrick moved toward Brenadier and began removing his tack, starting with the saddle bags. "How about we start some dinner? I'll warn you, though, I'm not much of a cook. How about you?"

Artra finally emerged from behind the pillar, a small smile gracing his young, but weathered face. "I do all right, if I may say so."

Garrick smiled and gestured toward the saddle bags he had set on the ground as he loosened the girth strap on the saddle.

I'll never be able to redeem myself as an Agaesi after this, he thought. Yet, as he helped Artra prepare dinner and chatted with the young mage, Garrick found he didn't care.

The open road and the miles embraced Ashik like an old friend. It may have been long seasons since he had last left his village, but his feet hardened immediately to the climb and the walking as though he had never stopped moving.

It wasn't all the same, of course. He wasn't travelling to trade this time, but to kill. In addition, this journey was far louder and the mountains seemed positively crowded with the group he now accompanied.

"This is Tethe," the UNITER had said the morning they left. Ashik was presented with a tall, broad-shouldered, poised woman of sienna complexion. She had more scars than hair, and Ashik quickly learned that she was sparing with praise, or anything other than commands or demands for information.

"She is the right hand of her empress and the commander of her army," the Uniter went on while Tethe regarded Ashik as she might a hunting dog in training. "She has won over forty battles and is renowned among the Makils for her strategic prowess. That is why I have chosen her to lead this mission."

Ashik bowed to her. "It is an honour to be of service." As she continued merely to stare at him, however, he felt himself wither like a dried flower.

Next to her, the ferocity of the eagle warriors seemed almost friendly. Mahogany-skinned and massive, they all had small, hard eyes and thickly muscled bodies buried under layers of leather and hide. Ashik prided himself on his ability to remember faces, but even he had a hard time distinguishing between these Kathecs. Not wanting to mistake one for the other, he scrutinized their faces each chance he had to try to remember them. The Kathec empires were almost constantly at war with each other, and the way some of these warriors regarded others made it clear that they were from opposing forces. Ashik would have to tread carefully in his interactions with these dangerous men.

The rest of the Makil warrior queens were slightly warmer than Tethe, in the way that a mountain stream pounding over frost-drenched rocks was warmer than an ice-crusted lake. Many wore their dark locks long, though tied back behind their heads. Most of them were tall and ropy with muscle.

Ashik couldn't help frowning as he had gazed at the force he would accompany. For all his travels across the free lands, of these cultures, he had only lived among the Makils, and they were naturally distrustful of outsiders. Even these, though they knew they had to rely on him, looked down their noses at him. All of the warriors seemed to feel the same way about him, and he felt as though he shrank in size with each passing moment. He spoke enough Kathec to get by and Tir Kerstet had promised to help him with his Rturan, but before they even left, Ashik felt out of place, uncertain that he could do what he had been chosen for.

Then, the Uniter had introduced the last member of their party.

"Ialla is a spirit singer," the Uniter had said, gesturing to a slight, tawny girl with long, elaborate braids trailing down her back. "She will find the fox-headed woman. Then, it is up to you to lead the warriors to her."

As Ashik watched her, her uneasiness with her task was clear. A wave of relief washed over Ashik that he wasn't alone in feeling so out of place, even though he felt guilty for her suffering the same disquiet.

Their departure passed sooner than Ashik could prepare for, even despite the extended farewells the people of the village gave him, and he soon disappeared into the mountains as though in a dream. Half a week had passed since then. Ashik tried to focus on the familiarity of the paths he traversed, and yet the journey was so strange compared to his travels in the past that everything felt different, even his surroundings. Throughout the days of travel, he frequently repeated to himself that the Uniter wished him to guide this mission.

He has faith in me, he told himself again and again, trying to quell his nerves.

Ashik led the way, Urda lumbering alongside him as he made his way down the faint trails leading through the mountains. Behind him strode Tethe. Unlike some of her countrywomen, she carried her spear with her, her dark eyes occasionally scanning their surroundings. She seemed prepared for anything. The rest of the Makil warrior queens trailed behind her, focused but occasionally chatting amongst themselves.

The Rturans, the slender, pale-skinned mercenaries from the south, had settled into natural scouting positions around the group with little instruction from Tethe. Ashik occasionally caught a friendly nod from Tir Kerstet when their eyes met, but the others ignored him.

The Kathec eagle warriors, on the other hand, largely kept more distance between each other than they did the rest of the warriors. They marched with their donkeys between them, purposely avoiding each other's gaze.

As Ashik glanced back at the group he led, it took him a moment to locate Ialla. His shoulders slumped as he glimpsed the look of discomfort that she had worn since they left. He wanted to speak to her, but after a long day of travel and Tethe's sharp commands, he'd yet to muster the courage to do so. He watched her for a moment, but she didn't seem to notice his attention.

Ashik faced ahead instead, appreciating the view unobstructed by all his travelling companions, though the noise of their steps and voices still drifted constantly from behind him. The warmth of sunlight drenched his face for the first time since they set out from Khaladon and he relished the feeling.

He checked the position of the sun as he led them around a rise. Finding it less than a hand's width above the peaks to the northwest, he turned to Tethe.

"We should begin finding a place to set up camp," he said to her in Trade.

She narrowed her eyes at him with a challenging look that made him swallow uneasily. "The sun is still up. Surely we can travel longer."

Ashik kept his voice unwavering, but found it difficult to continue facing those severe eyes. "It is bright now, but night falls quickly in the mountains. By the time we find a place and set up camp, it will be very dark."

While she still looked displeased, she nodded. "Do you know of a good site?"

Ashik nodded. "There is a ledge nearby that is sheltered from the wind."

Without acknowledging him, Tethe called over her shoulder, "We will make camp soon."

A few of the warriors replied, some looking pleased with the thought of stopping. Ialla appeared openly relieved.

They continued around a couple more bends until, thankfully,

Ashik found the ledge he recalled. It was wide enough to fit shelter for them all and surrounded on two sides by twenty-foot cliff faces.

Tethe began barking out orders the moment they came to a stop on the ledge. The Makils efficiently began removing their animals' tack while the Rturans split up, four tending to their horses while the other four began setting up shelters. The eagle warriors remained apart, a couple pairs working together, but each largely focused on his own supplies.

"Kathecs," Tethe snapped in her sharp voice.

The eagle warriors stopped their activities to face her.

"You might be enemies on the battlefield, but here, we are allies and you will work together. Go collect firewood, all of you."

Some of the eagle warriors grumbled and many exchanged dark looks with each other, but they complied without complaint. They grabbed axes and machetes from the others' supplies, leaving their own supplies and animals for the Makils to tend.

Ashik couldn't help being impressed with the Uniter's foresight as he watched the large, burly men leave. The Kathec empires were known for their near constant wars, and the eagle warriors were the deadliest of all. Their battlefield savagery was infamous. However, eagle warriors were not given to lead. They were loyal brutes who looked to the elite general class for orders and then were left to decimate the field.

The Makil warrior queens, on the other hand, were strictly regimented and tactically superior. Tethe should have no troubles getting them to obey, even if it went against their nature.

"Ashik!" Tethe's call barked through the yellow dusk in a voice that compelled people to obey.

Ashik leapt from where he had been tethering Urda after removing the goat's tack. He hurriedly knotted the lead rope around the branch of a small, spindly tree growing near the ledge and jogged to Tethe's tent.

"Yes, Tethe?"

The flap of her tent hung open. Inside, she sat cross-legged on the ground. A map of Elderra spread out before her, filling much of the remaining floor space. She gestured him to enter with a curt wave. Ashik stepped inside and sat on another side of the map.

She pointed to the illustration of the Orthys Mountains, on the eastern side, around where they had now reached. The range spread from nearly the southern edge of the continent all the way to the northern coastline, creating a natural barrier between the free territories and the western nations.

"Why are you leading us all the way around the mountains? It is far shorter to cross them."

Ashik swallowed, reminding himself that she naturally had a sharp tone of voice. She was, after all, asking him, despite the accusatory sound to her words.

"The mountains have become dangerous, even for experienced travellers," he explained, failing to keep his voice firm. "Let alone those who do not know which ground is safe at a glance. I would be very distressed if any warriors fell before we even reached the malakh."

"But going south takes us close to the Fanerian border."

He pointed at where the drawings of the peaks petered out to the south. "The only settlement of any size near the mountains is a village called Aether. We can stay higher in the foothills and keep out of sight of it, and we will be far enough north to avoid watch towers and border sentries. Besides, if we mean to cross Faneria to face the malakh, it is best if we stay to the south, where there is more open space."

Even before he finished speaking, she was waving her hand dismissively and rolling up the map. "Fine. Go."

Ashik opened his mouth, wondering if he should say something to the dismissal, then simply bowed his head and hurried out of Tethe's tent.

Outside, he looked around the busy camp for a moment, trying to calm his nerves. All the warriors were busy, yet he didn't know what he should be doing. He quickly moved toward the supplies he had removed from Urda, only to find that they had been moved. An awkward search followed through the covered lean-tos that had been erected around the ledge. He noticed that the eagle warriors had returned and a few fires had been lit. The burly men still seemed to regard each other with suspicion, but they didn't keep as much distance between each other as they had earlier.

Then, as Ashik moved around a shelter deeper onto the ledge, he heard a faint grunt and stopped. Turning, he found his supplies piled up near the corner where the cliff faces met. The expanse of murok hide he had brought for shelter lay draped across the ground, propped up in one spot by a wobbling branch. As it shifted, he caught a glimpse of Ialla's braids swaying underneath it.

Ashik stepped over, lifting the edge of the hide to peer underneath. "Are you all right?"

Ialla gasped, startled by his appearance, before giving him an apologetic smile. "I'm sorry. I just wanted to help."

He couldn't help smiling at that, relief washing over him. "Here, let me show you how I do it."

Hunching her shoulders, she released the branch to his grip and shuffled out from beneath the hide. As Ashik folded the hide over the top of the branch on the ground, he found several other branches laying with it.

"Here, put that branch under the fold over there like this."

Following his directions, they soon managed to get the hide propped up. They ended up kneeling together inside a small room made of the hide.

"There we go," he said with a smile, lifting a side of the shelter to pull the rest of his supplies inside.

"Wow," Ialla uttered, squinting around in the darkness. "It's warm in here."

Ashik nodded. "Murok hide is good for that. Are you warm enough in your shelter?"

She rubbed her arms underneath her heavy cloak. "Not as warm as this."

"You can stay in here if you like. I have extra hides, and the cold doesn't bother me."

Turning, she fixed wide, doe eyes on him. "Are you sure?"

"Of course." He smiled softly. "It seems like you could use the comfort."

She averted her gaze.

"You're feeling out of place here, aren't you?"

Her shoulders hunched. "Yes."

Letting out a breath, Ashik settled on the ground beside her, staring outside where the flap of hide hung open. "I know what you mean. All of this seems so strange to me. I have never travelled with warriors before."

Drawing her knees to her chest, Ialla wrapped her arms around them. "I had barely ever left my village before I was called to Veil's Edge last year."

Ashik glanced at her. He had always been fascinated by spirit singers. They crossed cultural lines, being referred to by different names and accessed through different means, but no matter their origins or methods, the highest of them were called to Veil's Edge, that strange, spiritual place respected by all the free peoples. He knew that Ialla had been there when the Uniter chose her for this mission, but Ashik knew little else about her.

He was about to ask more about her spirit singing, but before he could, she continued, "And Tethe makes me feel like a burden."

He frowned, setting aside his questions for later. "Tethe has a sharp tongue, even for a Makil, but she's not a fool." He spoke as much to himself as to Ialla. "She respects experience, and surely she must realize how important we both are to this mission. You're the key to finding the malakh. Me… well, what can I do that a decent map doesn't?"

A light touch on his arm drew him out of his thoughts. Glancing aside, he found Ialla laying a hand on him.

"You're worth much more than that," she said, the tone of her voice still uneasy but trying to be reassuring for him. "I've seen you speaking to the Rturans." A shudder passed over her body. "They frighten me."

Shaking his head, his attention drifted once more. "Tir Kerstet is a friend, but the others… they don't need a translator. They don't care about talking. They respect action." Pausing, he laughed. "I'm sorry, I was trying to make you feel better."

She chuckled, a faint but genuine smile lighting up her face. "It's all right. I'm glad to know I'm not alone."

Ashik smiled in return, though he couldn't quite shake his own feelings of worthlessness. He tried to focus only on her face. "Well, shall we get something to eat and sit by the fire?"

"That sounds wonderful. I've never been so hungry as I have this week."

Ashik stood and held the flap of his shelter open as she stepped out. "It's the cold, and the thin air makes your breathing harder. Let me make you some butter tea."

Digging into his supplies, they gathered some food and turned toward the fires. Ashik remained lost in his thoughts as they passed into the quickly deepening darkness, the sky violet and rose above them and stars winking to life in the east.

A hand waving caught his attention. Tir Kerstet gestured beside him where he sat before a fire. He scooted away from the other Rturans spread out on his other side as Ashik and Ialla approached.

Ialla hesitated as they neared the Rturan. "Is it all right if I join you?"

Giving her a brief look, Tir Kerstet nodded. Ialla sat beside Ashik as he began preparing food and butter tea. He said nothing as he reflected on the Rturan's offer to teach him to fight before they had left Khaladon. Neither of them had said anything about it since, but after his conversation with Ialla, Ashik tried to draw up the courage to ask Tir Kerstet about it. The murmuring of various conversations in different languages hummed through the air as the fires crackled and snapped. Nearly complete darkness settled over the mountains as the trees occasionally rustled in a breeze, their shadowy branches rippling across the deep blue of the night sky.

Ashik was most of the way through his meal when Tir Kerstet broke the silence.

"You're quiet tonight."

It was nothing more than a passing observation, and the Rturan hardly looked at him as he made it, yet Ashik bit his tongue worriedly.

Drawing in a breath, Ashik ventured cautiously, "Are you… would you please teach me to fight?"

Tir Kerstet arched an eyebrow. "Are you sure? I'm not going to waste my time if you're not dedicated to it."

Ashik swallowed. Ais Ainlan, the short-haired Rturan woman, watched him as she sat across the fire. The look seemed calculating. Testing.

Ashik drew back his shoulders as he faced Tir Kerstet. "Yes. I want to learn."

Tir Kerstet stared at Ashik for a moment, then nodded. "Very well. Finish up and follow me."

Ashik hurriedly gulped down the rest of his butter tea, stealing a glance at Ais Ainlan as he did so. *Does she look satisfied?* he wondered. Perhaps less annoyed with his presence, at least.

He glanced at Ialla as he set his cup down. "Will you take my things back, please?"

"All right," she answered.

To his surprise, he saw a slightly sad look in her eyes in that moment. He had no time to reflect on it, however, as the sound of Tir Kerstet walking away drew Ashik after the Rturan into the darkness.

CHAPTER 5
A BIGGER WORLD

SILENCE FELL OVER the room. Damian and her father frowned at each other with sadness tinged with both hope and resignation.

Claude let out a sigh as he looked up at Damian from the sofa. "I suppose nothing I can say will make you change your mind."

Damian's heart wrenched as she looked down at him. For several minutes, she had told him why she had to leave, and he tried to convince her to stay. He had a counter for all of her arguments, she a rebuttal for each of his entreaties. It was clear neither mind would change, and eventually both had given up trying.

"I'm sorry, Papa. I just can't stay here." Kneeling down, she took his hand. "I'll come back."

He smiled wearily. "Where will you go?"

It was the question she had dreaded and prepared for the most. She knew she couldn't lie to her father, so she looked into his grey-blue eyes and told him as much of the truth as she could. Her attempt to convince him of the truth of her words and the conviction in them reminded her of Garrick, and she tried to emulate him.

"Somewhere I can do some good."

The look in her father's eyes made it clear he knew she wasn't telling him everything, but he only said, "When will you leave?"

"Tomorrow morning, I hope. I just need to speak with Sir Kennar." She stood. "Is there anything else you need from me before I go? Anything you want me to get?"

His moustache twitched in a faint smile. "I'm fine. I have people to help me."

Damian turned away with a meagre smile of her own. "I know," she said softly. "We will be back soon."

Liam followed her outside her house and into the street. Damian stopped there, her eyes searching as she looked up and down the road. It was strange to be looking for this man, like trying to find her own shadow. After a moment, she spotted him leaning against the wall of a house half a block down. Setting her shoulders back, Damian strode to him, Liam silently walking after.

The usual boredom in Sir Miles Kennar's face shifted to curiosity as she approached. He was a middle-aged man nearly as tall and easily as broad as Liam, all hard muscle and sharp lines. His thinning brown hair was peppered with grey, his beard full but short and his face lined, weather-beaten, and scarred. He was armed only with a simple, narrow sword, a padded shirt, and a calf-length mail tunic, but his bearing and the sharpness in his brown eyes made it clear he was a knight.

He had arrived in Aether a few weeks after she returned to the town, sent by the king to watch her and ensure she didn't cause any trouble or use any magic. Despite his constant presence every time she left her home, she had rarely interacted with him. Damian couldn't help thinking of Garrick as she looked upon him, as she had every time she noticed her Agaesi escort. However, though they were both dragon knights, they couldn't be more unlike each other. Damian hadn't yet decided if that comforted or bothered her.

"This is somewhat unexpected," Sir Kennar said as she stopped before him.

Damian kept her face as neutral and complacent as she could manage. "Sir Kennar, I wanted to let you know that I'm leaving."

He raised an eyebrow. "Is that so?"

She hesitated. "Is that all right?"

He shrugged. "I don't see why not. My orders were to keep an eye on you. The king didn't say anything about you being confined to this town. However, you do realize that you're going to get worse than this out there." He tilted his chin up, indicating the village surrounding them.

Damian let out a sigh. "I know. But there's nothing left for me here."

"That's a pretty bleak outlook on your own home." He didn't refute the point, however. "Where are you going?"

"Misengrad."

He drew back, more surprised by that answer than by her announcement that she was leaving. "That's a very long way from here. Why do you want to go there?"

As she studied the look on his face, she wondered if she should tell him the truth, despite what Garrick had said of the rest of the Agaesi in his letter. She didn't like the thought of lying to Sir Kennar about her purpose. *But Garrick has much more experience with them than I do.*

She shrugged, trying to look nonchalant. "I just want to get away. I've never been to Misengrad."

Sir Kennar eyed her carefully and Damian wondered if he had picked up on the lie. Instead, he nodded. "When did you want to leave?"

"As soon as possible. Tomorrow morning, if we can."

He raised an eyebrow. "It's a bad time of year to be travelling."

"Yes… but winter would be worse, and I don't want to wait another half year."

"Are you sure?"

Damian watched a townswoman walk by on the far side of the road, glaring at her the whole time she passed.

"I'm sure."

"Very well. I should be able to get ready by morning."

"Thank you, Sir."

A wry smile crossed his face. "I doubt anyone thanks their armed escort very often."

Damian grinned faintly. "Well, I appreciate it all the same."

"As I appreciate your telling me you're leaving. I will see you in the morn."

She nodded. "Good night, Sir." With that, they parted ways and Damian returned to her home.

She was packed and dressed shortly after sunrise the next morning. A tear rolled down her face as she embraced her father in the common room, him squeezing her with strength that defied his injuries.

His voice choked up. "Be safe, little Dame."

She winced, the sound of his voice eating at her. "You too, Papa."

She felt him raise his head. "Take care of her."

Damian glanced over her shoulder to find a deeply solemn look on Liam's face. "I will."

She drew in a breath, trying to steady her voice. "I love you, Papa."

"I love you too, Damian."

"I will come back." She nearly promised it, but the words caught in her throat.

"Do."

Pulling back, she gave him one last smile before picking up her stuffed pack and walking out the door, Liam behind her with a large bag over his cloak.

Sir Kennar was waiting outside, now garbed in a full suit of what looked like parade armour, inlaid around the edges with silver and mother-of-pearl scrollwork, some of which was chipped, dented, or scuffed. On his left hip hung a large sword with an ornate bronze hilt shaped into a dragon, the pommel its head, a ruby gleaming in its eye, and the blade sheathed in dark leather stamped with intricate designs. At his right hip hung the arming sword, along with two daggers. A forked grey cloak hung over his shoulders down to his knees. Even with his head bare to the autumn sunlight, he looked formidable.

The effect was nearly ruined by the shaggy palomino pony he held by the lead rope.

Damian covered her mouth as she attempted to stifle a laugh. The knight had clearly chosen the pony for a beast of burden, as it had no saddle, but a harness holding large baskets on its flanks, each stuffed full with supplies.

The look on Sir Kennar's face seemed aloof, yet Damian almost thought he was daring her to say something. He glanced between her and Liam as she walked up to him.

"Are you ready to go?"

She nodded. Inhaling deeply, she led the way west. The walk through Aether never seemed so long as it did that time. Their passage was marked by conspiratorial murmurs, relieved outbursts or outright cheers, and occasional expressions of regret. A few times, their progress was stopped as someone still friendly toward Damian spoke with her, surprised that she was leaving so suddenly. The whole time, as she was flanked by the graceful flow of Liam's black cloak and the jingle of mail against Sir Kennar's armour, she felt eyes upon her. Damian tried to focus her thoughts on Niabi, but she couldn't ignore the attention of the townspeople.

At last, they reached the northern edge of the harbour along the river. The ferry operator looked from her to Liam to Sir Kennar doubtfully until he stepped aside and allowed them to board.

Across the river, the ferry man backed away from Damian's outstretched hand and she dropped their fare onto the deck of the flat boat and stepped off. At the top of the first hill, she couldn't help looking back. Her chest tightened as she looked over the village. Wiping her eyes, she turned and continued toward the path.

The travel was a quiet affair that made the hours and the leagues stretch long. The sun climbed wearily through the sky as they walked, its zenith still seeming low in the air. Damian was relieved when the sun hung just above their heads nearly directly before them and Liam touched her shoulder, pointing to a hill to their left. Squinting, she could just see some shapes at its peak.

"Sir Kennar?"

He grunted in response, following her pointing finger with his eyes. "That could be shelter. It's worth taking a look." They made for the distant formation.

Near the top of the hill, Damian realized the tallest structure was the remains of a half-collapsed windmill, choked with ivy. As they crested the hill, a field of other broken buildings laid out before them. Many stone walls had collapsed, thatched roofs were gone, wooden support beams rotted, and the flagstones that must have once made up the roads were broken and covered with weeds.

"What do you suppose happened here?" she asked quietly, looking at the ruins and wondering about the families that must have filled these houses.

"Who knows?" Sir Kennar replied. "It could have been fire, plague, attack, famine. Maybe they left. I don't see any sign of mass graves. Whatever happened, it was a long time ago. All it means for us is a little bit of shelter." He clucked his tongue to the pony and strode through the gaping doorway into the broken windmill.

Damian frowned, looking over the ruins and trying to imagine the village when it was alive. A prayer filled her mind, but she bit back the words.

"Who do you pray to over the dead?" she asked.

"I have never considered it," Liam answered.

She gave him a curious look. "You've gone this many years without encountering any dead?"

"No." His gaze over the ruins was steady. "I feel that any prayers I speak would be meaningless."

Damian frowned, her eyes drifting over the destroyed village.

"But if I had to choose, I think I would speak to Fortune."

She looked at him, but he simply stared ahead. It might be appropriate to speak to Fortune, though it seemed to her like death was the moment when luck failed all. Even those who died peacefully left behind others who grieved. A much more kindly face appeared in Damian's mind as she thought of the statues in the now destroyed Temple of Time in Trent.

She spoke hesitantly. "What about the Goddess of Change?"

That was easier to accept. Everything changed. Damian's life had certainly changed since touching the stone fragment at the feet of the statue of Veran. Accepting change brought with it some measure of peace or comfort, even if it wasn't entirely welcome.

Liam seemed to consider the question before nodding slowly.

Damian smiled. She briefly considered speaking a prayer aloud, but a lifetime of seeing the Gods of Time as evil stayed her tongue.

They dropped their burdens inside an abandoned building not far from the mill, then started a fire and ate. The sun was setting by the time they finished. Damian sat on the remnants of a low wall to watch it sink below the horizon, Liam sitting beside her. They watched the light diminish in a companionable silence, the tree-dotted grass around them and the distant road quiet.

"You did not tell your father the truth of where we are going."

Liam's voice, though soft, drove into the silence like a hammer. It was not a question, nor even a prompt, but a casual observation.

Damian's gaze dropped to the grass at her feet. "He didn't see the things we did. Raven Point buried by the... Gods of Light." It still felt strange not to refer to them as the 'true gods'. "Niabi destroying Albrith in her obsession to kill Nephrita. He heard what I told him, but he doesn't truly believe it." She looked back the way they had come. Aether was far over the horizon and she saw no sign of the Ivory River. "Nobody does. They believe too strongly in the Gods of Light to think that they might do anything bad. That's why I can't just stay at home knowing Niabi is building an army for them."

Sighing, she drew her knees to her chest and wrapped her arms around them. "And yet..." She turned to the broken windmill. Firelight flickered through the open doorway and against the far wall, visible above the broken side nearer to them. "I still believe in them. Want to believe in them. I did my entire life. Just believing in them gave me strength and helped keep me calm. Even when I had nothing else, I had them.

"When *everyone* feels that Niabi's doing the right thing, and I've had a lifetime of trusting in the Gods of Light and their malakhs... I can't help but wonder if I'm the one who's wrong."

Stars glinted to life down the road. A lump grew in Damian's throat.

Liam's deep voice came suddenly out of the darkness. "Any being that would destroy an innocent town..." He spoke slowly, thoughtfully, as though he only considered what he said as he talked. "And kill innocent people does not deserve devotion. Or to be part of this world."

Albrith in ruins. Raven Point. Those images were scarred into Damian's mind. She wished she could tell the world the truth about both, about the Gods of Light. She did know one thing. Niabi didn't care.

And with her leading an army devoted to the Gods of Light? Damian shuddered to imagine the atrocities that force could commit.

"So… you're ready for this?"

It was a silly question, she knew. Liam was undoubtedly far readier than she was to take on this mission.

However, his nod was considered, rather than immediate. "It is good to have a purpose again."

She lifted her hand, wanting to place it on Liam's, but hesitated. Instead, she dropped it on her lap. "Thank you. For being here with me."

For a moment, he looked at her as though he wanted to say something. But he only nodded again.

As usual, the dining hall was quiet. It was late in the lunch hour. Many of the Agaesi stationed in the tower, and their families, sat at the long tables across the hall, but far more seats remained empty. Redge's younger children had already left to play in the courtyard, leaving him at the table with his wife. Like a few of the other knights and their wives in the room, they rarely spoke as they focused on eating.

What is there to talk about?

He tried to run over assignments for the knights for the week as he ate, but his thoughts kept drifting to his eldest daughter, who, once again, had not come down to the dining hall while he was there. His wife told him that during the hours outside her chores, she had taken to wandering the long-unused upper floors of the tower simply for a change of scenery.

Redge sighed as he noticed he had nearly finished his stew, heralding his imminent return to the same office where he sat day after day.

No wonder she's sick of this tower. I'm tired of being here and at least I'm allowed to leave.

A conversation between a handful of knights one table and several seats down from Redge grew more animated, their words creeping through his introspection.

"I'm telling you, she's getting ready to attack us."

"Why would she? It's not like she's after land or resources or the throne or anything. She's a malakh, for goodness' sake."

"Then why assemble this army in the first place? It stinks, it does."

Redge looked up, frowning toward the conversation. The knights, of varying ages, didn't notice his attention, nor that of the others around who began to listen in.

"Look, she already has her force in the north. The only reason she would gather another in the south was if she was going to march against us."

"I heard she's already headed our way."

Redge stood, allowing his chair to scrape loudly across the floor. "That's enough."

The knights straightened, some with mild starts. "Sir Warwick."

"I don't want to hear such rumours," Redge continued with a pointed glance toward the women and elders watching the exchange.

"But Sir, we were only—"

"The stories are circulating all over the place, Sir Warwick. There's got to be some truth to them."

"I don't care," Redge insisted. "You're knights, not some petty lordlings looking for idle amusement. I won't have this tower become some gossip parlour."

Some of the knights grumbled and a couple turned with a muttered, "yes, Sir," but as Redge returned to his own seat, it was clear their conversation was over. Their reactions were not the only signs of disappointment. The wives and elders who had been listening to the conversation faced their tables with frowns.

Never mind, Redge thought, *that I've heard enough of the same stories to feel it's all but confirmed that the Army of Light is marching toward Faneria.*

With a brief goodbye to his wife, Redge picked up his bowl and spoon and carried them back toward the kitchen. His eyes were drawn to the two elder knights who now silently spooned stew into their mouths, looking bored with the end of the conversation. It was all too easy for Redge to imagine how desperate he would be for even the wildest rumours of the outside world once he had to hang up his halberd for good and stay locked in this tower for the rest of his life.

Redge shook off those thoughts as he returned to his office, but he had hardly begun to return to his duties when Brannik rushed in, clutching a paper.

"Sir Warwick," he wheezed. "Summons from the duke."

Redge's frown deepened as he read the note, brief as before. The rumours whirled through his mind as he waited until the appointed time.

The mood in the room was different this time. Redge could sense the tension thick on the air as he stepped through the doorway. It wasn't the same room where he had last met with the duke and advisors a season ago. This was a council room, dark and austere, dominated by a heavy, polished table with fifteen chairs and the walls decorated only with large maps of Faneria and Hesperia. This was a room where war was planned.

The crowd was different, too. There were fewer nobles in the room, mainly those that led notable standing forces, and the duke's son, the Markiese of Gredsk. One lady sat tall and proud among them, the Dowager Countess of Verchesse, a region directly on the border with Edan.

Redge knew everyone present from various military engagements over the years he had served as captain of the Agaesi, though one face he recognized he hadn't expected. He took a seat near the end of the large table.

As the last straggler arrived, the duke said, "Thank you all for coming, gentlemen, lady." He briefly introduced each of the people in the room. "I'd also like to welcome Sir Lyle Hitchcliffe, formerly captain of the Misengrad city guard, now training men in the city in arms and combat."

Sir Hitchcliffe, sitting farthest from the duke, nodded to the room at large. His eyes met Redge's briefly, but he showed nothing more than a flicker of recognition for their meeting back in spring.

If the manner of this meeting hadn't made its intent clear enough, the introductions served to prove to everyone what they had been gathered to discuss. Dread settled over Redge as an uneasy silence fell over the room.

"I know you have all heard the rumours," the duke began. "Unfortunately, they are true. The southern force of the Army of Light has moved out, and reached our border."

A flurry of whispers and murmuring rose up.

"Have they come to make war with us?" uttered a man near Redge.

The countess, sitting to the duke's right, raised her chin. "I received word from my son, the earl, last night. The Army of Light, headed by the," her nose wrinkled as she continued, "malakh, camped out along our border after asking to pass through and we refused."

Someone snorted in amazement.

"What can they be thinking?" said another. "Do they really expect to march an army up to our borders and expect we'll just let them through?"

"Evidently," the countess replied with arched eyebrows. "The earl reports that they did not bring any siege equipment."

More voices chimed in as the din in the room grew.

"No siege equipment?"

"Edan is supposed to be our ally."

"What are they after?"

Redge caught Sir Hitchcliffe's eyes and saw a similar look of concern mixed with mild annoyance in his eyes as in his own.

"Enough," came the duke's booming voice, and the others silenced. "We cannot be sure of their intentions yet, but the fact is we need to bolster the line, and fast."

"I can have two hundred men ready to march by the end of the week," spoke one noble.

"They will provide good support, but we need reinforcements sooner. The Army of Light may not be prepared for a siege, but we cannot know if or when they plan to storm the border. Sir Warwick, Sir Hitchcliffe, your forces are here in the city. Can you have men ready to march by tomorrow morning?"

Redge frowned. "I can spare a handful more knights, with horses, but the Agaesi aren't meant to counter sieges."

"It is still more blood and more eyes to watch the Army of Light encampment. Sir Hitchcliffe?"

Sir Hitchcliffe looked thoughtful. "If they continue their training, perhaps thirty are proficient enough with a bow to bolster the defences. I cannot prepare those training this morning, but I can send them along to catch up with the rest by mid-afternoon tomorrow."

The duke nodded. "Do that. Keep up your training regimen. If you can ready more archers, inform me at once, but depending what happens, we may have need of more infantry, as well."

Sir Hitchcliffe bowed his head. "Yes, Your Grace."

Others could contribute more men immediately, bringing over a hundred to reinforce the lines within the next few days, if they marched hard. Redge listened quietly, committing the numbers to memory and forming a map of the border defences in his mind.

Eventually, the planning wound down and the duke leaned forward against the table, his brow knitting seriously.

"Now, listen. I know I cannot keep stories and rumours from circulating, but we all know what danger spies pose. Nothing that we say in this room about the Army of Light shall be discussed to anyone not invited to these meetings. Similarly, if any of you receive any confirmed information regarding the Army of Light, you are to share it at these meetings with everyone present. We are all here for the protection of Hesperia, and as the first line of defence for the entire kingdom against the Army of Light. I have utter faith that I can count on each of you for that purpose, but I want to ensure that there will be no secrets among us.

"Are there any final questions before we adjourn?"

Everyone around the table either answered negatively, shook their heads, or remained silent.

The duke pushed his chair back and stood, all others rapidly following suit. "Then I thank you all again for coming. Be ready. We will be meeting about this again soon."

Those final words hung on Redge's mind as he walked out of the room and returned to the Agaesi tower.

CHAPTER 6
REUNION

A VILLAGE CAME into view over the horizon. Damian watched the buildings appear between the rolling hills of eastern Faneria. It looked slightly smaller than Aether. The houses and shops spread out to either side of the main road that ran through the village. Farmers worked in the fields and pastures beyond and people and animals passed through the streets within.

As they drew closer, Damian lifted the hood of her cloak. Her braid fell over her shoulder as she draped the hood over her head, trying to shadow her face or at least her eyes with it.

She caught Sir Kennar giving her a curious look. "Wouldn't it be easier to just wear a veil like you used to?"

Damian looked away, frowning, and fumbled for words. "It's not that simple." She tried to put voice to the thoughts that swam through her mind, but then, taking a cue from Liam, his soft footfalls beside her, she decided nothing else needed to be said.

Sir Kennar merely shrugged and faced forward, leading the pony to his other side. Damian wrapped her cloak closer about her, though not from the chill in the air.

"We should pick up a little more food for the road," the Agaesi said. He sent her a sidelong glance. "Do you want me to handle that?"

Already the villagers at the edge of the town looked curiously at the new arrivals. She sighed. "That would probably be best."

Heads turned as they strode down the main street of the village, but none approached. Some even seemed to give the three of them extra space. Their interest seemed more focused on Sir Kennar and a little on Liam rather than her, however. Damian felt relieved, along with a strange sense of disappointment.

Soon, they found a bakery. Sir Kennar regarded Liam for a moment before thrusting the lead rope of the pony in his direction. Silently, Liam took the lead as the knight opened the door.

Damian watched him for a second before she realized his eyes were on her as he held the door open. Her stomach twisted. "Can't I just wait out here?"

"I have my orders." Sir Kennar gestured inside the bakery.

Peering inside, she found a mostly open room crowded with counters along the walls and a large table in the middle. Shelves of jars and sacks of various sizes lined the walls above the counters. Flour dusted nearly every surface. A brown tabby and ginger tom cats rested on the counter near the door while several people kneaded dough and leaned over ovens. Shutters hung open on every wall and up onto the roof, leaving the room well lit. There would be little hiding inside.

She swallowed. "You didn't stay so close to me in Aether."

"In Aether, there wasn't much danger of you running off. It's my duty to keep an eye on you."

Damian's expression fell. While she hadn't interacted much with the knight at home, he had seemed to treat her respectfully and had given her more leeway than she anticipated, and certainly more than the guards who had escorted her to Aether from Albrith.

I guess trust is too much to ask, even from an Agaesi. Silently, she strode through the door. She moved into the corner beside the doorway as Sir Kennar followed her inside, standing near the main counter. The brown tabby watched him in interest as he called for one of the bakers.

"Come back later this…" said a stout man shorter than Damian, stopping himself as he saw Sir Kennar standing at the counter. Clearing his throat, he hastily handed his lump of dough off to the plump woman next to him and hurried around, dusting his hands. "Welcome, Sir! What can I do for you?"

"We need food that will travel well. Biscuits, hard rolls, that type of thing."

The baker glanced briefly at Damian when Sir Kennar said 'we,' but focused on the knight and brightened as he finished. "You've come to the right place, Sir! We pride ourselves on bread that stays fresh the longest. We just made up a batch of our famous mini crusty rolls, perfect portions that stay fresh for over a week, and our specialty is oat-currant-blueberry biscuits—very filling, excellent for travelling, and they'll stay fresh nearly as long as the rolls."

Damian watched the brown tabby as the baker spoke. It rose and stretched, then moved forward to rub its head against Sir Kennar's gauntleted arm, though he pushed it away. Undaunted, it spotted her and hopped across to the counter along the wall to walk toward her. She idly scratched between its ears as Sir Kennar and the baker talked, but couldn't help wincing when the baker stated an outrageous price.

She stepped forward. "Ah, Sir Kennar, perhaps some payment in barter might be to everyone's…"

The short baker turned to her as she approached. She trailed off as he saw her eyes, gasped, and lurched back, shielding himself with his arms as though she pointed a blade at him. All the other bakers stopped and stared at the commotion. Those who saw Damian's eyes before she lowered them spouted prayers to the Gods of Light with upturned palms or hid behind counters. Obliviously, the cat continued rubbing up against her.

"That's the… that's the…"

"That is the woman I am guarding," Sir Kennar cut in.

The short baker pointed a stiff finger at Damian that still remained well out of her reach. "We won't serve her kind here."

Sir Kennar shifted, putting himself between Damian and the baker. "You will serve me if you wish me to continue guarding her."

The baker sneered. "You're one of *her* ilk? You're not welcome in my bakery. Get out!"

The baker had barely finished speaking when Sir Kennar slammed a fist on the counter, the crash of metal on wood ringing throughout the bakery. Everyone, including Damian, flinched, and the other bakers who had begun to utter their support of the stout man fell silent.

"You will serve *me* as a knight of the realm and a dragon knight of Hesperia or I will arrest you for treason," Sir Kennar snapped in a voice of stone. With his other hand, he drew a few coins out of a pouch on his belt and slapped them on the counter.

The short baker paled and then his eyes widened as he looked at the coins on the counter. Damian's eyes enlarged as she looked at the offered payment, double what the baker had asked. It was enough to put them up at a luxurious inn for half a week.

The baker's gaze darted between Sir Kennar, Damian, the coins, and the cat still leaning against Damian. The room was so quiet Damian could hear him swallow.

"V-very well, Sir. Your order will be ready in the morning."

He made no move to collect the coins, but one of the bakers behind him turned to tend an oven that had remained open throughout the conversation.

"It had better be." With that, Sir Kennar turned and walked out of the shop, holding the door as Damian followed. The knight snatched the lead from Liam and stalked back to the main road. Damian nearly had to jog to keep up.

"I have never been treated like that." He glanced at her from the corner of his eye, his expression not unfriendly. "Perhaps you should stay out of sight next time."

"I'm sorry, Sir."

He made a dismissive noise in response. "I'm only surprised you spoke up."

"He was trying to swindle you. Those rolls were only worth half what he asked."

He shrugged. "It doesn't matter."

She watched him for a long moment as they continued walking. Over the years, she had seen knights who were boastful with their coin, though most still paid at least close to the going price for goods or services. She had never met another like Garrick, who was almost egregiously generous to those he favoured, beit friend or stranger, and who thought nothing of massively overpaying for things, without seeming like he was trying to impress anyone.

And now there was Sir Kennar, who acted as though coin wasn't an issue at all.

Are the Agaesi really that wealthy? she wondered and suddenly felt a little uncomfortable.

She caught a glimpse of Liam walking beside her. Had she not known him so long, she would not have recognized the faint questioning look in his eyes. She tried to give him a reassuring smile.

They obtained a few more supplies, this time with Damian quietly hiding her eyes by the doors of the shops they visited, before finding an inn for the night.

"Which room will you be staying in," Sir Kennar asked Liam, "or will you be getting your own?"

Damian blushed at the suggestion that Liam might share her room.

Liam answered, "Yours."

Was it her imagination or did he hesitate very briefly before answering? Damian stole a glance at him, but couldn't discern anything in his expression before she hastily looked away. She found it hard to subdue the warmth in her cheeks as Sir Kennar paid and they retreated to their separate rooms.

When Damian returned to Aether, her father had asked if Liam was courting her. She had smiled as she denied it and helped set up a bed for Liam in her work room among the fabric, sewing supplies, and mannequins. So why did the suggestion make her cheeks flush now?

She cast those thoughts from her mind as Sir Kennar pointed her to her room for the night, next to the men's but farther down the hall. If she left, she would have to walk by their door, and a glimpse at them entering their room showed Sir Kennar claiming the bed near the door. She went into the next room, shivered, and lit the wood stove in the corner.

Half a week in and a long way to go. She started thinking of Niabi, but her mind darted from topic to topic as she got comfortable. Before long, Sir Kennar, now out of all his armour but his mail, came to fetch her with Liam and they went downstairs for supper. They claimed a table in a darker corner and Sir Kennar ordered and brought their meals. Even as the inn filled up, the tables around them remained empty and those people seated beyond stared and whispered.

"I guess word travels fast in this village," she remarked wearily as she watched one woman raise her hands and face toward the ceiling after meeting Damian's eyes. The innkeeper watched Damian from behind the bar with a deep frown.

Sir Kennar glanced over his shoulder before returning to his meal. "We'll leave in the morning."

When they crossed the common room to return to their rooms, people shuffled their chairs aside. Damian felt eyes on her from every direction. She hurried up the stairs, overtaking Sir Kennar. It wasn't until she shut the door that she realized she should have wished Liam and Sir Kennar good night.

"Favourite dessert."

"Easy. Cinnamon flip-pockets."

As Garrick slid cautiously down the muddy, leaf-strewn hill, he caught a glimpse of the curious look on Artra's face.

"What are those?"

"It's a very thin pastry, folded over and tucked into itself, drizzled with butter and sprinkled with cinnamon."

Artra sounded wistful. "I've never had cinnamon before. I've heard it's delicious."

"You have no idea." Garrick's mouth watered merely at the

memory.

The morning light glared in their eyes as they made their way down the washed-out trail. It hadn't taken Artra much convincing to leave the desolate old fort behind. Loneliness may not have been his only problem.

Garrick grinned over his shoulder at Artra as he came up with another question.

"Favourite kiss."

Artra's reaction was as dramatic as Garrick had hoped. The mage flushed bright red and avoided his eyes.

"Er, well…"

Garrick raised his eyebrows.

Artra shifted. "Her name was Poppy."

"Yes? Go on."

"Well, she had brown hair. She was almost as tall as you. And very, um… shapely."

Garrick glanced back, finding Artra even redder. He decided to release Artra from his torment. He focused on the path before him, clutching Brenadier's lead tightly.

"She sounds lovely."

"She was." There was a note of pain he tried to hide in his voice.

Walking in front of Artra, Garrick allowed sympathy for the one-armed man to cross his face. It sounded as though this woman had been one of Yanuk's mages. For a moment, he considered telling Artra that he was only the first of the mages to turn their backs on Yanuk, and that others might be alive and free even now.

That would cause complications, however, as Garrick had not revealed that he knew where Artra came from. Soon, Garrick would be out of his life forever. If he could set the mage up with a new life where no one who wished him harm would ever find him, then it would be better if he didn't cling to hopes that he would reunite with some of his former companions.

Instead, he merely deflected attention from Artra's thoughts.

"All right, your turn."

To their disappointment, the westward trail became more overgrown and difficult to navigate, and the only town it led to, late in the day, was the remains of an abandoned logging settlement. The forest was rapidly reclaiming the land, the ground thick with ferns and undergrowth and a number of trees already reaching two or three stories high with branches breaking through walls or lifting thatched roofs off their supporting beams. Garrick, Artra, and even Brenadier took shelter in one of the sturdiest of the remaining buildings as it began to rain.

Artra fidgeted as he stared into the fire, speaking little but looking troubled.

"Are you all right?" Garrick asked.

Artra looked up, frowned, then returned his attention to the fire. "I'm just worried. I've... been living apart from society for so long." He glanced up, looking through the gaping window at the rain. "I don't know if I can handle it."

Garrick smiled warmly. "You'll be fine. I've seen plenty of people less able than you able to carry on their lives just fine."

"Really?"

Garrick nodded.

"And... you'll help me get on my feet?" The worry in his eyes increased as he looked at Garrick. Garrick couldn't blame him. He was still lying to the man, easily. However, the sincerity with which he spoke was entirely genuine.

"I swear it. Whatever I can do to help convince them to take you in and settle down, I'll do it."

Artra still seemed slightly wary, but nodded in relief.

Garrick smiled. *It's nice to be honest for a change, even if just a little.*

Shortly after leaving the settlement the following morning, the trail forked.

Artra looked down the northward trail. "This trail is better tended."

Garrick frowned, trying to recall the maps of Hesperia he had viewed so many times. "It is, but we're still not that far from the lake. I'm not sure the town is to the north." He glanced down the other way. "If we keep heading south, even if we miss the town we're looking for, we'll eventually make it back to the farms, or the road."

"I suppose so."

Clicking his tongue, Garrick led Brenadier down the muddy southward track, Artra walking alongside.

The sky remained overcast as the trail wended through the forest. Garrick thought he kept track of which direction they walked, but an occasional glimpse of sunlight through the clouds often revealed shadows that proved him wrong. The path, meanwhile, grew more leaf-strewn and overgrown with bracken and saplings. Eventually, it petered out altogether, and they could only tramp on through the forest as best they could. Garrick hoped he wasn't leading them around in circles. He frequently looked for signs of the sun breaking through the clouds, only to be disappointed time and again.

It wasn't until an hour or so after lunch that he noticed a niggling feeling that he realized had been building for a while already. At first, he dismissed it as the change in the air preceding another storm. Yet, he realized after a few more minutes of walking, despite the constant cloud cover, there were no other signs of impending storms. The wind was no stronger than normal, the air no damper than to be expected this time of year, the leaves of the trees put their dark sides toward the sky, and that peculiar taste in the air before rain wasn't there.

He tried to dismiss the sensation again. There was nothing unusual about this hilly, rocky forest, aside from its wildness.

But no, there was no ignoring that strange tingle along his skin. If anything, it seemed more potent than before.

"Garrick?"

Garrick blinked. Artra stood a few strides ahead, glancing curiously back at him. Garrick hadn't realized he had stopped while he focused on the sensation.

He shook his head. "Sorry. Just trying to figure out where we are."

Artra squinted toward the pale, featureless sky between the thick canopy of leaves. "Well, I think we're still going south, at least somewhat."

"That's good enough for now, anyway." Garrick moved on after Artra, guiding Brenadier between trees.

And nearly stumbled.

The sensation was gone.

He glanced around, but hurriedly fell back into step, lest Artra notice. The feeling had vanished so suddenly, while he was focused on Artra, that the normality of it didn't strike him until a moment later. His eyes swept across the hills, stones, and trees, but the tingling hadn't seemed to emanate from anywhere.

Shaking his head, he moved on.

Garrick was more watchful, but didn't let on anything to Artra as they continued through the forest. They continued clambering over the rough terrain, seeming to travel far for the constant change in scenery, but knowing that they had not made all that much ground for the day.

As they struggled to climb a rocky rise, Garrick ventured, "I guess we should have tried our luck at the lake." He grinned apologetically.

Artra shrugged with a smile. "It's all right. As long as we don't run into any bears or wolves."

That would be an unwelcome surprise, Garrick agreed. They carefully strode along the ridge at the top of the rise, the forest opening up to their left.

"Well, as long as we're going roughly in a straight line, hopefully we shouldn't have much more of this." He hesitated to name a time range, in case he turned out to be terribly wrong, but it seemed more optimistic to add, "Maybe a couple more days."

Artra rubbed his upper legs as they descended the far side of the hill. "I'll be in better shape after climbing all these hills, that's for sure." Another hill rose sharply to their right, quickly obscuring the view.

Garrick chuckled. "Nothing like a long hike through the wilderness to build up your strength."

Artra smiled. "At least the view's quite—"

He cut off abruptly as Garrick grabbed his arm, stopping in his tracks. They had just reached the base of the hill, another rising before them as the hill that rose to a small cliff face to their right curved around away from them.

Garrick froze, listening. He swore he heard leaves rustling under heavy feet nearby. Artra watched him curiously, nearly about to say something before Garrick shot him a significant look.

As soon as Brenadier fell still, they heard the thump of another horse's hooves just around the bend.

Hand still on Artra's arm, Garrick pulled the mage back. Garrick caught a glimpse of Artra paling as he handed Brenadier's reins to the mage's one good arm. Garrick drew his voulge from the harness on his back and crept forward.

A suspicious silence lurked around the corner of the cliff face. Garrick edged up to the rock without rustling his mail, keeping the blade of his voulge low. He expanded his senses. The rock and forest came into sharper relief, the shadows less dark and colours crisper. A breeze rustled leaves like the thunder of a galloping horse, and he heard the creak of leather and snuffling breath of a horse maybe ten paces around the bend. He could taste a faint aroma of steel on the air. Behind it, he could sense a powerful aura of magic.

His eyebrows rose. *Magic?*

As he focused on the presence of magic, he realized he could sense a few other, much weaker ones, around it. Dread crept over him, until a glint of light to the side caught his eye.

Sprites. The small, floating orbs of light drifted lazily through the air around the bend. Garrick settled his nerves. The sprites were drawn to the magic presence. That strong aura, not to mention the horse rider around the corner, was far more concerning.

He waited for a long minute, hoping the interloper would lose patience and advance first, but the rider was clearly well trained and didn't budge. Garrick did hear the gentle thump of another horse's hoof against the ground as it shifted in place.

He needed to assess the situation. Drawing upon more of Agasis's power, he felt strength fill his muscles, his body reacting far quicker to his thoughts.

Garrick crouched down silently, bringing his face nearly to knee level. Then, he craned his neck quickly around the bend.

He had only a fraction of a second to see the fully armoured, mounted knight lowering the aim of his bow before he released the arrow. In that moment, Garrick scanned the path around the knight's bay horse, seeing the hill rising to the left, memorizing the placement of the nearest trees, and taking in the other knight atop a brown horse some ten paces farther back, sword drawn and wearing a tabard marked with the sunburst of Edan, like the archer.

Garrick snapped his head back around the rock as the arrow shot past, immediately lunging to his feet and charging around the bend after. The bowman hurriedly reached for another arrow, but with the speed of an Agaesi, Garrick darted toward the nearest tree, jumping and kicking off it toward the bowman. Before the Edanese knight could draw the second arrow from his saddle-mounted quiver, Garrick sailed across the gap and swung his voulge. To his strength, the haft of his voulge just below the blade struck the knight in his full suit of plate and knocked him off the saddle like a sack of potatoes.

With a skip step over the horse's saddle, Garrick landed astride the fallen knight, lowering the blade of his voulge threateningly over the knight's neck.

Before it reached his intended position, however, a brick wall seemed to slam into him, throwing him backwards nearly as far as he had jumped. Fiery pain swept over his torso as he flew, but it faded swiftly under the power of Agasis. By the time he landed on his back, he managed to flip his legs over him and stand at a crouch, voulge held at the ready.

His eyes were immediately upon the knight just now rising, but a glint of gold and a flash of pastel colour beside the second knight drew his attention farther down the path. Garrick's eyes widened even as his brows drew down in anger.

"Niabi," he growled.

A swath of emotions rushed over him at the sight of the golden-haired fox woman. Anger, shock, suspicion, and yes, a thread of inescapable fear.

Niabi's black eyes narrowed, her muzzle wrinkling and fangs showing. "You."

The fallen knight drew his sword, but had yet to attempt to re-mount his horse. His eyes flicked quickly to the malakh. "You know this man, Lady Niabi?"

Garrick's eyes narrowed, his own gaze shifting between the knights and Niabi. "Why, didn't she tell you about the times we met? When she tried to murder an innocent young woman?"

The mounted knight looked briefly surprised, though the standing one merely returned a skeptical look.

Niabi sneered. "That girl held the power of Nephrita inside her."

"Which she was born with." Garrick surreptitiously examined their surroundings as he spoke. There didn't seem to be anyone else accompanying Niabi. The knights would be easy enough for him to handle, but he doubted he could defeat Niabi alone. "She *begged* you to help her control it and your response was to turn her into stone."

He wasn't likely to be able to run. Whatever Niabi was doing in Faneria, he was sure it wasn't good, especially if she and her knights had managed to slip through the border undetected. He had to get word through to Misengrad about her appearance, and he still had Artra to worry about. Perhaps he could get a message through to the mage to flee with Brenadier without Niabi or her knights knowing. Garrick could at least keep them busy long enough for that.

A low growl rumbled in Niabi's throat. "If you had not interfered, your cities would never have been destroyed."

Anger swept over him, flushed with guilt he quickly cast aside. The haft of his voulge creaked as he clenched his fingers around it. "*You* caused just as much damage to Albrith as Nephrita did. If you had ever pulled your muzzle out from under your own tail, you would have realized that I was trying to prevent Nephrita's return as well. We could have worked together!"

Niabi's hackles rose. Her sneer lengthened to show her full complement of sharp teeth. "You were never on the side of the True Gods. Nephrita escaped because of you!"

Nephrita escaped from the Battle of Albrith? Garrick couldn't ponder that tidbit any further, however, as the standing knight began to look impatient with the conversation.

And of course, Garrick couldn't help thinking wryly, *here I am again without my armour.*

"Lady Niabi, what shall we do with this man?"

Come on, Artra. I need your help. He raised his voice slightly, just enough to ensure that Artra would hear him. "Kill me if you must. I'm prepared to die to defend my kingdom. But you won't make it through Faneria without people finding out. Word will spread. And once Misengrad knows you're here, you'll be facing all the forces of Hesperia."

Unsurprisingly, Niabi was unswayed by his words. "Then they will be heathens all, and deserve whatever death they receive. Just as you do."

Garrick had barely registered the beginning of the tremor in the earth when he leaped, his body reacting to his thoughts quicker than he could comprehend them. Large blocks of stone crashed together with a deafening crack just behind his feet. He charged quickly over to the unhorsed knight, knowing that his best chance lay in being too close to one of Niabi's escorts for her to risk killing Garrick with stone. He spun in quick, unpredictable arcs around the knight, avoiding the ropes of grass that sprang up around his feet to ensnare him. Dodging or parrying the knight's seemingly slow and clumsy swings of his sword was easy, and Garrick slowed his movement to keep from killing or knocking out the knight too fast.

The other knight soon caught up, galloping in with his sword swinging down. Garrick nimbly leaped aside, but his movement was clearly expected, as a fern snaked around his ankle the moment he landed. Garrick swung his voulge down and tried to stab at the plant, but he had barely turned the long weapon before the fern yanked at his foot, throwing him toward the cliff face. Garrick could only brace himself, holding his head out and absorbing the crushing impact in his right arm and thigh.

He grunted as he smashed into the unyielding rock. The natural bumps in the rock dug in like daggers, while his arm and leg felt like they were completely flattened. He barely registered the sound of rocks shaken loose and tumbling down around the bend as his momentum faded and he slipped off the cliff wall.

The falling stones elicited a neigh, and a soft yelp, around the bend.

In the span of an eye blink, Garrick looked at Niabi and saw the tip of her nose raise, eyes enlarging slightly at the sound. The unhorsed knight seemed to pause as well, though Garrick had to block another swing from the mounted knight.

As the sword struck the ironwood haft of Garrick's voulge, he heard a rustle of plants around the bend. Another, louder whinny rang through the air, and a cry of pain.

"Artra!" Garrick cried. He let his voulge dip slightly, bringing the blade of the sword closer to his head, before he shoved out, pushing the knight's arms into his chest and throwing him backwards off the saddle. As he fell, Garrick darted around the brown horse and down the path around the bend.

He fell still at the sight that awaited him.

Brenadier huffed as he struggled to regain his hooves from where he had clearly been knocked onto his side. The stallion seemed little the worse for wear for the attack, though he had landed on the sack containing Garrick's armour.

Artra, however, lay unmoving on the ground. Three ropes of grass as thick as Garrick's wrist twined clear through his chest and stomach and out his back. Dark blood stained the grass and Artra's tunic.

Garrick clenched his fingers tighter around his voulge. More plants shot up from the earth to wind around his feet as the knights, mounted once more, charged toward him, swords out.

Spinning his voulge, Garrick neatly stabbed it through the plants grasping one foot, bracing himself and yanking the other out with a great heave.

He spun to face the two knights bearing down on him, swinging his voulge around. He didn't hold back this time. He swung his voulge with all his strength, smashing the blade into the ribs of one knight and shoving him so hard off the saddle that the brown horse stumbled and fell onto its side as well.

The other knight was now close enough to swing his sword, but Garrick shoved his voulge backwards, ramming the butt of it into the knight's chest and unhorsing him as well.

He lowered the weapon, glaring at Niabi with fire glinting at the edges of his vision.

"He did nothing to you!"

Columns of rock shot out of the ground toward him, but once again, he leaped clear before they crashed together. Garrick braced himself for further attacks, but Niabi merely stared back.

"As you said, I could not allow witnesses to spread knowledge of my presence here."

Garrick's breath rushed in and out of him, each making his blood burn hotter, fire pumping through his veins. He reached along the thread connecting him to Agasis, drawing more power than ever before. Rage flooded him and his muscles strained against his clothes, his skin digging into his mail. Pain and restlessness washed over his entire body.

Roaring like a beast and his entire body enflamed, Garrick stormed toward Niabi.

CHAPTER 7
GATHERING STORM

DAMIAN AWOKE TO knocks on the door.

"Miss Sires?" Sir Kennar's voice came through the door.

She sat up, shaking off sleep. "Yes?"

"The sun's been up nearly two hours. We should get moving."

She looked at the window in surprise. Bright, clear light filtered through the shutters to glow against the window.

"Yes, of course. I'll be right out."

She hurriedly dressed as the surprise gradually wore off. The travel had left her exhausted. It was little wonder she slept in, though she had rarely stayed in bed quite so late.

When she opened the door, Sir Kennar was standing outside, fully equipped with his elaborate armour and weapons. "Perhaps we should stay another night. I don't know if we'll be able to reach another village before dark now."

She averted her eyes, remembering the looks on the faces of the people in the common room the last night.

"I'm not sure that's a good idea. Can't we camp out?"

"I'm quite sure that's not a good idea." Sir Kennar sighed. "Unfortunately, I think you're right. We'll have to make do. Pack your things. We're all ready to go."

Damian hurried back into the room to gather her belongings, then followed Sir Kennar and Liam down the stairs. She ate a quick breakfast, cold and tough and served with a scowl, before following the men outside. The pony waited, its baskets stuffed full once again, and through the gap beneath one lid Damian could see the corner of a biscuit. She hunched her shoulders, ashamed that she had held them up so long.

With their late start, the day seemed particularly short. Their path through a valley was narrow and ill-tended. The main road leading from central to eastern Faneria skirted south around these foothills of the Orthys Mountains, and few people chose to go through them. The steep hills and stands of juniper and poplar trees made darkness descend quickly. They only stopped to rest twice before the sun dipped behind the hills. They had yet to come across any other signs of people.

"I didn't think we'd make another town before dark," Sir Kennar said. He pointed toward the top of a rise to the north, where a few slabs of granite jutted through the grass. "Let's make camp up there."

"Isn't that a little exposed?" Damian asked, thinking of the animals that occasionally wandered as far south as Aether, and of bandits.

"I'd rather be somewhere we have a good view." Sir Kennar led the way off the trail and up the slope. Damian exchanged a glance with Liam as they followed.

Damian gathered branches and lit a central fire as Sir Kennar and Liam assembled shelters and started smaller fires within them. Nighttime fell quickly and the chill in the air seeped through Damian's cloak. Chores completed, she began to sit down before the central fire until she noticed Liam, standing at the edge of camp and staring into the distance.

"Liam?" She walked up to him. "What is it?"

"Fire."

She followed his eyes as Sir Kennar joined them. Her eyes widened. A few hills over, perhaps half a mile off, the distinctive flickering glow of a fire glinted between the trees.

"Somebody else is out there?" Damian asked, surprised.

"I wouldn't count on it being anything good," Sir Kennar commented.

The light vanished.

Damian straightened. "They put it out."

"They probably don't want us knowing they're there." Sir Kennar turned back to their own camp.

Damian looked at him, trying to tamp down her fear. "Should we move our camp?"

She and Liam returned to the fire as Sir Kennar knelt beside one of the baskets. "It would take too long and it's too dangerous to stumble around in the dark. It's better if we get as much rest as we can so we can deal with them in the morning, if we have to."

Frowning, Damian sat before the fire. She doubted she would

sleep very well this night. It was strange that the people a few hills away weren't using the road, and stranger still that they moved north of it. There were very few villages in the mountains north of Aether and none of them were very large. If the people who extinguished that fire came from east of the mountains, they should be using the road. She couldn't imagine them as anything other than bandits.

Before she could say anything more, however, Sir Kennar stood. "Stay here. I'll be back soon."

Damian opened her mouth to respond, but he strode into the darkness before she could. She noticed that he hadn't removed any of his armour or weapons. The ensuing silence fell like a weight over her and Liam, one even the cracks and snaps of the fire couldn't break.

"He isn't going to…" she attempted.

Liam looked as confused as she felt. "I cannot see him doing so alone."

He can't be going after the people at that other fire, she thought. *He's here for me. But then, what is he doing?*

They could do nothing but eat and watch the darkness as the last traces of daylight faded in the west. Much as Damian tried to tell herself not to worry, that Sir Kennar knew what he was doing, she couldn't help staring down the path anxiously.

Finally, the distinctive jingle of Sir Kennar's armour came out of the darkness, as well as his shadow against the path.

Damian let out a relieved sigh. "Sir Kennar. I was beginning…"

Her smile faded and her voice trailed off as he approached. Someone else walked with him. Rather, he gripped the back of someone's collar and pushed them along in front of him. As he came closer to the firelight, Damian could also see a scowl marking his face.

Sir Kennar approached the fire and shoved his captive forward so he sprawled in the grass on the far side from Damian, and dropped an unfamiliar rucksack at his side. "We had a mage following us."

Damian's eyes widened. "What?" she breathed. Her attention was drawn to the captive just as he looked up and met her eyes, starting slightly at the sight.

Damian gasped. "You?!"

His eyes enlarged. "You?!"

Sir Kennar's eyes narrowed. "You know this boy?"

The 'boy' in question was a man not much older nor larger than Damian, wearing layers of faded and threadbare clothes, with a mop of dark curls on his head. As he leaned on his hands and knees on the other side of the fire, she saw the patches of bone-white skin against his otherwise olive-toned complexion that she immediately recognized.

"Yes." Her eyes narrowed. "I caught him stealing from the market in Windermere a year ago."

Sir Kennar's expression darkened further. "Is that right?"

The man with the patchwork face groaned softly as he looked away.

"I tried to report him to the city guard, but they didn't..." Drawing in a breath, her eyes widened. "...see him."

Looking frustrated, the captive threw himself back into a sitting position.

"You... you're one of Yanuk's mages, aren't you?"

"I was his apprentice," he answered in a defeated tone, not facing any of them.

The reaction was immediate. Sir Kennar drew his sword, Liam shifted to put a hand on his own, and Damian slid back from the fire in a crouch.

The mage glared sidelong at Sir Kennar, blade glinting in the light, and his voice hardened. "What do you think I was doing in that backwards little village? I didn't support what Yanuk did." Looking away, a faintly pained expression crossed his face. "I abandoned him."

Sir Kennar loomed closer, not relaxing in the least. "Why were you following us?"

The mage's eyes narrowed. "Apparently, I wanted to ruin my life."

Sir Kennar's sword moved silently toward the mage's neck. "Answer the question."

Leaning away from the sword, he snapped, "All right! I was tired of hiding who I am, okay? I was Yanuk's apprentice for fifteen years. We lived peacefully, not bothering anyone, and now my home and everyone I knew is gone. I heard that the 'witch' from the Battle of Albrith was in town, and... I just wanted a piece of my life back."

He let out a sigh, glancing briefly at Damian before looking away.

"Clearly, it was a mistake. I'm sorry. I was never out to hurt anyone."

Damian pursed her lips as she took in the misery in his expression. It was a far cry from the blank look he had given her when she caught him with an armful of items taken from various booths at the market a year ago.

"That may be," Sir Kennar replied, "but magic is forbidden. Mercenary, watch him."

Standing, Liam moved two steps closer to the mage, drawing his blade. Sir Kennar sheathed his and knelt behind the mage, drawing a length of rope out of the pony's supplies and tying the captive's hands behind his back. The mage didn't move or struggle.

He sent a frustrated look to Damian. "You see? This is why we had to go into hiding. My one spell was more than some of them did and they were all condemned to exile and starvation."

Damian shifted, avoiding his eyes.

"You knowingly and willfully broke the law," Sir Kennar snapped as he knotted the binds holding the mage's arms behind him.

"It's the only spell I've cast in half a year," he growled.

"The reason why doesn't matter."

"Well, it should!"

"That's enough." Rising, Sir Kennar turned to Damian. "We have to take him with us until we reach somewhere that can hold him."

Damian swallowed as she looked at the mage. He returned a look that maintained its hardness for only a moment before he slumped in defeat.

Sir Kennar glanced between Damian and Liam, looking unhappy. "I'm sorry. With only three of us, I have to ask you to help guard him through the night."

Damian nodded. "That's fine." Surprisingly, her voice sounded small.

They decided upon a night watch and Damian hurried to finish her supper. She stole furtive glances at the mage as she did. He merely sat cross-legged before the fire, arms tied behind his back. As soon as she finished eating, she rose to retreat into the small shelter, barely large enough for her to lie down around the small fire burning within.

As she turned, however, the mage spoke.

"My name is Rhyslen. Rhyslen Noskopoulos."

Damian stopped. She turned to the mage. A weary look was in his eyes as he gazed back. She glanced at Sir Kennar and Liam. The knight, unsurprisingly, sat hunched over his supper, glaring warily at Rhyslen. Liam, on the other hand, did not appear impassive as usual, but regarded the mage with an unreadable expression.

After a moment, she turned back to Rhyslen. "Damian Sires."

He nodded, his features softening slightly.

Pausing, Damian wondered if she should introduce the others, then gave up and disappeared into the tent.

Despite the thoughts rushing through her mind, sleep came quickly to her. Although it was hard to drag herself out of her bed in the blackness of night, she felt rested enough by the time Sir Kennar woke her and she emerged from the shelter.

Wrapping a blanket around herself, she hunched down beside the fire. Liam and Sir Kennar had kept it going, though the flames burned low, providing meagre light against the deep cloak of night. Her breath clouded on the air, though her heavy gown and cloak and the wool blanket kept her comfortable.

After adding a few branches to the fire and coaxing the flames higher, she glanced around. As Sir Kennar's movement inside the larger shelter settled down, soft sounds of Liam sleeping drifted out through the canvas walls. Damian smiled at that.

She turned toward where they had seen the distant fire when they made camp. The moon hung low, throwing long shadows across the hills tinted deep blue. No signs of anyone else could be seen. She could only hope whoever was out there didn't mean them any trouble.

Shuffling nearby drew her attention. Turning, she saw Rhyslen lying in the grass beside the shelter where Liam and Sir Kennar slept. His hands were still tied behind his back, and in his tossing, he had apparently pushed his blankets off. Between shivers, he attempted to use his feet and teeth and roll his body to tug the covers back over himself, with little success.

Frowning, Damian rose, leaving her blanket on the ground, and approached him. "Here, let me help," she said. He lay still, looking up at her. Carefully avoiding touching him, she grabbed the blankets and pulled them back over him.

He shivered again, this time in relief as the blankets radiated his warmth back into him. "Thank you."

With a curt nod, Damian turned back to the fire, sitting and wrapping her blanket around her shoulders. She tried to focus on the gentle flames, but her attention kept being drawn back to Rhyslen. He shifted as much as he could with his arms bound, trying to get comfortable against the ground.

"Why were you following us?" she asked.

His eyes shot open, betraying how far he was from sleep. "It's like I said." He sighed. "Living in that village, giving up my magic, it felt like I was torn in two. I went around town as half a person, while the other half of me was hidden beneath the floorboards." He curled in on himself a little more. "It had been so long since I was around anyone who understood who I really am. I was desperate for any connection to my old life, no matter how slim." He huffed. "I guess I was better off as half a person. Now I can look forward to going to prison the rest of my life, or hanging."

Silence fell over the campsite as Damian watched him uncertainly. "How did Sir Kennar catch you?"

"I lit a fire. I've never been good with flint or tinder, so I used a spell to make the kindling catch. I had no idea he was there until he leaped out of the shadows and put his sword to my neck."

Damian's stomach twisted.

He must have noticed her reaction, because his voice strengthened as he added, "I've never used magic to hurt anyone. Ever."

Her eyes narrowed. "You used Yanuk's spell to steal from the market in Windermere."

Averting his eyes, he muttered, "I gave everything back."

"You never even looked remorseful. The only reason you gave those things back was because I caught you. You never even thought it was wrong, did you?"

"Of course I knew it was wrong. Look, I was confused when you caught me because you're the only person who's ever been able to see through our spell. I didn't understand how you could see me."

Damian's voice hardened. "You were using that spell to rob people. I saw you, you never hesitated and you grabbed whatever you could carry. Those goods are the merchants' livelihood, the fruit of their hard work, and you didn't care."

"Stop calling me a thief," he growled. "I always thought stealing was wrong. I've just been doing it so long that I set those feelings aside. I had to. It was the only way we could survive."

"There's always another way. You just chose to steal because it was easier."

Damian could see his eyes narrow in his patchwork face as he stared at her. "You have no idea what hardship is like, do you? I was the fifth son of a tanner. Not the only child of a successful merchant."

Damian bristled and wilted at the same time.

"Nobody taught me any skills. I spent my childhood scrounging for scraps because there wasn't enough food to go around and I was too small to wrest any from my brothers and sisters. I was never going to inherit anything and looking like this, I sure wasn't going to marry any better." He couldn't gesture with his hands bound, but the tilt of his shoulders drew attention to the splotches of white skin on his face, and presumably the rest of his body. "It was only a matter of time before my parents sold me into servitude, if I didn't starve to death first. I had nothing to hope for."

He let out a sigh and the bitterness shifted to wistfulness. "Then, Yanuk found me, and he told me I was special. That I had a gift few people did, and that he needed me. I went with him that day and never looked back. And when I got to the home he had built and met the other mages he had gathered… for the first time in my life, they looked at me like I was perfectly normal. Before that, no one had ever looked at me without at least pity. Can you imagine what that's like?"

Damian turned away, thinking of the first time Liam saw her eyes, and every time since. "Yes, I can."

He paused, then nodded. "Yes, we had to steal. Those people, Yanuk's mages, had served their kingdom faithfully their entire lives, only to be blamed for something they had no part in and cast out with nothing. They had nothing to trade and no one would ever have given them a chance to do any honest work. Some of them tried, you know. Did you see what happened to them? Patrus had both his hands cut off for practicing magic, despite that he did so in service to the Earl of Marrows. Edrand, who had lived in the same village for half his life, those villagers tried to burn him alive. The people of Misengrad never even knew Yanuk was there until the people in the same castle where he had served the Duke of Hesperia for sixteen years called him out. The people of Misengrad gathered in the courtyard to condemn him and he took a stone to the head before he ever even knew why they hated him. So yes, we had no choice."

Damian's expression softened, though she still regarded Rhyslen with some suspicion. "They looked fairly well-off when I saw them."

His voice evened out as well. "It takes a lot of resources even if all you're trying to do is survive. Seeds to plant our garden, tools to work it, buckets to put the crops in, pots and knives and spoons to cook them. Digging a well and making furniture. It took years to build a home." His voice choked.

She stared at him as he tucked his chin into his chest.

"I just… I still can't believe that he's gone. All of them are gone." His legs curled tighter about himself.

"I'm sorry."

Rhyslen didn't look up. "Are you?"

Her eyes narrowed. "I'm sorry that you lost people important to you," she replied somewhat defensively.

"Is it true? What people say he did?"

She hesitated, wondering if he really wanted to know the truth. "Yes. He cast a spell that bound the Goddess of Chaos to him, and he used her to attack Albrith."

"Stars above."

She took a breath. "I tried to talk him out of it. He wouldn't even consider sparing the people of Albrith."

Rhyslen let out a sigh.

"You don't sound surprised."

"Yes, he was bitter about the way he was cast out. Anyone would be. But he never cared. He just wanted to build our community, create a safe haven. Where did he even find a spell to bind a god?"

She frowned. "I don't know the details. It was in a book he stole. Someone told him about it."

"It figures." Bitterness returned to his voice. "People say they don't trust magic, but they won't hesitate to use it if it's to their advantage. Clearly somebody couldn't leave well enough alone and manipulated him into casting that spell."

"Yanuk didn't need any encouragement," Damian returned darkly. "He rejoiced in the suffering and death he caused."

"He was pushed to the brink and used even in the end," Rhyslen growled.

"Well, that's not what I saw."

In the darkness, she saw the anger in Rhyslen's eyes before he deflated. "You only saw him at his worst. I only knew him at his best. As a leader. Someone who encouraged and supported his fellows, and who opened his home to other outcasts."

Silence fell.

Before Damian could think of anything to say, he shifted. "I'd better get back to sleep. I probably have a long march to my death tomorrow." His voice held hints of both frustration and defeat, and she couldn't tell which was more prominent. He seemed to try to roll over before deciding against it and merely making himself as comfortable as he could the way he lay.

She watched him as he fell still and his breathing slowed, then turned her eyes to the dying fire.

*   *   *

Ashik felt like a child.

Frustration knitted his brow as he paced in front of Urda, the goat contentedly grazing and ignoring Ashik striding back and forth with the end of his lead. Ashik stood with Ialla and a handful of the other warriors, surrounded by the animals and supplies.

Stopping his movement, he gazed uphill, where Tethe and the rest of the warriors gathered. They crouched along the crest of the hill, staring out where the Fanerians they had spotted the last night travelled.

He had not even been given a chance to study the mysterious group. When they came to this hill, Tethe ordered him and the others to wait with the animals and proceeded to the top.

I am here as their guide, he seethed as he resumed pacing, *their expert on Faneria! I should at least see who those people are so I can tell them if they're anything to worry about.* Instead, he was treated as a child asking to sit with the grown-ups at meal time, given a sharp glare from Tethe when he tried to voice his protest.

She has seen me training with Tir Kerstet, but I am still not a warrior to her. Not to be respected.

He frowned, wondering if it was even possible for him to earn the respect of the warriors he travelled with. Perhaps they only saw him as a burden.

He glanced aside at Ialla, hoping for reassurance. She met his eyes, returning an uncertain look.

Footfalls nearby drew his attention away, and he turned to find a Makil warrior queen skipping down the slope toward them.

"String your bows," the Makil ordered. "Tethe wants us in position before they round the next bend."

Ashik blinked as the Rturans hastily retrieved bows and the other warriors grabbed weapons.

"What?" Ashik asked. "Why—who are they? How many?"

The Makil shook her head as she removed her poleaxe from one of the horses' tack. "Four people, only two armed. We are not near a town, so this is the best place to do it. Animals will take care of their remains and no one will know we were here."

More of the warriors began to come downhill, though some remained to keep watch on the Fanerians. Ashik could only watch as they prepared for battle, dumbfounded. Four people, travelling alone through the mountains, only two of whom were any danger, against over twenty of the fiercest warriors of the free lands? The Fanerians hadn't even tried to find the fire they may or may not have spotted the last night. They had simply continued on their route.

"You are to remain with the animals," the Makil ordered as she twirled her poleaxe.

Around him, Ashik heard eager chuckles as hands hefted weapons. Ialla, on the other hand, only shook her head at him. A few of the warriors, now well armed, slipped into the woods to take positions on the other side of the path. Ashik watched them leave with a mixture of dread and disappointment.

This is why they don't respect me. I will never be this eager to kill.

But do those people really have to die?

Dropping Urda's lead, he crept up the hill.

A few of the warriors at the top of the rise turned sharp looks to him as he neared, and one eagle warrior grabbed his shoulder as he peered over.

"Ashik," Tethe hissed, her voice losing none of its sharpness for its lowered volume. "Go back."

Ignoring her command, Ashik pushed against the eagle warrior until he could see over the hill. He spotted the unwary Fanerians below, his heart clenching as he noticed the young woman with them. As he examined them further, however, he grew confused. What he saw didn't make much sense.

"Keep him out of the way," Tethe snapped quietly to the eagle warrior keeping a firm hold on Ashik. Then, to the other warriors remaining with her, she said, "Get into position. We strike soon."

"Wait," Ashik barked.

The eagle warrior's grip tightened threateningly on Ashik while Tethe shot him a dark glare at the level of his voice.

"Don't attack them," Ashik pleaded, trying to implore Tethe to believe him with his eyes.

"Silence him," Tethe ordered the eagle warrior.

The Kathec reached a huge hand toward Ashik's mouth, but he pulled his head away and said, "They are more dangerous than they appear!"

"Get him out of here," Tethe growled, and a second eagle warrior grabbed Ashik, glowering all the while. Ashik tried to protest again, but the first clamped a huge, meaty hand over his mouth. They lifted him bodily and began carrying him down the hill. No matter how he struggled, he couldn't break free of their grasp, and desperation turned to panic as the other warriors got into position.

"Let him go."

All eyes turned and even Ashik ceased his struggling.

Tir Kerstet stood calmly at Ashik's elevated feet, though his eyes were on Tethe. "He knows Faneria as none of us do. If he thinks this is a mistake, we should hear him out."

Ashik twisted his head around, eyeing Tethe sideways as he hung suspended in the eagle warriors' arms. Her eyes narrowed into a darker look than the one she had given him as she regarded the Rturan.

"We cannot allow them to tell others of our presence," she replied firmly.

"Maybe they won't," Tir Kerstet answered. "But more importantly, Ashik seems to think attacking them would present a danger to us."

Tethe sent her glare to Ashik, who nodded as fervently as he could with his head still clutched tightly in the Kathec's hand.

"Would it not be better," the scarred Rturan went on, "if we knew what awaited us before attacking?"

Tethe stared at Tir Kerstet for a moment longer. Silence hung over the hillside. Finally, she glanced at Ashik from the corner of her eye. "Speak quickly."

The eagle warrior removed his hand and the words poured out of Ashik as though out of an overfilled cup.

"The knight, do you see the style of his armour, and how he has no helmet?"

A Makil warrior snorted. "It shows dat he is a fool."

"No, it shows that he is a dragon knight. Their prowess in battle is legendary. The stories of their power surpass even those of the eagle warriors."

One of his captors twisted an arm and sneered into Ashik's face as he winced, biting back a cry. "You dare say we are weaker than these knights?"

"No, listen to me," Ashik struggled to say. The pressure on his arm eased and his next words rushed out. "They are known for travelling alone and they do not take on squires, and they certainly do not get assigned any mere escort duty, not even for royalty."

Tir Kerstet grasped the implication. "You think he is guarding the others?"

"It's the only explanation I can think of. It's like having an eagle warrior guard someone like that. Which one is he guarding? How dangerous must they be if a dragon knight must guard them?"

Ais Ainlan, the short-haired Rturan woman, had strode up during the conversation, strung bow in hand and quiver of arrows at her hip. "We still killing him all. What difference this making?"

Ashik, still hanging from the Kathecs' arms, replied, "The dragon knights are known for having almost inhuman senses. He might stop any arrows coming toward him. And we have no way of knowing how dangerous the others are. Please, Tethe, our mission is the fox-headed woman, not these people. It doesn't matter if they saw our fire. Don't risk any of our warriors over this."

Tethe stormed over to him, teeth bared as she glared down at him. "You do not give orders."

He flinched, though he couldn't gain any distance from her. Around him, however, he could hear some discontented muttering among the handful of warriors remaining on the hillside. Tethe continued staring hard into Ashik's eyes. He tried to continue meeting the look, but the strain of holding his neck up coupled with the discomfort of her gaze had him turning away after a moment.

Then, Tethe turned and marched back up the hill without a word. Silence fell as all the warriors watched her. Ashik twisted his head back to watch as well.

At the top of the hill, Tethe crouched, cupped her hands around her mouth, and let out a sharp triple cry like a jay.

The eagle warriors holding Ashik grumbled and unceremoniously dropped him to the ground. Some of the other warriors joined them in sulking off down the hill.

Ashik leaned forward, wincing as he rubbed his shoulder where it struck a rock when he landed. Looking up, he found Tir Kerstet holding a hand out. Ashik gratefully took it and the Rturan helped him to his feet.

"What happened?" Ashik asked.

"That was the call to stand down and return," Tir Kerstet explained. He began to say more, but Tethe appeared beside Ashik once more, her glowering, hairless face filling his vision.

"You do not *ever* question my orders," she snarled. "If you have a problem, you speak to me *alone*."

Without waiting for a response, she turned and stalked down the hill, snapping out orders as she went.

Ashik swayed in place, his knees trembling. When he leaned his hands on them, he found that nearly his entire body shook along with them.

"She is not happy," Tir Kerstet remarked as he watched her descend the hill toward the animals. "You've embarrassed her. That won't be forgiven easily."

He turned to follow the Makil woman, but Ashik stopped him with a hand on his arm.

"Thank you."

Tir Kerstet gave him a small grin and a short nod. "Those clubs of theirs are quite appropriate for their personalities. These people don't seem to appreciate a well-honed knife. Still, I would keep your head down for a while."

Ashik nodded earnestly and followed on unsteady feet as Tir Kerstet descended the hill.

"Ashik!" Ialla cried as he approached. She dropped the leads for both her antelope and Urda and raced forward, throwing her arms around him. He leaned back, startled briefly by the reaction, before gratefully embracing her as well.

Leaning her head back, she looked up at him with wide eyes. "Are you all right?"

He opened his mouth to respond, but before he could say anything, Tethe's voice cut through the air.

"Ashik!"

He and Ialla jumped back from each other with a start. "Ye—" he began.

"Get us away from here," she snapped over him. Her eyes narrowed further. "And those people."

Sketching out a short bow, Ashik hurried to pick up Urda's lead and began moving out as Tethe ordered the others to lead the rest of the animals. Some of the warriors who had taken positions on the other side of the path were still returning, but Ashik dared not ask if he should wait until they had formed up again. Instead, he led them down a gully toward the path a stone's throw back from where he had seen the Fanerians.

He couldn't help looking up the path as he crossed it, though the other group had disappeared.

A dragon knight and another swordsman with two young people, he thought. *What would bring people like that together?*

Chapter 8
Reflections in the Water

REDGE MOVED THROUGH his forms with precision honed through decades of training. He swung the pole, weighted very similarly to his own halberd, to the trainer's instructions. He reacted swiftly to each abrupt change the trainer barked out, halting abruptly mid-swing and shifting his stance effortlessly while the trainer tried over and over to surprise him.

Redge tried to keep his mind clear as he trained, but the movements came so naturally to him that the conversations of the other knights and families in the training yard burrowed through his thoughts like worms through soil.

"They're telling the truth. Come on, if they had any intention of attacking, they would have already. The Army of Light hasn't made one attempt against the border in two weeks. Not one!"

The trainer snapped another instruction. Redge hurriedly pulled back into a defensive stance that would allow an opening on an opponent using that attack against him.

"Have you forgotten who we really serve? We fight by the blessing of Agasis, not the Gods of Light. We're mages, for darkness' sake. We're heathens in their eyes."

Redge pushed harder through his next motions, throwing all his strength into his lunges and swings.

"She's a *malakh*. She serves the true gods. We should be celebrating their arrival, not turning them away."

The conversations came from all sides as Redge's muscles strained and sweat dripped down his brow and through his hair.

"He gives us our power every day of our lives. We owe Him our loyalty, not the Gods of Light."

"If they want to rid the world of the old gods, all the better, I'd say. When was the last time you even went inside the Den?"

"I can't believe I'm hearing such blasphemy. Agasis is the only reason any of us even exist."

Redge stopped his movements abruptly at the end of one form. He straightened, leaning on the pole and breathing hard. All around him, broken up by clacking sticks, panting breath, or pulling weeds, the discussions continued.

After a brief moment catching his breath, Redge lifted the pole and marched across the yard to where the training equipment laid. He strode forcefully between two knights practising their forms in mirror image, interrupting their conversation as he passed through. They said nothing as he passed, but continued talking soon after.

Redge leaned the pole against the wall of the tower beside the others, snatching up a towel to wipe himself off. Slinging the towel around his shoulders, he grabbed a cup beside a bucket of water and gulped it down. He caught a glance of Brannik, holding his clean clothes, as he tossed down the empty wooden cup. The young boy gave him a reluctant nod.

Redge swallowed a groan. "After lunch?"

"Yes, Sir."

Grabbing his clothes, he retreated behind the screen to change, then tromped up the stairs into the dining hall. He had been nursing an unspoken hope that perhaps he could delay his return to his office for a bath, but that would have to wait for another time. Again.

The discussion in the council room was even more heated than the ones in the training yard. Sir Hitchcliffe, he noted, did about as admirable a job of hiding his feelings as Redge himself did. Redge had to force himself to keep from rubbing his temples while Sir Hitchcliffe quietly tapped the table with two fingers as the other knights' and lords' voices rose.

"The king never officially took a side when Enseros split off from Edan. Now Edan is attacking Enseros and Enseros is entreating to us for help. If we provide it, we lose what faith we have from Edan, but if we don't, then we get Enseros as an enemy."

"Well, Enseros isn't the one besieging our border."

"Yes, but Edan is the one we have a peace treaty with. We've only an unspoken accord with Enseros."

"I should say they've broken the treaty already with this."

"Do you remember what it was like before we had that treaty with Edan? Do you? Because I do. And let me tell you, I do not wish to return to that. My province is finally beginning to build now that we are not constantly throwing men and resources at that border, and do not tell me that your people and resources have not benefitted from the end of those hostilities."

"Enseros deserves our loyalty, too. It doesn't matter who's king or emperor, their people have—"

"Enough," boomed the duke. He sent a firm look over each of the advisors as their voices fell quiet. "Politics are not at issue here. The defence of our realm is. The fact is, we have too many blind spots along the border and we need more men."

One of the lesser lords threw up a hand in exasperation. "That's just it, Your Grace. The Army of Light has made it clear they are not hostile toward us. Why should we sacrifice more of our men to defend against people who really aren't our enemy?"

Even as others raised their voices in agreement, the duke answered, "Because we are under orders to do so." He looked around the room again as the voices fell silent. "From the *king*. Until we hear otherwise, it is our duty to defend the border, and that means we need more men. Sir Hitchcliffe?"

Redge, just across the table from Sir Hitchcliffe, was probably the only one to see the irritation seep from Lyle's eyes before the duke turned to him.

"I can have another hundred and fifty ready within three days."

"Very good. Send my administrators the requisitions for supplies, as usual. Sir Warwick? Have you any more men you can spare?"

Redge shrugged helplessly. "Only a handful, Your Grace. Nearly half the Agaesi are already deployed to the border." *And with everything going on in Elderra at the moment, I think we want the rest of them to remain here in case something else happens that only we are trained to handle,* he thought, but couldn't say aloud. He tried to convey it to the duke in his expression.

The duke nodded. "That handful is still worth twice or thrice their number in other men. Get them ready to march." He turned to a lord whose territory lay to the south, along the bay where the Marble River emptied. "How goes the recruitment of sailors?"

"Very well, Your Grace. The water is getting choppy and more ships are harbouring for the winter every week. My men have a system in place to recruit more sailors and send them to the border. We're adding about thirty every week. They're not all well trained in combat, but if nothing else, they can provide more lookouts."

"Good," answered the duke. "Lady Petrochenko, inform the earl of these additional men and ensure that they are placed in those spots we have not been able to monitor regularly.

"Now, we need to address the problem of supplies."

Redge merely listened as the conversation turned to areas over which the Agaesi had no control, contributing little before the meeting ended.

The rest of the afternoon was a whirlwind of paperwork and meetings with knights he prepared to send to the border. However, he paused long enough to order Brannik to have dinner sent up to his suite, a once common luxury he had often forgotten to arrange of late. The thought of a quiet meal together with his family encouraged him while he struggled to remain on top of his tasks.

The waiting dinner also provided a convenient excuse for him to refuse to remain in his office past dark. He gratefully finished up his tasks and climbed the stairs to his apartment as the sun fell behind the wall outside his window.

As he opened the door, the aromas of roasted meat and vegetables wafted out. So did the excited voices of his sons and younger daughter.

"Papa!" they all cried out, rushing over to fling themselves into his arms. Redge couldn't help smiling as he held them close. For that brief moment, all seemed right.

"Hello, children," he greeted as they squeezed him tightly, ignoring how his mail must dig in to their arms. "How was your day?"

"Great!" they answered.

Redge turned to his older son. "And how was your training today?"

The boy began babbling excitedly about his lessons, but Redge's wife caught his eye as she approached. She leaned in to kiss him as usual, but there was an urgency in her eyes.

"Lenerre wants to speak with you."

Redge's eyebrows rose. Despite his best efforts, their eldest daughter had rarely spoken to him in weeks and spent much of her time either closed in her room or wandering the higher floors of the tower, long abandoned as the ranks of the Agaesi diminished.

"Papa?" his son went on. "Papa, are you listening?"

Redge put his hand on his son's shoulder and looked in his eyes. "I'll hear all about it at dinner. Right now, I need to go speak with your sister. Wash up, I'll be out soon."

The boy let out an exasperated sigh as only a child can and detached himself from Redge, along with the younger girl and boy, and hurried toward the washroom.

Without taking off his mail or arming sword, Redge marched

across the sitting room to Lenerre's door. He knocked.

"Lenerre?"

He heard shuffling and a muffled acknowledgement inside. Carefully, he opened the door.

As he swung the door open, he saw Lenerre standing at the far side of the room, self-consciously straightening her gown. A chair remained perched behind her, quickly abandoned from where it faced the window. The view outside looked over the wall to the glistening sheet of Aura Lake stretching to the horizon.

Her face was thinner and her eyes wider than his wife had been when he first courted her, but Lenerre was nearly of the same age now. While not quite an adult yet, she was certainly a woman. Gazing at her, he felt pride mix with guilt, while also truly feeling his age.

"Papa," she blurted out as though struggling to hold the word in. "I-I would like a word with you."

He had not seen her so nervous before. Thoughts rushed through his head as he watched her fidget, ranging from breaking some ancient Agaesi artifact to a dalliance with some young man in the tower. Most of them seemed highly unlikely, especially given her behaviour over the last season or two, but the sight of her unease heightened his own.

Still, he thought, *I must at least look like I have the answers. She needs that right now.*

Straightening, he smoothed out his features and stepped inside, shutting the door behind him. "Of course, Lenerre. What's on your mind?"

After attempting to answer for a moment, she bit her lip and averted her eyes. "I... I have been thinking a lot about this over the past weeks..." Her fingers twisted about each other, though she made a valiant effort to remain standing straight. "I just want you to know that I'm not just saying this on a whim, I really have been thinking about it."

Redge stared as she stumbled over her words. His mind raced even more as he tried to imagine what she was trying to say. "What is it?"

Lenerre pulled in a breath and drew herself up, meeting his eyes firmly. "Will you take me to the outside world?"

His eyes enlarged further. Before he could answer, more words spilled out of her.

"Just for a day, or even a few hours. Just out into Misengrad, I don't even need to leave the city. I'll stay by your side the entire time. I promise you I won't try to run away or anything. And no one needs to know I am your daughter. I-I'll dress up as a servant, or even a criminal you're escorting. You can bind my hands and everything."

Redge blinked against the onslaught of words. "I..."

"Don't just say no without thinking about it," she cut in, her expression hardening. "I'm not asking to leave and I'm not going to run away. I won't say a word about the Agaesi while we're outside. I'll do whatever you say I need to, but please, let me see something outside this tower. Some new people. Please."

He swallowed, considering what she said. She had been building herself up to ask this for weeks. And she was asking. She respected him enough to bring this to him, to take it seriously.

But it was impossible.

Gently, he said, "There's no way we could get you out without being seen."

Lenerre waved a hand. "So let the tower guards see me. What does it matter? You're the captain, you can order them to do whatever you like."

Redge was already shaking his head before she finished speaking. "Being captain only matters to the duke. I am equal to each of the knights here. If I used my captaincy to obtain special privileges, it would set a dangerous precedent."

"Then let anyone do it! What does it matter if we go outside once when we have to live the rest of our lives in this tower?"

"Lenerre..."

"I should have known you wouldn't listen to me," she spat, spinning around and folding her arms. "You don't care at all, you just have to uphold the ancient traditions."

"That's not true," he answered firmly, then calmed down as he crossed the room to stand by her. "I would love to be able to show you the outside world. I just don't know how we could get you out of the tower without being seen."

She still looked frustrated, but the anger diminished. "Well, what if we found a way? Would you at least think about it?"

He tried to imagine a way out of the tower that wouldn't be noticed, but failed to come up with an idea. Looking in her desperate eyes, he focused on the thought of taking her outside rather than the method of doing so.

"Yes. If we were to find a way to sneak you out of the tower, I would be glad to show you the outside world."

Turning, she drew her shoulders back as she looked up at him.

"You promise you'll try to think of a way?"

He took one of her hands in both of his. "I promise." A wry grin crossed his face. "After all, I suppose it won't be too much longer until I have to hang up my halberd for good. Then I'll be looking for the same thing."

Sighing, she leaned forward and hugged him. "Thank you, Papa." She sounded resigned, but there was a glint of hope in her eyes.

Redge smiled and embraced her as well, but his heart clenched all the same. *It's not an unreasonable request. It would do so many of the young people such good to be able to have brief, supervised visits to the outside world.*

Too bad it's not up to me. His mouth twisted to consider what the Scion would say about that idea.

Dinner was half cold by the time they sat down at the table, but with Lenerre speaking and eating alongside the rest of the family, Redge didn't mind.

Before the sun reached its zenith on the short, autumn day that rose over the foothills of the Orthys Mountains, another village came into sight.

Memories of the town they left the day before made Damian's shoulders slump at the sight. Trying to distract herself from the thought of her upcoming reception, she glanced over her companions.

Liam, as usual, showed little reaction, though he met her eyes with a warmth that radiated straight to her core. Sir Kennar, on the other hand, looked almost disappointed at the sight. Damian suspected she understood his feelings. They would be losing a lot of travel time that day if they stayed in the village overnight, but at midday already, it was highly unlikely they would find another town where they could stay before the sun set. Thoughts of what Niabi may be doing even now made her hope that the dragon knight would agree to continue their travel after resting and resupplying.

Those thoughts vanished like the breeze when Damian turned her attention on Rhyslen. Surprisingly, she found a despairing look on his face. She glanced ahead at the village. It looked small, and unlikely to have a prison where Sir Kennar could safely leave him. She watched Rhyslen for a moment, wondering what was bothering him, but didn't ask.

It wasn't until they were close enough to see people tending gardens on the edge of town that Rhyslen turned to Sir Kennar, despair giving way nearly to desperation.

"Can you please untie my hands while we're in this village? I promise I won't do anything."

Sir Kennar glared at him. "You're more likely to cause mischief or try to disappear among all these people than out on the road."

Rhyslen glanced furtively at the nearest people as they drew nearer. "Please? People stare at me enough as it is."

Damian raised her hood over her head, trying to shade her eyes. Hesitantly, she said to Sir Kennar, "Maybe we should avoid drawing more attention to ourselves…"

"In a small town like this," Sir Kennar answered, "any newcomers draw everyone's eyes. His hands remain bound."

Rhyslen slumped with a sigh. She gave him an apologetic look, but he merely frowned and stared at his feet while he plodded onward.

Damian remained silent as they entered the village. Few people were out in the streets, mostly children chasing each other with the occasional townsperson hauling supplies somewhere. As expected, they drew the attention of everyone they passed, though not as dramatically as Damian had feared. With his cloak covering his shoulders and upper arms, Rhyslen's bound hands were less obvious, and people stared far more at his patchwork face. Their eyes also lingered on Sir Kennar, as well as upon Liam. As Damian kept her eyes averted, most who looked at her only glanced curiously before turning to one of the men.

With no prison in the town, nor an inn with any rooms for guests, they merely restocked the pony's baskets and continued on their way, hardly speaking to anyone before they left.

The village disappeared around bends and behind hills as they marched ever westward, the sun slowly outpacing them. The travel fell silent and nothing broke the stillness of the hours of walking except for an occasional sighting of an animal.

Sir Kennar hovered close to Rhyslen as they walked, holding the pony's lead to his other side. Damian, striding alongside Liam, didn't realize that her pace had slowed until she noticed they now walked some thirty paces behind Sir Kennar.

She turned to Liam. She hadn't noticed his steps slowing, but he stayed with her throughout, and she began to wonder if she was the one who had slowed.

"Liam?" she asked quietly. "Is everything all right?"

He nodded toward the two walking ahead. "This will make things complicated."

She frowned. "I know. I certainly wasn't expecting to run into him… or be followed by him."

"He seems… truthful."

Rhyslen's words from the last night echoed in Damian's mind. Tugging her cloak closer, she uttered, "Yes…"

A few strides passed in silence.

"We know that not all of Yanuk's mages supported him," Liam eventually continued. "Some left for that reason."

"True," Damian replied thoughtfully, her eyes on the hunched figure ahead. "I'm not sure I trust him, though."

Liam nodded slowly. "But a mage would make a powerful ally against Niabi."

Damian straightened, her eyes enlarging. "I hadn't thought of that. But… I still don't know."

"We must be prepared."

A flash of guilt shot through Damian. She had been so focused on the travel, Rhyslen, and on getting Sir Kennar to take them to Misengrad as soon as possible that she hadn't stopped to consider what she was really doing. She rubbed her arm. In a hidden pocket inside her sleeve, she felt the lump of Garrick's letter folded within.

Niabi was building an army. She meant to roll across Faneria, all of Elderra, for the cruelty of the Gods of Light, and most people would support her conquest. This was no time for her to get swept up in petty squabbles.

Damian inhaled deeply. "I'll try to get him to help."

Liam nodded in agreement. "But be careful."

Warmth spread through Damian at those words, and she smiled up at Liam. His eyes softened and his mouth quirked. It wasn't quite a smile, but it sent a thrill through her heart all the same.

However, he soon sobered. "Have you decided when you will tell Sir Kennar?"

She let out a sigh. "I don't know. He doesn't trust me as much as I thought he did in Aether, and Garrick said even the other Agaesi don't see Niabi the way we do. I'm not sure he'll believe me."

"If there is anything I can do to help, please tell me."

Another smile crossed her face. "I will. Thank you, Liam."

His features softened again as he nodded, but before either of them could say anything more, a call from ahead drew their attention.

"Hey!"

Damian looked up to find Sir Kennar and Rhyslen standing still at the top of a rise, now only half as far in front as they had been.

Sir Kennar watched them approach apprehensively.

"You shouldn't fall behind," he said as Damian and Liam drew near. "We never know what might be out here."

Damian swallowed with a brief look to Rhyslen, but the firmness in the knight's eyes made it clear he wasn't worried about external trouble.

She cast her gaze downward guiltily. "I'm sorry."

"Come along." With that, he turned and nudged Rhyslen onward, the pony to his other side, and Damian followed with Liam walking alongside her.

The travel fell into silence again. Only a few hours passed, however, before the sun set and they set up camp. Supper was a quiet affair, after Rhyslen convinced Sir Kennar to untie his hands so he could eat. He clearly tried to focus on his meal, though even Damian felt uneasy from the close scrutiny Sir Kennar gave him as he ate. No sooner had Rhyslen finished than the knight rose to tie his hands behind his back again. Rhyslen never complained, nor even looked perturbed by the treatment. He merely obeyed, lying down on the ground with his blankets with a look of resignation on his face while Sir Kennar and Liam disappeared into a shelter.

Damian waited agonizing minutes as the stars came out, listening for sounds of slumber from the occupied tent. Liam fell still quickly, but she wanted to be certain that Sir Kennar was sound asleep before she made her move. She stole furtive glances to Rhyslen as she waited, hoping that he wouldn't fall asleep, or at least would be easily awakened if he did. She shivered beneath her cloak and blanket as she sat before the fire, wishing now that they had stayed in the village for the night, even if it meant being exposed to the townspeople. The feeling of being truly warm seemed like a distant dream. Her cheeks were sore from the gentle but insistent bite of chill in the air.

Silence descended over the hills. Damian looked slowly around, but saw no signs of movement anywhere.

Then, a grunting sigh from inside the shelter joined the sounds of Liam's breathing.

Carefully, she inched closer to Rhyslen. Reaching out, she shook his foot through the blankets. He awoke with a start, yanking his foot up as his head rose to blink at her. She quickly gestured for him to be quiet.

"I want to talk to you," she whispered, relaying the importance of the discussion in her expression.

His eyes widened slightly in understanding. "In my bag. There's a cutting of fennel. Break off some leaves and put them in my hands."

Damian's eyes narrowed suspiciously. "Fennel? Why?"

"For privacy."

She leaned back. "You want to use Yanuk's spell." He nodded, but she quickly hissed, "Not a chance."

Exasperated, he uttered back, "Do you want him to find out?" He nodded toward the occupied shelter, where sounds of both of the men breathing now emanated. "It's just to keep them from hearing. I swear. It's not like the spell affects you anyway."

She frowned at him for a long moment. She didn't trust Yanuk's apprentice with anything he would need to cast magic.

But, she thought, *that's exactly what I want him to do, just against Niabi. I have to start trusting him somewhere.*

Reluctantly, she rose and tiptoed to where the supplies had been laid out, well out of Rhyslen's reach. She found his sack of supplies amongst the baskets and everyone's personal bags and carried it to the fire to look through it.

Most of its contents seemed to be food, some of which was going soft or too hard. She dug through until she found a stalk of fennel about the length of her forearm, wrapped in linen. Breaking off a sprig of leaves, she re-wrapped the rest of it and returned it to the bag, taking the rucksack back to the rest of the supplies. Then, she brought the leaves to Rhyslen.

Standing over him, she hesitated a moment more.

Looking over his shoulder, Rhyslen gave her a steady look. "Fennel is only used in the unseeing spell." A wry grin crossed his patchwork face. "Besides, I came here to catch up with you. If I didn't have anywhere to go back in that village, I really don't have anywhere to go from here."

Damian's brow wrinkled at that, not sure she agreed with that logic. However, she knelt, pulling up the covers at his back. She found his hands splayed open against the small of his back, and dropped the fennel into them.

She replaced the blankets over him as his fingers curled around the herb. Shutting his eyes, he uttered something she couldn't make out under his breath.

After a moment, he opened his eyes again, struggling to glance over his shoulder at her. "There. Now we can speak privately."

Damian frowned, torn between revulsion and curiosity. "I don't feel any different."

He tilted his head aside. "Really? You can't hear how our voices change?"

"No."

"I guess it's because the spell doesn't affect you. Trust me, it's working."

She rose, still looking somewhat uncomfortable. "How does it work? Does it really make us... invisible?"

"Not exactly. It's like when you see something in the same place every day, so that you don't even see it anymore. It tricks people's minds into not seeing us, or hearing us."

She considered that for a moment.

"So what was it you wanted to talk about?"

The words drew her out of her thoughts. Straightening, she moved around him so she could kneel in front of him and give him a serious look. "I'm going after the malakh that attacked Albrith." Without giving him more time to react other than widening his eyes, she continued, "She's building an army in Edan and she means to move across all of Elderra, wiping out all traces of the old gods. But, I know it will be far worse than that. I have to stop her. I want you to help me."

Leaning forward, he answered immediately and emphatically, "Yes."

The reaction surprised Damian, and she let it show. "You're awfully eager to do this. Haven't you heard the stories of how powerful she is?"

"I have," he replied, "but this is what I always wanted to do, especially since Yanuk... since the Battle of Albrith."

"What?" she uttered.

Rhyslen let out a sigh. "All those years we lived in that abandoned fort in Hesperia... all we did was cast spells for good. Yanuk did so much damage to people's beliefs about magic. I want to undo that. To show that magic can help people."

She frowned. "Most people think the malakh is right, you know. Nobody is going to thank us for doing this."

"Maybe not. But she would condemn me anyway just because I'm a mage. And I did hear about how much damage she caused to Albrith. I'll help you. I swear it."

"Thank you." Her smile faded soon, and she bit her lip. "Could you... would you teach me?"

He gazed at her curiously. "Teach you what?"

"Magic."

Leaning back, his eyes opened wide. "How can I teach *you* anything about magic? If the stories are true..."

"They're not." She leaned back on her haunches, drawing her cloak closer about herself. "My magic doesn't work anymore." She hunched her shoulders. "I've tried."

Guilt crept over her. During the summer when she sat alone in her room in Aether, she had attempted to cast magic the way she used to before she ever started losing control over Nephrita's power. She knew what she was doing this time, but couldn't help herself, even though it was forbidden and she would likely be imprisoned if Sir Kennar ever found out.

Growing up, as she kept her distance from everyone else and watched the people around her live their lives without the same limitations, she clung to her magic. She needed something special, something secret, to make the isolation worth it. It comforted her as much as it frightened her.

But it hadn't worked. On three separate nights, she tried, increasingly desperate, to summon her magic, but nothing happened. That familiar, ever-present warmth, that tingle of energy she could feel rippling over her skin and coalescing at her finger tips, was gone.

She tried and failed to banish the aching emptiness that washed over her. She cursed herself for being so attached to something that caused her so much trouble and so many others such pain, yet the pervading loss remained.

"It can't be gone," Rhyslen said gently, drawing her attention back to him. "You used magic during the Battle of Albrith, didn't you?"

"Yes, but I don't know how. I can't make it work."

"Maybe we can figure it out." He frowned toward the occupied tent. "If we get the chance. Are we going to be dealing with him the entire time?"

"Probably." She rubbed her eyes.

"I don't understand. If you're free to go where you like, why are you being guarded by him?"

Her shoulders felt heavy. "The same reason Sir Kennar condemned you. Because I'm a mage. People see me the exact same way they see Yanuk, or worse. But because I helped save Albrith, the king and his advisors decided it wasn't fair to imprison me. However, they didn't truly trust me, so they sent Sir Kennar to keep watch over me."

"Even though you can't use magic anymore?"

She huffed. "It doesn't matter. No one believes me."

"Well, I do."

Damian looked up, surprised at the sincerity of the statement. "Thank you."

He twisted his head, but stopped short of looking over his shoulder. "The fennel's almost used up. The spell is about to wear off. Is there anything else you wanted to say?"

She shook her head, rising to return to the fire. "That's it."

For now, she added silently.

Ashik's arm trembled and his shoulder strained beneath his wool clothes. He narrowed his eyes, trying to set aside the pain of the action as he focused. Letting out a breath, he released.

The bowstring grazed his cheek as the arrow sailed through the deep orange evening. Ashik lowered the bow just in time to see the arrow drive into the narrow trunk of a tree fifty paces away, near two other arrows already planted within it. A smile spread across his face.

Turning to Tir Kerstet, standing beside him, Ashik said, "That's three in a row."

The Rturan nodded, his eyes on the tree he had designated as a target. "It's a fine start. Of course, your target won't be standing still for you." Seeing the disappointed look on Ashik's face, Tir Kerstet's scarred chin stretched in a smile and he said, "You've gotten a lot better these past several days. Go on, collect the arrows."

Nodding, Ashik looped the bow over his shoulder and jogged toward the tree. As he drew near, his smile spread again. The three arrows had struck within two handspans of each other. Leaning a foot against the tree, he managed to pull out each of the arrows and then returned to the campsite.

Around the edges of the shelters, the warriors did their own training in the failing light. Some sparred with others, and Ashik was pleased to see the different peoples mingling to do so. A Makil warrior queen faced off against another Rturan, the former using her poleaxe and shield while the latter held two single-edged short swords upside down, with the backs of the blades braced against his forearms. Another Makil struggled to fend off two eagle warriors, though they clearly weren't in their battlefield fury. Others simply practiced their forms or did strength exercises.

Ashik's eyes were drawn to the groups sparring. They had not seen any further sign of the Fanerians they had nearly attacked in the foothills, nor had they encountered anyone else as they passed out of the mountains into the low hills and snow-dusted open grasses of the great plains of southern Faneria. As such, Tethe had decreed it safe to resume training, and the clangs of metal and cracks of wood striking sounded through the evening.

As Ashik returned to his position, the retrieved arrows clutched in one hand, he caught a glimpse of Ais Ainlan. The short-haired Rturan woman looked sidelong at him where she moved gracefully through different positions with her sword. There was less hostility in her eyes as she met his gaze this time, but she still looked away without any sign of warmth as she swung her sword, the blade whistling through the air.

Ashik frowned as he came up beside Tir Kerstet. All the warriors who weren't busy tending to supplies or cooking were engaged in training with swords, cudgels, or polearms.

"Come on," Tir Kerstet said. "Let's do it again."

"Tir Kerstet," Ashik ventured. "Would you teach me to fight up close?"

The Rturan's eyes narrowed as he stared at Ashik. "You don't truly think you'll be able to fight the fox-headed woman face to face in a week of training, do you?"

Ashik looked away. The thought of attacking the malakh, or anyone, with a weapon made him feel ill, not to mention clumsy and awkward. *But even the Uniter is an accomplished swordsman,* he told himself. *And all of these warriors fight up close.*

He rolled his shoulder, trying to release some of the tension brought about by his archery. "What if I have to defend myself? I should at least know how, right?"

The disbelieving look remained on Tir Kerstet's face.

"I just want to learn," Ashik insisted. "At least a little."

Tir Kerstet shrugged. "Well, anyway, the Rturan way is not for outsiders, especially not for someone who 'just wants to learn.' I'm sorry. You'll have to ask one of the others."

Ashik blinked, momentarily taken aback. Tir Kerstet's apology had been sincere, however, and it wasn't surprising that Rturan battle forms would be kept secret. "All right," Ashik said with a nod.

Tir Kerstet walked away toward some of the other Rturans as Ashik turned to some of the others sparring. Inhaling deeply, Ashik approached the nearest pair, a Makil and a Kathec facing off. The eagle warrior wielded a large, heavy battleaxe two-handed while the warrior queen used a scimitar and a large shield. Both weapons were sheathed.

Ashik stepped cautiously up within several feet of the combatants and paused, clearing his throat uncertainly. Neither seemed to notice him for a moment. He began to say something, but the warrior queen's eyes flicked to him as she and the eagle warrior circled.

Crossing her scimitar and shield before her, she barked, "Break!" As the eagle warrior backed off, they both straightened and turned to Ashik.

Suddenly feeling nervous, Ashik swallowed and asked, "Would you teach me to fight?"

The Makil raised an eyebrow, but the Kathec, a bear of a man named Huathl, beamed, showing off a crooked canine tooth. "Yes!" he exclaimed eagerly. "I teach you to fight." He clapped Ashik on the shoulder. "You take axe, I get machete."

With that, Huathl swung his axe into Ashik's arms. Ashik struggled not to drop the heavy weapon as the steel-braced wooden haft slammed across his upper arms. Stumbling from the effort, he couldn't even respond as the eagle warrior hurried away to the supplies.

"You have been training hard dese last days."

Ashik looked up at the warrior queen, standing at ease and proud with her shield and sheathed sword. Her name was Masa. She still wore the dark sweeps of kohl from her eyelids to her temples that her empress preferred, making the whites of her eyes nearly glow within her sienna face. A scarf tied back the loose locks that fell to her shoulders.

Ashik opened his mouth to respond, but hesitated, realizing that the truth sounded pathetic. After a moment, he answered, "We were all chosen by the Uniter to complete this mission. I wanted to help as much as I can." He winced, struggling to shift the heavy battleaxe into a two-handed grip.

Masa grinned. "I t'ink de axe is not your weapon. Here, try dis." She flipped the scimitar over in her hand so that she held it by the sheathed blade, the hilt toward Ashik. Lowering the axe to the ground, Ashik gently took the sword. It was much lighter than the axe, though the weight would still take some getting used to. He experimentally swung the tip up and down a little.

Masa shook her head. "You don' chop like an axe." She unbuckled the shield from her arm as she stepped toward him. "You are a pant'er." Tilting her head aside, she looked him up and down. "Per'aps mountain lion." She gestured for him to hold his free arm out and strapped the shield to it. "Dese are your claws. Dey are a part of your body. Dey swing when you swing. Dey cut what you cut." Stepping back, she motioned for him to swing the scimitar.

Ashik frowned as he tried to understand what she told him. *My claws...* He tried a slash of the scimitar and was surprised when he found the blade slicing smoothly through the air, the weight flowing with his movement instead of restricting him.

Masa nodded and then pointed to the shield. "Dis is your paw. It may not have claws, but it can do more than protect." She picked up the axe and moved around in front of him. "It can deflect an' it can bash, and when an attack comes in, you t'row your arm in front to stop it."

She began swinging the axe and Ashik swept the shield in front of him, bracing himself as the sheathed blade clacked against the shield. She held the weapon there, though she didn't push hard against it.

"Now, you can turn your arm to push my axe aside."

Ashik tried tilting the shield to the side and was rewarded with the axe sliding away from him, leaving Masa open. She was obviously allowing him to do it, but he smiled at the manoevre all the same.

"You see?" she said, straightening and lowering the axe. "You do not *learn* to fight. You *feel* it. It becomes part of your blood and muscles, your eyes and ears. You don' train your technique. You train your body to know battle."

Murmured agreements rang out nearby, and Ashik looked around to find several other warriors watching and nodding along. Ashik immediately felt his cheeks heat up at the attention, but they all watched him in interest. Behind two of them, he noticed Ialla. In that brief glimpse, he saw a disappointed look on her face before she turned and walked away.

Ashik opened his mouth to call to her, but a deep voice barked out, "Bah! What is wrong with axe?"

Huathl stepped out from the crowd, machete in hand, scowling good-naturedly as he looked at Ashik.

Masa grinned back. "De axe is bigger dan Ashik is. Give him dat."

Smiling, Huathl approached and took Masa's scimitar from Ashik, replacing it with the machete he had retrieved. Ashik tried to look through the crowd for Ialla again, but Masa's voice drew his attention back.

"Dat is more like boar tusk," she said. "More for goring, but it is a good weapon to learn wit'. It will hone your body to fighting."

"Show us what you can do, goat man," called a Rturan. A round of chuckles circled the group watching. Aromas of food wafted on the air as darkness began to settle over the plains. Ashik hunched his shoulders, the tip of the sheathed machete lowering as he glanced around.

"If you cannot fight with o'ders watching," Masa called over everyone, "den you cannot fight at all."

"Yes," Huathl agreed with a clap on Ashik's shoulder. "We all start somewhere. That why we teach you now!"

Ashik still felt nervous, but the agreements that rang out with this statement eased his shoulders. He tried a few more swings with the machete and several of the warriors called out suggestions for his stance and movements. Masa and Huathl stayed close, adjusting his grip or motions as needed.

It wasn't long before the meal was ready. Masa walked beside Ashik as they strode into the light of the fires and the savoury smell of cooking meat.

"We will teach you to fight," she assured him. "Maybe not enough to fight de fox-headed woman, but it is good for you to know."

"Yes," Tir Kerstet added, approaching silently from the crowd that now hurried for food. "You should keep up with your archery practice, but this might be a good idea after all."

"Like you say," added another Kathec, "we all here for same reason. We make warrior of you." He laughed loudly but warmly, and others nearby echoed his sentiment.

There was a little good-natured teasing of Ashik as they ate, but the warriors were more open and friendly with him than it seemed they had been so far on the journey. Ashik stayed awake as long as he could, chatting with them about their homelands, the plains drenched in shadow and the fires gradually burning down.

Finally, Tethe ordered everyone but the night watchers to bed, and Ashik retreated toward the murok hide wrapping of his shelter with a smile on his face. It faded, however, as he lifted the side and noticed Ialla already asleep within. He'd barely had a chance to speak to her since he started practicing archery with Tir Kerstet. He had no idea how long she had been asleep. With a sigh, he pulled some unused hides out from beneath the shelter and settled down to sleep just outside it.

Chapter 9
Awakening

THE WORLD CAME back in a haze.

Light filtered red through Garrick's closed eyelids. His head felt stuffed with feathers, his mouth was parched, and he couldn't feel the rest of his body. He lay still for a moment, battling the urge to drift back to sleep.

Finally, he forced his eyes open. He lay on his back and stared up for a long moment. Gradually, his eyes focused and he found a simple wood ceiling above him.

Turning his head to the side, he glanced around. He lay on the floor of a common room furnished with little more than a pair of upholstered chairs, a desk, and floor to ceiling shelves lining every wall, stuffed full of books and strange trinkets. Directly across from him, a hearth burned modestly. Beside it laid a pile of twisted shapes that glinted dully in the firelight. Loose pages, writing instruments, and other odds and ends littered the floor in every corner. The room stretched back just far enough for him to see, with two doors visible behind him. Past his feet there was a small table with two chairs. The room ended at a door set between the only windows he could see, daylight gleaming against the yellow panes. Another doorway opened to the side near the front wall.

He blinked as he looked around the room. Then, he started to sit up.

Pain tore through his entire body. His limbs and torso seared in sudden, blinding agony.

Sucking in a sharp breath, he dropped back to the floor. His eyes shot open in surprise as he bit back a cry, panting heavily from the strain on his apparently battered body. He glanced around the room again, his brows knitting.

The sound of footsteps emerged from the doorway by the entrance.

"Are you truly awake this time?"

He squinted at the speaker, his vision spinning. About his age and slender, dressed in a plain off-white shirt, leather vest, and trousers, with short ginger hair, it took him a moment before he realized his companion was a woman.

"This time?" he asked.

She strode across the room until she stood directly over him. "You have been slipping in and out of consciousness for the past day."

He paused. "I don't remember waking up."

A smile tugged at the corner of her mouth. "You seem more lucid this time. You have already spoken more words than any other time you awakened. How do you feel?"

He cringed as he tried to shift. "I hurt. A lot." He blinked at her. "What happened?"

"You are safe. I brought you back here after I found you at the scene of your battle."

He stared at her. "Battle?" He glanced around the unfamiliar room, reflecting on the last, and only, battle he had taken part in. "So… I'm in Albrith?"

The smile faded as she gazed at him cautiously. "No, you are in the forest in central Hesperia. You do not remember?"

He shook his head faintly, afraid to incite more pain. "The last thing I remember, I was in Misengrad." He hesitated. "Or did I leave after that?" The memories were a jumble in his mind and he couldn't tell which came first.

Kneeling down, she looked hard into his eyes. "You might have hit your head. What is your name?"

He told her.

The woman leaned back on her haunches. "Well, Sheridan, I found you—"

"My name is Garrick," he cut in, giving her a curious look. "Sir Garrick Magni."

She paused for a moment before continuing slowly. "I found you in a Sir Garrick Magni-sized crater in the ground two days ago. It was an impressive, well, impression. You looked like you fell from the top of a tower, though there were far too many trees in the way for that."

Some of the words were lost on Garrick as soon as she spoke them, but the word 'tower' clung to his thoughts. "So I'm in

Misengrad."

His voice cracked on the end of the word and his throat seized in a fit of uncontrollable coughs. He winced as he struggled, the coughs sending sharp pains through his chest and back. The woman hurried out of the room and returned with a wooden cup. She held it to his lips, dribbling water into his mouth. He coughed a few more times against the water rushing against the back of his throat, but soon, they subsided.

"Thank you," he croaked. He watched her as she rose and nodded in acknowledgement. "I'm sorry, I don't remember your name."

"You did not ask it."

He blinked. "Yes, I did."

She smiled and kneeled before him. "Sleep. We will speak more when you awaken."

Damian spent much of the following days thinking about her conversation with Rhyslen, magic, and Yanuk. She continued feeling torn between wanting her magic gone and wanting to learn how to use it, though she knew that if she had any hope of helping to stop Niabi, she would need it.

She wanted to speak privately to Rhyslen more, but he wasn't used to travelling such long distances on foot, and the walk exhausted him. If they didn't stop at an inn and sleep in separate rooms, with Rhyslen closely watched over by Sir Kennar in the same one, the mage was simply too tired to talk. It was also too much of a risk to continue trying not to alert Sir Kennar to their conversation, or to cast the unseeing spell.

Damian was still contemplating another way of speaking to Rhyslen as they stopped for dinner just off the road a few days later. It was another quiet meal as they each nibbled on biscuit, dried meat, hard cheese, and apples. The pony grazed nearby, happily eating the apple cores that they threw toward it.

Rhyslen paused in his meal to reach up underneath the collar of his cloak and scratch at his neck. Suddenly, Sir Kennar's arm shot out and he grabbed Rhylsen by the wrist. Damian jumped at the movement, nearly dropping her food.

"Hey!" Rhyslen yelped, fighting fruitlessly against the knight's grip. His eyes were wide in alarm.

Sir Kennar's other hand reached toward Rhyslen's chest. "What is this?" he demanded, pulling something attached to a leather cord around Rhyslen's neck. With a quick yank, he snapped the leather and pulled the pendant off him.

The knight's eyes darkened as Damian peered worriedly at the pendant he now held. Tied to the cord was a plain crystal the size of a strawberry, cloudy and rough-hewn except for one smooth, flat side.

"How long have you had this?" Sir Kennar snapped, still holding Rhyslen's wrist tightly.

"That's not—" Rhyslen attempted.

"This is enchanted, isn't it?" the knight ploughed on. He tugged Rhyslen's wrist to draw him closer. "You've had this on you the whole time."

Damian was on her knees, realizing Liam had done the same beside her, her heart hammering in her chest as she looked between Rhyslen and Sir Kennar.

"It is, but it doesn't work anymore!" Rhyslen quickly spat out. "Yanuk had the other half, we used to use it to speak to each other."

"What else does it do?" Sir Kennar growled.

"That's it. It was only enchanted to speak with the other half."

"What other magical artifacts do you have on you?"

"Nothing, I swear it. I only have that because it was one of the few things I still have of Yanuk's. I forgot I was still wearing it." Rhyslen tried to lean away from the closeness of Sir Kennar's glaring face, though there was a glint of defiance in his eyes. "You've already caught me for practicing magic. I don't have anything left to hide."

Sir Kennar stared at Rhyslen, his expression still hard and hand still wrapped around the mage's wrist. "If you have nothing else to hide, then why were you in that village? Yanuk's stronghold was in Hesperia."

Rhyslen glanced at Damian. In that brief look, discomfort at the sight of her eyes was overshadowed by uncertainty and guilt. The sight filled Damian with unease. She hadn't considered that before, but she now realized how unlikely it was that they would come across Rhyslen so far to the east when she knew Yanuk's mages had come from Hesperia.

Rhyslen couldn't hold his gaze for long before turning away. "I was looking for Damian."

"I asked why you were there, not why you left."

"It is why I was there." Rhyslen shook his head, now avoiding Damian's eyes entirely. "After she caught me stealing from the market in Windermere, I went back and told Yanuk what happened."

"What?" Damian cried.

Rhyslen still didn't face her. "You were the first person who was ever able to see through our spell. Yanuk was insatiably curious. As soon as the snow started melting, he asked me to find you and figure out how you did it. But, by the time I reached Aether, you had just left. That's when he asked me to come back, because he was planning to march on Albrith. I started following his orders, but I made it as far as that village and just… stopped. I found a home, or at least room and board, from the town midwife for helping her out. I'd been there ever since."

A long moment of silence dragged out as a chill rippled down Damian's spine. Thoughts rushed through her mind. Rhyslen had been searching for her long before the fateful night on her father's barge that had set everything off. *Was I fated to cross paths with Yanuk all along? Did my discovering Rhyslen in the market in Windermere somehow affect my magic and start to make me lose control over it over the following year? Am I, even now, being pulled along by strings of destiny?*

Sir Kennar's voice cut through the silence. "You travelled halfway across Elderra just to speak with her?"

Rhyslen's eyes narrowed. "Yes. If I had found that she had talent in magic, I would have invited her to join us, but that's it. As I said, Yanuk had an insatiable curiosity when it came to magic."

Sir Kennar looked unconvinced. "You're awfully free with this information."

"What difference does it make?" Rhyslen answered bitterly. "Yanuk is dead now. They're all dead. I've nothing to gain by lying now. Besides, you've already decided that I'm guilty. You might as well just execute me now and save yourself the trouble."

Sir Kennar finally released Rhyslen's wrist, but his relief was short-lived. The knight swept smoothly to his feet and drew his sword in one fluid movement.

"No!" Damian cried as she stood.

Beside her, Liam rose swiftly, grabbing his own sword as he stepped forward. Damian raised a hand to stop him, but hesitated, and Liam stopped short.

Sir Kennar loomed over Rhyslen, staring down at him with a hard expression as he held his sword loosely in his hand. Damian's breath fell short. She still wasn't sure who she sided with more. Her eyes flicked to Liam, who half-crouched two paces away from Sir Kennar, waiting but ready to move.

Then, she finally turned to Rhyslen. He remained where he sat on the ground, staring up at Sir Kennar. His posture was unthreatening, but his eyes were unyielding.

He is truly ready to die for this.

Damian looked uneasily at the knight. Sir Kennar's attention never wavered from Rhyslen, not even sparing a glance toward Liam as he stood ready to draw his sword.

The moment felt like it lasted an hour. The cold breeze whistled across the plains and the pony continued grazing. Finally, Sir Kennar straightened and sheathed his sword.

"Let's go. We're wasting daylight."

With that, he turned and strode toward where the pony was tethered, an unreadable expression on his face and the pendant swinging from his gauntleted hand.

Damian and Rhyslen exchanged a started look. It was clear both of them realized the same thing. Sir Kennar had not bound Rhyslen's hands this time.

Liam crouched to pick up the fallen pieces of their forgotten dinner and Damian scrambled to retrieve her pack as Sir Kennar untied the pony and started making his way back to the road. She opened her mouth a couple times to ask either Rhyslen or Sir Kennar about him not tying the mage's hands, but eventually closed her mouth and followed him in silence. As Liam fell into step with her, she looked up at him curiously. He returned an uncertain, but relieved look.

They said nothing else as the travel resumed, and though Damian worried constantly about upsetting the fragile peace that had descended, she returned Rhyslen's grateful glances as he walked with his arms unhindered.

As they moved onward, her thoughts also turned to what Rhyslen had said to Sir Kennar. No more secrets, nothing more to hide.

How nice would that be? It seemed that every secret she held ate away at her. That included the ones she kept hidden from Sir Kennar.

Maybe I should just tell him why I'm going to Misengrad, she thought. Although it hadn't come up, it still felt wrong to keep her true purpose secret.

Garrick's letter stopped her short. She had read it several times over the journey and knew what it said by heart.

The Agaesis' hands are tied. Even my fellow knights don't believe Niabi is so dangerous.

Even if Sir Kennar sympathized with her cause, he would be risking his very title to go after Niabi. It was surprising enough that Garrick would do it. A frown crossed her face. Much as she hated it, she would have to keep him in the dark a bit longer. Perhaps by the time they reached Misengrad, Sir Kennar might have warmed to her enough for her to admit the truth. For the moment, she was lucky enough that Rhyslen was walking without his hands bound.

It didn't give her any more opportunity to speak with him, unfortunately. In fact, it seemed less likely than before that evening when they made camp just off the road, as Sir Kennar insisted Rhyslen share the larger shelter with him and Liam.

Damian sat through her watch in silence and boredom, now less concerned about Rhyslen but more aware of their surroundings. As they had made their way west, the foothills of the Orthys Mountains had dropped to low, rolling hills interspersed with stretches of flat plain where she could see animals sleeping in the distance, guarded by dogs.

At last, her watch ended and she woke Sir Kennar. Donning only his mail tunic, cloak, and sword belt, he emerged surprisingly quietly from the shelter and strode toward the fire. Nodding with a slightly forced smile, she rose to retreat to the smaller shelter they had built.

Before she made it, a hand fell on her shoulder.

"Damian, wait a moment, please."

She drew in a breath as she turned to Sir Kennar. In the flickering light of the flames, she saw a strange look on his face, though he didn't face her.

"I'm sorry."

She turned curiously. "For what?"

"It was crass of me to act as though I might kill Rhyslen in front of you. Such a thing would have been shameful."

Conflicting emotions swam through her, annoyance warring with tenderness and worry. Her voice came out hesitantly. "You're not going to when I can't see, are you?"

"No. As much as I hate to admit it, he is right in some respects. I still think he is wrong for willfully practicing magic, but I cannot execute him for it. He did leave Yanuk and, as far as I know, has not used his magic to harm anyone. If we cannot find somewhere to hold and judge him sooner, I will take him all the way to Misengrad to be tried."

Damian breathed a sigh of relief. "Thank you, Sir Kennar."

He finally faced her, with one raised eyebrow. "You seem awfully glad for the leniency against someone who followed you twice, and stole from your market."

Now she turned away. "I guess after hearing him talk about his life, I realized I have more in common with him than I thought. Maybe I would've done the same thing in his position. I certainly wouldn't have had the same outlook on life."

"Do you think that excuses his misdeeds?" To her surprise, his voice didn't sound accusatory, only curious.

Suddenly, she felt tired. "I think the problem is that the people who decide what are misdeeds and what aren't never try to understand people who are desperate. It seems like most people are much quicker to look for enemies than friends." Silence followed her statement.

Trying to ignore the slightly surprised look on his face, she finished, "Good night, Sir Kennar." With that, she retreated into her shelter for some much-needed sleep.

Late the following day, they came upon another village. Damian released a breath of relief as she saw the buildings come into view over the rolling hills, though that soon turned to unease as they drew nearer. She raised the hood of her cloak, draping it over her face enough to hopefully hide her eyes from the people in the village.

Rhyslen gave her a strange look as she adjusted the hood and tucked her braid inside it. "Didn't you used to wear a veil? Wouldn't that hide your eyes better?"

She averted her gaze, biting her lip. "I didn't bring any."

She glanced cautiously at the villagers as they entered the town. As usual, they drew stares, though the looks focused more on Sir Kennar and Rhyslen than her. They passed a couple blocks in silence, townspeople hurrying around them and carrying various burdens.

Finally, Rhyslen broke the silence. "Is it just me, or do these people seem…"

"Ill at ease?" Sir Kennar offered quietly.

Damian sighed softly. "It's just because I'm here."

"They don't know who you are," Sir Kennar replied.

"They're not even looking at us that much," Rhyslen said. "Not as much as I'd expect, anyway."

"It seems as though they're looking for something else," Sir Kennar clarified.

"Something must have happened here," Damian remarked, now noticing how the villagers' initial interest and scrutiny soon faded as they hurried about their tasks. "They look haggard. We should try to find out what's wrong."

"They won't talk to any of us," Rhyslen said.

Sir Kennar glanced askance at him. "They won't even talk to

you?"

Bitterness touched Rhyslen's voice. "People never talk freely to anyone who looks different, and I'm as different as they come." He cleared his throat as he noticed Damian's look. "Well, usually."

"Perhaps we do not need to speak with them."

Damian turned at the sound of Liam's voice.

He faced her. "But to listen."

"That's not a bad idea," Sir Kennar said. "They might not talk to us, but I'll wager they're talking a lot to each other."

Damian looked up at Liam. "Do you think you can find anything out?"

"I will try."

She nodded. "I think it is a good idea. I'd like to know what's going on."

With a final nod, Liam veered down another road.

The sky turned golden as Damian, Sir Kennar, and Rhyslen found their way to an inn, stabled the pony, and carried their things into two rooms.

More people stared when the three of them finally went down to the common room for supper. Damian felt more at ease than she had since she left Aether. However, as they sat down with their meals, she anxiously watched the windows for Liam. It felt like she was missing a part of herself, and it surprised her to realize how much it bothered her for him to be gone.

"Give him time," Sir Kennar said between bites. "It can't be easy finding out information without saying anything."

"He really doesn't talk much, does he?" Rhyslen asked.

Damian smiled faintly. "No." Liam did seem to speak more to her than anyone else. It felt like a secret shared. Her smile faded. "Do you think he's doing all right?"

"Why? Do you think something happened to him?" Rhyslen's voice betrayed his disbelief.

"If he wanted to leave," Sir Kennar said, "he could have done that anytime. Be patient."

She stopped herself from replying in annoyance. He didn't understand. She knew Liam wouldn't leave.

She had nearly finished eating when the door opened and Liam stepped into the common room. Damian's heart leapt and a smile split her face as he crossed the room to their table.

"Did you find anything out?" Sir Kennar asked quietly.

Liam took a seat beside Damian. "Provincial soldiers came through a week ago."

She looked at him curiously and Rhyslen straightened.

Sir Kennar's eyes narrowed faintly. "Duke's men came here."

Liam nodded.

"What were they doing here?" Damian asked.

"Questioning people. About loyalty."

She exchanged a glance with Sir Kennar and Rhyslen. The knight looked suspicious while the mage looked uneasy.

"They also collected a tax," Liam went on, "and recruited many able-bodied men."

"That explains why they looked so tired," Damian mused.

Rhyslen nodded. "Because the people left have to pick up the slack."

"This can only mean one thing," Sir Kennar stated grimly. "The duke is preparing for hostilities."

"No wonder they seem so tense," Rhyslen commented.

Damian shook her head. "What's happening in the kingdom?"

"It's the same things that are always at play," Sir Kennar answered. "There's nothing we can do about it."

"Still," Rhyslen murmured, "best we don't linger here."

"We can agree on that. It's still almost two weeks to Misengrad."

With that, they returned to their meals, each of them deep in thought.

Chapter 10
Breathing Fire

REDGE DID HIS best not to rub his eyes as the increasingly loud discussion bounced off the walls of the council room.

"With all due respect, Your Grace, we can't keep politics out of the conversation. That's exactly what's causing all the problems."

"Have we forgotten that a malakh is leading the Army of Light? You don't need to go to Albrith to find people who think it's heresy that we're keeping them out. There's plenty of people right here in Misengrad who object to blockading the border against them."

"Never mind King Greganis' word as regent that they won't harm our land or our people if we let them pass."

Politics bored Redge and he mostly tuned out the discussion, but he couldn't help noticing that each week, more of the members of the council began to shift their opinions toward letting the Army of Light pass. Redge hoped no one would ask what he thought. He wasn't certain where he stood on the issue.

"It isn't that simple and you know it," the duke countered. "No matter how careful they are, a marching army will damage the land and put a strain on the villages it passes by."

"But the malakh serves the Goddess of Life," replied another lord. "With her power, she might be able to heal our crops, maybe even increase their output. We could have a more comfortable winter than ever before."

"There is no guarantee of that," said another. "Remember what she did to Albrith. She made no reparations there, not even an apology for the destruction she caused."

"The fact is, our people are stretched thin and crops are rotting in the fields because we've sent so many men to the border."

"Enseros is getting ready to march. We don't want them as

enemies."

"Enough," the duke attempted, but the conversation continued unhindered.

"Enseros is a long way from here. The Army of Light is much more important to us."

"I've said it before and I'll say it again, this army is clearly on a mission from the true gods. We're all heretics to continue keeping them out like this."

"I heard it on good authority that over a quarter of the population of Albrith disagree with the king's decision on this. People have been thrown out of audiences with him for questioning his orders."

"Enough," the duke boomed loudly enough to make the others stop. "We must stay on task." He faced a baronet in charge of the smiths' guild. "Have you had any luck increasing production?"

"Not much, Your Grace," the baronet answered with a helpless shrug. "The smiths are working as hard as they can. Demand for horseshoes alone is enough to keep over half of them busy at all times."

"Do what you can. Too many of our men along the border have no weapons or insufficient ones."

"Of course, Your Grace."

Redge tuned out their voices again. He wished he was better at ignoring the fevered discussions about the rightness of the Army of Light's and the king's actions. Unfortunately, it reflected all too well the conversations he kept overhearing in the Agaesi tower. Even the women and elders, who would never leave it, began to worry about what this protracted siege would mean for them.

And then there was Lenerre. He truly wanted to give her what she desired, but puzzled over how he could smuggle her out of the tower. The windows weren't an option. The tower's isolation meant that none of the windows faced the rest of the castle, and he couldn't imagine climbing the sheer, featureless walls of the tower to reach anywhere beyond. It was equally unlikely that they could climb the wall surrounding the Agaesi training yard and garden, though perhaps there might be tools with which to do so.

Perhaps there was a loose stone somewhere or he could dig a hole in some hidden nook to crawl underneath the wall. It still seemed the most likely option, though Redge had had neither the time nor the privacy to investigate that idea further.

Luckily, nothing else was asked of Redge for the rest of the meeting, for he remained engrossed in his own thoughts. As usual, since he sat near the end of the table, he was one of the first to leave the room once the meeting adjourned. His pace slowed soon after he exited into the corridor outside, however. He moved to the side, nodding to or greeting the lords and other knights who passed him as they returned to their own duties.

"Sir Warwick."

There was a prompt in the voice, unlike the others merely returning a courtesy. Redge turned and straightened as he saw Cedryck Valikov striding up to him.

"Lord Gredsk," Redge answered with a bow.

Lord Gredsk held out a hand for Redge to continue and matched his pace. The markiese glanced around, checking the positions of the retreating lords, knights, and lady. After a moment, as the other council members moved farther away, the markiese spoke in a low voice.

"Have you heard anything from Sir Magni recently?"

Redge hid his frown. "I'm afraid not, My Lord. I don't usually get many updates from knights on assignment."

The markiese nodded once. "I suspected that, but... well, I had been hoping differently. Thank you, Sir Warwick."

"I will let you know if I hear anything from him, My Lord."

"I appreciate that." With that, the markiese increased his pace and moved to intercept the duke.

Redge's thoughts, however, remained on Sir Magni.

Damn that Scion, he thought. Ever since Sir Magni had been knighted and undergone the binding ceremony that gave him the powers of Agasis, the old man had made it his mission to make Garrick's life miserable. But sending a good knight away on a futile mission just to get him out of Misengrad at a time like this? It was inexcusable. Bad enough that he went over Redge's head to do it.

Redge casually examined the walls and corridors as he made his way back to the Agaesi tower, looking for any secret entrance Lenerre could escape through. Of course, if such an egress existed, it wouldn't be found by a cursory examination. Redge knew that, yet he checked anyway.

The guards at the entrance to the tower watched him intently as he approached, questions clear on their faces. Redge pretended to ignore the looks as he nodded to them and moved inside, hurrying to his office.

Another long afternoon passed as Redge tried desperately to get his backlog of correspondence under control. Before he knew it, sunlight streamed into his office through his windows, glaring over the pages on his desk. Nearly as promptly, the sun vanished behind the wall guarding the Agaesi tower and courtyard from the outside world.

Sighing, he stopped his work and left his office for the dining hall. His head still swirled with all the work he had left to do.

He was so preoccupied with his thoughts that he didn't realize something was different until he nearly ran into the small figure standing before him in the dining hall. Redge hurriedly steadied his tray before he dropped his dinner, giving his armful a brief look before returning his wide-eyed attention to the unexpected figure in front of him.

"Your Reverence."

The Scion had drawn the eyes of nearly everyone in the room. He was rarely seen outside the Den, the temple priestesses bringing him his meals and using a private bedroom and bathing room for his purpose.

"Why…" Redge attempted, stopping himself when he realized that statement might sound rude. "What brings you here?"

The Scion smiled at him, but there was no warmth in it. "It seems this is the only way I may speak with you. I have been attempting to arrange a meeting with you for two weeks now."

Redge released a sigh through his nose as he lowered his dinner to the table beside him. It wasn't his preferred seat in the hall, but the Scion stood in the centre of the aisle and did not budge.

"I'm sorry, Your Reverence. I don't mean to dismiss you. I've just been very busy lately."

"Is that right?" Sarcasm dripped from the Scion's voice. "You literally could not be closer to the Den unless you were me. You must be very busy indeed if you cannot find time to walk all the way down the hall from your apartment to meet with me. I'm surprised you managed to find time to eat, your schedule must be so tight."

Redge narrowed his eyes, but managed to avoid any other reaction. At a glimpse of the faces staring around them, he said, "Would you like to go somewhere private to speak?"

The Scion held up his hands, his voice growing gradually louder. "Oh no, I wouldn't dare impose upon your precious time."

Now Redge allowed his annoyance to show. "Fine. You have my attention. What is it you want?"

The Scion's false smile evaporated as he pointed at Redge's face. "That, Sir Warwick, is precisely the problem! I should not need to disrupt my meditations simply to have a word with you. Your priorities are backwards if you believe that I should be dismissed so easily."

"Yes, well, in case you hadn't heard, our border is under siege. I'm sorry if you think imminent war isn't as import—"

"Unless our lives are in immediate danger," the Scion interrupted, "*nothing* is more important than paying tribute to Agasis. I don't believe this siege is as dangerous as you are making it out to be. In fact, I have been hearing blasphemous talk that you think this Army of Light should be allowed to pass."

"I have said no such thing," Redge fairly growled.

"But you have allowed this to happen," the Scion retorted. "Do you know how many knights have come to pay their respects in the Den in the last week? Three! Three out of twenty."

Before Redge could reply, the Scion turned his accusing gaze upon the others in the dining hall watching the scene. "You feel the presence of Agasis in you, do you not?"

The knights he faced looked away uneasily, and even many of the women, elders, and children turned from the Scion's eyes.

"Your Reverence—" Redge attempted.

"He is with you every moment of every day! How arrogant must you be to think you do not owe Him your worship. He gives you your very lives!"

Redge had had enough.

"What lives?" he snapped. The Scion spun to shoot him an appalled look, but Redge refused to allow him a chance to speak. "Look around you! There are barely a hundred of us left. It's only a matter of time before we die out entirely. And what have us few knights to aspire to? The most distinguished order of knights in the kingdom and our elders are locked up in this tower like prisoners."

The Scion's eyes narrowed furiously, but once more, before he could answer, Redge went on, "And our women never even get to see the outside world. At best, they can spend their lives cooking or tending to your needs. Servants have better lives than our families do. Indentured servants, for shadows' sake! At least they can hope to one day buy their freedom."

The Scion's nostrils flared, rage written all over his pasty, wrinkled face. "You would dare defy the glory of serving Agasis?"

"I am doing no such thing. The Agaesi survived the formation of Faneria around their ancient home by joining with them. By adapting. It is time we did so again, rather than stubbornly hold on to traditions that benefit us none, like a suckling pig clinging to its dead mother's teat. We should be a part of society, not hiding outside of it."

The Scion opened his mouth to retaliate, but murmuring around him forestalled his objections. He glanced around to find those in the dining hall clearly considering Redge's words.

"You have no idea how precarious your position is, Sir Warwick. Talk like that could spell the end of the Agaesi."

"We're headed that way already." Redge glanced pointedly at Brannik, with his wheezing breath and his limp. "And we deserve better."

The mumbling grew faintly louder, though many in the dining hall still looked uncertain.

After a moment, the Scion squared his shoulders, sneering at Redge. "I won't forget this, Captain."

Redge didn't move as the Scion brushed past him, crossing the dining hall to the stairs. The dining hall remained utterly silent as the old man climbed the stairs to head back to the Den, his elaborate robe swishing on the stone steps.

Redge huffed out a breath and sat down where he had placed his tray. It wasn't too hot to eat now.

He took a few bites before he heard any movement from the rest of the dining hall. Looking up, he saw one knight trying to move back to his table, but froze as Redge noticed him.

Redge's eyes narrowed faintly as he glanced around at the unmoving figures. "As you were."

With that, the occupants hastily returned to their tasks.

Garrick dreamed of awaking, of a spasm of pain ripping through his body and strange hands holding him down. When he woke, his head felt thick and pounded inside his skull. Blinking blearily, he glanced at the common room around him.

"Have I been here before?" he muttered.

"You have not left."

He turned his head to face the one who answered. The orange-haired woman who dressed like a man. She stood near the kitchen. Through the windows by the front door, he could see sunlight shining in once more. Or still. His face felt scratchy, hair on his jaw rubbing against his neck when he turned his head. He thought back to the last time he remembered awaking in her home.

"How long have I been here?"

"Nearly three days now."

He glanced away, trying to remember what happened.

"How are you feeling?"

He moaned softly, squinting his eyes shut. He attempted to lift his arm to scratch his chin, but pain shot through him with the attempt and he groaned.

"Do not move!" The woman hurried over, but Garrick had already dropped his arm.

He gazed up at her, baffled. "What happened?"

Pausing, she glanced down at him. "What do you remember?"

He shook his head faintly. "I… I don't know."

She crouched before him. "Was the horse yours?"

Garrick tilted his head up, gazing at her. "Brenadier? My horse? The chestnut stallion?"

"He is here. He seems unharmed."

"Unharmed?"

Pieces started connecting together. Brenadier. His injuries. Battle.

His eyes widened. "The mage!" Garrick tried to roll over, but sharp pains stabbed through his entire body with the action.

"Do not move!" she exclaimed again, laying a hand on his chest. "I think you injured your back. I went to a lot of trouble to try to keep from changing your position. I even kept some of your armour on." As she said it, Garrick realized he could still feel his mail beneath him, though it wasn't on top of his body or his arms. "I would not appreciate it if you wasted my effort."

He spoke through clenched teeth, echoes of pain drifting over him. "I'll get bedsores if I don't move. Besides, I have an itch."

He attempted to shift his position, but she pressed down on his chest again, causing a sharp spike of pain to rise. "I do not think you understand how serious your injuries are. If you move too much, you could risk paralysis."

Garrick froze. Slowly, he turned his full attention upon her.

She held her finger and thumb a finger's length apart. "You left a dent in the ground that deep. I do not know how you even survived. But if you do not lie still, your injuries will get worse."

Garrick breathed slowly as he took in her words, his gaze drifting across the room. He could see the pieces of his armour piled up near the hearth. The pieces of plate were clean, but deformed, and part of his mail tunic lay pooled beside it. It looked like a number of rings had been pried apart. The ironwood haft of his voulge was snapped in half.

The woman shifted with a frown. "Now, where do you itch?"

His expression fell as he turned away, realizing he could be trapped immobile for weeks, if not the rest of his life. He gazed uncomfortably at the wall.

"I have to relieve myself."

"Oh." She cleared her throat. "I will get a bedpan."

He stared at the ceiling as she helped him, unable to do anything to assist.

"Well, this is the most humiliating thing I have ever done."

She stood, covering him with a blanket. "You are hurt. There is no shame in this." She didn't look at him as she said it, however. He said nothing in response as she took the bedpan outside to empty it.

As she stepped back in, he said without looking at her, "I'm sorry. I don't remember your name."

There was a smile in her voice. "You seemed a bit addled last time you said that, so I will forgive you this time."

He blinked. "Last time?"

Stepping forward, she grinned down at him. "My name is Kina Ukiel."

Chapter 11
Moving Pieces

Something was wrong.

Damian could tell that before they entered the village, and a quick glance to the others confirmed that they could see it as well. Down the main road, a huge crowd could be seen congregating in a square. Most, if not all, of the village's population must have been gathered there. One voice shouted something Damian couldn't make out at this distance, followed by a yell of support from the crowd.

Damian slowed her pace, swallowing uncomfortably as she watched the scene. Liam hovered close to her side and Rhyslen hung back as well, but Sir Kennar continued resolutely toward the crowd.

"S-Sir Kennar," she attempted.

With a glance back, he jerked his head toward the commotion. "This could be trouble. We need to find out what's going on." Damian exchanged an uneasy look with Rhyslen, but Sir Kennar went on, "Come along."

Shifting her shoulders, she followed as he moved toward the empty buildings and approached the crowd. As they drew near, she saw a dark-haired man standing on the edge of a fountain in the square's centre. She began to make out his voice.

"Trade is down," he was yelling, "bandits are running free, and enemies are closing in from all sides. And what does the king do? He hides in his castle!"

The crowd roared in agreement, and anger.

The leader pointed above the crowd vaguely to the northwest. "He's locked safe behind his high walls and leaves the rest of us out here on our own. There's this siege on the western border, Enseros arming for war, and even rumours that the barbarians are getting ready to invade. We're all in danger, yet there's been no sign of a patrol in weeks. They only care about us when it's convenient!"

The townspeople shouted assent, egging him on.

Sir Kennar began to stride into the street toward the crowd.

Damian quickly stepped forward. "You're not going to…"

He paused, but his gaze on her was firm. "He has the whole town riled up. If I don't do something, this is going to get much worse. Trust me, two hundred angry villagers can cause a big problem."

"You can't go in alone," she pleaded.

"Send for help," Rhyslen added.

Sir Kennar shook his head. "If a squad of soldiers comes in to subdue them, these people are going to feel justified and their anger will only escalate. I have to talk some sense into them. Stay behind me and keep close."

He turned and continued toward the crowd, and Damian and the others could only follow.

"If the king won't protect us," the instigator shouted, "then why should we support him?"

The crowd cheered again.

A chill crept up Damian's spine. *They're talking about treason.*

Suddenly, Sir Kennar's voice rose above the crowd. "What would you have the king do?"

All eyes turned to him and a surprised hush fell over many as they took in Sir Kennar's fine armour and bare head.

"Soldiers have to come from somewhere," he went on in a strong, but calm voice. "They must be fed, and armed, if they are to fulfill their duty. You cry about protection, but do you expect this protection to appear out of thin air?"

The instigator pointed an accusing finger at Sir Kennar. "The king should have foreseen these troubles before it ever came to this point."

Agreeing shouts rose from the crowd and some raised hoes, rakes, and other implements threateningly.

Sir Kennar shrugged, keeping his voice neutral for as loud as he had to speak. "Perhaps he should have. I don't understand the politics of running a kingdom. However, if you forsake him now, you'll be left even more vulnerable."

Damian could see some of the townspeople glancing at each other, clearly considering his words. Uncertain murmurs rose among the crowd and hope swelled in her heart.

It was dashed before she could breathe a sigh of relief.

"Don't listen to one of the warmongers of Hesperia," the instigator retorted. "Look at his armour. That costs more than Eldore produces in a year!"

The crowd yelled in support, their gazes darkening as they stared at Sir Kennar.

"That's not—" he attempted, but the instigator continued unswayed.

"If the king didn't lavish riches on his hired killers, we wouldn't be in this mess in the first place!"

"Yeah!" the crowd shouted.

"We work ourselves to the bone to support the king," added one man holding a hammer, "and he just hands out riches like that to his favourite cronies!"

Another yell supported him.

"This isn't about—" Sir Kennar tried again, but the voices drowned him out as the crowd edged in, making him back away.

"And what's he doing here now?" the instigator went on. "They sent him here to cow us into submission!"

The roar of the crowd was nearly deafening. Panic gripped Damian as the crowd pressed forward, expressions of fury on their faces. Liam loomed close, but even his protective presence didn't ease any of her terror. Sir Kennar continued backing away, but the edges of the crowd fanned out, trying to surround them.

"We are just passing through," he shouted, but none of the villagers listened.

"Well," the instigator said with a dark grin, "let's show the king just what we think of his fighting dogs."

The crowd shouted once more, holding their makeshift weapons high.

"We mean you no harm," Sir Kennar replied. His steps backwards hastened, but the crowd pushed outward so quickly that their escape would soon be blocked off entirely. "Let us leave and this won't get any worse."

Another voice in the crowd barked out a laugh. "It's only getting worse for you!"

Sir Kennar's voice darkened. "You don't want to do this."

Damian's hands shook. She looked desperately around. Liam stood close, not reaching for his sword but crouched and ready for a fight. Rhyslen gave Damian a pleading look and flicked his eyes toward his bag, tied to the pony's back.

The unseeing spell, she realized, then that hope vanished. The crowd had nearly surrounded them and stood barely four paces away. The unseeing spell wouldn't help them now.

Sir Kennar continued trying to herd them backwards, not daring to turn his back to the crowd, but they were rapidly becoming penned in. Screams of 'warmonger,' 'king's crony,' and, most distressingly, 'kill him' rose from the crowd.

"Get out of here," Sir Kennar hissed over his shoulder, and stopped his retreat to stand tall before the imposing crowd.

"Sir Kennar!" Damian cried, reaching forward as Liam pulled her back.

"It doesn't matter to me what you do here," Sir Kennar called out, meeting the eyes of the villagers in turn. They hesitated, watching him with wary eyes.

Rhyslen tugged at her sleeve. "Come on, let's go, while we still can."

"We can't just leave him," Damian uttered. However, she didn't fight as Liam and Rhyslen pulled her backwards, Liam holding the pony's lead.

"If you wish to bring the king's attention to your village, however," Sir Kennar went on, "this is a sure way to do it. Each of you had best be sure you're willing to risk your lives, your businesses, and your families to do something that will haunt you to the end of your days. As one of the 'king's killers,' I know all about that. Let us leave and nothing more will come of this."

Damian looked toward the instigator. She was too far away now to make out his expression, but he merely watched from his vantage point atop the fountain.

One of the men in the front row responded instead.

"I am doing this for my family!"

With a yell, he rushed toward Sir Kennar and swung his shovel.

Sir Kennar blocked the blow with his arm, not drawing his sword, but the crowd erupted into a frenzy of movement as they closed in on him.

"No!" Damian cried. She stumbled as she leaned forward, suddenly unhindered. Liam ran forward, grabbing the shoulder of a man trying to beat Sir Kennar with a club and throwing him off.

"Liam!"

The crowd swarmed around Sir Kennar and Liam. Though they both shoved back and disarmed the attackers admirably, more and more blows came through from the sheer numbers of people bearing down on them. Distantly, Damian realized Rhyslen rummaged through his pack on the pony. Consumed by fear, she could only run forward and try to help push people away.

"Stop this!" she pleaded, her voice drowned out by the madness of the crowd. "Get away from them!"

She tried to grab the arm of a large man holding fireplace tongs, but he threw her to the ground without so much as looking at her. Damian scrambled to her feet, but now the crowd was three people deep. As she watched, Liam disappeared beneath the crowd.

Rage and horror bubbled up within her in equal measure, trembling through her entire body. She let out a shout that echoed around the square.

"Leave them alone!"

A boom and roar filled her ears as her frustration shot out of her, and cries and screams filled the air as weapons clanged and people thumped to the ground. Damian swayed, suddenly dizzy and struggling to focus and stay on her feet.

Blinking, she could just make out the shapes of Liam and Sir Kennar rising and moving over to her. Liam took her arm, and she could make out a worried look in his crystalline eyes.

He and Sir Kennar started to move her back toward the pony, but she pulled herself free of their arms and took a step forward, glaring at the crowd. Some of those now lying on the ground yelped and tried to scramble backward as she spoke.

"Take up your grievances with the king if you must, but if your answer is to attack a man who has done nothing to you, then you're more warmongers than he will ever be."

Turning, she swept around and stalked back toward the men. Only two paces on, however, her knees trembled and she struggled to keep her balance. "I don't feel well." There was a tremor in her voice and the mere act of speaking seemed to drain her.

"Take the pony," Sir Kennar ordered. Liam swiftly stepped up with the pony, blocking the crowd's view of Damian as he helped her onto its back.

Her strength gradually flowed back as they hurried down the road into the fields beyond. She looked over her shoulder. The crowd was indistinct now, though she could still see raised arms and the lone figure on top of the fountain. Formless shouts rose on the air.

She hunched her shoulders, wrapping her arms around herself. "I'm sorry."

Sir Kennar looked subdued. "I should be punishing you for using magic, but you may very well have just saved my life." He sent Damian a cautious look. "How did you do that?"

"I don't know," she answered quietly.

"Are you all right?" Rhyslen asked. His eyes were wide as he stared at her, though it seemed as much in awe as in surprise.

"I'm… hungry."

Silently, Liam reached into one of the pony's baskets and pulled out an apple. She took it gratefully.

Sir Kennar let out a sigh. "Things are far worse than I realized. We have to get word through to the king somehow."

"Do you think all those things they were saying are true?" Rhyslen asked.

The knight shook his head. "I've been out of touch from any reliable sources of goings-on in the kingdom. I'm sure that person riling them up was embellishing things, to say the least." Sir Kennar frowned. "However, this isn't the first time we've heard about a siege to the west." He couldn't entirely hide the worry in his eyes. Damian only wished she could tell him what she knew of the Army of Light, thanks to Garrick's letter.

She stared at the pony's bobbing neck without seeing it. "And that's the second town we've visited that mentioned increased taxes and recruitment."

Sir Kennar only looked away.

They backtracked a long way, until the village was the size of a coin in the distance, before turning south off the road, finding a suitable campsite after the sun had set. Though they would lose as much as a day of travel, they all agreed that giving a wide berth around the village before returning to the road was best.

As a result, they didn't make much ground the following day, only barely reaching a farming hamlet with a dozen buildings at sundown. The town's smith allowed them shelter in his shop, still nearly sweltering from the forge. Sir Kennar seemed unusually quiet and pensive as they all lay down to sleep on the floor of the shop, but said nothing was wrong when Damian asked.

She was happy enough to agree to rouse the men early and leave by sunrise. Sir Kennar still drew the attention of the entire settlement, though at least it kept their focus off her. The knight gave the villagers his blessings, but excused himself from the other favours they asked of him, and soon, they left the hamlet behind.

The day continued as the previous ones had as they returned to the road and continued walking west, leading the pony along.

Dinnertime seemed to come earlier than ever, and they waited until the sun was noticeably past its apex before they stopped for a break. As they reached the top of a short hill, Damian noticed a copse of trees at its bottom, some forty paces south of the road.

"Let's stop there," Sir Kennar said, nodding his head faintly toward the trees. As Damian began to turn toward it, he added, "Wait. Let's go down a little farther before we move off the road."

Damian gave him a curious look, noticing Rhyslen mirroring her, but the Agaesi said no more. They climbed down the far side of the rise a handful of paces before Sir Kennar turned and led them toward the trees.

To Damian's surprise, however, as she opened the pony's basket to retrieve some food, Sir Kennar remained standing, swords still strapped to his side.

"You go ahead and eat," he said before any of them could ask the question. "Stay here. I'll be back soon."

"Where…" Damian attempted, but the knight jogged away before she could finish, mail rattling beneath the straps of his plate armour.

Rhyslen blinked, the biscuit in his hand untouched. "What is he doing?"

Damian could only stare after Sir Kennar, his form barely visible through the trees. Strangely, he moved south, farther from the road, toward the edge of the hill they had just descended.

She felt cold. Looking at Liam, she found him returning a look both knowing and uncertain.

"This is exactly what he did when he went to find you," she told Rhyslen.

His eyebrows rose. "You don't think someone else is following us?"

"I don't know." She couldn't imagine Sir Kennar leaving both her and Rhyslen alone for any other reason.

All three of them watched Sir Kennar diminishing in the distance through the branches of the trees for a moment.

"He has seemed preoccupied this morning," Liam remarked.

Rhyslen stared into the distance where Sir Kennar vanished. "We could leave." He turned to Damian. "Just take the supplies and go, right now."

Damian shot him a horrified look. "No."

He held out an arm. "This is our chance. We could be free, finally."

"We couldn't get far enough away," Liam piped in. "He would catch us up easily."

"Then let's use the unseeing spell," Rhyslen argued.

"He's trusting us." Damian's hands curled into fists.

"Damian, he's treating you like a criminal."

"Your hands aren't bound anymore. Are mine? Or Liam's?"

Rhyslen's eyes narrowed. "Just because he's not tying us up

doesn't mean he trusts us. We're still keeping secrets from him, remember?"

Liam stepped closer. "Trust must be earned. He's showing us some by leaving us alone. Is your first thought really to betray that?"

Damian turned a sly smile to Rhyslen. He sat back with a huff.

"We're not going to stop Niabi by alienating potential allies," Damian said. "She's doing just as much damage by making people believe in her. If we can convince Sir Kennar that stopping her is the right thing to do, it'll help keep her influence from spreading."

"Do you really think he's ever going to accept that?"

Damian shook her head. "We're not leaving." She glanced back to the hill around which Sir Kennar disappeared. "Anyway, while we have privacy, there's something I have to tell you."

Rhyslen pursed her lips, but didn't argue further.

"I've been thinking about how we might stop Niabi, and... I think you might be able to help us find more people to join us."

"Me? How could I help?"

She inhaled deeply. "Some of Yanuk's mages still live."

He straightened, breathless with obvious hope. "Really? Where?"

"I don't know where they are now, but some of the mages didn't want to march on Albrith, like you, and left along the way. I thought maybe you could help us track them down."

Leaning forward, he stared excitedly at her. "Do you know anything about them?"

She shook her head, reflecting on what Nephrita had shared with her when she was bound to Yanuk. "I know there were four desertions, at least before Raven Point."

"What's that?"

Visions of a ruined town flashed through her mind. A jagged seam the only reminder of half of the village that was buried below. Broken people lying on a hillside.

"It was a village. Yanuk ransacked it after binding Nephrita to his will."

A frown crossed Rhyslen's face briefly, but then he looked thoughtful. "So if we follow the same path he took before then, we might be able to find them. Where is Raven Point?"

"It was almost due south of the Bay of Glass. I... think it was a little bit north of Windermere. But they might have moved on by now. I can't guarantee we'll find them, even if we can follow their trail precisely."

"They will need food and shelter, and they won't have anywhere else to go. I wouldn't be surprised if they just settled down wherever they ended up, like me."

"I think it's worth looking, but I wouldn't get your hopes up."

Rhyslen nodded, though it was clear he longed to find his old friends. With that, they each retrieved some food and ate, their conversation lapsing into silence.

Damian was truly beginning to worry about Sir Kennar when Liam announced, "He is coming back."

Relief flooding her, Damian moved around the trees to stand beside Liam. Then she stopped still.

Sir Kennar strode down the hill toward them from the road, one gauntleted hand holding his drawn sword and the other wrapped in the collar of another person he pushed in front of him. The dark-haired man seemed to have his hands bound behind his back. As Sir Kennar came within thirty paces of their camp, Damian could see the satchel hanging over the knight's shoulder, and a large, dark bruise on the side of his captive's face. Sir Kennar looked unchanged, though the expression on his face was perhaps a little harder.

Rhyslen came up beside Damian, drawing in a surprised breath. She watched curiously as Sir Kennar led the man close. The captive tried to slow, only to be shoved along by the knight a few steps from Damian. The man winced and bowed his head from the pressure.

Finally, Sir Kennar stopped just before Damian, Liam, and Rhyslen. "Sit down," he ordered his captive, giving the man a shove on his shoulder. The dark-haired man grunted as he dropped to the ground, crossing his legs before him. He raised his head to stare flatly at Damian.

As she met his eyes, she gasped.

"Him," Rhyslen snapped, his voice somewhere between a question and an exclamation.

The instigator from the riot in the village two days earlier smirked up at her, blood staining his gums.

"Mister Gressel has been following us since Eldore," Sir Kennar explained.

"Why?" Damian asked, narrowing her eyes at the instigator.

"He hasn't been forthcoming with that information."

"Do what you will," Gressel said. "I'm not tellin' you anything."

"Perhaps you don't need to." Sir Kennar removed the satchel and tossed it to Damian. "Let's have a look at his effects."

She gave Gressel a glance. His expression betrayed nothing.

What does he want with us? she wondered. *We weren't able to sway the townspeople against him.* Opening the satchel, she looked inside. Rhyslen peered over her shoulder. Damian pulled out extra clothes, a water skin, a small and roughly drawn map of the kingdom, a tinder box, a dagger, a package of food wrapped in cheesecloth, a coin pouch, and other sundries. Then, she paused.

"There's paper in here. And ink."

Rhyslen pulled the near flap of the satchel wider, staring around the other items at the writing instruments at the bottom. "There's sealing wax, too."

Damian pulled the satchel closer, digging through the remaining items in search of a seal. She could feel nothing inside. Frowning, she began removing the remaining items from the satchel. Even after taking out the paper, she found none.

"There's no seal in here," she said, upending the satchel and shaking it for good measure.

"What did you do with it?" Sir Kennar growled, raising the blade of his sword toward Gressel's neck. The captive kept his mouth shut.

Liam moved around behind Gressel, glancing down. Kneeling, he grabbed at Gressel's hands. Damian couldn't see what he did, but Gressel grunted as he clearly struggled. After a moment, Liam rose, holding up a pewter signet ring.

"What's the seal on it?" Sir Kennar asked.

Liam handed it to Damian and she looked at it. "It's a duck in some reeds."

Rhyslen straightened. "That's the seal of Claxbury. I was born there."

"Wait," Damian said, "you mean he's an official from there?" She doubtfully examined the man's unkempt beard and ragged clothes. There was a trace of discomfort on his face as they studied the signet ring he had obviously tried to hide from Liam.

"It's more likely he's here on official business," Sir Kennar answered. He looked at Rhyslen. "Who's the thane of Claxbury?"

"I haven't been there since I was a child, but it's been held by the Haestus family for half a dozen generations."

"Haestus?" Damian interjected, straightening. "That name sounds familiar."

Sir Kennar looked at her in surprise. "Why would you be familiar with Lord Haestus?"

She screwed up her face as she tried to remember. *Why do I know the thane of a province I've never been to?*

She gasped as it struck her.

"The meeting with the king and his advisors," she uttered. "After the Battle of Albrith." Her gaze dropped to Gressel. "He was the one calling for my arrest the most."

Sir Kennar stared at Gressel. "So now you're spying on her for your thane, is that it? Is he so desperate to prove himself right?" His eyes darkened. "Or is it to prove the king wrong?"

Gressel chuckled darkly. "I'm not tellin', but you kill me an' you'll do both. Go on."

Damian's throat tightened. Sir Kennar's eyes didn't waver from Gressel, nor did the anger diminish in his face. Damian chanced a glance at Liam, but he only watched the scene intently. Rhyslen returned her uncertain look.

Gressel appeared not quite triumphant, but satisfied. There was no fear of death in his eyes.

The thump sounded in Damian's ears nearly before she registered Sir Kennar moving. His free hand swung in a blur she couldn't follow, smacking against Gressel somewhere on his neck. Damian started at the sudden blow as Gressel dropped bonelessly to the ground. Rhyslen took a step back, his eyes wide.

Sir Kennar sheathed his sword, staring down at Gressel with a frown. "Unfortunately, he's right. We can't kill him, but we don't have the resources to keep him prisoner until we reach somewhere that can hold him." He held a hand out to Damian. "I'll keep his signet ring, but we have to let him go."

She handed over the ring, but her attention was on Gressel. Damian felt a chill sweep over her back as she stared down at his unmoving form. She shivered.

"Damian?" Rhyslen asked. "Are you all right?"

She spun around and stepped a couple paces away, trying to fight sudden tears that were a mixture of anger, frustration, and terror. She hugged herself beneath her cloak.

"It's bad enough that people hate and fear me across the kingdom," she snapped, failing to keep the tremor out of her voice. "Now this lord is using me in his political schemes?"

Liam swiftly strode over and laid a hand on her shoulder. She leaned into the touch, wanting more.

"I'm sure it's not personal against you," Rhyslen said with a touch of weariness. "People like that, they'll use any leverage they can get to try to grab more power."

"It's more of a reflection on him than on you, to be sure," Sir Kennar added. "We had better keep moving. He may not be out for long."

Damian turned around, a look of surprise on her face. "But you didn't have anything to eat."

Sir Kennar untied the pony. "I'll eat as we walk. I want to put some distance between us and him."

Damian frowned down at Gressel's prone form one last time as they made their way back toward the road.

I'm being watched, she thought. *Even out in the middle of nowhere, trying to get away from everything, people are watching what I do.*

Garrick said nothing as Kina spooned soup into his mouth. He lay on his side, propped up and padded by piles of blankets and pillows and supported by sacks of grain. The broken mail had been removed, but the searing pain in his lower back like stones grinding against his spine was a constant companion. The bindings and splints Kina had made for his broken limbs pressed into him. The hip, knee, and shoulder he rested on flamed with growing agony, and he knew that the painstaking process of turning him onto his back would happen soon. He stared unseeing ahead, silently chewing and swallowing and moving no part of his body aside from his jaw.

"Do you remember anything yet?"

He shut his eyes and let out a breath. A single image had appeared in his mind, his only reminder of the event that had left him immobile, and even that had faded like a dream.

Niabi.

"Enough."

They both fell silent as she continued feeding him, and his thoughts drifted to what he could remember about the mage he had found. Artra. Garrick could no longer remember his surname, or some of the conversations they'd had. Eventually, Kina emptied the bowl and stood to take it back into the kitchen.

"The man I was accompanying."

Her footfalls paused halfway across the common room. When she replied, her voice sounded thick. "He did not survive."

Garrick closed his eyes.

I try to follow orders and people die. I try to do the right thing instead and people still die. One man, out in the middle of nowhere, and I couldn't even protect him.

"I'm a failure."

Kina continued toward the kitchen. "You did everything you

could."

"Clearly, it wasn't enough."

"You are too injured even to feed yourself. No one can fault you for not doing more."

His voice hardened. "I promised him I would protect him with my life. Now he's dead." Garrick let out a sigh. "And I'm not."

Kina set the bowl down in the kitchen. "Blaming yourself for surviving will not help him. I know how you feel, but clinging to guilt never makes it easier, or right."

He let out a scoffing breath.

She stepped out of the kitchen. "Trust me. In all my travels, I have learned this much. The only thing you can do for someone who is gone is to let go and look forward."

Garrick raised an eyebrow as he glanced around at her cluttered home. "I mean no offense, but I find it hard to believe someone of your… means has travelled very much."

From the corner of his eye, he saw her grin. "You would be surprised, then. Perhaps I will tell you sometime when you are not so grumpy."

He smiled wryly, examining the trinkets scattered about the room. Strange figures and decorated candle holders, boxes, and other items littered the shelves, all clearly very old and most of them very foreign. He didn't recognize the style of many of them and couldn't guess at their origin.

"I'm not grumpy."

Hands on her hips, she leaned her head back. "You are only saying that because you are curious about my stories. It will take a more sincere effort than that to convince me."

He donned his best courtly smile. "I am as vibrant as springtime wildflowers."

"I do not believe you."

"I could sing for you, but I'd probably muck up the words, what with the head injury."

Her grin widened. "Now that could be entertaining." She strode over and sat on the arm of a chair near him. "Perhaps if you sang me a song, I will regale you with a tale of adventure and heroism the likes of which you have never heard."

He chuckled wryly. "I find that unlikely. I am an Agaesi." She tilted her head aside, regarding him in interest, but his smile faltered. "I have to write a letter to my captain. I need to tell him what happened."

"Unless your horse can take it to him, it will not go anywhere."

"Please," he urged. "If you don't know how to write—"

"I can write," Kina cut across him. "I wrote most of these books."

Garrick blinked in surprise, glancing once more around the room. "But there is no one to take any message anywhere."

He studied her. "What do you mean?"

"I live alone, Sir Magni. Entirely alone. The nearest village is a two-day walk from here."

His eyes enlarged.

"Obviously, with you in your condition, I cannot leave you here alone for half a week."

He chewed his lip. "You could take Brenadier." His uncertainty was clear in his voice, for Brenadier wasn't built for sustained speed.

She shook her head. "It would still be days of travel. Until you are well enough to care for yourself, it seems I am stuck here as much as you are."

He squeezed his eyes shut. "I'm sorry. I don't mean to be such a burden on you."

"Do not be." The smile returned to her voice. "I have not had company in a long time. You have made my life very interesting again."

He could not smile in return. "I'm afraid I won't be very interesting for quite some time."

"You only say that because you cannot see what I see."

Casting a flat look to her, he asked, "What do you see?"

To his surprise, he found a knowing and mysterious look on her face as she studied him, but it disappeared as she answered.

"An Agaesi knight who is apparently unimpressed with grand adventure stories."

He smiled humourlessly. "Just call me Garrick. I don't feel like much of a knight like this."

"Well, whether you believe it or not, Garrick, it is a pleasure to meet you."

He fixed his gaze on her. "Thank you for helping me. I owe you my life."

Kina grinned. "I am glad to hear that you believe it was worth saving."

A wry grin crossed his face. "I'm not sure about that."

"Then how about we play a game and take your mind off things?"

Garrick watched as she walked to one of the bookshelves along the wall and pulled out a game board and a small velvet pouch.

"What do you have? Bridges and Towers?"

"Bridges and Towers would do me little good when I live alone."

"Any game would."

"Yes, but this one is a memento. Besides, you could hardly keep your tiles hidden from me if we played Bridges and Towers."

Garrick frowned at that. He looked curiously at the game board as she set it on the floor beside his head. "What is this?" The board was divided up in diamonds in a configuration he had never seen before. As she set the pouch down beside it, small stones rattled inside.

"Domination. This game is much simpler than Bridges and Towers."

"I've never even heard of a game like this."

"It is a very old game," Kina said with a knowing smile that Garrick began to associate with her. "The rules are very simple." Pulling out red and blue stone markers from the pouch, she laid them out in a certain arrangement on the board. "The object is to take your opponent's pieces until he is left with two. You can move two pieces per turn for a total of four spaces, though you must move two pieces at least one space. You take one of your opponent's pieces by surrounding it with your pieces. And if you reach the opponent's side of the board and make a triangle against the edge, then you can take one piece back for each empty space inside."

"That's it?"

"As I said, it is a very simple game. However, the strategies used can be quite complex. Would you like to give it a try?"

He frowned. "It doesn't seem that complex."

She smiled slyly. "Then how about we make it more interesting and place a wager on the winner?"

He laughed. "What would I bet? You already have everything I own."

"A story," she said with that knowing smile.

He studied her for a moment. Clearly she could see more to him than he thought he was letting on.

Everyone has their own agenda.

He glanced once more around the common room at the strange artifacts scattered throughout.

"Very well. A secret for the loser to share."

Her smile widened. "Agreed." With that, she moved her first pieces and began the game. For several turns, they played quietly, Garrick telling Kina where to move his pieces as he tried to figure out her strategy and how to defeat it.

The first time she took one of his pieces came as a complete surprise.

He blinked as he re-created the move in his mind.

She smirked. "You can see how easy it is to miss potential moves when you have such freedom with your pieces."

He grinned at her. "Yes, I'm starting to see that." He instructed her on his next move. Deciding it was time to be more aggressive, he pressed two of his pieces toward a defensive barrier she had made on her side of the board.

As soon as he began feeling satisfied with breaking apart her formation, however, it circled around and took three of his pieces at once. He frowned, adjusting his strategy, but failed to prevent her formation from reaching an open space on his side of the board and creating triangles to bring back some of her pieces. Soon, he found his pieces outnumbered two to one and it was all he could do to delay the inevitable.

As she set down a marker that completed a circle, leaving only two of his pieces on the board, he half grinned. "I see what you mean about the strategies being more complex. The movements aren't too different from Bridges and Towers, but the game play is nothing like it."

She smiled as she slid the pieces off the board and re-arranged them into the starting configuration. "Yes, I like it much better. Easy to learn, but difficult to master. I have not played Domination in a long time."

"I wouldn't have thought so with the way you played."

That knowing smile crossed her face again. "I remember successful strategies." Finishing her arrangement of the game board, she looked into his eyes. "Now, I believe you owe me a secret. Perhaps you would like to tell me the truth of the Agaesi?"

He felt trapped, the walls of the common room that had been his world for most of a week closing in on him. Summoning all the lessons of court politics from his mother, he gave her an innocently curious look. "Truth?"

She leaned back on her hands. "I know the rumours of the Agaesi knights, as well as the common knowledge. That your skill is without equal, and that no one joins the Order of the Dragon who does not seem to already be there."

"The Agaesi are very selective."

"That is not an answer."

He looked warily at her. "You ask something that no one outside our order knows. In any case, I thought it was my choice what I shared."

She shrugged, idly dropping extra pieces in the velvet pouch. "It is up to you. But the next time we play, I will tell you a story of equal importance."

He raised his eyebrows dubiously. "You have secrets that rival what has been kept within the oldest order of knights in the kingdom, going back to the Time of Gods and Magic?"

She merely smiled at him. "Yes."

For a moment, he could only stare at her. Then, his eyes were drawn to the trinkets scattered about the room and the game they had just played. He tried to get a measure of her, surprised that he hadn't before now. She might have secrets, very large ones, but nothing she had said or done hinted at any sense of deceit, manipulation, or desire for any gain other than sated curiosity. Speaking with Kina had been so different from dealing with nobles that he hadn't even thought about his mother's instructions until now.

Besides, Kina had treated him better than any of the Agaesi ever had, and he might never return to that life. *What do I have to lose?*

"What you ask is not something easily accepted."

"I have seen very strange things in my life. I will not be disturbed by what you tell me."

He had a suspicion she was not exaggerating. If anything, he suspected that was a gross understatement. He inhaled deeply, staring toward the ceiling.

"The truth is… we're mages."

All she said was, "Is that right?" There was some curiosity, but no surprise in her voice.

Garrick eyed her warily. "Yes. That is where our power comes from… and likely, that's why I survived Niabi's attack."

"But your magic is different from most."

He stared at her.

She shrugged. "Well, this secret would not have remained hidden so long if you simply shot fire from your hands like many mages."

That wasn't what she meant, that much was clear, but he nodded. "Yes, that's true."

Leaning back again, she glanced at one of the shelves. "I will share a secret with you as well."

"Oh? I need not win it?"

"Would you like to know why I took such interest in you to bring you back here, rather than simply send for help?"

A dry grin crossed his face. "I thought it was the 'Sir Garrick

Magni-sized hole in the ground.'"

Her smile widened. "I will admit, that did make me curious. But that is not it." She leaned forward, facing him again. "In truth, Sir Garrick, I have the gift, or sometimes the curse, of mage sight."

He looked puzzled. "What's that?"

"Essentially, I can see magic."

His eyes widened. "What?"

She smiled at his reaction. "You have horns. On your head." She held her hands up to the sides of her head, the first finger on each pointing up. "I have seen my share of magic, but I have only seen one other who had some spell that was a part of him rather than something summoned on command."

Garrick blinked. The Agaesi could sense magic, but he had never heard of someone able to see magic. "How did you end up with an ability like that?"

"That is a story for when you win a game." She gestured to the board. "Would you like to play again?"

Chapter 12
Pride Abounds

THE FOLLOWING WEEK of travel ended up far less exciting than the previous one, much to Damian's relief. The nights grew colder and they pushed their risk of discovery to find shelter in towns, rather than camp out in the open. Fortunately, none of the other villages they passed showed the same level of tension as Eldore. Still, they all agreed it was best not to test the villages' reception of them, often leaving Liam to secure lodging and additional supplies. There was no further sign of Gressel and Sir Kennar didn't detect any other spies, but Damian couldn't help looking over her shoulder, especially when they entered a populated area.

The journey otherwise became surprisingly comfortable. Her feet hardened to the travel and the four of them became friendly. Even Sir Kennar and Rhyslen grew amiable toward each other. Sir Kennar still didn't fully trust him, though he did allow Rhyslen to carry his own supplies. However, as they followed the road, they occasionally passed other travellers who increasingly supported the assertions of Gressel and the mob in Eldore. Furtive whispers of the Army of Light, the malakh leading it, and the recruitment efforts to repel them at the border accompanied these brief meetings. Damian couldn't help noticing Sir Kennar's lips pursing and his gait increasing following such encounters.

Sir Kennar did spend long enough in one town to send a message to the king with news of Gressel spying on them for Lord Haestus, though their pace remained hurried. Damian could understand his anxiousness to reach Misengrad, though as the daylight hours shortened every day, she wondered if he was simply trying to cover as much ground as they could with less time to do it.

As they entered another village as another autumn afternoon sent long bars of sunlight and shadow between buildings, she watched the people carefully. Aside from any signs that they might meet with hostility, despite Rhyslen and Liam's advance scouting assuring them otherwise, Damian wondered if they might find one of Yanuk's missing mages here. Their travels had brought them within a couple days of Aura Lake and she was relatively certain that they were south of Raven Point. She couldn't guess what the missing mages might have been thinking when they left Yanuk's group, but this was one of the larger towns in the area. If she had been left suddenly on her own, she would have gravitated toward a place like this, somewhere with greater access to resources and less likelihood that all the inhabitants would know each other and recognize a stranger.

Unfortunately, that also meant a larger area to search. She glanced at the people around as she walked, hoping that her study was surreptitious enough not to arouse Sir Kennar's suspicions, or the villagers'. Of course, she had no idea who she was looking for, so eventually she gave up looking.

When they came up to a butcher in search of more food for the journey, however, a voice across the street caught her attention.

"As I live and breathe, tha's Rhyslen!"

Damian's eyes enlarged. She turned her head to face the source of the outburst, but stopped herself before she looked back. None of the others had reacted to the woman's call.

A male voice grunted in response.

Quick, scuffling footsteps followed, but they stopped short as Damian and Sir Kennar came up to the butcher shop.

"Tha's a dragon knight," the woman said. "What's 'e doing with one o' *them?*" Scorn dripped from her voice.

Nobody on the street seemed to react to or even notice their conversation, despite that the woman wasn't trying to keep her voice down. Damian's heart raced as Sir Kennar pulled some coins out of a pouch to hand to Rhyslen.

"Should he come with me?" Rhyslen asked, nodding toward Liam.

Sir Kennar grinned wryly. "It's probably best if he does. He knows how to haggle."

Damian couldn't help smiling. She had seen Liam's style of haggling. It involved staring unmoving at whatever poor merchant was subject to his scrutiny until they meekly offered a lower price. It was surprising how effective it was.

Her mind raced as Rhyslen began climbing the stairs into the shop, wondering how they could speak with the mages hiding in plain view behind her.

She stepped hastily forward before Rhyslen walked inside. "Wait, Rhyslen. I'll hold your bag for you."

He turned, giving her a curious look, and she stared at him, hoping it was firm enough to clue him in to her intentions without alerting Sir Kennar of the same thing. It was a delicate balance, and she couldn't help thinking of Garrick as she did it.

Her heart wrenched as Rhyslen said, "Sure," and slid the pack off his shoulder to hand to her. She hated keeping such secrets from Sir Kennar. It would be difficult enough to hide these mages from him if they were willing to join her. She vowed to tell him the truth as soon as she met with the mages.

The man behind them emitted a strange set of soft grunts.

"An' who's that fella Rhyslen went in the shop with?" the woman added. "I don' like this one whit."

Damian forced herself not to react to the voices as she moved around the other side of the pony from Sir Kennar. Her heart pounded as he watched her heft the pack up on the animal's back.

"A trick my father and I learned on our market journey," she said with a smile she hoped looked genuine. "If you look like you're ready to travel, merchants often get the impression that you're in a hurry and hike up their prices."

Sir Kennar *hmph*ed but said nothing in response. His gaze wandered from the closed door of the butcher shop across the town to his other side.

As swiftly and quietly as she could, she reached into Rhyslen's pack and pulled out paper and charcoal. Hiding herself on the other side of the pony as Sir Kennar, she scribbled out a quick note.

She had barely finished writing when the door to the butcher shop opened and Rhyslen and Liam emerged. Liam nodded as they climbed down the stairs.

"We got what we need," Rhyslen said. "They said it could be ready by tonight, but since we don't know where we're staying, I said we would pick it up in the morning." He held out the leftover coins from the purchase, but Sir Kennar merely waved it off.

"Good. I think finding an inn next would be best. We can search for the other things we need once the horse is stabled."

Liam strode around the pony to take the reins from Damian. She allowed her mask to slip, looking up at him with the anxious excitement of having found some of the missing mages. Doubtless he didn't understand what had her worked up, and he gazed curiously back at her.

As they began walking, Damian folded up the note and dropped it on the ground. She glanced over her shoulder directly at the couple who had been talking.

Both of them were dressed in faded, fraying, dirt-stained clothes. The woman was tall and curvaceous, with a shock of curly brown hair barely pulled back into a tail. The man was slightly shorter than her, skinny with dark hair and a wide, square jaw. The woman gasped and clutched the man's shoulder as Damian looked them square in the eyes. At this distance, she wasn't sure if they could make out the colour of her eyes or merely reacted to the fact that she saw them. She tried to convey friendliness in her look, though she couldn't help wondering if urgency won out.

She faced forward, not giving them another look as Sir Kennar and the others continued down the street in search of an inn. She hoped the note would be enough and wouldn't simply scare them away. The fact that they were using the unseeing spell in the middle of town this long after the Battle of Albrith made her wonder if they had spent the entire time since they left Yanuk in hiding.

What would that be like? Did they live in constant fear of discovery or, like Rhyslen in the market in Windermere, had they become so comfortable in their trust in the spell that they no longer had any fears?

Sadly, whereas a year ago Damian could never have imagined living that way, now she thought it might be convenient. She was used to being ignored, and it was better than being reviled.

Soon, they found an inn, and Damian's heart pounded again. Lately, when they sought shelter in a village, Sir Kennar went inside alone to arrange for a night's stay, more concerned about Damian being recognized in a crowded common room than worried that she would leave. Still, she couldn't help fearing that this day would be different.

However, the knight didn't say a word. He merely nodded to the rest of them, handing the lead of the pony to Damian as he stepped inside.

As soon as the door shut, she turned to Rhyslen.

"I saw them," she said, softly and urgently. "Two of Yanuk's desertions. They recognized you."

Rhyslen perked up. "Really? What did they look like?"

"A tall woman with curly brown hair and a stout man with dark brown hair."

"Poppy and Merle!" he uttered eagerly. "Where were they? I never even saw them."

"They were using the unseeing spell." She spoke as much to Liam, listening silently, as to Rhyslen. "I left a note to meet with them tonight, but I don't—"

The door to the inn opened. She started and looked at Sir Kennar as he stepped outside.

"We are all set," he said.

He began unstrapping the baskets off the pony and Damian busied herself helping to remove the pony's tack. She looked over its back at Liam. He simply nodded in return. She wished she had the freedom to speak with him unrestrained, as she had the night after they left Aether. But since Rhyslen had joined them, Sir Kennar stayed too close to allow them any privacy. Briefly, she even missed being in Aether. The long walks they had taken through the streets or out into the surrounding pasture, his closeness making the looks and insults from the townspeople less hurtful.

Tomorrow, she vowed. *I can't wait any longer. I have to tell Sir Kennar the truth.*

She followed the men inside and up to her lone room, as usual, while the others shared one. She frowned. Unseeing spell or no, it would be impossible for Rhyslen to sneak out of the same room as Sir Kennar to go meet with Poppy and Merle. She would have to meet them alone and hope that they were willing to trust her.

She waited, tense, as the sun set and the next room grew quiet. Agonizing minutes became an interminable hour. Finally, the moment arrived. Moonrise. Her heart thrummed and skin crawled.

All she could do was move carefully and step softly as she slipped on her boots, wrapped a heavy cloak around herself, and crept out of her room. She listened carefully at the men's door as she passed, but heard no stirring within.

At the entrance to the inn, she hesitated, flinching when she saw that the door was locked. She sighed. There was nothing else for it. She unlocked the door and stepped out, hoping that no one else would rise and notice the unlocked door, or that the innkeeper wouldn't lock it again while she was out.

Damian slipped into the night, struggling to orient herself in the darkness. Her breath clouded on the air and a scattering of tiny snowflakes drifted down as she walked. The silence and stillness, made heavier by the snow, made her feel as though she travelled through an abandoned town.

She hurriedly backtracked the way they had come through the

village until she turned a corner down the road from the butcher shop. Cautiously, she approached, looking at the shops all around for any signs of people.

"Poppy?" she asked softly. "Merle?"

As she came up to the butcher shop, figures stepped out of the shadows on the other side. Damian took in a breath. It was the same people from earlier that day. Moonlight glinted off the strands of Poppy's wild hair that peeked out from underneath a hood, and off the blade of a dagger Merle held out.

"Who are you?" Poppy demanded.

Damian straightened. "My name is Damian Sires. You have probably heard of me as the witch from the Battle of Albrith."

Poppy's eyes widened, though they remained hard. Merle shifted, looking like he was about to say something before Poppy continued, "How do yae know Rhyslen?"

"I met him in Windermere last year." Damian had already decided that telling the mages the truth was best, and didn't hesitate. "He was stealing from the market and I saw through the unseeing spell. Yanuk sent him away to find me and he ended up in a village in eastern Faneria when Yanuk decided to march on Albrith. I found him while travelling this way and he wanted to come with me. He told me about you."

"And why isn't he here now?"

Damian glanced briefly at Merle, who stood holding the dagger in one hand, the other methodically flapping back and forth. He seemed content to let Poppy speak for both of them.

"He is sharing a room with the dragon knight. He wanted to come, but there's no way he would be able to get out without being noticed. I'm risking a lot as it is."

"Fine," Poppy answered without seeming satisfied. "What do yae want with us?"

"I want you to help me." Damian took a step forward. "The malakh from the Battle of Albrith is gathering an army. I don't know what her plans are for it, but from what I know of her... it's going to be bad. I have to stop her."

The hardness in Poppy's eyes faded for the first time, replaced by confusion. "What, by yaerself?"

Damian gave her a wan smile. "That's why I'm looking for help." She sobered. "Rhyslen wants to see you. He couldn't go along with Yanuk's plan, and that's why you left, isn't it?"

Poppy looked surprised.

"You wouldn't have to hide anymore," Damian went on,

gesturing around her at the town. "And you'd be among friends."

Poppy shuffled her feet uneasily. "But… we're not fighters."

"We don't need fighters. What we need is someone who can give us an edge. Who can do something unexpected."

The two mages exchanged a glance.

"I don't know if we can really help… but I sure would like t' see Rhyslen. What about the dragon knight?"

"Yes," answered a dark voice.

Damian gasped and spun. Sir Kennar stood barely five paces away, close enough that in the moonlight, she could see the anger in his eyes.

"What about the dragon knight?"

Poppy yelped and she and Merle backed a pace away.

"S-Sir Kennar," Damian uttered.

"What are you doing out here, Damian?" The knight's voice was dangerous and his hand was on his sword. Though he was garbed only with mail and his arming sword, he looked imposing.

"Sir Kennar," she attempted, her voice tremoring. "I'm sorry, I wanted to—"

"Answer. Me."

She drew in a breath, heart thundering. She had never seen or heard him so threatening.

"They're mages," she spat out.

Poppy snapped her gaze to Damian. "What're yae doin'?!"

The words spilled out as Damian continued. "I'm so sorry I deceived you, Sir. I was going to tell you in the morning. I'm going after—"

"Mages?" Sir Kennar fairly snarled the word. Damian quailed. "You're sneaking out in the middle of the night and *recruiting mages* behind my back?"

She flinched. "It's not like that. I have to—"

"Don't you move," he growled fiercely enough to make Damian jump. She saw him staring at Poppy and Merle and turned to find them frozen a couple paces farther away.

"Sir, I—"

"I thought I could trust you."

Damian winced. It was like a blow to the stomach. She spoke hurriedly. "Sir, please. I have to help stop Niabi and her Army of Light. Look."

Poppy chirped out a warning as Damian pulled Garrick's letter out from inside her sleeve and stepped forward to hand it to him.

"I'm sorry I didn't tell you sooner, but I didn't know if you would believe me. At least, not at first. Then I couldn't find the right time to tell you. It's the truth, I swear it." She breathed hard, her hopes rising as he read the letter.

Then, his expression darkened further. "Even if Sir Magni," he said with particular distaste, "is telling the truth, then he is also directly defying orders." Sir Kennar crumpled up the letter and tossed it on the ground. Damian's breath caught as he moved forward. "I've given you a lot of leeway, but this is crossing the line. This is conspiracy against the crown. You need to come with me right now."

Damian backed away, her whole body trembling. "No, wait, Sir Kennar, please…"

Suddenly, his eyes widened and he lunged forward. Damian barely stepped out of his reach with a yelp before he could grab her.

"Damian!" he roared, his voice ringing through the deserted town as he drew his arming sword in one swift motion. He snapped his gaze all around the street, but didn't look at her. "Show yourself right now!"

She blinked, unmoving beside the stairs up to the butcher shop. Then, she looked at Poppy and Merle. The curly-haired woman beckoned with furtive motions, something clutched in one hand.

"Come on!" she snapped.

"No, wait—"

"Damian," Sir Kennar yelled again, more serious this time. "This is your only warning. Show yourself right now or I will use lethal force to stop you. You have to the count of three." He turned slowly in the street, looking all around. His eyes passed across Damian without seeing her.

"Sir Kennar…" Damian's chest clenched as though her ribs shrank.

"One…"

Poppy appeared beside her, grabbing her arm and tugging hard away from the knight. "We have t' ge' ou' o' here, yae daft girl!"

"Two…"

Damian fought against Poppy's grip. "No! Drop the spell!"

"Are yae bleedin' crazy?"

"I need to talk to—"

"*Three*!"

Sir Kennar launched into a flurry of motion, his sword slashing in vicious arcs. Poppy leaped away with a shriek, rushing past Damian back toward Merle. Damian barely tracked Sir Kennar's movement before he veered toward her, the blade whistling through the air.

She screamed.

A wave of dizziness swept over her as she heard Sir Kennar grunt and a heavy, metallic thump, followed by the clang of his sword. She fell to one knee as everything grew quiet again.

"Whoa there!" Poppy cried, grabbing her arm. "Are yae all right?"

Damian blinked, swaying in place as her vision refocused. When it cleared, she found Sir Kennar lying unmoving in the street. Merle stood beside him, one hand held toward the knight and the other clutching a stone and an herb of some sort.

She gasped, covering her mouth with her hand. "Sir Kennar!" Pulling herself from Poppy's grip, she stumbled over to the knight.

"Storms an' shadows, lass, 'e tried to kill yae!" Poppy snapped.

Damian watched, some relief reaching through her horror to see the rise and fall of Sir Kennar's chest.

"See? Nothin' to fret over, but we need to get gone from this town an' fast. Come on."

Dazed, Damian allowed Poppy to pull her to her feet and begin moving down the road. Her thoughts were murky and her knees trembled.

"Wait!" she cried, lurching to a stop. She blinked as she tried to focus on Poppy's freckled face. "Liam… Rhyslen. We have to go get them."

Poppy looked over Damian's shoulder for a moment, then nodded. "All right. Looks like yae've got us for now. Which way to yaer inn?"

Damian stumbled as they made their way back down the street, past where Sir Kennar lay, and she reluctantly leaned on Poppy for support. She could barely form coherent thoughts and focused on finding the inn.

Her strength bled away as they continued. By the time they reached the inn, she couldn't stand on her own. Moments disappeared and she heard little of the frantic conversation largely between Poppy and Rhyslen. Liam's arms wrapped around her and she finally drifted into blackness. The last thing she noticed was the smell of Liam's leather breastplate.

Garrick could only stare at the game board beside his head and the red pieces that lay alone across its surface. The triumph at defeating Kina was gone in place of astonishment at what she had just said.

"A sword that belonged to Nephrita."

She nodded. "Yes."

He raised his eyes to her. "And an actual dragon tried to stop you?"

She grinned. "With scales and fire breath."

He let out a breath, his gaze drifting to the ceiling. "I admit it, you were right."

"About what?"

"You do have a secret to rival the Agaesi."

She chuckled. "The other half of the tale is even more incredible."

His eyes widened. "It gets stranger than that?"

"Much more so."

He shook his head. "Well, of all the places I might have ended up, this is by far the most interesting."

Kina grinned. "Does that make up for my cooking, then?"

Garrick laughed. "I know better than to answer that. So does my victory get me more than the teaser for this epic tale?"

She smiled briefly. "In my youth, I ran with a mercenary named Drago Kramoris."

He raised an eyebrow at the claim of her youth, but she didn't react to the look.

"He led a band of sellswords that achieved some notoriety in Edan. We were known for finding treasures in ruins, the ancient remains of forgotten civilizations. They often still held treasures inside. Likely some still do. I found the sword as we were hired to do. It was buried with a long dead king, along with a small crystal he wore around his neck. I soon found that the crystal was part of the sword, but when I made it whole again, it changed me."

He gave her a curious look.

She smiled mirthlessly. "I gained... features of a beast. The people of Brighton immediately began hunting me. It was by accident that I fled with the sword, but once I discovered what it was and that our client planned to use it for an ancient spell, I vowed to keep it from him at all costs."

Garrick's eyes enlarged. "He wanted to bind Nephrita to his will."

She blinked, caught off guard for once. "How do you know that?"

"Because it's precisely what Yanuk Alganov did for the Battle of Albrith."

She pushed herself out of her chair. "What? But that is impossible! I still..." Clamping her mouth shut, she stopped herself short, but not quickly enough.

He stared at her. "You still have the sword."

Slowly, she sat back down. "Yes."

For a moment, he simply watched her. Then he nodded. "So you kept it from your, ah, client."

She seemed to relax a little. "Yes, ultimately."

He raised an eyebrow.

She smiled. "He got it back at one point, thanks to that dragon. I managed to take it back and stop him before the ceremony completed, however."

Garrick gave her a surprised look.

Kina straightened, putting her hands on her hips and cocking her head aside. "What? You think me incapable of dashing heroics?"

He laughed. "I'm starting to think you capable of far more than I imagined, but I'll admit I have a hard time picturing you doing it."

Tossing her head, she let out a scoffing sound with a smile on her face.

He considered what she had said. "You said you stopped him before the spell completed? Does that mean it was in progress when you intervened?"

She sat back. "Yes. They had begun casting the spell, but I stopped them before it was complete. Although, one of my companions said that something was released that night."

Garrick frowned. From what he had learned, Nephrita had been a part of Damian for her entire life. "When did all this happen?"

"The Century Storm. It was the wrath of the Gods of Light for attempting to summon Nephrita in Brighton."

His eyebrows rose. "When Damian was born. That was when Nephrita became a part of her." He glanced at Kina curiously. "But that would make you…"

"Old enough to be your mother," Kina finished for him with a sly smile.

He blinked, his eyes sweeping up and down her body, then grinned. "The years have treated you well. I would have sworn you were hardly any older than me."

"I do not believe I have merely aged well." Her gaze turned distant. "Though the sword restored my humanity during that ceremony, it left me with a few gifts. My mage sight and an apparently lengthened life. My appearance has not changed since that day."

He paused, staring at her in surprise. "Is that why you live in seclusion?"

"It is among the reasons. The people in the nearest village are only beginning to talk. I have not been here too many years, and everyone knows someone who looks much younger than they are. But questions will become accusations eventually, so I keep my distance as I can."

He watched her, seeing more in her eyes than she let on. "It sounds very trying."

She shrugged. "I am comfortable with solitude. If I were truly lonely, there are places I could go." She grinned at him. "Though it is quite satisfying to have such accepting company."

He smiled dryly in return. "Even though you have to wash me and feed me like a babe?"

Waving a hand in dismissal, she turned toward the kitchen. "The most interesting part of you is still intact."

He chuckled as she disappeared into the kitchen, and he took the moment to examine some of the baubles scattered around the common room once more.

Yes, he thought, *there is definitely more to your story than I suspected.*

CHAPTER 13
NO TURNING BACK

VOICES ROSE OUT of the silence, followed by pain. A fierce headache made itself known at the same time Damian's stomach twisted. She became aware of a swaying motion and the fact that she was lying down on a narrow surface at the same time as she felt soreness in her limbs.

She moaned and the swaying stopped.

Strong hands pushed her upright. She brushed stray hairs out of her face and opened her eyes to see Liam before her. His eyes were on a level with her collar bone as he reached up to support her. The baskets of supplies hung over his shoulders.

"Damian!" a voice called out and running steps sounded behind her.

It was morning and they were surrounded by farmland. She sat atop the pony bareback, where she had clearly ridden for a while. For a moment, she couldn't remember what happened.

"Are you all right?" Liam asked softly, his deep voice thrumming over her and his brow creased in worry.

The footfalls came up beside the horse.

"I told you she'd be fine," Rhyslen said.

"Well, yae certainly gave me a scare. How're yae feelin'?"

The sound of that voice and the glimpse of Poppy's freckled face and unruly hair brought it all back. Damian gasped, then doubled over with a groan as hunger gnawed at her stomach.

Liam released her to rummage in one of the baskets and hand her an apple and a biscuit. She hurriedly choked them down. They tasted like ash with the image of Sir Kennar lying in the street lingering in her mind.

With a nod, Liam led them on, Rhyslen and Poppy drawing back to walk with Merle. The mages chatted, though Damian couldn't hear their words as she sated her hunger.

"How long have you been walking?"

"Since you returned," Liam replied.

Damian's eyebrows rose. "All night?"

He nodded.

She looked up at the sun. It hung low, the sky having just shifted from the warm hues of sunrise to the blue of day. This late in the season, however, it rose late. They must have been travelling for a long time.

Twisting around on the pony's back, she looked behind her. She could see a few small hamlets rising out of the fields of barley and potatoes, but no sign of the town where they had met Poppy and Merle.

They needed to move fast. As soon as Sir Kennar awoke, he would go after them, and probably a lot faster than they were moving.

Damian's stomach twisted again, but not from hunger. She halted the pony and climbed down to continue walking on foot, letting Liam strap the baskets to the animal. Her head was down and she held her cloak close in the chill air. Guilt weighed down her shoulders as thoughts whirled through her mind.

How could I do that to him?

I betrayed him.

I attacked him, for the sake of people I don't even know.

He will never forgive me. Not after that.

After all that time spent gaining his trust, I ruined it in only a minute. In one bad decision.

No... in weeks of lying to him and keeping my plans secret.

I betrayed him.

A hand fell on her shoulder.

She looked up, startled out of her introspection. There was a softness in Liam's blue eyes that she had rarely seen from him.

"I'm sorry," he said solemnly. "I wish it hadn't happened this way."

She was surprised at how heartbroken he looked. *He wasn't really that close to Sir Kennar, was he?* she wondered.

He squeezed her shoulder gently. "I know how much it must hurt."

It struck her. Liam must have felt the same guilt, only a hundredfold, when he betrayed the Red Hawks. He hadn't meant to, he hadn't wanted to, but he had still done it. Just like her.

Reaching up, she placed her hand atop his. Surprisingly, she found herself wanting more. Instead, she let out a sigh.

"I was a fool. I should have told him. I should have told him what I was doing right from the start." Yet, she frowned as she recalled Sir Kennar's anger the last night. "Although, he probably still wouldn't have believed me. Maybe…" A shocking thought struck her, and filled her with as much relief as guilt. "Maybe it had to happen this way."

Voices drew up from behind them as Rhyslen and the others approached.

"So, what now?" Poppy asked.

Damian sighed again as Liam's hand slipped off her shoulder. She stopped walking, staring over the farmland in front of her. "Where are we going?"

"South," Poppy answered. She waved at Liam. "He started leadin' us this way when we left town, but he wasn't exactly forthcomin' with the details."

"Or answers to our questions," Rhyslen added flatly.

Damian paused, thinking for a long moment. "He's right. We need to continue to Misengrad."

"Are yae mad, girl?" Poppy snapped before Rhyslen could answer, hands on her hips. "Rhyslen told us about yaer lofty summons, but yae can't possibly think it's a good idea t' go walkin' into the den o' the dragon knights when yae just laid one out on the road in the middle o' the night an' buggered off."

"There's no way we would even make it into the city," Rhyslen added. "We can't meet up with your knight friend. We have to focus on finding the malakh ourselves."

Damian spun on them. "And do either of you know how to defeat a malakh? Any of you?" she added, eyeing Merle between them. He stared back, unmoved by her reaction. "We need more information on malakhs if we hope to have a chance of stopping her. Nobody is more likely to have that than the Agaesi."

Rhyslen held out an arm. "We won't even make it through the gates. And if they see you without Sir Kennar…"

"Don't you think I know that?" Frustrated and miserable tears gathered in her eyes. "Gods afar, I'm a *fugitive*. With the way people think about me, they probably won't even arrest me. They might kill me on sight. I… I can never go home again." Her voice choked.

"I'm sorry, Damian." Rhyslen reached toward her, but she backed away from his hand.

Even Poppy's visage softened. "We know how yae feel."

Damian turned away from them, facing Liam instead as she struggled not to cry. His expression softened, concern clear in his eyes as he looked at her. Behind her, the mages shifted.

Damian struggled to calm down. *They're counting on me. I have to lead them.*

She straightened, breathing slowly. "We still need to know more about malakhs." She turned back to the mages. "The unseeing spell can get us into Misengrad. There must be a way we can get a message through to Garrick." She faced Poppy and Merle. "I know you didn't really get a chance to answer me last night, so, will you join us? We could really use your help."

Poppy frowned uncomfortably. She glanced at Merle, who glared at everything and huffed and looked away when she turned to him. Then she faced Rhyslen, who looked thoughtful.

Poppy let out a sigh. "I s'pose so."

"No!" snapped Merle.

Damian leaned back at the vehement response, but Poppy merely faced him with a placating smile.

"I know, Merle. Don't worry, this will be better fer us in the end."

Merle clearly remained unconvinced, but said nothing more as he stood scowling into the distance and waving his hand.

Rhyslen cleared his throat. "Well, this gives us the opportunity to teach you the proper way to cast magic."

"Oh." Damian's eyebrows rose. She had never considered actually learning to use magic. Part of her still quailed at the thought.

I've been using my own magic for fun most of my life, she chastised herself. *Now that I have a good reason to learn, I'm going to balk at learning it the right way?*

The Gods of Light are the ones building an army to attack innocent people. They're the ones setting Niabi against the world. It's time I use the weapons of the old gods against her.

With a nod, she answered, "Thank you. I would be glad to learn. As we travel, at least."

"Of course," Rhyslen answered with a smile.

"What about Sir Kennar?" Poppy chimed in. "He'll know just where to find us."

Damian considered that. What would Sir Kennar do once he awakened in the town? Her expression fell. "After what I did last night, he'll be expecting anything from us. He's a skilled knight. He will probably be able to track us no matter what we try to do. We should just stick to the road so we can travel as quickly as we can and hopefully stay ahead of him." She looked at Liam, who nodded in agreement.

Poppy exchanged another look with Merle.

Rhyslen shrugged, resigned. "Lead the way, then."

With a nod, Damian turned and began walking again, the mages falling into a line behind her and Liam.

"D'yae really think we can stop that malakh?"

Memories of her encounters with Niabi sent a chill up Damian's spine. "I don't know. But I have to try."

She didn't tell them just how true that statement was.

The mages fell back and conversed among themselves as they continued walking across the farmland. Although Damian largely remained lost in her own thoughts, she frowned when she heard their laughter, though Merle still snapped out something occasionally.

Exhaustion caught up with the rest of them by dinnertime, and Damian stood watching for signs of Sir Kennar's approach while Liam, Rhyslen, Poppy, and Merle dozed in a grove of trees beside the fence surrounding a pasture.

With no signs of pursuit that she could see, Damian woke the others around halfway through the afternoon and continued. Shortly after, they saw another village in the distance.

"We goin' into town?" Poppy asked.

Rhyslen gave Damian a cautious look. He didn't need to say anything for her to know what he was thinking.

"We need more food, but I don't think I should be seen. At best, it would be like an arrow pointing straight toward us for Sir Kennar to follow, and at worst..." Her thoughts drifted back to Eldore. Shaking her head, she turned to the mages. "I think it would be better if I went around. Would you mind buying what we need?"

Poppy gave her a curious look. "Why don't yae just cover yaerself up like one o' those Seers at a temple o' Wisdom?"

Damian couldn't help frowning. She'd been hearing that the entire trip since she left Aether.

"Well, she does have a point," Rhyslen said cautiously.

"No," she answered. "I spent eighteen years keeping my eyes covered and I'm tired of it. I don't want to have to hide myself anymore just to be accepted."

Silence met that pronouncement. Rhyslen returned a look that was part wistful and part sad. Merle didn't seem any less antagonistic than he had the rest of the time he had been with them, but Poppy regarded Damian more gently.

The tall woman nodded. "All right. We'll go stock up."

"I'll stay with you," Rhyslen said to Damian, his patchwork face twisting in a wry grin. "I'm not exactly inconspicuous, either."

Damian handed Poppy the reins of the pony and fished out some coins for her. Damian's heart tightened as she passed over money she had largely gotten from Sir Kennar.

"We'll meet yae back along the road on the far side o' town." With a smile to Merle, Poppy led the way towards the village. Merle stomped after her.

Damian, Rhyslen, and Liam turned off the road into the fields. Her eyes were on Poppy and Merle as they approached the town. She frowned.

"Did I do something to upset Merle?"

Rhyslen looked weary. "It's not you personally. He just doesn't take change well. And he has a difficult time talking to people in the first place." Rhyslen scoffed. "Most of the people in the village where he grew up thought he was simple. Imbeciles. He's one of the smartest people I've met. He remembers the incantations and the exact amount of ingredients needed for every spell he's ever heard or learned. Even Yanuk had to consult books for most of the ones he knew. Merle just couldn't interact with people properly.

"Poppy was the first person who ever really got through to him. She pretty much taught him how to talk, until he seemed just about normal." His expression fell. "He's gotten worse since I last saw him."

Rhyslen turned to Damian. "These are the people Yanuk and the others gravitated towards. The outcasts, the misfits. The people who nobody else would give a chance. You would have been welcome there. Everyone would have treated you just like everybody else."

She averted her gaze. It bothered her how much that thought enticed her, and how it brought feelings of pity and regret for what happened to Yanuk.

"But you were still living outside the law," Liam remarked suddenly.

Rhyslen scoffed, holding out a hand. "And we're not now?"

Liam's eyes shifted, and Damian saw a trace of discomfort or concern in them.

Rhyslen's attention was on the distant town, his brows drawn down. "They certainly would have accepted you more than any of the villagers we've come across." He held a hand out toward the village they had to avoid. "These are the people you want to save?"

Damian's eyes narrowed. "Now you're starting to sound like Yanuk."

"Well, maybe he had a point."

"It's not about saving them," she answered firmly. "The only reason they're treating me this way is because the Gods of Light have decreed that magic is evil. They demand loyalty from their followers, but they don't really care about them or want to make their lives better or give them guidance or anything. No, they demand loyalty so that their followers will fight and subjugate people for them. The Army of Light, all of it. It's the Gods of Light manipulating people just to further their own interests. And I know that to the people who truly believe in them, that makes me evil. But I can't just let them do that." She fixed her gaze on him to find him giving her a wry grin.

"Oh, so we're not out to save thousands of people who don't want to be saved, we're out to take on the gods themselves." The humour in his eyes and grin remained as he spoke, but Damian looked away at that.

"I know, it seems silly. It's just…" She trailed off.

"It's okay, Damian. Maybe it's too much for us to handle, but I think you're right."

Liam added, "Someone has to stand up against them."

She looked in his eyes and smiled faintly, then turned to Rhyslen.

"Exactly," he agreed.

"Thank you," she answered, her shoulders feeling lighter. "That's what we need to focus on. And, I hate to say it, but now we have fewer things holding us back."

It was like turning her back on her past. It was painful, but it gave her purpose.

Stopping Niabi is more important than ever.

Silence lay over the plains. Only the howl of the wind stirred the rolling hills covered in dried grass, occasional copses of trees, and rock outcroppings breaching the earth like stone whales.

Ashik stood amongst the openness, strands of hair torn free of his topknot brushing against his face as the brisk breeze blew uninterrupted across the land. During brief lulls in the wind, he heard the rest of the warriors milling about and speaking softly behind him, but his eyes remained fixed ahead.

Ialla sat on the ground several paces away, legs crossed and hands resting on her knees with her palms open to the grey sky. Her eyes were shut. She sat so still that Ashik could barely see her breathe.

The only indication that she was doing anything other than merely sitting there was the faint, glowing lights of sprites hovering around her. Ashik could see and hear nothing out of the ordinary. Only a distant, strange sensation tickled the edge of his awareness. He didn't quite feel it. It was like a thought he couldn't grasp, a dream that's starkly vivid while asleep but fades just out of understanding moments after awaking in the midst of it.

Giving up on attempting to identify or understand the sensation, he focused on the sprites. They were real enough, for all that they appeared to be featureless motes of light floating on the air like dust in a quiet room. Ialla remained seemingly unaware of their presence and they slowly circled her in a flowing dance.

What is it like? he wondered as she reached into the spirit realm. He tried to imagine the nebulous sensation just beyond his awareness as stronger, overwhelming him, but it was so alien that he couldn't be certain he wasn't merely imagining it. Ialla's abilities were clearly far beyond his understanding.

One of the sprites drifted closer to him as it continued swaying around her. It looked as though it drifted on the breeze, but for the fact that the steady, sometimes intense wind that rocked the open plains in southern Faneria blew contrary to the sprite's course. The whole image was surreal, as though it existed in a different world from the one he inhabited.

There was little use for magic in the mountains, and most of the societies he had lived among, including those he now travelled with, guarded their spells jealously. He had witnessed ritual magic among some cultures, but those often amounted to little more than flashy displays or visual representations of the health of the people and land around them.

Spirit singers were an entirely different matter. Unlike other mages, who seemed only to borrow power for their spells, spirit singers could see the magic in the world like shades of colours to ordinary eyes.

At least, it was rumoured as such. While the spirit singers at Veil's Edge and elsewhere didn't covet their abilities like the Makils or Kathecs, their knowledge was meant only for those with the gift.

Ashik had never been so close to a spirit singer reaching into the realm of magic itself. He had rarely been this close to any display of magic, let alone one so intimately attached to it. Slowly, he knelt in the short, brown grass, leaning forward and reaching a hand toward

Ialla.

Her eyes shot open and she sucked in a gasp.

Ashik jerked his hand back as the sprites streaked straight up into the air, soon disappearing from view. Firm footfalls crossed the grass and he scrambled to his feet as Tethe approached.

"Well?" she demanded of Ialla.

Ialla hurried to stand and face Tethe. "She is very much close. And she is clearly heading this way. We are heading straight toward her now."

"How long?"

Ialla cringed. "Not long. Maybe in a few days?"

Ialla looked like she was about to elaborate, but with a curt nod of acknowledgement, Tethe turned and strode back to the rest of the warriors.

"I'm sorry," Ashik said as Ialla approached him. "Did I disturb you?"

She smiled. "No, not at all. I just hope my reading of the *shikar* was right."

"I'm sure Tethe has all the information she needs to make a battle plan now."

"I hope so. I could definitely feel the fox-headed woman." Ialla looked uncomfortable. "She is very powerful. More than anything else I've felt before."

He hesitated a moment, taking in the disturbed look on her face. Then, he put on a smile. "Well, that's why we have the deadliest warriors the free lands have to offer. Come on, we'd better get back to the others."

That night, after they set up camp, Tethe gathered the group around a large fire to present a battle plan.

"The scouts found a ravine," she said, drawing in the dirt beside the fire with a stick. "The fox-headed woman will likely have to cross it. We will ambush her there. Ashik."

Ashik started. He sat up straight at the edge of the group. "Yes, Tethe?"

"You know the most about this fox-headed woman. Tell us what we can expect."

He cleared his throat uncomfortably as all the warriors turned to him. "Well, I only know what I have heard from the stories…"

Tethe impatiently gestured for him to continue.

Shifting, he went on, "She attacks using the very land around her. Rocks rise at her will and the earth opens up beneath her enemies' feet. She commands grass to bind and trees to move. She is very powerful, and from what I heard, not even the Goddess of Chaos could stand against her. I don't know if she holds sway over animals, but her command of life means she turns the ground itself against her enemies."

A few of the warriors turned to each other and some murmuring rose.

"That," Tethe said, "is why *we* are attacking *her.*"

Another Makil nodded. "Nothing is invulnerable. And if we surprise her, then she will fall."

An eagle warrior added, "Attack hard and fast. She cannot stop us all."

Tethe made marks around her drawing of the ravine in the dirt. "We will attack her in two waves. The warrior queens will attack first. When she is weak, the eagle warriors will come finish her off. The Rturans will stay along the sides of the ravine and attack with bows and knives."

Excited murmuring and bloodthirsty chuckles rose as she outlined the battle plan and placement of the warriors, with help from the scouts who had found the ravine.

Ashik tried to share their enthusiasm, but thoughts of the upcoming battle only made him uneasy. His discomfort was slightly assuaged by Tethe's meticulousness and confidence in the battle plan.

However, the more she detailed the attack and the more Ashik thought about it, the more uncertain he felt.

He tried to approach Tethe when she signalled an end to the meeting, but she walked off too quickly and started speaking with a few of the other Makils before Ashik could catch her attention. He hesitated, watching her and wondering if he should draw closer.

"Ashik."

Ashik turned with a start. Tir Kerstet stood nearby.

"Are you training tonight?" the Rturan asked, slightly impatiently.

With a glance back at Tethe, Ashik answered, "Yes, of course." He followed Tir Kerstet into the shadows at the edge of their camp site, though his thoughts remained on Tethe's battle plan as he took the sheathed machete the Rturan tossed to him.

Ashik tried to focus on the training, Tir Kerstet now willing to spar with him, though his thoughts were embroiled in the upcoming battle. Tethe hadn't said anything to Ashik after he shared what information he had about the malakh. Would he be expected to fight alongside the others? He had crossed sheathed blades with most of the warriors at this point, and while he knew he couldn't truly hold his own against them, he was feeling fairly confident in his reflexes and stamina. However, the thought of actually attacking someone with the machete he held, bare blade against flesh, made him feel ill.

Trust in Tethe, he told himself as he blocked Tir Kerstet's thrust with his shield. *She has won dozens of battles. She knows what she's doing.* Even as he thought it, however, his brow furrowed.

A smart rap on Ashik's knuckles jarred him out of his introspection. He jumped back, dropping the machete and shaking his hand with a yelp.

"You're not paying attention," Tir Kerstet said evenly as Ashik massaged the bruised hand. The Rturan hesitated before his expression softened. "What's wrong?"

"It's nothing," Ashik mumbled.

The Rturan only raised an eyebrow.

Ashik looked away. *Tethe knows battle as I never will.* Memories of the anger in her eyes when he talked her out of attacking the Fanerians in the foothills made him shudder. *I'm a fool if I think I should be advising her on battle plans.*

"You don't think we should be attacking her?" Tir Kerstet ventured.

"No," Ashik replied, then hurriedly added, "that's not it."

Returning his attention to Tir Kerstet, Ashik found the Rturan giving him an annoyed look. Ashik cringed. The Rturans were a very direct people. One of the reasons they tended not to respect traders was a belief that the Rturans felt them duplicitous, dancing around a subject rather than addressing it directly.

Ashik let out a sigh. "It's just that I'm not sure the Makils should be attacking first."

Tir Kerstet cocked his head to the side. "How so? It made sense to me."

"I know the Makils are more disciplined, and they have the advantage of reach with their spears, but the eagle warriors are far more brutal. They attack hard and fast, and are used in their wars to cut through enemy lines. I would think their ferocity would be best used first and then the Makils can come in and exploit vulnerabilities."

Tir Kerstet's brow creased. "So tell her."

Ashik frowned as he looked toward Tethe's shelter. She had already disappeared inside. "I don't know…"

"Does she know this?"

Ashik felt like an imbecile. His shoulders hunched. "She must. I'm sure she has a much better idea of how to utilize the warriors than I do."

"Still," Tir Kerstet went on, "a good leader listens to all advice she gets."

"Even from one as uninformed in battle as me?"

The Rturan shrugged. "If you really believe what you just told me, then tell her. Otherwise, trust her." With that, he raised his narrow sword in its sleek leather scabbard and assumed a fighting stance.

He's right, Ashik thought, picking up his fallen machete. *She's the one the Uniter chose to lead this mission. I need to trust in her.*

And yet, as his sword clacked against the Rturan's, Ashik couldn't help but worry about the coming battle.

Chapter 14
Not Alone

GARRICK LAY ON his back, his head turned to the side to read a book propped open next to him. The script was careful and practiced, but the letters were plain in design and slightly uneven, not the flawless calligraphy of scribes. There were no illuminations and a few ink smudges marred the pages. The binding of the book was also careful but uneven and it was covered with an unmarked leather board. The text within, however, was unlike anything Garrick had ever read.

"This is incredible. I'll admit I didn't entirely believe you when you said you remembered everything, but this…" His eyes scanned a block of text in a language he had never seen before. Kina had copied it from a wall she saw in Brighton, in northern Edan, when she visited the city nearly twenty years ago. "This was before you even knew how to read?"

Over the top of the book, Garrick saw her grin. "A few years before." She tapped her head. "Everything is up here, but finding and organizing it is proving difficult. How is that one reading?"

"I'll admit, the version you told me was more interesting. A little too much detail in this." Cringing at the pain that rippled over his arm and into his back, he lifted his left hand and turned the page. He blinked as a few words caught his eye. "Wait, Lyle Hitchcliffe?"

"Yes. I met him after I found Nephrita's sword and fled Brighton with it."

"As in Sir Lyle Hitchcliffe, formerly of the Misengrad city guard?"

She turned from her desk to face Garrick as he spoke, but her surprise turned to confusion by the time he finished. "Sir?"

"He was knighted following the Battle of Albrith. He was the one who killed Yanuk."

Kina's eyes enlarged. "Because he knew. He knew that the only way to break the binding spell was to kill him." She shook her head. "I knew you were both from Misengrad, but the city is so large that I did not think you knew him."

"I didn't mention his name because I never suspected you knew him. Although that does explain some of his rather uncommon knowledge." Garrick half grinned. "It must have been fate that I would come into your care."

She smiled enigmatically, a hint of almost worry in her eyes. "I feel it is something else. It seems from the moment I found that sword that I have been drawn into the continuing story of Nephrita, much as I might try to keep to myself."

Garrick was surprised at the seriousness in her words. Instead of pursuing the topic, he grinned. "Chaos follows you? I believe that's what's called a bad omen."

Her smile lightened. "I have lived here in peace for years, Garrick. If chaos follows me, then it has kept its distance for—"

A knock on the door interrupted her. The two of them stared at the door and then at each other for a moment. Shaking her head, Kina set down the quill she had been writing with.

"Who would that be?" Garrick asked worriedly.

"I doubt anyone who would cause trouble, if that is what you mean."

Then, a voice came through the closed door. "Kina? Are you in there?"

With a broad smile, Kina strode to the door and opened it. From his angle and with the light shining through the door, Garrick could make out little more than a silhouette. Their visitor was large and well built, if not without some extra flesh on his stomach.

"Therrus, welcome."

"Hello, Kina." Therrus ducked under the door frame as he stepped inside.

"It is good to see you."

"Well, I'm pleased to hear that. After I heard you came into town and didn't come to see me and then went this long without coming to resupply at all, I was beginning to think I'd done something to offend you." Therrus had a strong, booming voice that rang throughout her small home. Garrick felt a strange wash of emotions at the appearance of the first visitor he had seen since he awoke in Kina's home and tried to settle his racing heart.

Kina laughed. "The last visit was a mere oversight. I was

planning to make it up to you this time, but as you can see, I have been held up with unexpected company."

"Oh?" Therrus followed her gesture to Garrick lying on the floor, and his eyebrows rose. "Well, what have we here?"

Garrick smiled wryly at the large man. "Hello. Forgive me for not getting up."

Kina led Therrus over to him. "This is Sir Garrick Magni. I found him badly injured in the woods a few weeks ago. He still cannot move, so I have been unable to leave to resupply."

Therrus stopped beside Garrick, staring down his large form at the knight. "Is that so?" From up close, Garrick could see the grey in Therrus's receding brown hair and beard, and the lines on his jaw and at the corners of his eyes. "Sir."

"Garrick, this is Therrus Osterian."

Grinning, the large man elbowed Kina in the side. "On a first name basis with a knight, eh?"

She brushed his arm away. "It is not like that."

Therrus barked out a laugh. "Sure it isn't, having him lying here prone in your home like this. I doubt it's any mistake he's lying on his back, eh?" He winked suggestively.

Garrick's smile faded.

Kina pushed Therrus back a pace with a roll of her eyes. "As you can see, I do not keep company with him for his sense of humour. He and I went on some adventures across Elderra a number of years ago."

Folding his arms, Therrus scoffed. "You make me sound like an old man."

"And how is your wife?" Kina asked with a sidelong glance.

"Pregnant." Therrus's voice was matter-of-fact, but he smiled.

"Congratulations."

Therrus waved off Kina's remark, blowing out a breath. "Save that for when the tyke's born. Besides, a third child isn't as interesting as what you have here." He squatted down to look closer at Garrick. Garrick blinked and focused on Therrus's brown eyes. "So what happened to you, Sir?"

"Truth be told, I don't remember."

"Nothing?" Therrus's eyebrows rose.

"I believe he was thrown down into the ground," Kina offered. "He hit his head and his back and had many other injuries besides."

The old adventurer cringed. "My sympathies, mate. I wouldn't want to be in your shoes right now. And you don't know how it happened?"

"I know what caused it." Garrick's eyes narrowed. "The malakh from the Battle of Albrith, Niabi."

Therrus blinked. "She attacked you?"

"Don't look so surprised. Didn't you hear what she did to Albrith?"

"To stop the Goddess of Chaos, sure. But why would she attack you? She's a malakh, for Light's sake."

Garrick's throat tightened. He found a sour look on Kina's face at the conversation.

"Anyway, I thought she was leading that Army of Light to the west."

"What?" asked Garrick and Kina in unison.

"Yeah. You hadn't heard?"

Kina gave him a flat look.

Therrus shifted. "Right. Yeah, apparently they've been besieging the border for a few weeks now."

"*What*?" Garrick repeated.

"Right? So I don't see what she would be doin' in Faneria."

Garrick shut his eyes, breathing deeply. "It was her. That's the only thing I know, but I'm sure of it."

"That's odd indeed." He looked at Kina. "And you didn't see her?"

Kina shook her head. "I had no idea she came so close until Garrick woke up after I brought him here."

"So you haven't left since then?"

"He would not be able to care for himself long enough for me to go."

Therrus turned back to Garrick. "You can't move at all?"

Garrick flexed the fingers of his left hand, wincing at the fire that rippled up his arm. "Some of the bones have started to mend, but I don't know how bad my back is."

Kina faced Therrus fully. "We need supplies badly. Flour, yeast, meat, candles, soap. Would you like me to make you a list?"

Therrus waved a hand. "No, it would do me no good. Amary knows what you get each trip, right?"

"Yes, but please have him double it this time." Kina glanced at Garrick. "And perhaps some tender tea."

The knight gave the former adventurer a mild smile. "The pain's not so bad these days."

"He needs to be seen by a healer badly."

Therrus nodded. "I'll have the old gal come out as quickly as she can."

He turned to leave, but Garrick said, "Wait." He glanced at Kina. "The letter?"

Kina nodded and moved to retrieve a folded letter from her desk, one Garrick had dictated to her two weeks ago for Sir Warwick. "This needs to go to Misengrad."

Therrus took the letter. "I'll see what I can do."

"Oh," Garrick added before Kina could speak. "And can you bring my horse? He should be around outside, on hobbles. He probably needs his hooves trimmed and shoes replaced."

"No worries, Sir."

"Thank you for your help, Therrus," Kina said. "Please hurry and bring Pecca back quickly."

Therrus nodded. "I'll run the ol' backstabber as hard as she'll go." Garrick shot him a strange look, but it went unnoticed as the adventurer opened the door to leave. Therrus paused there, looking back. "And Kina… I'm glad you're all right."

She nodded with a smile. "Thank you for coming, Therrus. Safe travels." The door closed and silence fell over the room once more. A long moment passed as Garrick focused on his breathing, struggling to steady his racing heart.

Kina paused as she turned to face him. "Are you all right?"

Garrick swallowed, realizing his mouth was dry. "I've never felt uncomfortable talking to someone before, especially someone as interesting as him."

Shrugging, Kina approached the desk. "Well, we have been alone for weeks now. It has been quite some time since you even spoke with anyone else."

Garrick frowned, but didn't press the point. He tried to take his mind off his discomfort and his thoughts shifted back to Kina's moment of losing her composure.

"You follow the Gods of Time, don't you?"

"I do not follow them so much as I believe it wise to remain in their favour."

He couldn't help smiling wryly. "You realize how fickle their favour is, of course."

She chuckled. "Believe me, I am aware. I have met a goddess as well."

"Right, that younger sister of Nephrita's. She sounded about as fickle as Nephrita, from the way you told it." Bile rose at the back of his throat at the thought of Nephrita and the one day he had known her… and one night they spent together.

"I am not certain that I would say fickle. She knows much and sees more, and not by any virtue of divine powers."

Garrick gave her a strange look. "What does that mean?"

Kina looked amused. "It means she has lived many lifetimes, and that she can see more about a person than even they are aware of."

"Sounds like a power unto itself."

"It can be." Kina gazed wistfully across the room.

He merely watched her for a moment, but one question from the conversation with Therrus still nagged at him.

"So... backstabber?"

She smiled. "His horse. The name stemmed from an incident when it backed up against him with an unsheathed sword strapped to its saddle."

Garrick chuckled. "I suppose someone with a perfect memory would have a wealth of stories to tell. You have been sparse with your details."

She picked up her quill. "Likewise. In fact, after I finish this page, perhaps we should go over our separate stories of the attempts to bind Nephrita, and this time, be more thorough in the telling."

"Good idea." Garrick swallowed as she turned to face her work and tasted the bitterness at the back of his throat. A shudder rippled over his spine as he thought again of Nephrita. Why did that memory disturb him? Nephrita's beauty had been stunning and the experience more profound than any other woman he had lain with. And yet, he hadn't desired that intimacy since.

What's wrong with me?

Despite his best efforts and staying in his office late nearly every night, the stack of papers on Redge's desk only seemed to grow. He ignored the rumbling of his stomach as he worked through lunch, hoping to finish up a few more letters before his next meeting with the duke and his advisors afterward. He wrote out yet another letter, his hand cramping from holding the quill so long.

He focused so intently on the letter that it wasn't until he wrote his closing lines that he noticed Brannik standing in front of his desk.

"Yes, Brannik?"

"Messages for you, Sir." The boy held out a handful of papers.

"Very well." He couldn't keep a frown off his face as the boy dropped the papers on top of the stack and slipped out of his office. Redge grabbed the pile and pulled it closer to him. He glanced briefly at the page on top before setting it aside. Confirmation of measurements received by the blacksmith to begin work on a new suit of Agaesi armour. No response needed.

He looked at each page momentarily before setting it aside, finding nothing requiring his immediate attention. Most were added onto a pile he made for correspondence needing a response.

He paused as he set the last note aside. At the bottom of the pile was a sealed, folded letter that had clearly come from outside the city. His name was written in neat but strangely styled script. He flipped the letter over. The seal was unmarked. There was merely a glob of wax holding the letter shut. Breaking the seal, he unfolded and read the letter.

His eyes widened.

He dropped his quill into its stand on his desk, not bothering to sign the letter he had just written, nor to empty the quill of its excess ink. Shoving out of his chair, he hurried out of his office.

"I will be back after the meeting," he announced to Brannik as he strode through the records room, the letter clutched in his hand.

The duke turned out to be in a private meeting, so Redge continued to the council room. He was the first there and he sat at his usual spot at the table and read the letter again.

Eventually, the other advisors began to arrive. Redge had managed to calm his nerves by that time, but he still watched each arrival anxiously, desperate for the meeting to begin.

Finally, the duke and the Markiese of Gredsk arrived. Redge stood as the duke crossed the room to sit at the head of the table, the markiese stopping a little farther down.

"Thank you all for coming," the duke announced as he took his seat, the lords, lady, and knights following suit. "We have much to cover today."

"My Lord Duke," Redge cut in, still standing, "if I may?"

All eyes turned to him, not a few looking appalled at his interruption.

"I have just received urgent news about the Army of Light," Redge added.

The duke waved a hand, not showing any sign of offense. "Go ahead."

"The malakh Niabi is in Faneria."

The reaction was immediate. Gasps and exclamations rang through the room, some leaning back in their chairs while one lord half stood, his chair scraping loudly across the floor.

"What?!"

"That's impossible!"

"How could you possibly know this?"

"There's no way she could have crossed the border without us knowing."

The duke boomed, "Enough." He waited a moment for the commotion to die down, then focused intently on Redge. "Please continue, Sir Warwick."

"She might not still be here," Redge admitted. "One of my knights encountered her while on patrol a few days outside Misengrad, but this was a while ago."

The duke noticed the letter beneath Redge's hand. "May I?"

Redge nodded, sliding the letter down the table toward the duke.

"She couldn't have crossed the border unseen," one of the lords insisted. "It's far too well guarded."

"It is now," Redge answered, "but he's been away from Misengrad since the beginning of autumn." The advisors returned curious or bewildered looks. Redge gestured at the letter the duke read. "Niabi injured him badly. He's been in the care of a hermit with no way to get a message out until recently."

"So she might not be here any longer," suggested one.

"She might not," the duke agreed, setting the letter down. "But she might."

Another knight leaned forward. "What does it say, Your Grace?"

"Not much. Unfortunately, Sir Magni was injured badly enough that he has few memories of the encounter."

From the corner of his eye, Redge just caught the markiese tensing before quickly smoothing his features again. Sir Hitchcliffe also looked thoughtful for a moment.

"We have no idea what her intentions are," the duke added.

"Is she alone?" someone asked.

"It doesn't say," Redge said.

"What could she be here for?"

"She couldn't have gotten a force through the border. Even back then, it is doubtful she could have brought more than a handful with her unseen."

"Why is this the first we're hearing of this?"

"Obviously, she is trying to keep her presence in Faneria secret," the markiese said. "It must have been chance that brought Sir Magni to her."

"None of that is important," said the Countess of Verchesse. "What matters is what we are going to do about it."

"What should we do about it?"

"She can't just remain free to wander around Faneria. She has an army besieging our border!"

"She must be involved in some sort of espionage or sabotage."

"Surely we would have heard something if she had any intention of doing that."

"Then what is she after?"

"Maybe she's here for peace discussions."

"I highly doubt that. But it is curious."

"What would people do if they knew she was here?"

"There would be riots. We cannot let anyone outside this room know of this."

"I agree," the duke said. He faced Redge again. "Sir Warwick, your men are best equipped to handle her. I need you to send as many as you can out to look for her, as soon as possible."

Redge nodded. "Of course, Your Grace." He added hesitantly, "What are their orders if they find her?"

The duke paused, rubbing his bearded chin in thought.

"Malakh or no," the countess said evenly, "her army is besieging our border, and she snuck across illegally for reasons unknown to us and is actively trying to hide her presence here."

The duke nodded. "We need intelligence on her activities, Sir Warwick. Order your knights to observe, not to engage, but if she does anything that poses a threat to Faneria, they must stop her immediately."

"Yes, Your Grace."

Another advisor began to say something, but the duke continued, "Unfortunately, that isn't the only piece of dire news to share today. I just received word that the Zahni are gathering."

This elicited another wave of shock through the room, and even Redge added his own exclamation at the news.

The duke held up a hand against the clamour. "It's true. Many different tribes are marching as one."

"Who leads this force?"

"Why are they here?"

"Are they waging war against us?"

The duke answered, "They are led by a man known to them as the Uniter. At this stage, we do not know anything else about him, but from observations, he clearly commands great respect from the Zahni.

"As to why they are gathering, we have no confirmation, but rumours suggest they mean to meet the Army of Light in battle."

Another round of murmurs rang through the room.

"The Army of Light to the west and a Zahni army to the east...

Faneria is beginning to feel very crowded."

"You realize what this means," another lord remarked. "Nearly all of Edan in the Army of Light and the tribes of Zahn all marching together in their army… we're going to have to take a side."

"That," the duke said over those who tried to answer, "is not for us to decide. If and when we receive orders from Albrith regarding the Zahn army, we will deal with it then. Right now, they are far from Hesperia, and we must hold the border against the Army of Light."

The advisors dropped the topic as the conversation turned to the siege, but Redge could see at least most of the others still deep in thought over this turn of events. It ate away at Redge's mind even as he tried to focus on the current discussion. His eyes drifted down to the letter from Garrick lying on the table before him.

Faneria is beginning to feel very crowded indeed.

CHAPTER 15
A BITTER DRAUGHT

THE DRUMMING OF horse hooves stirred Garrick from sleep. He opened his eyes with a start, his heart racing as the sound thrummed through the walls and murmuring voices accompanied them.

Kina emerged from the kitchen and approached the door. Several voices drifted through the door, along with a cold blast of air as she opened it. After spending so long in Kina's quiet home with only her for company, the activity of the crowd of five people seemed frenetic to Garrick.

"Therrus could not come?" Kina asked as an old woman stepped into her house.

"He was busy assisting with some repairs back in the village. It's already started snowing, after all."

"Of course."

That gave Garrick pause. Inside Kina's house, dug out from the side of a hill as he had come to learn, with the hearth burning constantly, the temperature never changed. Since he also couldn't see out the windows at the front of the house, he hadn't realized how late the season was.

The old woman barked out orders to the young men who accompanied her to bring in the supplies they had carted outside, and Kina instructed them where to take everything.

Still trying to take in all the commotion, Garrick didn't realize the old woman had drawn close until he found her standing over him.

"So this is your injured knight?"

Garrick smiled wanly and held up his left hand. "Sir Garrick Magni, miss. Thank you for coming."

She reached down to shake his hand with her wrinkled fingers.

"Well, we couldn't leave you stranded, now, could we? My name is Pecca. Folk call on me for healing around here. My gran taught me my herbs and how to treat sprains and bites, but I'm no fancy physician like what you have in your city."

He grinned dryly. "To be honest, I've never had cause to see a healer of any kind before now."

"That's good, then, what with a knight's duty. Now, tell me what happened to you again."

He told her what he knew and what Kina had told him of his injuries and how she found him at the scene of the fight. "It seems I hit my head and my back fairly hard, but pretty much my entire body was injured in some way or another."

Pecca nodded. "Kina, some more light, please." Kina hurried over with a handful of candles, lighting them from the hearth fire as the old woman knelt before Garrick. "Now, let's have a look at you."

Pecca began by holding a candle close to his face and waving her hand back and forth, watching how his eyes reacted, while the youths continued unloading the wagon and Kina returned to guiding them to the proper storage spots.

"That's fine," Pecca said as she unravelled an old dressing on what had been a long scrape deep enough to cut. She looked under the other dressings that remained. "This is all healed. Are you getting any headaches, memory loss, confusion?"

"Not since a few days after I was injured."

She nodded. "You should be careful with any bumps to your head for at least another two seasons, but you should be fine."

He chuckled. "I think I'll be lucky if I can even leave here for another two seasons."

"We'll see about that." With that, she began pressing her fingers over his bones, starting from the shoulders. He cringed at intervals as she pressed on a spot that sent a jolt of pain through him. He alternated between holding his breath and panting as she made her way down his body, commenting on his injuries. His voice was strained when he answered her questions about his recovery. Otherwise, he could barely focus on what she said.

After she inspected his upper body and with no ceremony, she pulled off the blanket covering his bare legs. Garrick shut his eyes tightly, unable to keep an embarrassed scowl from crossing his face.

Pecca continued her prodding. The muscles of Garrick's thighs seemed surprisingly soft and thin as the old woman felt for further injuries. Just below his left knee, Pecca paused. Spikes of pain ripped up his leg and all through his body as her fingers pressed over the bones around his knee for a long moment. She murmured thoughtfully. When she spoke, her voice was matter-of-fact.

"This break didn't set properly. You may not be able to walk on this leg."

His eyes shot open and he stared in horror at the ceiling.

Not noticing his reaction, Pecca leaned back. "All right, time to take a look at your back." She called over two youths and instructed them to turn him onto his stomach.

"Careful now. Do it slowly and don't twist his body at all. Sir Magni, do not move, you must keep your body relaxed. Slowly, slowly, keep him in the same position. Roll him over his arm."

Garrick cringed as the young men gradually rolled him onto his side, his wounds searing with the movement, gentle as it was, and he fought not to tense his muscles.

"Grab him! Don't let him fall, lower him slowly down. That's it."

Finally, he lay on his stomach, his head twisted to the side so his cheek rested on the pillow and he faced the wall. Pecca's fingers brushed his shoulder blades and hips first, his skin hot and tingling at the touch.

"You have some minor bedsores, but not much to be done for that in your state. Kina's done a pretty good job keeping them down."

Garrick didn't bother telling her how he had to force Kina to move him so frequently in the first week, or how dearly he wanted to resist or complain ever since.

Pecca's touch down his spine was gentler, but it still eddied in waves of pain through his body as her fingers reached the part of his back that hurt the worst. Wincing, he clenched his teeth and shut his eyes tightly, his breath heaving out of him in ragged gasps. She murmured the same way she did over his knee. His chest tightened with the sound.

"Everything's healing well back here." She rubbed her finger with a feather-light touch over his spine just above the small of his back. He could barely hear her over the spear of pain shooting through him. "It was definitely broken, and so were a number of other bones, but they've mostly set by now. You might be able to stand in a week or so." She did a quick inspection of the bones around his shoulders before stepping back and standing up. "Boys, go bring in the straw."

Kina stepped forward to cover Garrick with the blanket as the young men who had turned him scampered out.

"We've also brought bedclothes and a quilt, so he'll have a

proper bed when he's able to move to it."

Pecca spoke to Kina as the boys brought in armfuls of straw straight through the common room to one of the back rooms Garrick had yet to see. Garrick's mind was so clouded with residual pain from Pecca's inspection that he couldn't listen to their conversation if he wanted to. His entire body felt as battered as it had when he awoke in Kina's house for the first time and it was all he could do not to moan as he lay on his stomach.

He didn't know how much time had passed and couldn't even guess at how many trips the boys had made between their wagon outside and the room in back before silence fell and Pecca took her place by his side.

"Kina's done a fair job caring for you and I've told her some other things she can do for you. You're very lucky your injuries weren't worse."

Lucky, he thought bitterly. As he tried to calm himself, however, he realized he was very fortunate to have healed so well in only a few weeks. Considering he had lost his fight against Niabi, it amazed him that he was still alive. *Luck has nothing to do with it. Agasis, I owe you my life.*

"You need to stay off your feet for a while longer and it'll be quite some time before you're back to normal, if you ever are again."

A lump formed in his throat as he thought of her comments on his leg.

"As long as you continue taking it easy, you'll survive. You're out of the woods for now, but don't push it."

"Believe me," he said with a weary look at the wall he faced, "I don't intend to."

Pecca nodded. "That's for the best. I'll come in every now and again to check on you, but you're going to have to stay here for a while yet. We've brought plenty of molka and a few pinches of tender tea. We've nothing stronger for the pain in our village."

He donned a weak smile through the pain that still wracked his body. "Thank you again for taking the time to come here. Let me repay you for your trouble."

"There's no need for that."

"I insist. Kina, whatever she normally asks, give her double from my coin pouch."

He heard Kina cross the room and return with coins jingling in her hand.

"You're very kind, Sir Magni. I recommend you stay on your

stomach for as long as you can handle to try to ease up those bedsores before you turn back. Get plenty of rest, Sir Magni. It's the best you can do for now. Oh, and we brought your horse back. Our smith assured me he's in good health." She turned and nodded. "Kina." With that, Pecca strode across the common room and walked out, followed by the youths who had accompanied her, and Kina's house faded into silence once more.

Once they left, Garrick's expression fell and he let out a sigh.

"What is it?" Kina asked.

"I guess, lying here without moving for so long, I thought most of my injuries might be almost healed by now and maybe I'd only have another few weeks before I'm up and going again." He closed his eyes. "But I guess I'm going to be out for a long time still, aren't I?"

There was a pause before Kina answered. "Yes." The silence stretched out for a moment.

"I've never been like this before. Helpless. Waiting to get back to normal while the world goes by."

The sound of Kina's footsteps crossed the floor. "You are beginning to give in to despair again. I think it is time to have another game of Domination."

He attempted to smile, but failed. "Sorry, I'm not really in the mood right now. I'm still hurting a lot from her attention."

"Would you like some tender tea?"

"I think I'm just going to try to sleep." He sighed defeatedly. "I'll probably need it later, anyway."

She said nothing else as he closed his eyes and tried to relax. Dark thoughts continued tumbling through his mind for a while before he finally drifted to sleep.

For years, Damian had marvelled at her secret ability to cause things to happen. To create fire or wind or light, move things without touching them, even affect how plants grew. Now, she was amazed at the normalcy of it.

How simple this is, she thought as she watched the flames crackle, sparked by a fire that had risen from a stone and a series of words. *Like learning to read.*

How different would our lives be if this wasn't forbidden? How many things could be made easier, or more advanced, if we only utilized this power?

However, those thoughts made her recall the unseeing spell, and she could imagine all sorts of unsavoury uses for that spell alone. And, of course, Yanuk had abused that power and left many innocent people dead as a result.

Magic must be respected, and it must only be used for good. I'm doing this to stop Niabi.

At that, however, she frowned.

"Is there any faster way to cast spells?" she asked Rhyslen, reflecting on the meditation, preparation, and incantation required to create this small flame.

Sitting on the other side of their camp fire, Rhyslen shook his head. "Not with conjury. Sorcerors, mages who have forged a spirit bond with some innately magical creature, can cast magic quicker, and enchanted artifacts are generally much quicker to use too."

Damian looked at Liam. "Like your pendant."

She hadn't seen the effects of his bloodstone amulet when he used it to save her from Niabi back in the spring, but she later learned that it had allowed him to move inhumanly fast to reach her in time. She had also learned that it would work only once more. The thought that he had chosen to use its precious gift for her still warmed her heart.

Liam nodded in response. To her surprise, he looked pleased as he watched her learn to use magic from Rhyslen and Poppy.

Eyes widening, Rhyslen leaned forward. "You have an enchanted artifact? Where did you get it?"

"It was given to me by a scholar with a particular interest in magic."

Poppy sat up straighter. "Another mage? Where is 'e?"

Before Rhyslen could say anything else, Liam quickly stated, "She is dead."

"Oh," Rhyslen replied, sitting back with a disappointed look.

"Tha's too bad," Poppy added.

While they spoke, Damian stared at the tiny bead of carnelian in her fingers, reflecting on the magic she had loosed over the years, intentional or not. It had always come instantaneously, and the thought of having so much time involved in casting even simple spells frustrated any ideas that it could be used effectively in battle.

"What if," she wondered aloud, "I could use my power to bring out the power in magic ingredients? You know, cast the spell without having to say the incantation or anything?"

Poppy glanced between Merle and Rhyslen.

"Could she do that?"

"I don't know," Rhyslen answered. "Nothing—no one like you

has ever been recorded in history. You could give it a try."

Merle only nodded in agreement.

Holding up the stone, Damian focused her attention on it. The sensations that had flowed through her in the past, before Nephrita was released from her, were gone, but she reflected on the way they had felt. A warmth, a tingling, like her blood was alive and she could feel it swimming through her body.

She stared intently at the carnelian, trying to find that same energy within it. Did she feel the power inherent in the stone, radiating into her fingertips, or was she just imagining it? It was difficult to tell if it was different from the energy she felt when she had cast the spell with the incantation moments earlier.

Closing her eyes, she pictured the magic of the carnelian entering her, flowing down her arm, and gathering in her heart. Her eyes opened. Reaching out her free hand, she opened her fingers and tried to release the power she thought she felt.

Nothing happened.

Damian huffed out a sigh and dropped her hands. "It doesn't work."

"It may just take some more practice," Rhyslen offered, though a frown marked his patchwork face.

"When did yae do it before?" Poppy asked.

Damian shrugged helplessly. "It seems to come when I'm in danger." She frowned as she remembered the mob in Eldore, which hadn't paid her much attention at all until she intervened. "Or when people close to me are in danger. I'm not sure."

"Well, we can keep trying, but we should focus on learning more spells through conjury," Rhyslen replied. "I know magic takes a while to cast, but it can be used effectively with proper planning."

Planning, Damian thought. That was something she certainly needed to do more of.

She nodded. "Let's get to sleep."

Damian's nerves grew more strained as they made their way from Alden into Hesperia. She avoided being seen and they saw no signs of Sir Kennar pursuing them, but she knew it was only a matter of time. With each passing day, she grew more anxious to reach Misengrad.

Garrick will make everything right, she kept telling herself, trying not to think of the disgust in Sir Kennar's voice when he spoke of Garrick. *One way or another, something will be resolved.*

When they finally caught sight of Misengrad in the distance, however, tromping through the sodden, slushy path of ankle-deep snow on the well-used road, her relief was soon overcome by more discomfort. A towering curtain wall surrounded the city. Within sprawled a sea of buildings that pressed up against the outer wall, bordered to the north by the massive castle and the glimmering waves of Aura Lake. A handful of buildings laid outside the city wall, though none were close to the gates. Crisscrossing trails of trodden snow branched out from the gates to the many small farming hamlets within a league or two of the city. None of them was close enough to Misengrad to potentially offer a secret passage in. The river leading south from the lake was no help, either, as there didn't appear to be any variation in the wall where it emerged.

Fortunately, even from a distance, Damian could see that the gates looked wide, so as long as there was some gap in the line long enough for them to pass, they could gain access to the city without being noticed. Despite knowing that she could rely on the unseeing spell, she couldn't help feeling uneasy at the thought of sneaking into Misengrad, or guilty for doing it.

"Well, there it is," Poppy remarked as the city came fully into view. Her voice sounded resigned, and Damian wondered if she felt uncomfortable about entering the city as well.

Rhyslen frowned, clearly about to say something, but stopping himself short. Instead, he asked, "So, what's the plan?"

Damian frowned as well. Getting into the city shouldn't be too much of a problem. But up until they fled from Sir Kennar, she had been counting on notifying the guards at the gates to pass word through to Garrick that she had arrived.

"Let's just get into the city first," Damian said. "We'll look for a city guard away from the gates, someone who won't know that we didn't enter... properly. Then..." She glanced at Poppy.

The curly-haired woman gave a wry smile. "Yae want me to pass along word to yaer knight friend."

Damian gave her an apologetic half-smile. "I'm sorry to make you do this so much."

Poppy shrugged. "Well, 'tis only fair to do my part. The burden o' lookin' normal," she added, leering at Rhyslen. He pouted in mock offense.

However, as they crossed the open fields leading to the castle, with the sun glaring off the surface of the lake and the snow, Damian slowed, looking all around.

"Yae thinkin' what I'm thinkin'?"

Damian stopped in place with a sigh. They were still most of a mile from the gates, only a few people tromping down the road ahead of them while others made their way across the fields from the hamlets toward the city.

"The horse," she answered in a weary tone.

"Yes," Rhyslen said uncomfortably. "I'm not sure the unseeing spell can cover it."

"Even if it could," Poppy added, "it can't cover 'er tracks. Guards watchin' the gates are goin' t' notice that. We might be able t' slip past, but the pony…"

"It would be harder to go through the city with it, anyway," Damian said.

"So what do yae think? Leave it?"

Damian frowned, considering. It was absurd to simply leave the pony behind, no matter that she had done the same with Hope nearly half a year ago. That thought brought a pang of sadness, but she forced herself to concentrate. Perhaps they could sell the pony at one of the hamlets nearby, but it was unlikely the villagers could give anything remotely of similar value in exchange that wouldn't be impossible to carry. Even if they received some appropriate payment, they would still have the problem of needing to find other pack animals inside Misengrad, which would be even harder. They needed more supplies than ever now, and they needed them much more than when Damian travelled across Faneria in the spring. Her mind flitted across ideas of loaning the animals to one of the villages, but that didn't take hold before she dismissed it as even less likely to arrange.

Finally, she turned around. "Merle, would you stay outside the city with the pony?"

Merle had remained grumpy and annoyingly particular about how things were done during the journey, including rearranging their supplies in the pony's baskets. Yet, as they travelled, it had become clear to Damian that his foul mood wasn't personally directed toward her, and he seemed to relax substantially when caring for the animal every day.

"Yae can't—" Poppy attempted.

"Damian, I don't think that's a good idea," Rhyslen replied slowly.

Damian held up a placating hand. "He knows how to care for her, and he'll be more help out here with her than he will be in the city with us." She focused on Merle, gentling her voice. "Besides, I suppose you might be more comfortable out here than you will in there?"

While Merle struggled to say something, Poppy stepped forward and announced, "Then I'm stayin' out here, too."

"No, I need you to help get word through to Garrick. I certainly can't talk to anyone. Rhyslen might not be as well known, but he's too easily recognizable." The same was true of Liam, she thought, but didn't say. The small villages they had passed might know the name of the Crow, but the people there didn't know enough to recognize him. In a big city like Misengrad, however, she couldn't count on that. Memories rose of him being arrested at the gates into Trent.

Poppy harrumphed and put her fists on her hips. "I don' like this. Merle shouldn' be left all alone."

Rhyslen's eyes passed between them. "I could stay outside the city with him."

"I can stay with the horse," Liam said abruptly, silencing them all.

Damian chewed her lip as she looked at him, ignoring Rhyslen and Poppy's agreements with him. It did make the most sense. Damian couldn't think of a good reason why Liam shouldn't stay outside the city other than that she didn't want him to, though she frantically scrambled for a better excuse.

Before she came up with one, an unexpected voice cut in, "No."

Everyone looked at Merle. He shifted uncomfortably, staring at the ground. Damian faced away, though she kept her attention focused on him.

"I'll stay out here with the pony," Merle said in his stumbling accent. "We're here to stop that malakh." He flapped his hand, his eyes focusing on it. "We all have to do our part."

Poppy placed a hand on his shoulder. There was a hint of worry in her eyes mixed in with immense pride. "Are yae sure, Merle?"

He simply nodded in response.

"Thank you, Merle," Damian said as Liam handed Merle the reins of the pony.

Merle looked up nearly enough to meet Damian's eyes and smile.

Damian looked around at Liam, Rhyslen, and Poppy. "Ready?" The others nodded or spoke their assent. "We should cast the unseeing spell now, so they don't have reason to wonder where we went." She tilted her head toward the gates, where city guards inspected every person and wagon entering Misengrad.

Rhyslen frowned at the distance to the gates. "I don't have a lot of fennel left."

"I've some," Poppy added, "but it's past its season. It'll be hard to find any more."

Damian glanced uncomfortably toward the city gates. How carefully were the guards watching the approaches to the city? Would they notice a group of people suddenly seem to disappear?

The anger in Sir Kennar's face the last time she saw him flitted across her mind. She repressed a shudder. Though it left a lump in her throat, she replied, "We can't risk being seen. We'll deal with finding more fennel later."

As they cast the spell and began making their way toward the outer wall, she couldn't help wondering how often they would need to hide from view. Would she ever be able to show herself in public again?

Even when I'm not a criminal, I'm better off not being seen, she thought.

She shook off those thoughts as they made their way to the city, walking single file so as to step in the trampled slush behind other people and hopefully not leave any sudden tracks. From the number of times Poppy apologized for stepping on Liam's cloak, it was clear Damian wasn't the only one anxious to get into the city. She forced herself to keep a gradual pace, trying to avoid notice. She felt alone leading the group, which bothered her more than she expected. An occasional glimpse back at Liam following her soothed her nerves.

Near to the towering gates, the snow had been entirely trampled and the paved road was spattered with mud. She carefully watched the gates and the guards as she approached, waiting for a lapse in their attention and a gap in the flow of people wide enough for them to pass.

"Just go!" Poppy said behind Liam. "They won't even notice if yae bump into 'em."

Frowning, Damian moved forward. Despite Poppy's assurances, she tried to avoid touching anyone as she crossed through the gates. She looked at the nearest city guard as she passed, who watched the line and yawned without noticing her at all. Hurriedly, she passed him and edged through the crowd to the nearest clear space she could see. There, she stopped and waited for the others to catch up, though they weren't far behind.

Poppy spread her hands as she strolled up. "See? Nothin' to it."

"So what now?" Rhyslen asked, eyeing the fennel in his hand.

Damian looked around the city. It was the first time she had ever been to Misengrad and a slew of mixed emotions overcame her as she took it in. The village girl in her marvelled at the size and bustling crowds here, probably the largest city she had ever been in, with the possible exception of Albrith, while the merchant longed to explore the market and study the differences in this city from the ones she was familiar with. Another part of her felt almost disappointed that after trying so hard to reach here in the spring with Garrick, she had finally made it to little fanfare. And still, guilt gnawed at her stomach for entering the city illegally.

As her eyes passed across Liam, Rhyslen, and Poppy, she tried to focus on the problem at hand. "Let's get some distance from the gates and we can drop the spell."

"All right," Poppy agreed as she followed Damian deeper into the city, "but how're we goin' t' find this knight friend o' yours? This place is awfully big."

Damian considered it as they crossed a few blocks through the city, trying to stick to less popular roads where they wouldn't stick out. When they travelled far enough into a secluded area to drop the spell, Damian turned to the others.

"I know someone who might be able to help us."

"Who?" Poppy asked.

"His name is Lyle Hitchcliffe. He—"

"Hitchcliffe?" Rhyslen cut in, an incredulous look on his face. "As in captain of the guard Hitchcliffe?"

"You know 'im?" Poppy said.

"I know of him. The Hitchcliffes have been commanding the city guard in Misengrad for generations. You really want to get help from the captain of the guard after sneaking into the city?"

"He's not with the city guard anymore," Damian quickly answered. "He was knighted after the Battle of Albrith."

"Oh, great!" Poppy exclaimed, throwing up her hands, but Rhyslen only looked perplexed.

"He was at the…" He straightened and drew in a breath. "Wait a moment." His eyes narrowed, his hands clenching into fists. "I did hear about him. He killed half the mages single-handed."

"He what?" Poppy replied.

"That's a lie!" Damian said.

"Well, that's what I heard," Rhyslen growled.

"And you believed it? You know how stories get. He arrested them! He didn't kill them, just…" She stopped short, her throat tightening.

Rhyslen looked as if he had been struck. "Yanuk. He killed Yanuk. Didn't he?"

"He had to," Damian answered softly.

"Had to? Did he even give Yanuk a chance to surrender?"

"It was the only way to break his control over Nephrita."

"Are you sure of that?"

"He was. And for all the innocent lives Yanuk took, he deserved what he got."

"Are you even listening to yourself? You can't take the moral high ground when you're defending someone who murdered his opponent without giving him a chance to surrender. Last time I checked, that's called a war crime."

Damian looked away, but a shadow loomed over her.

"You weren't there," Liam replied dangerously, and Damian was shocked at the trace of anger in his eyes and voice. Even Rhyslen faltered at the look on Liam's face. "A man who commanded a god walked through the city unseen and Sir Hitchcliffe had only a moment to react when he finally saw Yanuk. What would you have done?"

Rhyslen managed to recover his composure, returning a sneer. "So you think that makes it right?"

"Rhyslen, yae know he had to be stopped," Poppy offered gently.

"I don't care!" Rhyslen snapped. "I am not walking up to the man who killed Yanuk and asking for a favour."

Damian fixed him with an icy glare. "You don't care?"

"Don't give me that. You're asking me to make nice with the man who killed the closest thing to a father I ever had."

Damian's jaw set. "If that's how you really feel, then leave right now and don't ever come back."

"Don't you turn this around on me—"

"Of course I'm turning this around on you," she snapped, stepping closer and jabbing a finger toward his chest. "You're letting your personal feelings for someone you *know* had to be stopped get in the way of stopping someone who's trying to lead an army against Faneria. That's not what someone who wants to give magic a good name would do."

Rhyslen's patchwork face reddened as he backed away from Damian, spluttering in anger.

"I'm not asking you to be friends with him, but right now, we need his help. And if you can't accept that, then just leave right now."

Rhyslen's jaw worked. "You would really get rid of me over this?"

Damian didn't relent. "Yes, I would. If I cannot trust you to do what's right, even if it hurts, then I do not want you on my side."

Poppy took a step toward Rhyslen, her voice soft. "He wasn't the same, Rhyslen. What this knight did… it's tragic, but truly, it was a blessin', and a mercy to the man Yanuk used to be."

Rhyslen stared at each of them, his eyes still hard. After a moment, his shoulders tensed and he looked away. "Fine."

Straightening, Damian let out a stiff breath. She rubbed her temples. "Poppy, can you find a city guard? I need to speak with the captain."

"I thought yae said he was a knight now?"

"Sir Hitchcliffe is, but the captain of the guard will know how to find him. But, I need to speak with him privately."

"If word gets around the city guard that we're here, then the Agaesi will find out that we escaped Sir Kennar," Rhyslen said. A trace of annoyance remained in his voice.

Damian began to answer, but a soft weight fell on her shoulder. She looked at Liam.

"I will go."

A faint smile crossed her face. "Are you sure? I still don't think he trusts you."

Liam nodded.

"Thank you. We'll meet up back in that courtyard we passed." She hesitated as he began to walk away. "Fortune be with you."

Glancing over his shoulder, he nodded solemnly.

"Are yae sure yae can trust this knight?" Poppy asked as she watched Liam turn the next corner. "I mean, it is his duty to report crimes, or sentence them."

Damian thought back to the last time she had seen Sir Hitchcliffe, at the briefing with the king and his advisors.

"I'm sure."

Damian, Rhyslen, and Poppy backtracked to a courtyard they saw while they were making their way unseen through the city. It was a small, brick-paved plaza between buildings and connected by alleys, scattered with leaves from an apple tree growing beside a fountain bubbling up from a well. The three of them sat on a stone bench across from the fountain as people occasionally came and went, the courtyard largely quiet.

"You're right," Rhyslen said suddenly, swirling snow around with his toe.

"Abou' what?" Poppy asked.

"Yanuk."

Damian looked at him.

"It's just hard to let go of everything you have."

Poppy sighed softly. "It's even harder to walk away from

everythin' intentionally."

Rhyslen faced her. "I'm really glad we found you."

"Not near so much as I am to have found you. I mean, Merle and I have each other, but we've been feeling so lonely since we left. I jus' wish we hadn't had to ruin Merle's whole routine to do it."

Damian frowned at that.

The chill in the air deepened as the afternoon waned and the flickers of candles glowed behind shuttered windows. Finally, when movement from one of the alleys caught Damian's eye, she perked up and leaped to her feet as she saw Liam emerge.

"Did you find him?"

Liam nodded. "He lives just across the river from here." Gathering their belongings, they hurried after him.

"Did you have any trouble?"

Liam shook his head.

"And Gravier? He helped you?"

There was the briefest hesitation. "Eventually. He did not want to trust me by myself. I didn't let him know you were here. But he seems well."

Damian smiled, though it was wistful. She recalled the journey to Albrith from Raven Point in the spring with Lyle and his second, Tauros Gravier. Despite his initial suspicions, Gravier had turned out to be a loyal companion. *I wish I could have seen him.*

Liam led the way through the darkening streets as people hurried to finish their tasks and escape indoors. Damian wrapped her cloak tighter, rubbing her hands for warmth as she walked after him, Poppy and Rhyslen following.

The buildings opened up as they made their way into a cleaner, older part of the city, the larger houses surrounded by snow-covered yards. It was in front of one of these that Liam stopped.

Poppy stamped her feet as she looked up at the house. "Pretty well-to-do this bloke is."

Damian couldn't help being impressed as she looked at Sir Hitchcliffe's house. It wasn't quite a manor, but it was larger than any non-noble house she had been inside.

"Strange that he's not in the Knights' Quarter, though," Rhyslen commented.

Damian wondered about that for a moment, then led the way through the trodden path up to the front door and knocked. After a pause, the door opened.

Lyle's frame, even larger than Liam's, nearly filled the doorway. He stared down at Damian in surprise, his eyes passing across each of them in turn as the breeze tossed his grey-streaked, dark brown hair.

"I need your help," Damian said.

His face tightened and he looked away as a woman's voice inside called, "Who is it?"

Straightening, Lyle opened the door wider. "Unexpected company."

Damian smiled her thanks as she stepped inside, followed by Liam, Rhyslen, and Poppy. Damian wiped her boots on the straw mat inside the door as Lyle shut the door behind them. Warmth rushed over her so swiftly that the chill in her own clothes made her shiver. Damian looked up, but got only a glimpse of the spacious common room before she saw a girl looking at her from a nearby sofa and ducked her head.

"Oh," came the voice of the woman in the kitchen.

She began to say something else, but Lyle swiftly said, "We'll be in the drawing room." Grabbing a candle, he led the way across the common room and through double doors down the hall from the kitchen. Damian nodded to the woman as she passed while keeping her eyes downcast.

"Ah," the woman attempted, then said in a resigned voice, "all right."

Damian hurried into the drawing room, the others following her as Lyle used the candle to light others in the room. Sofas, chairs, and accent tables were arranged over the carpeted stone floor. Large windows covered with heavy drapes hanging shut occupied two walls of the room, and across from the doors, a hearth lay empty and cold. It was still notably warmer than outside, but after the pervading warmth of the common room, the chill in this closed-off room made Damian shiver even more than she had outside. She looked longingly toward the hearth, but it was clean with no sign of any logs nearby.

After Lyle lit enough candles to give the room a modest illumination, he crossed to the doors, closing and locking them. Then, he turned and stared at Damian, folding his arms.

"How did you find me?"

"Gravier showed us."

Lyle's eyes narrowed faintly. "Where is he?"

"He left," Liam answered.

Damian shifted. "He… doesn't know I'm in Misengrad."

Lyle's eyes narrowed a little more. He gestured to the sofas in the room as he strode to an armchair. "Talk."

Sitting down beside Liam, Damian took a deep breath. "I got a letter from Garrick a few weeks ago, telling me that Niabi is building an army. He said the Agaesi can't do anything about it, so he asked for my help to stop her. I need to speak with him."

Lyle's brows knitted. "Sir Magni?"

She shifted. "I can't go see him myself." She fumbled for words.

"She had an Agaesi escort," Poppy supplied. "But he didn' believe 'er when she said she was tryin' to stop Niabi."

Lyle stared at her. "Who are you?"

"Poppy Arnsley." She spoke it like a challenge.

Damian held out a hand to her and Rhyslen. "They're the ones who left Yanuk on his march to Albrith." Rhyslen stiffened, but said nothing.

"Mages?" Lyle uttered. His frown deepened with each passing moment. "And your Agaesi escort?"

Damian bowed her head. "It's my fault. It was... a big misunderstanding. We escaped from him."

Lyle groaned, rubbing a hand over his eyes.

"I know I've made mistakes," Damian answered forcefully, "and I will accept the consequences for them. I just want to help stop Niabi."

"You never should have left Aether."

"I can't just sit at home doing nothing while she's gathering an army and everyone else thinks it's the right thing to do. I want to help Garrick."

"When did you receive that letter?"

Damian considered, annoyed at the change of subject. "About... four weeks ago."

Lyle sighed and pinched the bridge of his nose. "You have no idea the depth of trouble you have gotten yourself into. The Agaesi are scouring the countryside."

A chill settled over Damian. "Looking for me?"

"No. For Niabi."

She leaned forward. "What?"

"Yae mean her army's in Faneria?" Poppy said.

Lyle shook his head. "Just her."

Damian nearly leaped from her seat. "Then this is our chance. I have to see Garrick. We have to help him."

"Damian," Lyle said. "Sir Magni has not been in Misengrad since summer."

Damian froze, a chill colder than the room settling over her.

"What?" Poppy uttered.

"That's impossible," Rhyslen chimed in. "I saw the letter. No one could have faked what he said. It had to have come from Misengrad!"

"It was his report that informed us she was in Faneria," Lyle went on. "She attacked him at the beginning of autumn. He has not returned to the city since."

Damian slowly sat back on the couch, the strength washing from her limbs.

"Yae mean this whole thing was based on a lie?" Poppy snapped.

"I don't understand," Rhyslen said, "how could someone even do that?"

"I think the more pressing question is why," Lyle remarked.

Damian listened to them speak, feeling numb. All the secrecy in finding Rhyslen, Poppy, and Merle, attacking Sir Kennar, Damian releasing her magic to the angry villagers in Eldore, all of it was for a fraud.

"Tha's it, then," Poppy scoffed. "All o' this was fer nothin'."

"No."

All eyes turned to Damian. She faced Lyle steadily.

"It's all true, isn't it? Niabi's gathered an army?"

Lyle merely stared back, his eyes narrowing faintly.

"She still has to be stopped," Damian went on, as much for herself as anyone else. "That's why I'm here. Why we're here." She thought furiously. "The Agaesi must be doing something. And their library... Garrick told me they have more knowledge than anyone. They must know how to defeat a malakh." She faced Lyle. "Can you get me in to see them?"

His response was unwavering. "No."

"Please, Sir, if you just—"

"This was a grave mistake and I doubt you appreciate how much trouble you are causing both to yourself and to those around you."

Poppy folded her arms. "We knew what we were gettin' into."

"I told you," Damian replied, "I will accept the consequences of my actions, but—"

"You do not get to choose when you will face this," Lyle answered. "The Agaesi will arrest you when they see you, not when is convenient for you. You may think you are doing the right thing—"

"I am doing the right thing," she said, eyes narrowed.

"But what you have done makes you a criminal, and by associating with me, you are a danger to me, which is a danger to my family, and I will not put them through that."

Damian drew in a breath as he glared at her. She bowed her head. "I'm sorry. You're right. I didn't mean to endanger you."

Lyle's voice softened. "You mean well, but there is nothing more you can do. You should go home."

"I can't. I'm in this too deep already."

"You saw what Niabi did at the Battle of Albrith. Now she has an army. How can you hope to defeat her?"

"She is alone right now, and at her weakest." At the curious looks Rhyslen and Poppy sent her, she continued, "She serves the Goddess of Life. Her power comes from living things. We must strike her now, before winter ends."

"Damian…" Lyle began.

"I can't walk away from this," she said before he could finish. "I won't ask you to risk yourself, but I am going after Niabi." She stood, Liam rising beside her, and with mixed confusion, exasperation, and relief, Rhyslen and Poppy followed suit. "Thank you for seeing us, Sir Hitchcliffe." Raising the hood on her cloak, Damian moved toward the doors.

Lyle's voice held her back.

"I know someone who can help you."

CHAPTER 16
WHERE PATHS CONVERGE

TENSION SQUEEZED ASHIK'S shoulders as he crouched at the top of a rise, peering into the ravine below. Ice coated the creek at its bottom, dusted with the snow that painted everything else. The snow looked pristine, untouched by anything except the occasional animal track. The silence was absolute, and Ashik thought he could hear his own heartbeat as he watched the bend at the end of the ravine.

A light touch on his hand drew him out of his reverie. He glanced aside at Ialla. She returned a look that flickered between anxiousness, hope, tension, and fear. He attempted to give her a reassuring smile, but his own uncertainty kept it from feeling genuine. Turning his hand over, he grasped Ialla's fingers with his own.

They knelt alone at the top of the ravine. The rest of the warriors were in position below, hidden behind scraggly bushes and rock outcroppings. They crouched like statues in the ridges of the ravine. They had even managed to hide their tracks in the snow. Had Ashik not known they were there, he would never have spotted them.

They were ready. The fox-headed woman was coming.

Tethe had ordered Ashik to wait with Ialla in a voice that brooked no argument. Secretly, Ashik was relieved, though he refused to admit that to anyone else. The warriors were as prepared as they could be. They had come up with backup plans and signals and covered as many contigencies as Tethe could imagine. They had to succeed.

Ashik knew by occasional glimpses of the sun behind the featureless, pale grey of the sky that about an hour had passed since he and Ialla took their positions. The time felt interminable as he waited, and his anxiety never eased.

Finally, a flash of colour appeared around the bend in the ravine below. He drew in a breath as it came fully into view.

The malakh. Even from a distance, her golden fur and silken gown glimmered against the pale, late autumn light. Alone, her unnatural slenderness made her look tall, but from such a distance, it was difficult to tell. However, when her two escorts came around the bend behind her, Ashik could see that the malakh's eyes were on a level with the shoulders of the mounted knights. Her pointed ears reached nearly as high as their helmets.

The malakh and her escorts walked leisurely alongside the creek. Ashik glanced around the ravine. The Rturans waited in their positions, hidden from sight of the malakh, bows and throwing knives held at the ready. Closer toward the creek at the bottom, the eagle warriors and Makils crouched with weapons in hand.

Ashik clenched and loosened his fingers as he watched the malakh approach their hiding place at what seemed an agonizingly slow pace from so far away. Ialla's hand tightened around his, a comforting embrace, though his eyes remained focused on the fox-headed woman.

The malakh and her escorts stopped.

Ashik held his breath as his eyes returned to her. Her long muzzle swivelled to one side, then the other. It rose faintly as she scented the air. Ashik's heart pounded. He wondered if the call to attack would come, even though she wasn't close enough to the position they had chosen. The malakh's mouth opened to say something to the knights, but at this distance, Ashik could hear nothing.

Finally, they began moving again. Ashik let out his breath, but braced himself as she came toward the position. He held his breath once more as she drew close to the shrub that marked where the attack would begin. Just as quickly, she reached it.

A keening cry like an eagle split the air.

The first sound that broke the silence after that was the yelp of one of the knights as his horse stumbled beneath him. Ashik watched as though in a dream, stunned by the silence as arrows and knives flew toward the malakh and her companions from three directions. The other knight grabbed a shield off the back of his horse and covered himself, nudging his horse forward to put himself between the archers and the malakh. Before he did, however, Ashik caught a glimpse of a handful of feathered shafts sticking out of the malakh. The first knight pushed off and rolled free of his collapsing horse, diving for cover behind the shrub. The warrior queens withheld any battle cries and charged silently toward the group.

The malakh's gaze darted between the attackers in the moment the battle began, and for that brief moment, Ashik's heart swelled with hope that they were about to cut her down.

Then, by the time her unhorsed companion reached the shrub, she threw her arms out to either side, billowing sleeves sweeping after them. There was a boom and crackle and with a few yelps, the ground beneath the Rturans shook and slid down the slope, taking the warriors with it.

Ashik gasped, rising a little from the ridge as he watched the Rturans tumble down the slope, only a couple managing to stop their descent before collapsing to the floor of the ravine.

Before he saw what happened next, his eyes were drawn back to the malakh as the Makils closed in. The malakh showed no sign of concern, nor did she move as some of the warrior queens stumbled and tripped, sprawling face-down five paces from her. Only when the second wave of Makils dodged and darted around the first ones could Ashik see the rocky ravine floor sprouting up in sudden, jagged outcrops or sinking into ankle-deep pits. Those that managed to get through the undulating rock became quickly ensnared by spindly roots and grasses that sprang from the earth to twine around legs and weapons.

The knights, both now armed with swords and shields, turned to face the Makils who managed to draw close. Coupled with the uneven ground the warrior queens fought against, the knights deftly manoevred their blades aside. Some of the archers began to regain their feet and ready their weapons, but there was another boom and more, larger boulders broke free of the slope and careened down after them.

Ashik leaned forward, clenching his fingers over the rock before him while he desperately watched the Makils spar. Funnelled between the horses and the knights, they were unable to draw close and their spears couldn't land a blow.

The eagle warriors then began to charge in, but the tumbling boulders drew Ashik's attention, and he emitted a strangled cry as some smashed down on the archers. One let out a howl of pain as a rock slammed onto his leg, while another who had barely stopped tumbling from the initial fall was laid flat by another boulder crashing onto their head and shoulders. The boulder rolled once more, leaving behind a red stain in the trampled snow.

"Oh no," Ialla uttered.

The eagle warriors drew in, only some succumbing to the uneven ground, while the Makils pressed their attack. The malakh quickly scanned all sides of the battle. Then, a ring of needle-like columns of stone shot out of the ground, surrounding the malakh and her knights three paces out on all sides. Facing outward, the stones ripped through one Makil's shoulder and impaled another, lifting her body off the ground as it rose. Her limbs waved feebly, but soon her head and arms drooped.

Ashik felt like all the air was being pulled out of his lungs. The Rturans who had evaded the falling boulders continued their assault, but between the shoulder-high wall of stone and the knights' shields, nothing got through. The eagle warriors hacked at the wall with their cudgels and axes, but more spires shot up from the ground, felling even more. The fox-headed woman merely watched from behind her shelter. She casually yanked one of the arrows from her side, not seeming to react at all to its barbs.

Ialla's thickly padded hand grabbed Ashik's upper arm. "We have to do something."

At least a quarter of the force lay unmoving around the area, while the malakh and her knights looked completely at ease as rocks and grass took care of the rest. Some of the warriors switched tactics as they tried to follow the backup plans Tethe had made, but the broken ground kept any of them from landing a blow. Ashik swallowed roughly and cupped his hands around his mouth.

He let out a loud, triple cry like a jay.

He could see their enemies' heads turn in his direction, but he repeated the call. Some of the remaining warriors reacted immediately, fleeing either way down the ravine or up a safe passage on one of the slopes. Some closest to the daggers of stone hesitated, then followed suit. An eagle warrior still pounded away at the stone wall, despite more pillars shooting out of the ground toward him. A Makil grabbed him roughly by the arm, barely avoiding his swinging cudgel, and dragged him away as she fled.

Ashik waited, watching the surviving warriors as they cleared the scene, some limping or clutching bleeding wounds. A sick feeling rose in his stomach as they fled, leaving only bodies or warriors too wounded to flee.

When it was clear that the malakh and her knights would allow the surviving warriors to escape, Ashik rose to retreat himself. He stumbled as he found his knees barely able to support his weight, and leaned on Ialla as he struggled to get away from the scene.

*   *   *

Hunger gnawed at Damian's stomach as she lay on the sofa. It seemed to intensify as the warmth of the newly lit fire in the hearth spread throughout the drawing room, her body seeming to exchange one discomfort for another.

She glanced across the room. Liam slept on another sofa against the opposite wall. The sight made her smile. For all his impassiveness, there was a peace about him while sleeping that he didn't show while awake, and his steady snoring seemed charmingly normal.

Her stomach clenched again and she winced. Refusing supper out of guilt at the trouble she was bringing upon Lyle now seemed foolish. All their supplies, including their own food, remained outside the city with Merle.

She pulled back the blankets and rose. Lighting a candle from the hearth, she tiptoed across the room, around Poppy and Rhyslen's sleeping forms, to the doors. Cautiously, she stepped into the hall and moved toward the kitchen.

As she pushed open the door, her candle's light flickered onto Lyle, leaning against a counter inside with a steaming cup in his hand.

Damian gasped, her heart racing, and she backed out the door again. "Sir Hitchcliffe. I'm sorry, I didn't mean to—"

"So you are hungry after all."

Damian paused before she had shut the door entirely. Lyle reached behind him to slide a bowl down the counter toward her.

"Your pride will only hurt you."

Her cheeks burned as she stepped into the room. "I just didn't want to impose." She set the candle on the counter and picked up the bowl. A scent of herbs rose from the broth within, but the bowl was cool to the touch.

"It is not imposing if it is offered. If you only see through your own eyes, you will not succeed."

Before she could think of an answer to that, Lyle gestured with his head and led the way into the common room. Frowning, Damian followed him across the large room to the hearth, where the logs still glowed brightly and distorted the air above them. She let him take the bowl and place it on a grate above the embers.

"Thank you."

He added more fuel to the fire and used a poker to arrange the logs. "You have changed."

She watched him, equal parts cautious and curious.

"You were determined before," Lyle went on, "but only for your own sake." As the flames reignited and the new log caught, he set down the poker and took a seat in an armchair beside the fire, facing her. "They follow you, and not in the way your mercenary does."

She shifted. "I needed their help."

"That is not enough. Why are you doing this?"

She looked at him carefully. "I told you, I can't just sit at home doing nothing while Niabi builds an army."

"You will not succeed."

Damian pursed her lips.

"You cannot do something this dangerous merely because you cannot do nothing. Niabi is dedicated to her cause. Absolutely. Are you?"

"Yes."

"Why?"

She bristled. "I have to."

"Nothing says you do."

"My conscience does."

"There is plenty else you could do other than face her yourself."

"Not anything that would be of any use."

"You are wrong. You chose to do this. Why?"

"Because if I don't, no one else will!"

Silence fell.

Lyle continued watching her steadily. "Remember that."

Irritation waning, Damian stared at him.

"Niabi is doing this because she believes in it, probably enough to die for it. Unless you believe in your cause as strongly, your resolve will falter, and your friends may die for it."

Her insides clenched, and not from hunger this time. Her voice dropped. "You've seen it, haven't you?"

"Yes. I have led men to their deaths."

Damian's shoulders hunched.

"That follows you to the end of your days. But you cannot let it cloud your mind in the midst of battle. If you do not fight on, more people will die.

"There is more to being a leader than simply having a goal that people will follow. You need a plan. You need the presence to enforce it, and to ensure your companions will stay in line. You need to understand and utilize your companions' strengths and weaknesses. You need to be focused, and flexible, and think quickly.

"I believe you are strong enough to lead them true. But you have much to learn, and little time with which to do so."

Lyle rose. At a scraping sound, she looked up to find him holding the bowl of soup out to her.

Slowly, she took the bowl, now warm from the fire. "Please come with us. We need someone with your expertise. You know what the Gods of Light are doing is wrong."

Returning to his chair, he gave her a hard look. "I know that more than you do." He glanced around the room, ensuring no one else was near. "This is not the first time I have seen the Gods of Light do something terrible."

Something hardened inside Damian. "Raven Point."

"No. You."

She gave him a curious look. As she met his gaze, she remembered something he said the first time they met. Her eyes enlarged. "The Century Storm?"

He nodded.

"That… that was them?"

"Their wrath, much like at Raven Point."

Damian's breath fell short. She couldn't decide whether to sink wearily into the cushions of the couch or lean forward in excitement. "You were there? In Edan? It originated in Edan, didn't it?"

"Brighton," he clarified. "Birthplace of the Gods of Light."

She could hardly breathe now. Brighton was oft touted as the holiest of cities, but she had no idea it was where the Gods of Light came from.

"The Century Storm was their reaction to the Duke of Deverell attempting to summon Nephrita that night. The spell must have partially completed for the way everything turned out."

Even Damian's hunger seemed to have vanished. Damian's entire life had risen from that moment, in more ways than one. Nephrita's presence attaching to her, the storm that killed her mother. The Battle of Albrith had been nineteen years in the making.

The battle…

"Why didn't you ever tell anyone this?" she uttered. "If magic had never been blamed for the Century Storm, Yanuk might never have attacked Albrith."

"Do not think that does not weigh on me as well. Yet I could not, or I might not be here today."

"What do you mean?"

He fixed his gaze on her. "I was a city guard of Misengrad, deep inside Edan, years before the peace treaty was signed, interfering with the Duke of Deverell at a time when he fought for the throne of Edan. Now do you understand?"

She straightened. If anyone had learned of Lyle's involvement, it could have meant war. It didn't matter if he had been there in a personal capacity rather than official. Instead of the two kingdoms finally finding peace, Edan might have blamed Faneria for everything from subterfuge to assassination of the previous king. Faneria would have little way to prove otherwise, and Lyle's efforts to stop a madman from attaining ultimate power could have brought down both kingdoms.

"I have kept this hidden for nineteen years, even from my own family. I would appreciate you not sharing this information as well."

"I won't speak of it to anyone."

"I should not have been there. But I had to stop him. Now, you have to stop Niabi. She holds the power of a god and her army is sweeping across Edan. So you must be ready to face her, in every way."

Damian couldn't help feeling small, helpless, and terrified as she considered everything her mission meant, the power Niabi held, and the potential for her friends, or her, to die in the process.

Yet here was Lyle, a knighted veteran of many battles and a man who had seen the wrath of gods and mages before she was born, showing faith in her cause, and in her.

She nodded. "I will do everything I can to stop her." She pushed away the voice inside that told her she didn't stand a chance.

"You may have to, more than you anticipate." Lyle rose. "I am going to bed. You should too. You will need your rest."

She couldn't help agreeing as he crossed the common room and disappeared up the stairs, and she hurried to finish her soup.

The next morning, they awoke early and Lyle let them out through the larder onto the quiet back lane usually only used by servants. Each of them was loaded down with more stores of food.

"Thank you again, Sir Hitchcliffe," Damian said.

"Good luck," he replied as Damian, Liam, Rhyslen, and Poppy stepped into the fresh snow outside.

"Are yae sure this friend o' yours can really help us?" Poppy asked.

"I am certain. Kina is a collector of knowledge." Lyle gave Damian a significant look. "And she has seen things few people have."

Straightening, Damian nodded her understanding.

With Misengrad awakening around them in the red-gold light of dawn, they didn't walk far before casting the unseeing spell. They made their way back through the city to the gate where they had arrived the previous day. With a last, disappointed look over her shoulder, Damian led the way through the gates just as they opened. They soon rejoined Merle and began following Lyle's directions west around the city toward the distant forest.

Damian walked in silence, her thoughts on all the things Lyle had told her.

If you only see with your own eyes, you will not succeed.

"I'm sorry," she said suddenly.

"Beg pardon?" asked Poppy.

"Sorry for what?" Rhyslen asked.

"For giving you such a hard time over Yanuk yesterday," Damian answered him. "And this whole time."

He smiled wanly. "It's all right. I realized yesterday that I need to let him go. I keep trying to hold on to his memory, but it's only hurting my present."

From the corner of her eye, Damian saw Liam turn away. She faced him to find a thoughtful and perhaps slightly sad look on his face.

Before she could ask him what was on his mind, Poppy said, "Well, that's all well an' good, but since we're not meeting with your knight friend now, do we have any ideas how we're goin' to stop that malakh?"

Damian frowned. "No," she answered slowly. "We can only hope Kina does."

Niabi gazed at the four figures before her. Her knights had to drag the injured easterners through the snow over a mile from the ravine where they ambushed her. Only there, on the banks of a creek winding through the hills, could they find enough trees gathered together to lash the warriors to. They were awake now, the two most injured roused from their stupor as the two knights tied them upright against the trees, arms spread apart in tight, binding knots. They stared at her with a mixture of defiance and exhaustion.

Niabi couldn't help smiling as she watched them back. She ran her finger along the length of purplish-green plant stem in her hands, thicker than her wrist and organically severed at either end. She could feel the stiff hairs along the stem and the sap coating it, but of course, it didn't affect her. Sprites hovered around her, but she ignored their constant presence.

"So what do you want with them, Lady Niabi?" asked one of the knights, sneering at their captives. His horse nosed contentedly through the snow in search of grass, the wound on its side from the fight now healed over, thanks to her touch.

Her dark eyes didn't move from the easterners. "Actually, these people with their clumsy attack upon us has made our mission far easier. We can get precisely the information we seek from them."

The knights shifted and Niabi could hear the eagerness in their chuckles.

"Is that so?"

She didn't begrudge them their excitement. It had already latched onto her, though her long life had given her the patience not to show it.

The Army of Light was on a mission, a crusade. The people had been more than willing to give their lives to the cause, but for it to succeed, they needed a target. They needed to attack the Gods of Time directly.

But where had the old gods gone after the ancient war? No one seemed to know. Even their few remaining followers were too scattered and kept in the dark.

Then, Niabi had learned that the Gods of Time had more followers than she realized. Followers that weren't even aware of it.

She could feel the presence of the old gods on these easterners. She could almost smell it. All of them knew how to find the Gods of Time, and none of them was aware of it.

Niabi was going to find out.

"Remove their clothes," she ordered.

The knights leered as they approached the easterners and drew their daggers. The first woman spat in the knight's face as he ripped at her clothes. He flinched, then backhanded her across the face, his gauntlet cracking against her cheekbone. A harsh red scrape and a few bleeding scratches marred her face, but she still didn't speak.

It took several minutes for each knight to cut through one and then another easterner's clothes. Eventually, they were torn away, leaving only tatters of cloth where the ropes held them up.

"We tell you nothing, demon!" spat one of the men, even as his body paled and he shivered from the cold.

Niabi's smile widened. He was one of the most savage warriors from the battle, who had smashed at her stone barrier with an obsidian-bladed cudgel and now sported a deep gash beneath his ribs and several dark bruises across his dark skin.

She approached, grabbing his hair and yanking his head back against the trunk of the tree.

"We shall see."

Raising her other hand, she touched the tip of the stem up underneath his earlobe and drew it gently across his face, ending beneath the other ear. She pulled her hand free of his hair and stepped back.

The knights had drawn close behind her as she approached the easterner.

"What does that thing do?" one asked, pointing at the thick stem.

"Nothing yet," she answered, moving them back with a wave of her free hand. "But give it time. Sunlight shall do our work for us."

The knights gave each other a confused look. Niabi ignored them as she strode in front of the easterners.

"This is simple," she began. "There is some place sacred to all of your cultures, a place where all of you find closeness to your own 'gods'."

She stepped toward another man, sliding the stem over his exposed torso. This one seemed promising, as his fair complexion might be more susceptible to the stem's sap. He sucked in a sharp breath, the ropes creaking as he strained against them.

"You will tell me where this place is."

The effect on him was immediate, his skin turning red where the stem touched him.

"We will die before we tell you anything."

The first woman spoke almost matter-of-factly, not defiant like the cudgel wielder, but with utter confidence.

Niabi smiled as she moved to her. "Death is an easy promise to make." Niabi slid the stem along the woman's body. "Life brings much more suffering." Lifting her free hand, Niabi brushed her fingertips against the woman's lips. "Answer me this one question and I can end your pain."

Niabi moved back down the line, drawing the stem across the second woman's arms. She tapped the stem lightly against the second man's stomach, eliciting a choked groan through clenched teeth. Blisters began to form along the angry red line across his ribs and chest.

After touching the stem to a few more choice places on each of the captives, Niabi stepped back, allowing the full brunt of the late autumn sun to shine down on them.

It took time, but one thing Niabi had was patience. She watched as their shivers came more frequently and more violently and their skin paled. The invisible strokes of her plant stem emerged as burns and angry red welts. The second man had it worst. Niabi simply watched and waited. Gradually, the captives began to moan, pant, or hiss from pain. The first woman's lips swelled and she groaned through a puffy mouth.

The weakest link in the chain was clear. Niabi administered more gentle touches of the stem to the pale man, who, as the sun crawled on across the sky, began to scream. Sweat poured down his face, even as his extremities turned white from the cold. The others, through their own pain, implored him not to say anything. His howls were primal, and it was clear he could hear nothing they said to him.

Finally, it came out.

"Veil's Edge!" he shrieked. "Atop Rukhwara!"

Niabi grinned, striding closer to him. "And where is Rukhwara?"

"Table mountain," he howled, panting through clenched teeth. "Northeast Orthys Mountains." He barely got the words out before he screamed again.

"That's it?" one of the knights said eagerly. "That's what we were after?"

Niabi touched a fingertip to the man's chest. Even though another rash bloomed where she touched from the sap clinging to her fur, she drew the pain from him and he passed out, drooping against the ropes.

"That," she answered, "is what our army is after. That is where the heathen gods reside and where we will finally snuff their presence from Elderra."

The knights shuffled excitedly. "Is it time for us to return, then?"

"You two go," Niabi replied. "The army must know its destination."

The surprise, even alarm, was clear in the knight's voice. "But what about you, Lady Niabi?"

"I will be along after you, but you can reach the army much quicker on your horses."

Her response came without hesitation. They didn't need to know that the battle against the easterners had taken far more out of her than she let on, and with the cold sapping so much life from the plants and earth around her, it was becoming increasingly difficult to regain it.

The knights also didn't need to see what she planned for their captives. Even among their enemies, the humans' peculiar sensibilities would be offended.

The knights hesitated.

"Go," Niabi ordered. "I will follow, but this information must reach the army."

Reluctantly, they gathered their supplies and tightened the harnesses on their horses. "Be safe, Lady Niabi."

The other muttered to himself as he mounted his horse. "Veil's Edge, Rukhwara, northeast Orthys Mountains. Veil's Edge, Rukhwara, northeast Orthys Mountains…"

With that, they turned and began riding west through the snow.

"Demon," the first woman snarled thickly, though it lacked some of the fire she showed earlier in the day. "You are a… coward."

"I do what I must." Niabi strode over to her. "And this is so much greater than you."

The woman's howl of pain was brief, weakening swiftly before it faded into silence.

CHAPTER 17
RECOVERY

GARRICK TRIED TO breathe deeply, but as the movement squeezed at his ribs and spine, he settled for drawing in quick and even breaths.

Today is the day.

He clung to the determination, as though this was the first time he told himself that.

Slowly, he lifted his hands off the bed. Eyes squeezed shut, he winced from the pinching in his back as the weight of his upper body shifted from his shoulders to his spine. It wasn't pleasant, but it was better than lying flat on the floor. Sitting up was getting easier.

Kina placed her arm across his upper back. "Are you certain you wish to do this?"

He glanced at her from the corner of his eye, not daring to turn his head if he could avoid it. "Yes."

Nodding, she gently lifted his right arm over her head and draped it over her shoulders. He bent his knees, sliding his feet closer to him.

"Are you ready?"

With two more shallow breaths, Garrick leaned forward, Kina's arm firm behind him, and began pushing to his feet. He tried to keep his back as steady as possible, using momentum and Kina's strength to get him started.

As his full weight pressed on his legs, a spike of pain stabbed through his left knee and he buckled with a cry. Only Kina's grip kept him from collapsing to the floor, and she swiftly but carefully began lowering him again.

"No," he choked out through teeth clenched so tight his head pounded. He pushed harder with his right leg, trying to support himself without unbalancing his back too much. "I'm doing this."

Kina frowned, but helped pull him upright until at last he stood on his own feet. His legs trembled, barely able to support his weight, and the room spun. He blinked, breathing rapidly to try to make his vision settle. Stiffening nearly every muscle in his body, he pushed his left leg in front of him. Kina no longer held him up, but she kept her arm against him.

Garrick wobbled precariously and as his weight shifted toward his left knee, another spasm ripped through him and he moaned. He struggled to hobble over the bad knee onto his right leg, stumbling about like a man inebriated.

The pain in his leg rose with each movement and each moment, but he kept his eyes fixed on his goal. Kina's plain dining table, barely large enough to seat four, lay eight paces from his bed of the last half season.

The aches mounted, agony overtaking every other feeling in his body, but he forced himself onward. At the last two steps, he all but flung himself into the nearest chair, resting his elbow on the table with his head in his hand, panting heavily as his legs trembled.

Kina hurried around the table, sitting down across from him. "Are you all right?"

He only let out a long, low groan in response.

Gradually, the pain lessened. It remained ever present, but he could feel his fingers twined in his hair, could feel his tight grip pulling at his scalp. It was too long. His hair mostly stayed out of the way while he lay down, but without tying it back, it seemed continually in his face whenever he sat up. He needed to do something about that.

Kina's firm grip on his wrist pulled him from his reverie. He gave her a curious look before he noticed the knife in his hand. It was already drawn up near his neck, his other hand holding his hair out behind his head. He dropped both handfuls with a start.

He noticed a concerned look on Kina's face before she smiled pleasantly at him. "Well, congratulations. You have walked again."

Garrick's voice was faint and breathy. "Yeah." A moment of silence passed as he stared, disturbed, at the knife. *Did I really come that close to cutting off half my hair on a whim?*

"Can I ask you something?"

"Sure," he answered distractedly, struggling to understand what had just happened.

"Who is Sheridan?"

He tore his eyes from the knife and stared at Kina. "What?"

She looked amused. "When you first awoke here, you said your name was Sheridan before you corrected yourself."

"I did?"

"You did. Who is he?"

"It's me." Garrick grinned mirthlessly. "That's my middle name."

Kina leaned her chin on the heel of her hand, smile widening. "Sir Garrick Sheridan Magni. Sounds regal."

He laughed, not without some bitterness. "Hardly. I'm only a knight, and not a very well respected one at that."

"You are still the grandson of a duke."

"Well, those two generations create a pretty big gulf, especially only being related on my mother's side."

She watched him for a moment, her smile fading. "Why is it the Agaesi think so poorly of you?"

His expression fell as his attention focused completely on her. "Because I'm not pure." They had long since given up trading secrets for victories in Domination after Garrick began winning most games. In truth, he relished the opportunity to speak of the things that had defined his entire life, yet which he could discuss with no one.

"Every other Agaesi can trace their lineage, both sides of their family, straight back to the valley where they first met Agasis. Every single Agaesi ever has come out of that tower, except me."

Kina cocked her head aside. "So why are you different?"

"Because we needed help." At the curious look on her face, he explained, "Each generation is smaller than the last. Fully half the tower isn't even in use anymore. Not to mention that we don't command the same respect we used to."

She looked skeptical. "Not from what I have seen."

Garrick rubbed his forehead. His eyes were still drawn to the knife. "It's harder to see when you're not close to it. I was revered a lot more when I got away from Hesperia. In Misengrad, though, the Agaesi don't have the clout they used to. And people don't like the persistent rumours about our abilities."

After a moment, Kina ventured, "So…"

He smiled wryly at her. "So here I am. The old captain went to the previous duke and they reached an agreement. The duke married his oldest daughter to one of the finest Agaesi knights—my parents. My mother brought in both prestige and new blood to help the Agaesi line."

Kina's brow knitted. "But you have no siblings?"

"My birth was hard on my mother. She was never able to conceive again."

"So she was taken from the world of privilege that she knew and given to one that did not accept outsiders, and she could not fulfill the purpose for which she was uprooted? That must have been hard for your mother."

He nodded. "Especially after my father died. The captain makes sure that the others respect her, at least to her face. She did improve the Agaesis' standing to the people in power, after all. But that's why she spends so much time attending court. She never belonged in that tower."

"And you?"

He raised a weary look to Kina. "Me? I should be an Agaesi in more than name and ability, but I have spent my entire life constantly reminded that my very existence came as a last resort."

Sadness fell over Kina and she reached forward to lay her hand on his. "I understand how it feels to be treated as worthless as a child."

He shrugged, wincing at the pain with the movement, and smiled faintly. "What can I do? It's my life and it's all that I've known. So I've tried to prove myself, trained and studied as hard as I could with all that time spent by myself." He chuckled. "Turns out all I had to do to be accepted was leave." He looked down at her fingers gently rubbing the back of his hand. It was more soothing than he could recall any simple touch feeling. "But it sure is nice to be able to talk about all these things I've kept pent up inside."

Kina smiled. "It is."

He smiled in return and even the pain in his back and knee seemed to lessen.

The following day, he was able to walk far enough to move into the room Kina and Pecca's boys had set up for him. It was even less furnished than the common room and cluttered with more of Kina's artifacts, but he was glad for a space of his own. Aches accompanied every move he made, but his spirit rose as he began to walk around her house, eat at the table, sit upright for longer periods, and attend himself.

A week after his first unstable steps, he went outside for the first time since he awoke in Kina's house. The chill air seeped through the blanket wrapped around his shoulders, but a smile spread on his face as he stepped through the door. The open air and smell of trees, an earthy-sweet tang he had never noticed before, filled his senses. He shut his eyes and inhaled deeply as he leaned against the door frame, feeling the breeze on his face and in his hair, though he squinted against the glare of sunlight against snow when he opened his eyes.

"How are you feeling?"

He looked at Kina, shadows dark on her skin and clothes. Sunlight glinted gold against her ginger hair.

"Good, as long as I stay right here." He leaned against the door frame, using its support to keep his back straight without putting much weight on his bad leg.

"Is it still difficult to walk?"

"I think it will be for a while." Garrick glanced at the world outside, barren trees lining the gully outside Kina's house. A fallen tree trunk lay across the ground some fifteen paces away. It felt like a mile to him. He shook his head. "My arms and legs feel so weak. I can barely stay standing here." He tried to fix his shirt where a fold of cloth pressed against his arm, but it only shifted the loose fold under the blanket. His clothes hung off him and his trousers barely stayed on his waist.

"Your strength will return," Kina said.

"It's just strange." He shifted. "My arms feel like sticks. I never noticed how much smaller they got while I was lying down."

A dry grin crossed her face. "They have not gotten *that* much smaller."

"Maybe not, but it feels like a big difference."

"Well, there is only one way to build up those muscles again."

He raised his head as she strode around to the right side of her house, toward a half-frozen stream winding through the gully. A rough lean-to constructed of fallen branches and old blankets in a cluster of trees was visible around a bend, and between the trees, he could just see movement beside it.

Straightening, Garrick leaned forward and stepped into open air. He limped over his bad leg, wincing faintly with each step, as he made his way toward the lean-to. A smile spread on his face as he approached, the form of a horse coming into view.

Brenadier looked a little unkempt, but as magnificent as ever, clad in nothing but leather hobbles around his front legs and a blanket over his back. His head shot up from the ground where he grazed, ears pricked up as he saw Garrick. Nickering, the stallion turned and approached Garrick, head lowered and snuffling.

"Hey, Bren." Garrick scratched Brenadier behind the ears as the horse nuzzled his side in greeting. "Oh, so you were mad at me for leaving you before, but you're happy to see me now after roughing it for half a season?"

Brenadier snorted and tossed his head, pawing at the ground.

"Yeah, I'll bet you were sucking up to Kina, you big baby. You may have good taste, but she's anything but a pushover."

Restricted by the hobbles, Brenadier shoved his nose up under Garrick's arms.

Garrick sighed, a deep ache forming in his chest. "I can't, Bren."

"What does he want?" Kina asked.

"He wants me to ride him, but I don't think my back can take that much jostling."

The stallion snorted and shoved his head against Garrick.

Garrick straightened as he turned to Kina. "You could take him for a ride."

Her eyes grew large. "Me?" She eyed Brenadier uneasily. "I have very little experience with horse riding."

"It's not hard. All you have to do is stay low and hold on with your knees."

She frowned. "What if he throws me?"

He grinned. "He won't throw you, he's tame."

She folded her arms.

"You'll be fine. One of us should have some fun."

"I do not consider an uncontrolled ride on such a large animal 'fun'."

"I meant him. Horses need to run." Dropping his teasing tone, he smiled warmly at her. "It's perfectly safe. He'll know if you're falling and slow down. Trust me, you'll enjoy it. It feels like you're flying."

Kina rolled her eyes. "I am not certain that flying is a good thing. But very well, I will exercise him for you." She fetched the saddle and bridle and strapped them on to Brenadier under Garrick's instruction. Then, Garrick removed the hobbles and Kina mounted the stallion.

She shifted, trying to get comfortable on the saddle. "How do I guide him?"

"Don't worry about it. He'll be keeping to the trail. Just let him run and hold on. When he slows down, pull the reins to one side to turn him around and walk back." He handed her the reins. "You ready?"

"I suppose."

Garrick let go of the reins and took a step back. "Show her what real freedom feels like, Bren." He slapped the horse's rump and it let out a snort and took off, snow spraying up from his hooves.

Garrick got a brief glimpse of the worried look on Kina's face as Brenadier galloped through the gully. Then, he could only see the back of her head as she bounced atop the stallion's back.

Garrick cupped his hands around his mouth. "Remember to stay low! And try to avoid any rocks."

Kina leaned forward over Brenadier's bobbing neck as he went up one of the hills bordering the gully. Garrick smiled as he watched the stallion's long, wavy mane and tail flow behind him, his thick, sinewy muscles rippling as he moved. Even from a distance, Garrick revelled in the rhythmic thump of Brenadier's hooves, the ground sliding away beneath him.

A hint of wistfulness touched his eyes as Brenadier crested the hill and Kina slipped out of sight, but the ache in his chest had eased watching the stallion gallop. He limped over to the fallen log and sat down, wincing against the ache in his back and leg and panting from that small effort. The edges of thoughts touched Garrick's mind in the silence left behind: hope for the day when he could again move like Brenadier, anxiety that that day would never come, dread for the day he would return to Misengrad, and more, but he brushed them away as he gazed around at the outside world he had not seen in so long.

A few minutes passed. Garrick thought it had been long enough for Brenadier to wear himself out, though likely the stallion could go no faster than a canter, or even a trot, through the forest trail. Garrick put his fingers to his mouth and whistled as loudly as he could. Silence reigned for a few minutes longer, then suddenly, Brenadier appeared over the hill, head bobbing as he walked with Kina sitting upright astride him.

Garrick smiled as they reached the bottom of the hill and Kina rode up to him. "So what did you think?"

Her hair was more mussed than usual and her knuckles remained white. "Let me simply say that I look forward to the day you are well, so you need not live vicariously through me."

Garrick rubbed the stallion's neck. "That smile on your face says otherwise."

She let out a scoffing sound as she dismounted. "The last time I rode a horse that fast, I was fleeing for my life."

"And this time?"

Kina glanced at Brenadier. "I suppose I can see how it might feel freeing."

Garrick moved his hand to the horse's forehead. "There's nothing else like it. With nothing but the wind in my hair and the sound of his hooves on the ground… I'm untouchable."

"I must admit, it did make me pine for the days when I travelled, exploring ruins and unearthing lost history."

Garrick grinned at her. "I'm sure there's plenty more for you to discover."

A knowing smile crossed her face. "There likely is." Taking up the reins, she led Brenadier toward the stream. Garrick watched her walk away. Thin, almost boyish, looking like a man from the back with her short hair and trousers.

Not what I would have thought of as my type of woman, and yet, I think I'd be perfectly happy if I never spoke to anyone else.

The thought surprised him, but he didn't refute it.

In the end, ten warriors of the twenty-four that had set out from Khaladon perished.

Ashik knelt beside a crude litter holding the tenth. Tir Kerstet. He still breathed, but it was shallow, and Ashik knew the moment he saw the Rturan that he wouldn't survive.

"We fought… well," Tir Kerstet had rasped when he first noticed Ashik. "Made… ancestors proud."

One of his legs ended above the knee. Ais Ainlan explained that they had to amputate after his foot was crushed by one of the falling boulders. It wasn't enough. Above the scarred, seared skin where they had burned the wound to seal it, Ashik recognized the same deadening of flesh he had seen enough times in the mountains. There, it was usually the result of cold, but the outcome was the same. Tir Kerstet's ashen, clammy skin and the inane mumblings he let out now attested to that. It was unlikely he would last through the night.

Ashik was surprised to find that the thought didn't hurt him. For years, he had cried with outsiders at sombre death ceremonies across the free lands. Yet now, as he faced his first true loss since he had returned home, he wanted only to celebrate Tir Kerstet's life and the kinship he had given Ashik over the past weeks. Ko would guide Ashik past this world one day, and perhaps she helped Tir Kerstet on his journey even now. The thought brought him comfort and a sense of peace.

The hollow where they rested, where their supplies had been stored before the fateful encounter with the malakh, rang with movement as warriors tended to injuries. Tension lay over the group like a bubble, ready to burst. A few of the survivors had already snapped out their own opinions of what they should do next, but the question hadn't been answered yet.

Tethe was dead. Though there were a couple warrior queens she had called upon for help carrying out orders during the journey, she had not officially named anyone her second. Most of the surviving Rturans and Kathecs weren't eager to allow them to take command, nor even were the other surviving Makils, as they were each as experienced as the other in battle. Grief caused some to lash out, others to bemoan the hopelessness of ever defeating the fox-headed woman now. A few, like Ialla, simply hid away from the others as much as they could. Tears and curses fell in equal measure.

Now, two days after the battle and a couple hours after all the survivors had reunited, Ashik could feel the frustration growing in those around him. Voices were rising, feet were stomping, and people were working themselves up for a fight.

"Look around you, fools! We could not beat her with twice our number. It is over."

"Coward! Weakling! No wonder you still live, you were probably first to run."

"How dare you—"

"We were given this mission by Uniter himself. Even if we fail, let us have honourable deaths, not a shameful retreat."

"Honourable? You call crushing and stabbing by rocks honourable?"

"Dere is nothing to be gained by dying pointlessly. I was close to Tethe, I say we—"

"She never name you second. You do not give us orders."

"I will not back down from this fight!"

Ashik laid a hand on Tir Kerstet's shoulder as the arguments bounced around him. The Rturan didn't seem to notice the touch.

"Warriors," Ashik called out over all of them. A few ceased their bickering, and the rest trailed off as Ashik repeated himself and stood. Slowly, he glanced around, meeting the eyes of each of the survivors. Many nursed wounds, though few were serious.

"Our friends," Ashik began, "our brothers and sisters in arms who fell fighting the fox-headed woman, lived great lives. They devoted themselves, body and soul, to everything they did, including death. They fought with bravery and honour to do what was right." His voice strengthened. "They deserve a death ceremony, and they deserve for us to carry on their spirit by completing what we set out to do."

A couple of the warriors looked surprised at his words, and most looked moved or humbled.

Huathl, one eye swollen shut and his hides torn and bloodstained at the shoulder, took a step forward and squared his shoulders. "Ashik is right. We must honour dead by fighting on."

Murmured agreements rang out and Masa nodded solemnly. "Well spoken, Ashik. We need to rest, but tomorrow, we must return to de ravine and give our fallen comrades de death ceremony."

"And then we hunting fox head woman," Ais Ainlan added darkly.

A shout of agreement rang out, and the warriors returned to their tasks with vigor. As Ashik watched the movement about the hollow, he caught a glimpse of Ialla standing in the entrance of his shelter, smiling at him.

When he awoke the next morning, the first thing he saw was Ais Ainlan drawing the blanket covering Tir Kerstet over his head. Placing a hand over his heart, Ashik bowed to the draped body, then set to packing supplies.

By the time the sun was high in the pale grey sky, they returned, horses and all, to the ravine where they had faced the malakh. The scene that greeted them was grisly, particularly since animals had found the bodies. Ashik grew ill at the sight and gladly allowed others to handle gathering the remains and building a pyre. Meanwhile, he followed a Rturan scout and a handful of others who found the malakh's tracks leading farther east from the ravine, with what appeared to be drag marks in the snow accompanying them.

The sight that greeted him when he moved around a bend where the ravine levelled off, however, stopped him short. His heart felt like it collapsed in on itself.

Curses and hisses emanated from the warriors with him as they stood before the four trees beside the creek. Bile rose in Ashik's throat as he gazed upon the bodies tied to them and he had to force himself not to retch.

"What did she *do* to them?" a Rturan uttered. Others muttered epithets in their native tongues.

The bodies were barely recognizable. Oozing, red blisters stood out angrily against their pale, faded skin. That, however, seemed the least of the suffering the fox-headed woman had inflicted upon them. The bodies were shrivelled, almost mummified. Their discoloured skin stretched across protruding bones with hardly any flesh between them, as though they had been starved for weeks.

"How could she do dis in a day or two?" hissed Masa. "What foul spell did she cast on dem?"

"And why?" growled an eagle warrior. "What honour is there in this?"

"This not honour," sneered another Rturan. "Fox head woman have no honour doing this."

Swallowing roughly, Ashik passed his eyes across each of the bodies again. Animals had not even found these remains. He could tell that two of them had been Makil, one Kathec, and another Rturan, but their faces were so sunken that he couldn't tell who they had been. Their eyes bulged out of their skulls in a rictus of horror.

"She is a monster," snarled the first Rturan.

Masa shook her head, a sneer contorting her face. "No respect for life or death. She deserves de most painful death we can give her." She fixed her stare on the others, her muscles taut and hands trembling in rage. "Dis insult cannot go unanswered. We *must* kill her."

"We need to give them the death ceremony," the eagle warrior cut in.

Masa looked ready to argue, but hesitated. Ashik glanced at his companions. Above their heads, he could see smoke wafting over the hills behind them, where the pyre burned. Masa, the eagle warrior, and the Rturans with Ashik all looked steadily at the bodies, showing no signs of unease at the sight.

Slowly, Masa nodded. "Deir souls deserve what comfort we can give dem." With that, she strode forward, drawing a knife from her belt. The others followed and began cutting the ropes holding up the bodies.

Ashik had to look away as the bodies were released.

"Go on back, Ashik," Masa said. Glancing at her, he found her gently lowering one of the bodies onto a cloak laid onto the ground. She nodded at him. "We will be dere soon."

Nodding gratefully, Ashik turned and followed the creek back to the ravine. When he returned to the site of the battle, it was to a brilliant pyre with flames licking high up into the sky. Even the warriors keeping watch from the top of the ravine stood near its edges and occasionally looked down to watch the fire burn. The rest of the warriors gathered in a ring around the pyre. Some chanted or spoke in their native languages, some sang low, keening songs, and others simply watched with heads high and shoulders back. Ashik watched for a moment, warmth spreading through him at the sight.

Then, Ais Ainlan and Huathl, standing beside each other, stepped to either side to allow him to take a place between them. With a nod, Ashik joined them and began a Khurali celebratory chant. As he did so, however, he noticed Ais Ainlan wince and suck in a breath. Finding him watching her, she quickly smoothed out her features once again.

Ashik paused his chant. "Are you all right?"

"I am fine," she answered tightly.

Ashik hesitated, but decided not to press her on it.

Masa and the others returned soon, and the mood quickly turned fierce as the warriors at the ravine saw what happened to those at the four trees. Ashik stepped aside, allowing Masa to explain what they had found while he sought out Ialla.

She had wandered nearly around the bend where Ashik had first caught a glimpse of the malakh, well upwind of the pyre and almost out of sight of the grim scene.

"You shouldn't wander off so far by yourself," Ashik said gently as he approached her from behind.

"I'm sorry," she answered in a strangely muffled voice. "I find it hard to concentrate on the *shikar* with so many people around."

"Were you able to find her?" As he came around and looked at Ialla, he was surprised to see a distant, almost worried look on her face. His brow creased. "What is it?"

Finally, she met his eyes. "Ashik, there's… something else."

"What?"

She shook her head. "I don't know. When I reached into the *shikar*, I saw something… I'm not sure what, but it was just as powerful as the fox-headed woman. And it's just as close."

Ashik pursed his lips. "Something… evil?"

Ialla shrugged. "Spirits are not good or evil. They just are. All I know is it's not like anything I've felt before."

A frown crossed Ashik's face as he looked back toward the pyre. This strange, new presence was highly unusual, yet they had to focus. Ialla hadn't seen the shrivelled bodies that had been tied to the trees, though Ashik had the feeling that that sight would stay with him for the rest of his days.

"Well, we will have to be careful with… whatever that thing is you sensed, but we need to find the malakh. Did you locate her?"

Shaking herself, Ialla nodded. "She is moving west, but I don't think she is moving too fast, and she isn't far ahead of us. I think we can catch her up."

"Good. Then we had best get moving if we are to stop her." He turned to walk back to the rest of the warriors, but Ialla's hand on his arm stopped him. Glancing at her, he found her smiling at him.

"Thank you for taking charge, Ashik."

A small smile crossed his face, but he shrugged. "I haven't exactly done much. I've only been trying to keep everyone focused."

"You've done more than you think," she said. With that, she released his arm and they walked back toward the pyre together.

CHAPTER 18
FATE'S DESTINATION

THE CHILL IN the air was deepening. Garrick had taken a swig of molka before stepping outside, but the heat that had surged through him from the drink had long faded. He could barely keep from shivering wearing his forked Agaesi cloak and a blanket. He tried to wrap the blanket closer about his legs.

"Are you all right?" Kina asked, sitting on the fallen log beside him.

He smiled wryly. "It figures. Just as soon as I'm well enough to start going outside again, it gets too cold to stay out here." He cringed as his shifting made a stab of pain shoot up his back. He fell still, looking around at the world outside Kina's house. It was a monotone landscape of bare trees and snow. He had missed the autumn colours entirely.

"Shall we go inside? This seems like a good day to add more illustrations to my books."

He chuckled as he carefully rose from the log. "I'm not that good at sketching from memory."

"You are still better than me."

"Really?" He grinned sidelong at her. "When you remember every minute detail of everything you have ever seen? I just think you haven't…"

He trailed off, stopping in his tracks halfway back to Kina's house.

"What is it?" she asked.

Garrick paused. "I thought I heard something."

Kina fell still and listened. A moment passed as all they could hear was the breeze rattling the branches and few shrivelled leaves clinging to the trees.

Then, as the wind passed, he heard it again. Distant conversation and the thumps of horse hooves. It sounded like several people.

He exchanged a look with Kina. The surprise and confusion on her face made it clear she heard it, too. The people came from the same direction as the village where Therrus lived, but they weren't expecting any supply deliveries for another few weeks. Kina's home was buried in the thick of the woods, far off any provincial trails and over rough terrain. No sensible people would come this way and certainly no one would expect to find anything.

Unless Kina was betrayed.

A determined look crossed her face, though not without traces of worry. She nodded up toward the eastern side of the gully, flanking the visitors, then moved in that direction and began climbing the rise. Garrick briefly wanted to protest as he followed, but he realized that they would be no better prepared to face the intruders in her home than outside. Even if he had a weapon on him, he was in no condition to use it.

Kina moved with the breeze, using the sound of the trees creaking to mask her boots crunching through the snow. Garrick did his best to follow, though his back and knee flared with each step up, the climb quickly winded him, and he had to support himself heavily on the trees they passed.

Halfway up the rise, Kina paused as the wind died. She tilted her head as though to listen. Then, she perked up, her eyebrows rising curiously. Abandoning stealth, she continued her climb. Garrick followed, confused.

Kina reached the top of the rise and smiled, gazing through the forest to the north. To Garrick's surprise, she called out.

"Good afternoon. Is it me you are seeking?"

Assuming the intruders presented no threat, Garrick halted his progress, leaning back against a tree trunk and panting from the exertion.

But then a familiar voice answered.

"Are you Kina Ukiel?"

Garrick's eyes widened.

It can't be.

He pushed himself off the tree and struggled to climb the last few feet until he stood beside Kina. His eyes enlarged when he saw who stood twenty paces away.

"Damian?"

It was her, unmistakably, accompanied by the Crow and three people Garrick didn't know, along with a pony loaded down with supplies.

She straightened. "Garrick?"

"What are you doing here?" he and Damian asked in unison.

At least one of Damian's companions looked like she was about to speak, but Garrick and Damian's mutual question gave everyone pause.

Kina grinned sidelong at him. "Perhaps we should go inside and we can catch up. It seems we have much of that to do."

Garrick nodded and Damian said, "Thank you." With that, they all turned toward the gully. Kina wrapped an arm around Garrick's back, supporting him on the descent. He tried not to wince at the strain on his back and knee, feeling eyes on him while he climbed. At the bottom of the gully, he pushed himself harder, limping worse with each pace before he made it back inside Kina's house. He hurried to the clay bottle of molka on the table and hastily took a pull. It was larger than he intended and he fought a cough as the large swallow burned its way down his throat. Kina stared at him as he carefully lowered onto a chair at the table. The sounds of Damian and her companions tending to the pony drifted through the open door.

A swarm of emotions swept through Garrick when Damian stepped inside. She was still beautiful and exotic with those gleaming golden eyes, her hair and gown fashionably styled. Yet the timid, deferential girl he had met in Trent nearly half a year ago, still wanting to cower beneath a veil, was gone. Now she stood tall at the front of the companions she led into Kina's house, the set of her shoulders radiating confidence.

She seemed untouchable, certainly by Garrick. His throat grew thick as he thought of the last words he had spoken to her, after they had saved Albrith and she was being held captive in the king's castle while Garrick was awarded a medal for his bravery.

There's a lot you don't know about me.

He swallowed hard as the Crow and the others filed into the common room after her. They were odd companions, the young man with patchwork skin, the tall and buxom woman, and the hunched man practically clinging to her skirts. Kina lugged a pot she had filled with water in the kitchen to the hearth, but Garrick's eyes remained on Damian.

"It's good to see you, Damian."

She smiled at him, warmly and without any hint of bitterness. "It's good to see you, too." Her smile faded. "Though I'm sorry it has to be with you in this state."

Garrick gave a wry grin and took a swig of molka. He knew he shouldn't have much, but his back was hurting worse, and his head. He braced himself with the warmth of the drink, knowing he would need to focus for this discussion.

Damian stepped closer, sizing him up. "I didn't realize Niabi hurt you so badly."

Garrick's brows drew together. "How did you know?"

The tall woman piped in. "Sir Hitchcliffe told us."

His brows tightened further. "How did *he* know?"

Kina cleared her throat as she strode back to the table. "Perhaps we should begin with introductions?"

Damian straightened. "Of course."

"Please, sit down." As Damian and her companions struggled to find seats in Kina's sparsely furnished home, she went on, "My name is Kina Ukiel. I am an explorer of ancient ruins and a collector of knowledge. Though I suspect you know that already."

Damian sat across the small table from Garrick and nodded at Kina. "Yes. Lyle—Sir Hitchcliffe—sent us here. I am Damian Sires."

Garrick nodded at Kina's unspoken question. "The same one." At the apprehensive look on Damian's face, he said, "I've been here a long time with little to do but talk."

"All good, I hope," said the tall woman. She grinned wryly, but there was a faint edge in her expression, not easily noticeable.

"Garrick has told me much of Damian's determination and sense of duty," Kina answered. "And you are?"

"Poppy Arnsley. This is Merle Flecelle. He doesn't talk much."

"I'm Rhyslen Noskopoulos. I'm here to help Damian."

Damian held out a hand to the Crow. "And this is Liam Henricksson."

Garrick had forgotten the name the mercenary had given at the meeting with the king and advisors. It didn't change his opinion of the Crow, but he tried not to let it show on his face.

"So what brings you here?" Kina asked.

Straightening, Damian took in a deep breath and faced Kina fully. "Miss Ukiel—"

"Kina," Kina cut in with a smile.

"Kina. Can you tell us anything about malakhs?"

The realization struck Garrick like a hammer.

"You want to stop Niabi."

Damian looked at him without any hint of uncertainty. "Yes."

Garrick's throat tightened. Images lodged in his mind and his back and knee seemed to ache worse with the thought. Damian lying on the ground with a vine as thick as his leg run through her, twice. Crushed beneath a rock slide. Buried in the earth, never to be seen again. Or worse, her lying broken as he had been, but with no help in sight.

And these youths accompanying her. All of them soft, none of them armed. She didn't stand a chance.

He, an Agaesi knight, couldn't protect her from the fox woman before, or from herself. And now he was helpless and she was marching against Niabi. The images in his mind wouldn't fade.

The look on her face was unwavering. She was determined to do this. And he knew he couldn't let her.

He swallowed and settled his nerves, focusing on what would make her turn back. "You don't have to do this. Stopping Niabi isn't your responsibility."

She looked thoughtful, but as determined as ever. "If I don't, no one else will."

He had to get through to her. He *had* to. "That's not true. The Army of Light is besieging our border. Niabi is an enemy to all of Hesperia."

A dark look crossed her face and she scoffed. "Nobody really believes that."

"That doesn't mean you have to risk yourself to stop her."

"I couldn't live with myself if I didn't do everything I could to try to stop her."

"The Agaesi have dispatched a force to go after her. I know they're not the only ones. They might already have succeeded, for all we know."

An apprehensive look crossed her eyes. "And if they have, then I will be glad to return to Aether, but I told you, I can't bear to just sit safe at home while she prepares for war."

Garrick almost told Damian that Niabi's crimes weren't on her head before he realized he already had. He took a pull from the bottle. It was less than half full. Why hadn't his pain faded yet? Damian was so determined to fight Niabi, when neither of them had been able to land so much as a scratch on the malakh the previous times they faced her. He carefully considered his next tactic.

"Damian, we never stood a chance against her before. Don't you remember what she did in the red forest?"

"I remember what she did in Albrith," Damian answered quietly.

"Then you should turn back now."

Kina cleared her throat and Poppy tried to say something, but

Damian didn't give either of them a chance to speak.

"I knew this before I left, Garrick. It doesn't change anything."

Garrick leaned forward, frustration hardening his tone. "You're in over your head, Damian."

"Maybe—"

"Maybe?" he cut in. *Doesn't she remember how powerful Niabi is?* "You don't even realize how overwhelmed you are. Don't do this."

She pursed her lips. "I didn't travel weeks to get here only to turn back now. I have to try."

Garrick gestured sharply at her companions. "With them as your only support? What can they even do?" Damian opened her mouth to respond, but Garrick turned a piercing gaze to Rhyslen, sitting next to her. "Have you ever gone to battle before?"

Rhyslen stammered, flustered. "Well, no, but—"

"Have you ever faced a malakh, endowed with the power of the gods?" Garrick asked Poppy.

Poppy put her hands on her hips and narrowed her eyes at Garrick. "Who has?"

"Garrick," Kina attempted, fidgeting where she stood beside him.

"What about him?" Garrick pressed, peering around Poppy at Merle. "Are you willing to lay down your life for Damian?"

"You leave him out o' this," Poppy growled.

"Garrick—" Damian attempted.

Garrick held up a hand. "These are the people you're taking to go after Niabi? You don't stand a chance."

She let out an irritated sigh. "They are stronger than you real—"

"You will die." He said it slowly, emphasizing every word.

Instead of backing down, however, Damian's eyes narrowed. "Well, it is reassuring to hear that you have such faith in me. Did you always think me completely incapable?"

Now she's twisting my words? What is wrong with her? Garrick's gaze darkened further. "That's not what I meant and you know it."

"Do I? I haven't seen any sign of the Garrick I thought I knew since Padura. I'm beginning to wonder if that Garrick was a lie."

Garrick clenched his fist and teeth, trying unsuccessfully to control his frustration. "What I'm saying is that you don't have any experience with this. Any of this. You know that this is exactly what I was trained to do, and look at what she did to me." He sat back and spread his arms, showing off his diminished form. "I couldn't even sit up for weeks. I should be dead."

"Garrick, I know that you're suffering—"

"Oh, you know?" he cut in sharply. The condescenscion jabbed at him like a needle. "Really? You know what it's like to live with pain every hour, every day for a season. You know what it's like being unable to feed or bathe yourself or use the latrine on your own."

Kina stepped closer and placed a hand on his shoulder. "Garrick, I think that's—"

"You even know how it feels breaking your leg in a way that will never heal?" Garrick continued, shaking off her touch. "Well, then I guess you don't need my help."

Rhyslen stared at Garrick in surprise and disappointment.

Poppy glared at him. "Just who do yae think—"

Damian held up a hand, stopping her objection, but a hard look was etched onto her face. "Garrick, I am sorry that you have suffered so much, but I am not turning back now. And if you will not help me—"

"I've been trying to help you from the first day we met." Garrick's fingers tightened around the bottle. Irritation overcame his desire to protect her. "Not that that has made any difference to you. Sorry for trying to save your life." He took another swig.

Kina's voice grew more forceful. "Garrick..."

Damian's eyes darkened. "I'm trying to do some good in the world. I thought you would have appreciated that. I thought that was what knights did."

Garrick's eyes widened and his jaw tightened. Slowly, he lowered the bottle to the table and faced Damian, his eyes burning.

"What knights do is keep their emotions under control. Maybe if you had done that in Padura, Nephrita never would have been released from your body."

Damian could only stare speechless at him.

"Now wait a minute—" Poppy attempted, her voice low and dangerous, but Garrick spoke over her, his eyes never moving from Damian's.

"Maybe if you had acted more like a knight, all those people she killed in Albrith and Raven Point would still be alive."

Damian flinched as if struck.

"Hey—" Rhyslen began, his gaze darkening.

"Maybe you should talk to all the people who lost someone to her hands and tell them what knights do."

With that, he shoved himself out of his chair, still hanging onto the bottle of molka, and stalked through the common room. The voices of the others rose, yells following after him, and through it, Garrick could hear Damian running through the door and outside.

Garrick didn't look back as he slipped into his room and shut the door heavily behind him.

The gazes of the others weighed on Damian like stone. She could only stare after Garrick as he marched through the common room and disappeared behind a door. The shouting voices of the others rang through her ears as incomprehensible noise as her thoughts latched onto memories of Albrith and Raven Point. The room pressed in on her, her chest tightening, and finally she threw herself out of the chair and raced out of Kina's home, ignoring the calls that followed her. She sank to her knees in the snow coating the gully, arms wrapped around herself. The bite of frozen snowflakes and hot tears ran down her face.

It's my fault. All those people…

Breathing hard, she didn't hear the crunch of approaching footfalls until they were nearly upon her. She turned to demand her solitude, but by the time she glimpsed Liam's legs, he was already kneeling beside her.

He laid a hand on her back and she leaned into him, crying in earnest. Wrapping his arms around her, he gripped her tighter than he ever had. She sank into the embrace, a wave of warmth rushing through her before the chill of her thoughts overwhelmed her again.

She didn't know how long they crouched, snow muffling the hills as she leaned against him, thoughts whirling through her mind. The guilt felt like needles sticking into her from all directions, but she focused on the sensation of Liam's strong arms holding her.

Gradually, Damian's thoughts calmed. She leaned against Liam for a while still, his embrace making her feel safe like she rarely had.

It was a while before she noticed the tremor in his arms and his ragged breath.

She leaned back, his firm grip finally relenting, and looked worriedly up at him. "Are you all right?"

His face showed most of its usual impassiveness, but his jaw was set and his eyes squinted shut. She saw a twitch in his cheek as he inhaled. "I have… not been so angry since I betrayed the Red Hawks."

Damian's eyes widened.

He held her by the arms, the touch his own for once and not initiated by Damian. Opening his eyes, Liam stared at her, his features softening slightly. "You did not deserve that."

More tears came to her eyes. The movement almost felt painful, but Damian smiled faintly. "Thank you." She dipped her chin, leaning her forehead against his breastplate. His arms slid around her once more and she savoured the warmth and comfort.

Her thoughts flitted from one topic to another as they sat there long moments more. Guilt mingled with a recollection of Lyle's words with anger at Garrick with a wish that she and Liam weren't so bundled up. She grew cold and her gown became wet from kneeling in the snow.

Finally, she raised her head and looked into Liam's eyes once more. Deep discomfort still shone in his blue eyes.

"We should go back inside."

He nodded. Together, they rose and crossed the gully back to Kina's home. Damian opened the door to find Rhyslen pacing, Poppy standing near the table, and Merle looking entirely nonplussed by the whole scene. Kina had moved deeper into the living area of the common room, sliding away from the light of the hearth. The tea pot rested on the table, forgotten. Poppy turned and Rhyslen straightened as Damian and Liam stepped inside.

"Damian," Rhyslen said, taking a couple steps closer. "Are you all right?"

Damian nodded. "Yes. I'm sorry about that."

Poppy scoffed. "There's no need for you to be apologizin'."

"I'll say," Rhyslen replied, his face darkening. "That was completely out of line."

Damian glanced around the room cautiously. She noticed a deeply uncomfortable look on Kina's face as she rubbed her arm. "Where is Garrick?"

Poppy stuck a thumb over her shoulder. "The big, fat jerk went t' his room."

Kina looked away.

Hesitating, Damian stepped around the table. "Kina? Miss Ukiel? Could I please ask you a few questions about malakhs?"

The ginger-haired adventurer raised her head. She glanced between each of her company for a moment before her eyes lingered on Damian.

"Very well. But I would like to speak with you alone."

Damian nodded, but behind her, Poppy's sharp voice rang out. "I don't think we're the—"

"Poppy," Damian snapped over her shoulder.

Poppy recoiled, blinking in surprise. She recovered just as Rhyslen nodded and said, "Of course. We'll get out of your way."

He led the way out of Kina's home. Poppy shrugged, took Merle's hand, and followed.

Liam only briefly met Damian's gaze before he turned to depart as well. In that moment, however, Damian could see the turmoil still present in his eyes.

The door shut, closing Kina's home into silence.

Damian turned. Kina still looked uncomfortable.

"I'm really sorry about all that," Damian said quietly.

Kina merely waved at the table in response. Damian took a seat as Kina approached and sat across from her. A moment of awkward silence ensued as Damian struggled to think of what to say.

Kina saved her from the dilemma, though her focus was on her clasped hands. "You are really trying to stop Niabi."

Damian braced herself, but spoke as calmly as she could. "Yes."

"You mean to kill her."

Damian swallowed. "Yes."

"With them." Kina gestured toward the door.

Damian nodded.

"But they are not warriors."

"No. Well, Liam is, but not the others."

Kina tilted her head, a prompt on her face.

Damian hesitated. It seemed unfair to them for her to reveal their secret so many times, even if she felt that she could trust Kina with it. Although, she had brought far too much unpleasantness into Kina's house not to tell the truth.

Finally, Damian replied, "They're mages."

"All of them?"

"Not Liam. But Rhyslen, Merle, and Poppy are."

"How did you find them?" Curiosity began to overtake Kina's discomfort.

"They were part of Yanuk's group. They left because they disagreed with what he was doing," Damian hastily added.

Kina seemed to ponder this for a moment. "Garrick has told me of you. Enough that I believe I understand you, even if he might not. But I would like to hear of it in your own words."

"Hear what?"

"Everything."

Damian's eyes enlarged faintly, but the look on Kina's face was steady and genuine.

So Damian told her everything. Beginning with her magic and the challenges of growing up while keeping her eyes covered at all times, she spoke of her life and her abilities, told the story of the journey in the spring that ultimately led her to stopping Yanuk's mages in Albrith, and detailed her journey since she left Aether a few weeks ago. She spoke of meeting Rhyslen, both a year ago and within the last few weeks, how they were able to find Poppy and Merle, and how she escaped from Sir Kennar. How they snuck into Misengrad, tracked down Lyle, and he led them to Kina.

All the while, Kina listened with an attentiveness Damian had not often seen. Occasionally, Kina asked questions to clarify or elaborate on something. Most of the time, however, her full focus was upon Damian, even though Damian felt she wasn't telling the best story she could.

To Damian's relief, Kina's posture relaxed as she spoke. The tension in her own shoulders faded as she realized how nice it was to be able to share so much with someone who didn't have her own bias or agenda. Kina simply enjoyed hearing the story.

"I admire your drive," Kina finally said after Damian finished. "Living a life like you have, I do not think I would be able to dedicate myself to fighting Niabi. A malakh is no ordinary foe."

Damian leaned forward. "What can you tell me about malakhs?"

"Well, as you know, a malakh's power derives from the god it serves. Niabi serves Ganodu, does she not?"

It still seemed strange to Damian that the Goddess of Life had a name. Yet, somehow, it felt more fitting now. "Yes."

"So her power will be connected to living things. Plants, animals, even the earth itself. She will have the ability to control them."

Damian nodded, though she frowned. She had enough experience with Niabi to know this already.

"A servant of Ganodu is a powerful malakh indeed," Kina continued. "Malakhs have immense strength and speed, and with abilities tied to Ganodu, Niabi's touch could have the power to bring life, or death."

A chill seemed to settle over the room. Damian shivered as she remembered when Niabi touched her in the red forest. That touch had nearly turned Damian to stone.

"But if we attack her in winter, won't she be weak?"

Kina tilted her head. "I suppose she would be at her weakest when plants are dead and animals sparse. Her connection to life may be diminished. But she still holds the power of a god. She will not be easily defeated."

Damian sighed. "I know. Is there anything else you can tell me?"

"I suppose you have encountered her more than many. Very well, then I shall tell you something almost no one knows any longer, and which will be of great interest to you.

"Malakhs are not born. They are created."

Damian straightened. "You mean, they're not… alive?"

Kina murmured uncertaintly. "Not quite like we are, but the difference is hard to notice. They bleed like us, and breathe, although I read once that they do not need to, but often, they do not need to eat. I am not certain if they sleep."

Kina paused, her gaze drifting as she looked intensely thoughtful. After a moment, she faced Damian again. "When a god or goddess wishes to create a malakh, they take an artifact of some sort and imbue it with their power. Then—although my research is incomplete here—I believe they take some materials to help craft the form of the malakh. In Niabi's case, Ganodu may have taken a fox's tail or whiskers, perhaps leaves or moss or other materials tied to life, and shaped her using them.

"But the artifact imbued with Ganodu's power, that is what holds everything together. That is the core of the malakh. Remove or break that and Niabi will perish. Well, such as it is for something that can arguably not be called living."

Damian sat back slowly. "Her… core."

"The malakh's heart, as it were. Mind, it is often made of stone, or some equally hard material. And as a malakh who serves Ganodu, Niabi is likely to be able to harden her body like stone, or at least wood."

Damian frowned deeply. "So you're telling me that I have to get close enough to Niabi to break this core when her body might be as hard as stone and I can't let her touch me?"

Kina raised her hands, palms up. "I am not a fighter. I am the last person you want to ask for help with battle. But if you want my advice, magic will be the key to defeating her."

Damian raised a tired look to Kina. "But I don't know how to make my magic work when I need to."

A knowing smile crossed Kina's face. "Is it not obvious? You are touched by Nephrita. Your magic manifests with the presence of chaos."

Damian straightened, her eyes widening. The thought had never occurred to her. So far, since Nephrita was released from Damian, her magic had merely seemed to appear when she needed it to. Her magic had protected her. As she considered it, however, she realized that it happened when she was surrounded by or faced with chaos.

Yanuk's mages attacking her in Albrith. The mob in Eldore. Sir Kennar.

She was still thinking about it as Kina stood. "And I believe I have something that can help. Come with me."

Puzzled, Damian rose and followed Kina around the table. Picking up a candle, Kina led Damian across the common room and past one closed door to another. Kina stepped into the second room and Damian followed.

Kina's bedroom was small and sparse, with a simple straw pallet and a plain, old wardrobe. The floor was cluttered with wrinkled clothes, books, and a number of strange objects Damian could hardly identify in the flickering light of the lone candle. There wasn't even a looking-glass in the room.

Kina crossed to the wardrobe and opened its doors. There was no space to hang gowns inside, only shelves of clumsily folded shirts and trousers. To Damian's surprise, Kina began pulling shelves out from the wardrobe. Damian was about to ask what Kina was doing when she saw a glint of metal appear at the back of the wardrobe, behind all the clothes. Damian stared as a sword in an ancient scabbard emerged.

When Kina had pulled out enough shelves to completely expose the sword, she straightened and held out a hand to it. Damian gave her a curious look.

"I have kept this hidden for years," Kina explained, staring at the sword. "But before I did, I saw enough of it to know that few would touch it, and those who did would hear a voice in their head, should the sword decide they were unfit to wield it. The sword never spoke to me... until recently. I believe it was telling me that it now belongs to you."

Damian blinked at Kina. "But... what is it?"

Kina turned to face Damian. "This is Vashnir, the sword of Nephrita."

Damian drew in a breath.

Kina gestured toward the sword with the candle. "If anything can help you defeat Niabi, this is it."

Cautiously, Damian stepped forward and reached into the wardrobe. She braced herself, then grabbed the sword by the scabbard. She paused for a moment, waiting to see if anything would happen, then pulled the sword out. The hilt looked in surprisingly good condition, though the scabbard was grey and cracked. Aside from the strange style of the hilt, it looked like any sword she had seen.

As the candlelight glinted off a cracked crystal embedded in the crossguard, she started.

Kina took a step closer. "Did it speak to you?"

"No," Damian said slowly. "I've seen this before."

"What? When?"

"In a vision I had. A memory… of Nephrita's." Damian shivered as she recalled the vision of the immense battle many centuries past that took over her mind over a season ago.

"Yes." Kina stared a little sadly at the sword. "This belongs to you now."

Damian turned a baffled look to her. "Surely Liam would be better suited to—"

"Vashnir chooses its wielder," Kina interrupted seriously. "Not the other way around. If the sword does not defy you, then you are its owner."

"But… how…"

"That sword has great power," Kina went on. "I unlocked I suspect only a fragment of its power by invoking the name of Veran. The Goddess of Change. I suspect with your connection to Nephrita herself that you can utilize that sword to its greatest potential."

"I…" Damian attempted, unable to believe she had to explain this. "I can't use this."

Kina grinned once more. "I never could either."

Blinking, Damian could only stare at Kina.

"However, it has use beyond a weapon. Nephrita used it as a focus for her power, and it flared with its own power when I called upon Veran. It will help you."

Damian considered the sword anew.

Kina's eyes dropped as she frowned at Damian's gown. "Now we need to do something about that flimsy dress."

Damian struggled for words, lifting a corner of the skirt. "This isn't flimsy. This is kingsweave! You couldn't cut this with a knife."

Looking up, she found Kina busily flipping over clothes from the shelves of her wardrobe strewn over the floor.

"What are you doing?"

"These should work," Kina said, tossing some garments onto the bed. Rising, she dusted her hands and smiled at Damian. "Give them a try." Then, without giving Damian a chance to respond, Kina turned and strode out of the room, closing the door behind her.

Damian blinked for a moment before her gaze fell back to the sword still in her hands. It was growing heavy.

For a long moment, all she could do was stare at the sword and the cluttered room around her. The entire situation seemed ridiculous. Speaking with Kina alone in her home, Damian felt more normal than she had anywhere else, and the rest of the world seemed far away. That alone was so unusual she didn't know what to make of it.

Me, use a sword? she thought.

Another thought answered it as quickly.

Nephrita did.

That thought didn't comfort her. It did help gradually return her focus, however. She reflected on what Lyle said to her, and what she said to him.

I will do everything I can to stop her.

She glanced back at the clothes on the bed, then once more at Vashnir.

You may have to, more than you anticipate.

Damian focused on Niabi. The encounters she had with the malakh and the destruction the fox woman had caused to Albrith. And now, an army besieging Faneria.

If I don't stop Niabi, no one will. Remember that.

She gripped the hilt in her fingers, feeling how it balanced in her hand.

Damian emerged from Kina's bedroom a while later. She put her shoulders back as Kina turned to her, but couldn't help fidgeting. She had pinned up the front of her skirt nearly at waist level and beneath it she wore close-fitting trousers lined with wool. After taking in the sleeves of her gown, she had put on a supple leather vest. Her long, auburn hair was tied into a tight braid that circled her head and Vashnir hung off her hip from an old belt.

Kina smiled appraisingly. "You look much more prepared for a fight now."

Caught somewhere between a smile and a frown, Damian could only grin wryly. It seemed that every few moments she needed to convince herself that this change was not only best, but what she needed to do. Her eyes were drawn to the closed door beside Kina's. Garrick's own doubts tried to creep into Damian's thoughts, but she pushed them back.

If I don't stop Niabi, no one else will.

Touched by Nephrita and wielding her sword. That thought made Damian straighten. It may be difficult for her to realize, but she did have great power, especially with Vashnir by her side. Now she only needed to learn how to use it.

Kina held a hand out toward the front door. "Your friends are growing impatient." As Damian glanced toward the windows at the front of Kina's underground home, she saw the light turning golden-orange. "I do not have much room, but you are welcome to stay here the night."

Damian nodded. "Thank you for all your help, Kina."

"It was my pleasure. I enjoyed hearing your story. I only have one request."

"Yes?"

"Do not share what we spoke of." She gestured toward the door. "Not to them or anyone else."

Damian was reminded of Lyle asking her to keep his secrets as well. She bowed her head. "I won't. I promise."

Kina grinned. "And if you can, please return after… after you are finished and tell me what happened." With that, she opened the door.

Damian took in a deep breath and stepped outside. Rhyslen, Poppy, and Merle sat just a few paces outside Kina's door, though they had built a fire they gathered around. All turned to Damian as she emerged.

"Damian?" Poppy said, staring at her as though she had suddenly sprouted a second head. "What happened to yae?"

Rhyslen stood, gaping alongside her. "Is that a *sword*?"

Swallowing, Damian steeled her nerves, hesitating faintly as she considered Kina's reminder not to speak to them of her history. "It's... just in case."

Glancing around, she caught sight of Liam, standing at a distance from the others. To her surprise, she found him looking at her with deep emotion in his eyes, a powerful expression of... hurt? Fear? It was still too well guarded to tell.

"But," Rhyslen attempted, "you're not planning—"

"Kina said we can stay here tonight," Damian interrupted.

"Are yae sure yae want to do that?" Poppy continued to regard Damian with shock, but there was an edge to her words.

Admittedly, Damian didn't relish the idea that Garrick might emerge before they left. The chill in the air, biting even through her layers of clothes without the cloak she left inside, made her decision.

"It'll be a lot more comfortable than out here. We'll leave first thing in the morning." She glanced at Liam once more, but caught only a brief look of his unchanged expression before he turned away.

CHAPTER 19
GUIDING LIGHTS

DAMIAN, SLEEPING NEAR the front door in Kina's home, awoke as the windows began to brighten with dawn. She sat up and looked around. The fire had long since guttered and deeper inside, the room was nearly pitch black. She made out the lumps of the others beneath their blankets nearby.

Pulling back her covers, she stood and stretched. She wished she could give them more time to rest. She wished she could sleep longer herself. With the short days, however, she knew they needed to get moving as soon as they could.

As she glanced over her companions' sleeping forms, however, she paused. On the far side of the table, she saw a dark square of bedding that was clearly unoccupied.

Liam.

Damian's breath caught in her throat. She looked around the room once more, but saw no sign of Liam. His black cloak, which had hung beside Damian's near the door, was gone.

Looking back at the blankets, and the satchel beside them, tamped down her fear. *He wouldn't have left that behind if he was going to leave. He's probably just outside.*

She slipped on her boots, then hesitated. After a moment's consideration, she buckled Vashnir around her waist. Grabbing her cloak, she crept to the door. It was unlocked. She opened it as quietly as she could and edged outside.

There he stood, not five paces outside Kina's door, his back to her. He glanced over his shoulder as Damian stepped out, then quickly faced away again.

"Liam?" she asked softly, afraid to disturb the early morning winter silence.

His hair and cloak hung still as a statue before her. His tracks in the snow moved back and forth in various directions, never more than ten paces away.

Damian approached, moving around to his side to see his face. "Liam? What's wrong?"

He merely turned to keep his back to her.

Her chest constricted as she stopped moving. *What happened?* As she lowered her gaze, she caught a sight of the new clothes she wore. She looked completely different.

Her voice fell. "It's me, isn't it?"

"No," he answered immediately, and with more force than he usually showed.

Damian started. Looking up, she found him looking over his shoulder at her again.

He let out a soft breath and repeated, gentler, "No."

"Then what is it?" She tried to move around him again. This time, he allowed it, only turning his head away as she circled around.

She gasped when she saw the shadows beneath his eyes. A line was still drawn between his brows, an echo of the emotion she saw in him the last night.

He only shook his head in response.

A frown crossed her face. Her heart ached as she recalled him holding her in the snow the previous afternoon. She wanted that again.

Maybe it's best if we don't, she thought, reflecting on her mission. She forced back the tears that gathered in her eyes at the thought.

"Are you planning to use that?"

Looking up, she found his disturbed eyes riveted on the sword at her hip.

She bit her lip. Damian wanted nothing more than to tell Liam everything, but she wouldn't break her promise to Kina.

"It's... a focus for my power. My magic."

Would Vashnir finally allow her to utilize the innate energy in spell ingredients without taking the time to cast magic the proper way? Her attempts over the past days as Rhyslen and Poppy taught her spells had failed to yield any success the way her unintentional magic discharges had.

Yet, it seemed silly to carry a blade she had no intention of using as such when a perfectly good swordsman stood before her. Kina had told her of the sword speaking to her, but to Damian, it was just dead metal. She didn't disbelieve Kina, but maybe it wasn't as bad as Kina made it out to be. It would certainly be a lot simpler, and probably more effective, for Liam to use the sword than for Damian to carry it in the hopes that it would help her use the magic she was already learning.

She drew Vashnir, the sound of the blade sliding out seeming to ring through the quiet morning. The sword looked surprisingly well-kept. Not quite new, but the blade showed no nicks, scratches, or rust and retained a polished finish.

Turning the blade around, she held out the sword hilt first to Liam. "Would you like to try it?"

His throat bobbed in a swallow and he eyed the weapon cautiously. Damian watched him curiously at the reaction, but he gave no indication of his thoughts. After a moment, he hesitantly reached out and gently took it from her.

He raised the tip, examining the blade as he wielded the sword with practised ease. As he turned the sword, Damian caught a glimpse of her reflection in the blade. Her yellow eyes widened. She hardly recognized herself. Although she dressed more effeminately than Kina, her new fashion still made her look more like a boy than a girl.

She shook off that thought as Liam swung the sword around in a circle a couple times. For a brief moment, it seemed like he could hold the sword just fine.

Then, mid-swing, he dropped it, sucking in a sharp breath and hunching over, a hand over his face.

"Liam?" Damian asked urgently, stepping closer. She reached her hands out, but stopped before touching him. The sword laying in the snow looked, again, like dead steel.

She raised her eyes, trying to peer between the fingers of his glove to look at his. "Are you all right?"

After a long moment, he straightened and lowered his hand, and his features smoothed to their usual impassiveness.

"What…" she asked quietly. "What did it do?"

He stared down at the sword.

"It… is for you to wield. Not me."

Damian blinked.

Before she could say anything else, Liam turned and strode back to Kina's home. Damian could only watch as he disappeared inside, wondering what had happened.

As silence settled over the gully once more, Damian knelt and retrieved Vashnir. It continued to act just as a sword should.

"I just hope you can do more than choose who uses you," she

muttered as she dried off the blade with her cloak.

By the time she stepped back inside, Liam had finished packing and the mages were rising. Damian helped Kina prepare a quick breakfast and then they stepped outside to get the pony ready.

"Good luck," Kina said as she let them out her door, gazing wistfully at the sword hanging on Damian's hip.

"Thank you again, Kina," Damian said as the others harnessed the pony.

"Remember," Kina added quietly so only Damian could hear, "Veran is watching. I think she would be most interested in seeing how this ends, and perhaps lending her aid."

Strangely, Damian didn't find that thought chilling as she might once have. The Goddess of Change had intervened once already, when Damian touched a fragment of an artifact imbued with her power in Trent. Damian's life had changed irrevocably as a result of that.

If she's watching, maybe she will help us.

Smiling, she nodded at Kina, then led the way across the gully and up the side, heading north. Finding Niabi would be the trickiest part now. They had decided to start with the one place they knew she had been, the part of the forest where she had attacked Garrick. Damian could only hope that they would find some clue there to where she had gone or what she was doing in Faneria.

As they reached the top of the gully and began going back through the forest the way they had come the previous day, Damian glanced at Liam. He still seemed to be avoiding her. The thought made her heart constrict.

Other thoughts swirled through Damian's head as they walked, though she spoke little. The forest was barren, the ankle-deep snow making the trees look more uniform, the trail less obvious. Their tracks from their journey the previous day were the sole indicators of their path. The only signs of life were deer or rabbit prints in the snow. Silence hung heavily over the land under the blanket of snow and Damian relished the solitude.

The sun rose quickly and they didn't stop for a break until dinnertime. Rather than retrieve something to eat from the pony's baskets, however, she stepped aside and wrapped her fingers around Vashnir. A shudder rippled up her arm.

This is Nephrita's sword. The same one she used in that vision I had. This blade cut down dozens of warriors in but a few blows... and who knows how many others before that.

Damian swallowed hard.

It's just a tool. It belongs to me now.

She drew the sword. From her satchel, she pulled out the bead of carnelian she had been using to practice the fire-making spell. Clutching the carnelian in one hand and Vashnir in the other, she tried to focus on the energy within the stone.

Movement from the corner of her eye caught her attention. Turning, she noticed Liam across the clearing, distinctly moving away from her.

What did I do? she thought, tears welling in her eyes. Liam had said she hadn't done anything, but he had changed since she walked out of Kina's home dressed in trousers and with Vashnir hanging off her belt.

She drew in a shuddering breath, shutting her eyes. *I have to focus on Niabi. I can ask him what's going on after she's gone.*

Reluctantly facing away from him, she sat on a fallen log and focused once more on the carnelian. Rhyslen and Poppy had been teaching her the fundamentals of how magic worked. Even Merle had chimed in with a surprisingly detailed and technical explanation of how etherea was in everything, which types of objects held specific types of power, and how even the language used to conjure magic was not a direct link to the power itself, but used more as a focus for the mage to cast a spell. However, they'd still failed to unlock Damian's own power, the kind she had tapped into against Yanuk and against the people of Eldore, and which Kina was convinced she still held. Perhaps with the aid of Vashnir, she could use that same magic from the stone with the speed of her own power.

She had yet to achieve any success when Rhyslen stepped close and said, "The pony's had enough rest and food, I think. Should we get going?"

Nodding, she sheathed her sword and slipped the stone away.

Damian followed Rhyslen back to the others. Hunger now gnawed at her stomach, but she didn't pause as Poppy and Merle stood, the baskets strapped to the pony once more, and they began making their way through the forest again. She reached into the pony's baskets and stuffed down a quick meal as she walked, focusing once more on trying to find the site of Garrick's fight with Niabi.

The scenery constantly changed around them, making Damian feel as though they travelled far that day, though she knew that wasn't true. Slowed by manoevring the horse between the trees and over uneven terrain, and with their unfamiliarity with the unmarked area, it took them far longer to reach their destination than Kina suggested.

An exhausting evening followed, spent split between learning spells with Rhyslen and Poppy and attempting to use Vashnir as a focus for her power, before they settled in for a long, cold night. The following morning, they awoke early and continued.

Shortly after dinnertime, they found it.

"Are yae sure this is it?" Poppy asked as she looked around. With the short cliff face to their left, a steeply rising hill to the right, and more hills ahead with what could be a path winding around the corner of the cliff face, the area looked much the same as the rest of the forest they had gone through.

"It's exactly as Kina described, and look." Damian pointed toward the cliff wall near where it rounded a bend to the left. The cliff face was fairly vertical, except for one incongruous spur of stone about as thick as Damian's waist jutting out about two paces. "That's the part that Kina said looked different when she found Garrick here." She glanced around.

"So what are we looking for?" Rhyslen asked.

Damian shook her head. "I'm not sure. Just see if you can find any traces of Niabi's passing, any clue at all."

She began walking around, beginning at the strange outcropping of stone, eyes passing all around as she studied everything in sight. The others did the same in different areas. She examined the trees and the rock face, both looking up close and trying to take in the entire scene as she gradually made her way around in a circle.

No signs of Niabi or the fight presented themselves. Damian continued looking around, but her spirits fell as she thought she had no way of finding out where the fox woman had gone.

Then, after climbing atop the cliff face, she looked down and noticed Liam. He was halfway up the hill across from the cliff, bent down and digging out snow and even the dried leaves beneath it.

Curiously, she descended the cliff again and approached. By the time she reached him, he had unearthed a span of ground larger than him. He knelt at its center, one glove off as he carefully touched the hard-packed earth.

"What is it?" she asked as she drew close. She heard the others approach behind her.

He gestured around the edges of the patch of ground he had cleared. "There is an indentation in the ground here." Then he pointed at the centre. "It is a little deeper in the middle, and I believe…" Shutting his eyes, he ran his fingers over the area he was inspecting before. "…there is an impression of mail here." He looked up at her, replacing his glove. "I believe this is where Sir Magni fell, and where Kina found him."

Damian's eyes widened as she stared down at the patch of ground he had uncovered. It was an uneven circle nearly four paces across, smashed flat as if an enormous fist had struck it.

"Stars above," Poppy uttered. "How could 'e do that?"

"How did he even survive it?" Rhyslen added.

Damian could only stare at the indentation, at a loss for words. Broken, dried vines and abnormally long grass lay on either side of the slightly deeper pit in the middle, and she began to get an idea of what Niabi must have done to Garrick. Damian had seen him perform inhuman feats, but she couldn't imagine how he could have flattened the ground so much and lived.

And Niabi still beat him, she thought uncontrollably.

Suddenly, a rhythmic tapping rang out through the woods.

Poppy raised her head as the strange pattern repeated itself. "That's Merle. I think 'e found something."

Damian followed as Poppy made her way down the hill, followed by Rhyslen and Liam. Around the corner, they found Merle, holding a rock that he banged in the regular rhythm against the cliff face. He stopped as everyone appeared and pointed with a grunt. Just across the path from where he stood, strange shapes jutted out of the ground, around which the snow had been cleared.

Damian cautiously approached. Even from several paces away, she could see what looked like bones poking through dried flesh.

As she came close, she put a gloved hand over her mouth and had to suppress a gag. Merle clearly had no problem with the sight, as the snow was carefully removed around it and it lay exposed to the cold autumn air.

It was definitely human remains on the ground. Animals had gotten to it, some parts of the body separated from others and little flesh remaining over the bones. Damian could spend only a moment looking at the skull before turning away. There was no way of identifying who it might have been.

At least, she thought as much until Rhyslen gasped.

"Poppy," he exclaimed.

Damian followed his eyes to find him pointing down at a few bones separated slightly from the rest of the remains. Following its path back to the shoulder blade lying in between, she surmised that he examined arm bones.

As Poppy strode over and looked closely at the arm bones, she drew in a breath and uttered, "Oh no…"

Frowning, Damian followed them and looked at the bones. There was no sign of a hand anywhere, and the forearm bones were fused together and ended a finger's length past the elbow.

Damian gave them a cautious look. "Maybe animals got to it?"

Poppy shook her head, her eyes fixed on the bones. "That's not broken. It was like that when 'e was alive."

Damian raised her head in surprise. Rhyslen trembled, and she realized that it was from anger.

"You knew him?" she asked quietly.

Poppy nodded, looking weary. "With an arm like that, it has to be Artra. 'E was one of Yanuk's mages. One of our friends."

A stab of pity shot through Damian, and she opened her mouth to offer her sympathy, but Rhyslen spoke over her, still staring at the remains.

"How *dare* she," he snapped, his voice ringing through the empty woods. "What did he ever do to her?"

"Rhyslen," Damian attempted.

He stabbed a finger toward the remains, turning his hard look upon her. "This. *This* is why we had to live in hiding, why we still have to hide. The Gods of Light and the people who follow them see us like bugs, like some kind of infestation. They think anything we suffer is justified. Artra never did anything to anyone, we were the only ones to give him a chance, and this is what he got for wanting a better life."

Poppy straightened, putting her shoulders back. "'E's right. I'm sick o' bullies like her decidin' our fate."

"She's going to pay for this," Rhyslen growled. "For all of it."

Damian smiled faintly, heartened by their determination.

Poppy, on the other hand, frowned. "How are we goin' to find 'er, though? I don't see anythin' here that shows where she went after this."

Damian turned to Liam hopefully, but he only shook his head. She averted her eyes. Even if the ground wasn't covered in snow, most of a season had passed since this fight, and Niabi left no traces of her passing. Despair crept in at the edges of her mind.

A glint of light some thirty paces away caught her eye.

Turning, Damian peered at it curiously, wondering if it was something metal reflecting the sun. At least, she did until it drifted to the side and into the shadow of a tree without diminishing. Then, she noticed another fleck of light a few paces away from it.

Her eyes enlarged. "Sprites!"

"Say again?" Poppy replied.

Damian took a couple steps forward. A handful of sprites were visible, spread throughout the forest as far as she could see, all of them drifting gently westward.

She spun to face the others. "Sprites appeared every time Niabi did. They're drawn to her. If we follow them, they might lead us to her!"

A skeptical look crossed Rhyslen's patchwork face. "That seems like a stretch…"

Damian shook her head. "It's all we have. And look." She turned, gesturing to the sprites. All of them flowed slowly in the same direction, as though riding a current. "They're all going the same way. It has to mean something." Hesitating, she glanced at the others. "If you have any better ideas, I'd love to hear them. But this…" She watched the sprites once more. "I have a feeling they're following Niabi."

A moment of silence fell over the woods.

Finally, Poppy shrugged. "Well, like yae said, it's the best idea we got. We might as well take a chance."

Rhyslen nodded. "You're right. It's better than nothing."

Damian smiled. "All right. Let's go."

By the time Garrick awoke, Kina's house was silent. He had heard some movement as he dozed through the morning, but now, all he could hear was Kina shuffling about in the common room and kitchen. Garrick lay for long minutes staring into the room. His mangled armour, broken voulge, crumpled spare clothes, and saddle bags were piled up in the corner. The empty clay bottle lay near it where it had rolled after he dropped it the night before. Bile rose in the back of his swollen throat, and it had little to do with the molka.

Kina's footfalls retreated in the direction of her bedroom. Wincing, Garrick slowly rose from the bed, his entire body stiff and head throbbing. He limped across the floor and opened the door. The common room looked like it had the entire time he had been here. There was no sign that anyone else had come.

He hobbled across the common room, past the armchairs and hearth and the table, and stepped out the front door.

Blinding, hazy light assaulted him the moment he opened the door, along with a bite of cold in the air. He shut the door behind him, swaying as he tried to keep his balance while keeping most of his weight off his left leg.

It was earlier than he realized. The sun was a blinding orb shining through the grey-white veil of the sky and web of barren trees. The cold seeped into Garrick, but he ignored it. His shoulders sagged and he let out a sigh.

A nicker broke the still morning air in response.

Garrick lifted his head. Brenadier approached, bobbing his head in greeting. Garrick's expression fell at the sight. The magnificent horse wanted to gallop again, Garrick could see it in the toss of his head. Brenadier's long mane and tail were tangled, his hooves in need of trimming, and he was thinner than Garrick remembered. The blanket Kina had covered him with had fallen off.

Garrick edged away as Brenadier drew close and nuzzled his side. The touch of the horse's leathery nose felt like daggers in his sides. He tried to push Brenadier back, but the stallion persisted.

Frustrated, Garrick reached down and tore the hobbles off Brenadier's legs, then pushed the stallion's head away.

"Go on!" He waved the horse off, but Brenadier only retreated a pace and stared at him, ears pricked up.

"Get out of here!" Stepping forward, Garrick tried to shove the stallion away. Brenadier snorted and gave a warning nip in the direction of Garrick's fingers, but once again, moved just out of reach and stopped.

"Why won't you run?" Garrick snapped.

"Because he remains devoted to you," Kina's voice came behind him, "even if you feel unworthy of it." Garrick straightened as Kina stepped around him and touched the agitated horse on the neck. "And likely he knows that he would not survive in the wild."

A heavy weight settled in Garrick's stomach. He let out a sigh and bowed his head.

"I'm sorry." He couldn't face Kina as she led Brenadier toward the lean-to where the horse slept, gathering the hobbles and fallen blanket along the way.

Garrick rubbed roughly at his eyes. "I made an ass of myself yesterday, didn't I?"

There was a brief pause before Kina said, "If you do not remember, perhaps it is best if I do not say."

"I remember enough." The conversation yesterday was fuzzy in his mind and he remembered being too frustrated to take in Damian's reactions, but he could recall the look on her face. It made his insides twist.

"I can't believe I did that."

Kina approached cautiously after getting Brenadier safely

beneath the lean-to. "Do you truly believe Damian stands no chance of defeating Niabi?"

He frowned. "No."

Kina looked him in the eye. "Then why did you try so hard to make her turn back?"

His shoulders sagged. "I just didn't want her to get hurt."

The look on Damian's face etched into his mind. His throat tightened and the air felt colder.

Idiot. I hurt her more than anything Niabi could do to her.

He remembered the way she looked when she walked in the door yesterday. The way she smiled at him. His legs and his entire body felt weak and trembled.

After everything I've done to her, she was still willing to forgive me.

His voice cracked as his chest tightened. "Gods, I'm such a jerk."

He covered his eyes and wept. He felt Kina's hand on his shoulder before she leaned close and wrapped her arms around him. He embraced her and leaned his head into her shoulder, trying and failing not to grab her too tightly. The snow absorbed the sounds, making his choked noises seem empty and isolated.

Gradually, Garrick calmed down. He wiped his eyes as he straightened and attempted a wry smile. "Well, you've seen me at my worst, in every possible way."

Kina smiled. "If this is you at your worst, then you are a much better man than many I have met."

Garrick looked at her. The sight of that crafty smile upon her face was like a ray of light brighter than the pale, distant sun, an image so comforting it ached.

He reached out, taking her hand. "Thank you, for everything. I owe you more than I could ever repay."

She placed her other hand on his. "You owe me nothing except perhaps one of those cinnamon flip-pockets you love so much. You have given me some of the most interesting stories I have ever heard, little say some of the best conversations and a wealth of useful information. That more than makes up for those weeks caring for you."

His heart quickened. "Kina... come back to Misengrad with me."

She blinked. "Would the Agaesi not take issue with you bringing a stranger to their secluded home?"

"I don't care what they think. I don't care what anyone thinks anymore. I've finally found somebody with whom I can just be myself. And I don't ever want to lose that. I don't want to go back to Misengrad alone."

She moved closer, lifting a hand to touch his cheek. "Then do not." She reached up, her eyes closing. He leaned down, each wrapping their arms around the other, and kissed.

And for the first time, it felt completely natural.

Chapter 20
Eyes Opening

Firelight flickered along the smooth blade of Vashnir and against the cracked crystal in its crossguard. Damian watched the light glint against the ancient steel, the forest so dark and silent around her as to not exist at all. Only the sounds of her companions snoring or stirring in their sleep beneath their shelters broke the enormous stillness. Sprites still shone silently, either drifting aimlessly through the forest or hovering nearby.

Damian paid attention to none of it as she focused on the blade she held before her.

Chaos, she thought. *What is chaos? Disorder. Randomness. Unpredictability.*

It didn't sound so bad that way. After all, what was the alternative? Stagnation? Predictability?

Chaos is part of change. The unknown and the uncertain. The new and the strange. Disorder.

Chaos is all around us. Not just riots in towns or people attacking other people. Any interaction with someone is unknowable, unpredictable. Even the forest around me is chaotic. There is no order to the way the trees and plants grow. They are at the mercy of the weather and the terrain, neither of which can be controlled.

Chaos is everywhere. It is within me. She gripped the hilt of the sword tighter, her leather gloves creaking. *And it can be beautiful.*

Shutting her eyes, she focused on thoughts of chaos. She tried to reach for the spark of power she had felt when she faced Yanuk during the Battle of Albrith, and when Sir Kennar was overwhelmed in Eldore. She imagined her power reaching toward the sword in her hands, connecting with it, unlocking it.

After a long moment, she opened her eyes.

The sword was unchanged.

With a sigh, she lowered the blade. *If I can't figure out how to use this sword's power, then it will be dead weight in my arms.* Niabi was bigger, stronger, and faster than Damian, she would not be using a sword, and she had her additional control over living things. Vashnir was becoming more comfortable in Damian's arms and grip, but she held no illusions that she could ever use it in battle against a malakh.

But she had to do something.

There must be a reason this sword came to me.

She reflected on what Kina had said about her utilizing its hidden power. Damian raised the flat of the blade close to her face.

"Veran," she uttered. "Goddess of Change. Please show me how to use this sword. I need to stop Niabi. I have to keep the Army of Light from running through Faneria. If I can use the power within this sword, I am sure I can do it." Her thoughts drifted back to the Temple of Time in Trent, where she had touched a fragment of an artifact imbued with Veran's power. It seemed like a nightmare now, when Damian's own power had flowed out of her strongly enough to knock down the entire temple. "I… I think you chose me. Maybe not for this specifically, but I felt your touch that day. Please, help me now and show me how I can beat Niabi."

Closing her eyes again, Damian tried to feel for any change in the sword or in her, any indication that the sword was reacting to what she said or invoked.

After another long moment, she opened her eyes again. The sword was still unchanged.

Frowning, she slid the sword away in its old scabbard. She wouldn't give up trying to unlock the blade's power, but she could only hope that her magic would appear as it had since Nephrita was separated from her: when she needed it to.

She gave no indication of her thoughts when she roused Rhyslen for his watch and disappeared inside the smaller shelter where Poppy slept.

They continued following the sprites as they had over the previous days. Damian had veered south while they made their way west until they found where the forest ended at open farmland a few miles from the road. They stayed near the trees in case of any need for a quick escape, but she preferred to travel outside of them, as they moved much quicker than they did through the thick, rocky wood. The sprites led them on at their lazy pace, appearing and disappearing at times, particularly when they were out in the open. After several days of travel, however, they had nearly crossed half of Hesperia, and they would need to catch Niabi soon before she could escape back into Edan.

Most of a week after leaving Kina's home, Damian stopped them for dinner along the edge of the forest near a half-frozen stream. No one could be seen and no tracks except animal prints marked the smooth blanket of snow over the fields to the south. The naked branches of the trees reached skeletal fingers toward the overcast sky.

They ate in silence, few of them looking at each other. The mood of the group had become sombre as they tracked down Niabi. Rhyslen, Poppy, and Merle often spent breaks studying or refreshing their minds of spells as best they could, seeming to focus on any that would help them against Niabi. No one said anything, but Damian thought she could feel the worry, even dread, taking over their minds as they drew closer to catching the fox woman. Damian refused to bring it up or even entertain the thoughts that scratched at the edges of her mind, the ones that told her they weren't enough.

She should be training with Vashnir, she knew, but the travel exhausted her, and she was eager to move on as quickly as possible after stopping to eat and rest the pony. Those dark thoughts she refused to acknowledge also told her that it didn't matter how much she trained in a few days, she wouldn't be skilled enough to defeat Niabi, but she forcefully pushed them aside.

Suddenly, Liam straightened and stared back into the forest, as rigid as a deer alarmed by a sudden noise. The movement drew everyone's attention.

"Liam?" Damian asked. "What is it?" She hadn't heard or seen anything, but his attention didn't waver.

Without moving his eyes from whatever had caught his interest, he dropped the rest of his food in the snow and stood, quietly drawing his sword. Half crouching, he crept through the snow as softly as he could back toward the trees.

"What did you hear?" Damian attempted and began to stand. Liam forcefully held up his free hand, gesturing them to stay, and slipped between the trees. Damian's brow creased and she glanced between the others uncertainly.

Rhyslen swiftly dug in his bag. "I'll follow him." Leaning over his hand, he uttered the incantation for the unseeing spell and rose to jog through the snow after Liam.

Damian waited uncomfortably, unable to eat while she watched the area where they vanished.

"I'm sure it's nothin'," Poppy said, though her tone was far from reassuring.

Damian was about to ask Poppy to help her recite the unseeing spell when a sharp whistle cut through the air from the forest.

Damian threw herself to her feet. "Stay here," she told Poppy and Merle and swiftly ran through the forest where Liam and Rhyslen had disappeared.

She didn't travel far before she saw Liam's large frame, Rhyslen crouching beside him as they stared at the base of a tree that hid the source of their interest from her. When Damian came around the tree, she gasped.

A woman sat against the roots of the tree. Short, dark hair framed an ashen face nearly as pale as the snow. Her angular features and dark clothes looked unlike anything Damian had seen before. She panted shallowly and clutched at her side, though her sharp blue eyes faced them all defiantly. A crossbow lay in the snow where it had clearly been tossed from her hands, and Liam held his sword at the ready as he stood over her.

"She seems to have been following us," Rhyslen said, "but I don't know why. She hasn't said anything yet."

"She has not been following us for long," Liam added.

Damian blinked at him, then faced the woman again. "Who are you?"

The woman's nose wrinkled, but she didn't answer.

Damian lowered her gaze to where the woman held her side. "You're hurt." She tried to reach out, but the woman pressed herself back into the tree with a hiss.

Rhyslen put a hand on Damian's shoulder. "I wouldn't get too close. I'm sure she has more weapons on her."

Frowning, she sat back, absently shaking off his touch.

"What should we do with her?" Rhyslen asked.

For the first time, the woman spoke. "I not being captive."

"We don't want to take you captive," Damian answered.

The woman nodded resolutely. "Then you killing me."

"No," Damian exclaimed.

"Damian, we can't just let her go," Rhyslen said.

Damian focused on the woman instead. "Why were you following us?"

The woman still didn't respond.

Damian's eyes drifted to the crossbow lying in the snow. "Were you trying to kill us?"

The blue eyes flicked briefly over to her. "If I needing to."

"Why would you need to?"

The woman turned her face away. From the side, her pallor was even more obvious.

"Let's just leave her," Rhyslen said. "She's not going to be causing us any trouble the way she is. We've got to keep moving."

"She might not be alone," Liam replied. "She could bring more to us."

Damian merely stared down at the woman. Part of her knew they should just leave the woman. They didn't know anything about her, and even if it hadn't been her intention, she had been following them. As Damian continued staring at the woman, however, she found herself wanting to help.

She's in a lot of pain, Damian thought.

Ignoring the warnings of the men, Damian stepped forward and knelt before the woman. "What's your name?"

The woman continued staring to the side, saying nothing.

"My name is Damian Sires."

Damian caught a brief glimpse of a flat look on the woman's face as she turned. Then, when she saw Damian's eyes up close, she gasped and leaned her head back, eyes going wide.

"It's all right," Damian quickly said, holding up a hand. "We don't want to hurt you." After a moment, as the woman's eyes flicked over Damian's body and back to her yellow eyes, she tried again, "What's your name?"

The woman's eyes and brow twitched as different expressions raced across her face. Then, she swallowed and said, "Ais Ainlan."

Damian smiled. "Ais Ainlan?" she repeated, trying to match the pronunciation.

She said nothing.

"Can I ask why you were following us, Ais Ainlan?"

Ais Ainlan's eyes darted between Liam and Rhyslen before she looked away. "Not here for you." Before Damian could respond, she asked, "Who are you?"

Damian took in a breath. "You may have heard of me as the witch from the Battle of Albrith."

Confusion took over Ais Ainlan's features. She shifted, but then sucked in a breath and bent over, a pained grimace crossing her face.

Damian reached forward, stopping short of touching Ais Ainlan. "Please, let me help you."

"Damian," Rhyslen warned, and Liam took a step closer.

Ais Ainlan hissed toward them, but clearly, she had no real fight left. Her teeth gritted and her eyes squinted shut as her fingers trembled, though she didn't grip her side any tighter.

After a moment, Damian reached closer. Ais Ainlan's eyes shot open as Damian touched her fingers, but didn't resist as Damian pulled her hand away from her injured side. She clutched just below her arm, and Damian wondered if she had broken or cracked ribs.

Reaching out with her other hand, Damian touched her gloved fingertips to Ais Ainlan's side. She shut her eyes.

Chaos.

If I can create disorder, I must be able to remove it.

She tried to reach her senses into Ais Ainlan's body. She thought she felt where something was wrong, something against the natural order. Squinting harder, she tried to push her own power into Ais Ainlan, focusing on the problem, the disorder.

A strange shudder rippled through her. Ais Ainlan gasped in a pained breath. Damian's strength gave out and she fell backwards, barely caught by Liam's free hand before her head hit the snowy ground. She blinked as she focused on Ais Ainlan.

The woman stood beside the tree she had been lying against. Rhyslen had moved around her and watched her warily, a dagger clutched in his hand, but she paid him no attention. Ais Ainlan's eyes remained wide as she drew in successively deeper breaths. She finally sucked in a huge breath, her chest expanding as she straightened. Then, she felt at her side, her brows knitted expectantly, but she showed no signs of pain.

She turned her incredulous look on Damian. "Who are you?"

Damian struggled to her feet with Liam's help and managed not to sway as she stood before the taller woman. "I have been touched by the Goddess of Chaos." She gestured at Liam and Rhyslen. "And we are here to stop the malakh Niabi."

Forest now surrounded the warriors as they continued making their way west. Ashik strode near the front of the group, the rest spread out between the trees as they picked over the snow-coated ground. Now and then, he caught a glimpse of tracks in the snow that drew him onward. Bare feet larger than his boots, with depressions of paw pads beneath the toes, accompanied occasionally by brushes of snow where a gown disturbed it. The tracks did not often cross their path, as they trod north of the malakh's trail so that they could set up an ambush once they caught up to her. However, he was not the only one who straightened and marched harder when he did catch sight of her tracks.

Over a week had passed since they left the ravine behind in pursuit of the malakh. Most of the warriors' injuries had healed, and though they didn't have a battle plan for when they would reach the malakh, they all remained focused on their mission.

Too much so, perhaps. One of them often had to remind the others when to stop and rest. Ashik immediately thought that was the problem when Ialla laid a hand on his arm, and he turned to apologize. When he faced her, however, he found instead a startled look on her face. She had stopped in her tracks.

"It's here," she uttered.

"What is?" Ashik asked quietly as the warriors following them closed in, watching Ialla curiously or cautiously.

Ialla turned wide eyes to Ashik. "The thing I sensed in the *shikar*. It's nearly upon us."

"What does she speak of?" asked a Rturan as he approached. The scouts did not range as far as they had before they encountered the malakh, but even they drew in as the group came to a halt in the woods.

"Ialla sensed something else in the spirit realm at the ravine," Ashik explained. "It is close now."

Huathl's eyes narrowed. "What thing?"

"Is it dangerous?" asked a Makil.

Ashik glanced quickly over the group. He spotted most of the warriors, except... "Where is Ais Ainlan?"

Heads swivelled around as people tried to spot the missing Rturan woman. Murmurs rose, until Masa hushed them.

As soon as the voices fell silent, the sounds of a group of people crunching through the snow nearby rang clearly through the trees.

Masa swiftly drew her scimitar and shield as she turned to face the sounds, and the other warriors followed suit. Ashik could just make out movement between the trees some fifty paces away.

"Hold," called a voice. Ais Ainlan.

Ashik stepped around the warriors, holding up a hand as he peered into the woods. A dark shadow seemed to shroud the group that approached.

"Ais Ainlan?" he called out. "What's going on?"

The Rturan emerged from between the trees, and Ashik was surprised to find a faint rosy colour to her cheeks that had not been there for the past several days. Whatever had happened, it must have affected her far worse than she let on.

She stopped as she came within ten paces of the warriors, some of whom relaxed their stances and lowered their weapons at the sight of her casual posture.

She fixed her eyes on Ashik. "I finding someone we needing meet."

Another figure stepped out from behind Ais Ainlan, cloaked in the shadows that seemed to follow her. Ashik's eyes widened and gasps and exclamations rang out from the assembled warriors.

A woman stood beside Ais Ainlan, her eyes gleaming gold like the summer moon. Shadows glimmering with motes of light billowed behind her like clouds, as though the night sky draped about her.

Ko, Ashik thought in wonder as he stared at her.

As he blinked, however, the shadows seemed to recede and the flakes of snow hovering about her in the breeze gradually drifted back to the earth. He took in her auburn hair, braided tightly against her head, and her skin, nearly as fair as the Rturans', and yet he couldn't quite shake the feeling that had come over him.

"Who are you?" he asked, unable to entirely keep a tremor from his voice.

"My name is Damian Sires," she answered. A handful of other people, with a laden pony, emerged from the forest behind her. "And Ais Ainlan tells me you hunt the malakh Niabi."

Murmurs rippled among the warriors. Ashik stared at Ais Ainlan in surprise. The Rturan woman stood at ease beside Damian, her expression stoic, yet Ashik could see something in her eyes. *Is that awe?* Damian must have done something very impressive to earn her confidence.

"Yes," Ashik answered.

"Do you mean to say," Masa ventured, still holding her bare scimitar, "dat you are hunting her as well?" Her eyes flicked back and forth between Damian and the large, black-cloaked man standing just behind her. Ashik's eyes enlarged as he realized these were the same people they nearly attacked back in the foothills of the mountains, though there had been some changes to the group since.

"Yes," Damian replied. She swept her gaze over all the warriors. "And I think we all stand a much greater chance of defeating her if we work together."

Another round of murmurs circled. Ashik looked around. There was a lot of uncertainty among the warriors, but little open hostility to the suggestion. He also noticed many of the warriors showing the same sense of startled wonder that he felt when Damian appeared.

"I think," Ashik said slowly, "that we need to discuss this."

Damian nodded, seemingly unmoved by the reactions she created. "I understand, but perhaps we can talk while we travel? We need to catch Niabi before she leaves Faneria."

Ashik glanced over the warriors once more, many of whom nodded or agreed. "Very well." Weapons were sheathed or lowered. "Scouts, resume positions. Let's go."

The scouts, including Ais Ainlan, swiftly melted into the trees as they moved ahead of everyone else. Damian gestured her companions forward. They kept to the edges of the group, aside from Damian herself, who strode to the front beside Ashik, and they all began moving west again.

"My name is Ashik."

Damian nodded. "It's nice to meet you, Ashik. Are you the leader of your people?"

"No, no, no," he answered quickly. He let out a sigh. "Our leader was killed by the malakh."

Damian's eyes widened. "So you fought her already?"

"Yes, though it did not go so well for us."

As they trekked through the forest, they shared their stories and introduced their companions. Ashik was amazed by her history with the malakh, as well as the Goddess of Chaos, and the serendipity of their groups coming together. Aside from the extraordinary things that had happened to and with her, however, he was also stunned that the so-called witch from the Battle of Albrith was so… normal. From everything he had heard about her, he had supposed she had to be one of the exiled mages who had attacked the city, or hid some other dramatic, mysterious upbringing. The truth couldn't have surprised him more.

"So are your family mages, then?" he asked.

She shook her head. "My father is a cloth merchant. I used to help him with his trade journey across Faneria."

Ashik's ears pricked up. "Really?" Damian seemed surprised at his interest until he smiled and explained, "I'm a trader."

She perked up then. "You are?"

"Yes. I spent almost ten years travelling through the free lands, learning cultures and languages and establishing trade between different peoples. That's why I was chosen to accompany this mission." He gestured at the warriors following them. "I know these peoples and speak most of their languages, and I've travelled into

Faneria many times. I was chosen to translate and guide them."

Damian glanced over the warriors. "They all look so… different. You must have done a very good job."

He followed her eyes, taking in the surviving Makils, Kathecs, and Rturans. "I suppose, though I haven't done much. I just try to get them to talk to each other."

"That's no small feat." A distant look crossed her face. "It seems to me one of the most important, and hardest, things to do is just to get people to listen."

Ashik faced ahead thoughtfully. "I suppose so."

Their conversation lapsed to silence, and after a while, Ashik fell back into the group he led. He found himself walking beside Masa.

"So," she prompted quietly, "what have you learned?"

"She is," Ashik answered, considering, "surprisingly open and honest. I think her intentions are true. She seems to feel somewhat responsible for the malakh, and she is dedicated to stopping her. Enough that she is willing to trust us."

"But do you t'ink she can be trusted?" There wasn't nearly the amount of suspicion in her voice as Ashik would expect. He wondered if she had seen the same strange vision as he had when Damian appeared.

He shrugged. "As I said, she is dedicated to stopping the malakh. That's why she approached us. I don't see any reason why she would be deceitful in a way that would harm us."

Masa nodded slowly. "I agree. Next week, she may be an enemy, but today, she is a powerful ally." A sad look crossed her face as she flicked her eyes over the diminished group around them. "And I t'ink we will need dat if we hope to kill de fox-headed woman."

Frowning, Ashik nodded in return.

Huathl was a little less accepting. "Who is this westerner, thinking she join us like old friends?"

Shaking his head, Ashik replied, "I don't think she means to be presumptuous. She's just trying to stop the malakh, like we are. Why shouldn't we join up with her when we are out to do the same thing?"

The eagle warrior looked sour. "We know nothing of her."

Ashik considered his response. He wasn't certain why, but he trusted Damian, and he wanted the warriors to trust her. As he had said, it would be foolish not to accept the help she offered when she was out to do the exact same thing they were. However, Huathl wouldn't put much stock in the trust Damian had placed in them, or in what she had told Ashik. Huathl wanted to know that they weren't adding a burden to their group.

"Of the stories I heard about the Battle of Albrith," he said, "aside from the Goddess of Chaos and the fox-headed woman, the most tales were told of an extraordinary girl with uncanny power, who helped to stop the mages attacking the city. Damian is her."

The Kathec's eyebrows crawled high up his forehead as he turned to Ashik. "Truly?"

Ashik nodded. "Do you remember when we encountered her group in the mountains? She is the one the dragon knight was guarding. And she still managed to escape from him."

Huathl straightened, his beady eyes going wide. "That… small girl managed to defeat the special knight?"

Smiling conspiratorially, Ashik nodded again. "Her power comes from the touch of a god."

Huathl looked toward Damian again, still looking surprised. He murmured curiously. "Maybe we can give her chance after all."

Gratefully, Ashik left Huathl to his thoughts and moved on to another of the warriors.

The snow kept the forest bright enough to see well after the sun set, and all pushed on with the same urgent need to catch up to the malakh. Eventually, Damian called a halt. Shelters were assembled, fires were lit, animals were tended, and food was prepared.

When everyone had settled down to eat, Damian stood. Voices fell silent as she looked over everyone.

"I want to thank all of you for agreeing to join forces. As much as it pains me that my own countrymen won't support me, I'm heartened to have found all of you. Your strength, together with our magic, will defeat Niabi." Her gaze intensified. "*If* we are all willing to work together. I know this is hard for a lot of us. There has been a lot of distrust and suspicion among many of us for many years, but that divisiveness is exactly what the Gods of Light want. It's what they've fostered, not only among Fanerians, but with your people as well, by demonizing you in the eyes of their followers. For centuries, the Gods of Light have taught that different is dangerous, different is not to be trusted, but I've seen the truth. Different is dangerous for *them*. But us? We are more alike than we are not.

"We are all people. We all have families. People we love. Homes we want to protect. Beliefs worth fighting for. And for us, I think those things are more similar than we know.

"We all know that the Gods of Light don't care about us. Niabi has no love for the life she claims to serve. Her only loyalty is to her uncaring masters, and there is no evil she won't inflict to ensure their prosperity."

Nods and grumbles of agreement rippled among the warriors. Ashik suspected he wasn't the only one reflecting darkly on the shrivelled remains of the warriors tied to the trees.

"Niabi has spread her cruelty for too long," Damian continued, her voice rising as murmurs escalated. "She is beyond redemption, and if I have to be the judge of that, then so be it. I won't let her torment people any longer. I won't let her continue this path of destruction through my home." She hesitated, but seemed to galvanize herself for her next statement.

"Niabi needs to die."

More murmurs and nods spread through the group.

"But," Damian called out over the noise, "we must be careful. Even though she's weakened, Niabi is extremely powerful, and she has utterly no shame. The only way we can stop her is together. Coordinated. Cohesive. We will not defeat her fighting as two units. We need to work together." She squared her shoulders. "Following me."

Huathl was the first to break the ensuing silence. "You are not warrior. What you know of battle?"

"I don't know battle," Damian admitted, "and I would appreciate any insight anyone can give me. But I know Niabi. And…" She drew the sword sheathed at her hip and held it aloft. Dark sparks of energy crackled around the hilt and along the blade. Her voice strengthened. "The power of the Goddess of Chaos is with me."

Her eyes passed over the crowd as she let that comment hang a moment. Ashik glanced discreetly around as well. Some of the warriors looked impressed or surprised at the proclamation, though others seemed more interested in the energy flowing around the blade.

"I will lead you to victory," Damian announced, addressing her comrades as much as the warriors. "But I must know that I have your confidence, and your trust. Niabi will show no mercy, so we must be certain to show her none. Will you follow my orders? Will you fight Niabi with everything you have? When the time comes, can you do what needs to be done without hesitation? Can you abandon your fear, your prejudice, and fight together as one? Are you prepared to lay down your lives for what we all know is right?"

She lowered the blade to her side. "If your answer to any of these questions is no, then step aside now. There is too much at stake for any uncertainty." With that, she swept her gaze over the group.

Ashik held his breath as silence descended. Movement at the edges of the group caught his eye, and he saw her mage companions locking eyes uncertainly.

Then, Rhyslen stood, his eyes narrowed and shoulders back. "I'm with you, Damian. We have to stop Niabi."

Closer to Ashik, Masa got to her feet. "Well spoken. I may not know you, but I can see you have de heart of a true leader. I will follow you."

Ais Ainlan then rose. "I also following you. We must working together killing fox head woman."

More warriors rose and added their agreements.

"Just show me where to swing axe!" Huathl barked out with a raised fist. "I be glad to fight for you."

Gradually, all the warriors stood and joined in. Liam did the same, though he did so silently and with a distant look in his eyes that made Damian frown softly.

Ashik then noticed Poppy laying a hand on Merle's shoulder with a sad smile before she, too, moved to her feet.

"I'm with yae too, Damian," she said. "Maybe this wasn't what I was plannin' on doin' with my life, but even if I die fightin' Niabi, I can be proud o' doin' somethin' right."

Cheers rang out and a grateful smile crossed Damian's face. "Thank you," she said earnestly. "We will need to work out a battle plan soon, but first, let us eat. We must keep up our strength."

Another round of agreements rose and everyone tucked into their meals with relish. Many finished in short order and quickly spread out to the open field just outside their camp site to spar and practice with their various weapons. Ashik watched as Damian slipped through the trees after eating. Curiously, he trailed after her.

She stopped near the edge of the trees, a little away from where the warriors sparred. To Ashik's surprise, she then drew the sword sheathed at her belt. She didn't practice with it, however. She simply held it loosely within one hand while the other pulled something out of her bag.

He stood several paces away while she leaned over both items, occasionally holding up the hand she clutched something small within. With the clacks and clangs of weapons ringing nearby, he couldn't hear anything from her, though he thought he saw movement that suggested her saying something under her breath.

For a long minute, he merely watched her, wondering what would happen. Gradually, he grew bored, and he was about to walk away when Damian held up her hand and a gout of flame flared above her fingers.

Ashik leaned back at the display, and Damian seemed as surprised as he did. Then, she half-crouched, paused a moment, and then swung her arm around. As she did, a streak of fire fed by nothing swept through the air after her gesture. It lit up the trees for a brief moment before, lacking fuel, it swiftly burned out.

Ashik tilted his head. "How did you do that?"

She spun, her yellow eyes enlarging as she saw him standing a few paces away.

"And why do you hold the sword?" he added, brows knitting.

Her attention drifted to the bare blade in her hand. "It's a focus for my power. I..."

Before she could say more, a voice opposite Ashik called out, "Hoy!"

They both turned to find a Makil staring at Damian.

"You fight with a sword?" the woman said. "Come spar with us!"

"No, no," Damian answered. "I don't know how to fight with a sword."

The Makil looked only more incredulous. "You have a sword but don' know how to use it?"

"Come!" boomed a Kathec now standing behind her. "We teach you."

Damian faced them with a look like a cornered mouse. "I don't..."

"Come, come!" the Makil pressed, stepping forward to take Damian's arm. "What's de use of having a sword you cannot use?"

Damian gave Ashik a helpless look as the warriors urged her toward the open space. He grinned and shrugged in return.

"It wouldn't hurt to know some basics," he said, recalling his own lessons with the machete. He may not have wanted to fight, but Damian was preparing to battle the malakh, and she had some of the best warriors of the free lands to teach her.

As the Makil and Kathec pushed her past the tree line, however, her gaze shifted, and a stricken expression crossed her face. Curiously, Ashik followed the line of her eyesight. Liam strode away, back into the forest and farther from Damian.

Ashik turned to follow. Cloaked in black as he was, he melded with the shadows as he made his way around the edges of the camp site. Only the snow gave him away.

Stepping in his prints, Ashik followed as Liam moved around the camp, keeping out of sight of those who remained near the fires. The mercenary finally stopped near the tent he had erected before the meal, his breath clouding on the cold air as he stared into the forest.

For a moment, Ashik simply watched him. His face had been an impassive mask from the moment Ashik first saw him, yet he had given subtle clues showing turmoil within. Even now, under the moonlight dappled by the bare branches, his eyes were faintly narrowed in an expression of weariness, or pain. It looked more like the same upset that showed on Damian's face when she looked toward him throughout the day.

"You have been cold toward her," Ashik said softly.

Liam spun, his shoulder-length hair whirling around his face as he turned a suspicious look to Ashik.

"She doesn't seem to understand why," Ashik went on.

Liam turned away again.

Cautiously, Ashik strode around the mercenary, trying to see his face. "In my experience, there are only a few reasons why someone would act that way unexpectedly. You're still here, so it isn't that you don't care or your feelings have changed. So it seems to me that either she did something wrong—which seems unlikely, since she doesn't understand your reactions—or you have."

Liam didn't move as Ashik stepped in front of him. The mercenary was as tall as Huathl. Not as muscular, but equally as intimidating. He stared at Ashik with unfathomable blue eyes.

"Have you ever killed anyone?"

Ashik leaned back, startled by the question. "No."

"Neither has she." His eyes drifted toward the edge of the forest, where the sounds of sparring and cheering could faintly be heard in the distance. A deep sadness fell over his eyes. "She doesn't know how it kills part of yourself." The mask returned, and he turned toward his tent. "She is better off without that kind of pain in her life."

With that, he strode off. This time, Ashik merely watched, his brows knitted in confusion.

Liam hadn't denied it when Ashik implied that the mercenary had done something wrong. He recalled the hurt look in Damian's eyes as Liam walked away, a pain that didn't know why. Clearly, Liam held some guilt that would take more than a few minutes' digging to uncover.

Shaking his head, Ashik returned to the camp site, taking a different path through the trees than Liam had. Focused on his steps through the snow, he didn't realize he came upon other people until he stepped between two trees and nearly ran into them.

"Oh," Ashik said as Rhyslen made a little yelp and Poppy and Merle looked at him in surprise.

"I'm sorry," Ashik added with a smile. "I didn't mean to surprise you."

"It's all right," Rhyslen assured him, his shoulders relaxing as he gathered up a handful of satchets scattered around him. Poppy, however, gave Ashik a tight smile, her eyes flitting to Merle as the other man stared at Ashik.

Ashik tried to give the curly-haired woman a disarming look. "I appreciate you giving Damian your support tonight. It takes a lot of courage to be willing to fight for what you believe in, especially if you're not a warrior by nature."

A wry grin crossed her face. "Well, I wouldn't necessarily say that."

Ashik tilted his head aside as he stepped closer to the fire they sat around. "Oh?" Rhyslen scooted aside and gestured at the ground beside him, and Ashik nodded gratefully as he lowered to the frozen dirt.

"It's always been in my nature to protect people," Poppy explained.

Rhyslen smiled at her. "I did notice how you immediately took to Merle back at the fort."

Reaching over, Poppy playfully tousled Merle's hair. "'E clearly needed someone to help 'im out o' his shell. Plus, 'e reminded me of my brother."

"Did you have many siblings?" Ashik asked. He had often found that willingness to reach out to others and empathize with them in people from large families.

"Eight of 'em," Poppy answered. "I was the oldest." Her face soured. "Pa didn' take too kindly to lookin' after us all after Ma died. I ended up doin' most o' the work 'round the house."

"Is that how you ended up coming to Yanuk's?" Rhyslen wondered.

"Huh!" Poppy barked in a half laugh, half scoff. "I wouldn'a' minded just takin' care o' my brothers and sisters. The trouble were how much Pa liked his drink, an' his strap." She sent Rhyslen an even stare. "When ol' Helena found me, I was in the town stocks for hittin' back."

Ashik and Rhyslen's eyebrows rose simultaneously.

"Figures, dunnit?" Poppy's attention was now on Merle as she rubbed his back. "Man can raise his hand to his own family much as he like, but when a girl fights back, that's a crime."

Rhyslen seemed to deflate. "I never knew… I'm sorry."

She shrugged, showing no sign that her disinterest was feigned. "It's all ancient history now. But I never had much stomach for bullies, like this Niabi. I just hope my brothers and sisters are doin' all right."

Ashik shook his head. "It's unfair how women are treated here."

"Hey." Poppy straightened and faced Ashik. "Tell me about those women warriors. They don' look like they got any men among 'em."

Ashik smiled. "That's because men aren't allowed to wield weapons in the Makil empires. Women control everything there— the nobility, the armies, guilds, their own families. Men don't have many rights."

Her eyebrows crawled high up her forehead. "No kiddin'?"

Rhyslen, however, frowned, scrawling on the dirt in front of him with a stick. "It's always one or the other. It seems like Yanuk was the only one to make sure men and women were treated with equal respect."

"There are a number of free peoples who treat men and women as equals," Ashik countered. "In Rtura, for instance, there is hardly any difference between what the two can do. And Ialla's people don't even refer to each other by gender. They might be a simpler people, but it seems they are much more advanced in how they treat each other."

Merle suddenly stared at Ashik curiously, and spoke for the first time. "Aren't Zahni all barbarians?"

Ashik turned to him, eyes widening at the bluntness of the question. As Rhyslen and Poppy sputtered out apologies, Ashik found a surprisingly guileless look on Merle's face, full only of childlike curiosity. He didn't even seem to react to Rhyslen's embarrassment and Poppy's discomfort.

Taking in a breath, Ashik calmly said, "First, please do not call us 'Zahni'. It is seen as an insulting generalization, based on a western misunderstanding of the term 'zahan'. We are the free peoples."

Poppy watched him speak with cautious optimism, though Rhyslen's patchwork face remained slightly red.

"Secondly," Ashik went on, "let me ask you, how do you think the free peoples see westerners such as Fanerians?"

Merle blinked. "Smart? Enlightened?"

Both the others looked uncomfortable again, though they didn't interrupt.

Ashik shook his head. "In the Makil empires, all citizens enjoy clean, running water, and even the destitute are cared for. Their knowledge and technology is unparalleled. Rtura has a culture and traditions far older than Faneria. And that's not to speak of any of the other free peoples that aren't represented here."

He gestured to Poppy. "They see women treated inferior to men. People who look different, or act different," he added, waving a hand toward Rhyslen and Merle, "are ignored, if not actively harmed. Many of the free peoples cannot fathom this kind of treatment toward a country's own citizens."

Ashik gave Merle a moment. Brow knitted in furious concentration, Merle considered before speaking slowly. "So… the free peoples think we're barbarians?"

Ashik nodded slowly. "I have travelled enough to know that neither is true. Damian is right; our similarities far outweigh our differences. I only wish more people on both sides of the mountains understood that."

He watched his audience carefully. Poppy and Rhyslen exchanged a glance, surprise and understanding written all over their faces. Merle appeared only satisfied to have his curiosity sated.

"I'm sorry I've been so cold to yae," Poppy eventually said.

"Me, too," Rhyslen said.

Poppy added, "I didn' mean… it's just…"

Ashik gave her a warm smile. "I forgive you. It takes strength to face one's own prejudices, and I deeply appreciate your willingness to open your mind."

"Thank you," Rhyslen replied, and then grinned wryly. "After growing up in Yanuk's care, I always try to treat everyone with equal respect… but I guess I still have a ways to go."

Reaching out, Ashik laid a hand on Rhyslen's shoulder. "We can all better ourselves, and we should all strive to do so. That you can recognize that is the first step in the right direction."

"You seem pretty open-minded already."

Ashik shrugged. "I have travelled around much of the free lands, and into Faneria and Enseros. I've seen many different peoples and the value in all of them."

"So what are your people like?" Merle piped in.

Leaning his head back, Ashik looked up through the trees. He could barely make out the outlines of the bare branches against the deep night sky. "I'll tell you tomorrow. I think we should get to sleep while we can for tonight."

"I agree," Poppy said.

"Thanks for speaking with us," Rhyslen remarked. "It's nice to meet you properly, Ashik."

Ashik stood, smiling. "You as well. Sleep well."

The rest called out 'good night' as Ashik moved around the fire deeper into the camp. Movement at another fire between the trees caught his eye and he approached it, finding Ialla sitting alone and eating.

She looked up as he drew near and brightened when she saw him. "Ashik!" Setting down her food, she stood, taking his hands. Then, she glanced through the forest toward where the sounds of clacking weapons continued to ring. "Is everything all right?"

He smiled at her large, dark eyes. "Yes. The warriors don't need to focus on leading me by the hand with a machete I will never be comfortable holding. I think I've found my place now."

Redge's mind whirled as he made his way through the castle, unable to focus as his attention flitted from topic to topic. He strode swiftly and purposefully toward the meeting room, servants darting out of his way as he walked.

He had entered the council room and the door had nearly shut behind him before he stopped, blinking. The room was empty, save for him and the duke, already seated at the table.

"Sir Warwick," the duke greeted, standing.

"My Lord Duke," Redge stammered. "I beg your forgiveness— did I misread the time of the meeting?"

"No," the duke answered with a discernably false calm. He nodded toward the doors and the servant standing outside shut them, closing Redge and the duke in silence. The duke stepped slowly around the table toward him, his voice lowering. "I asked you to come before the meeting began so that I could speak with you personally."

Dread settled over Redge. A hundred dire thoughts rushed through his mind and he could no longer decide which was worse. He tried to keep his face straight and voice steady. "What can I do for you, Your Grace?"

The duke let out a sigh, and suddenly Redge could see the weariness in his eyes. His voice dropped further so that Redge could barely hear his next words.

"Is it true that your knight who was set to guard the witch from the Battle of Albrith lost her?"

Redge's eyes widened, both in surprise of this pronouncement and fear of repercussion. There was no accusation in the duke's words, however, only a tiredness that spoke of a futile hope that he was wrong.

"Yes. She attacked him in a village about a week from here and fled from him in the night." He hurried to add, "I only learned this last night."

The duke nodded slowly. "I have no doubt of that. If nothing else, I know you are loyal." He turned away to face the large map of Faneria on the wall. "Unfortunately, the problem is far larger than that."

A curious look crossed Redge's face. "Your Grace?"

"There are those in Albrith who are flaunting this as proof that the king's decision to spare her was wrong, the latest in a long line of ill choices they say make him unfit for rule."

Until that moment, Redge didn't think his back could feel any tighter. "They speak of open revolt against the king?" He couldn't keep the incredulity out of his voice.

"It hasn't come to that yet, but this faction gains more power every day. Especially since this news. I assume some spy of theirs heard of the incident and made haste to Albrith to further their cause."

Redge ran a hand through his hair. It felt thinner than he remembered. "Is there anything we can do, Your Grace?"

The duke inhaled deeply, rolling his shoulders back. "You've done plenty. This knowledge has helped me to come to a decision long in the making."

The door opened then, admitting the first of the other advisors into the meeting. Redge quietly greeted the lord who arrived and took his usual seat near the end of the table as the duke moved around to the head.

By the time the meeting adjourned, Redge walked with a smoother gait and straighter posture than he had in weeks.

Chapter 21
Shadow and Light

THE TREES DISPERSED and snow-covered farmland, barren at the onset of winter, spread out as Damian led her new band of warriors. The empty land of gentle hills, dotted with an occasional copse of trees, stretched as far as the eye could see. The stark openness, the emptiness of the massive sky, allowed them to see Niabi long before they were able to reach her. Even at such a great distance, the fact that she travelled alone, on foot, without any pack animal or other visible supplies, made it clear that they had found her.

Hiding their own supplies in a sheltered nook below a snow-coated outcrop, Damian sent the first two groups ahead after they passed Niabi to the north. Poppy led the way south with Ashik and some of his warriors. Merle followed, along with Liam and more of the free peoples. Damian watched them go, seeing no discernible change as they made their way across the plains, but as she glanced down at Rhyslen, she saw him focused not quite on his friends, but on the footprints in the snow they left behind.

"You're sure you have enough fennel to maintain the unseeing spell?" she asked him quietly.

"Merle is never wrong. If he says we have enough, then we do. As long as you're ready to do this."

Damian straightened in her seat atop the black horse, one of the free people's pack animals. She was the only one mounted. "We are." She didn't have to strengthen her conviction with her merchant voice. Deep inside, unease writhed, anxiety that she was leading experienced warriors into battle, but it remained buried beneath determination. She had been planning for this moment for weeks. All that mattered now was stopping Niabi.

The warriors accompanying them seemed satisfied with her answer, and Rhyslen nodded faintly.

Damian watched Poppy's and Merle's forces cut nearly due south across the plains, well ahead of where Niabi continued marching through the snow. Poppy's group pulled ahead, and Damian urged the horse forward, Rhyslen and the warriors continuing on foot beside her.

A twinge of discomfort crept over her skin as she watched Niabi continue her trek, heedless of the force bearing down on her. Much as Damian hated Niabi and understood that this was the only way they could hope to stop the malakh, it still felt wrong to attack unseen. A few of her companions had echoed the sentiment when she suggested it, but agreed that it was their best hope for success, and survival. The free warriors, even those who agreed with Damian, insisted she deserved no such consideration.

She had considered approaching Niabi in plain view, perhaps call out Niabi or offer for her to surrender. Memories of the disdain in the fox woman's eyes as she threatened to murder Damian or her companions, and Ashik's stories of their battle with her and Niabi's treatment of the captives, abandoned that thought.

Niabi had no honour. If Damian wanted to keep her force alive, she had to acknowledge that.

Gradually, the malakh's tall form crept out of the distance as Damian continued her approach. Poppy's force had moved south of Niabi's path, Merle's group nearly in position directly in front of the malakh, and Damian was close enough to see Niabi's head swivel from side to side.

"She senses something," Rhyslen said.

"Are you sure she cannot see us?" asked another of the free warriors as Niabi's muzzle lifted and she scented the air.

"Steady," Damian said. "She might suspect something, but the spell works on creatures of magic as well as humans. If she knew where we were, she would already be attacking us." She noticed some of the others looking roughly her way across the plains. Raising the crystals tied around her neck, she rubbed them with her thumb and spoke the incantation to activate the far-speaking spell on them both.

"Keep going."

Poppy and Merle muttered acknowledgements through the crystals and continued.

By the time they were in position, Niabi moved at a half-crouch, clearly aware that something was amiss. Poppy's group was arranged a hundred paces south of Damian and Merle's force was fifty paces west of Niabi, forming a triangle with the malakh at its back edge. Poppy and Merle, with their warriors, moved into place atop small rises from a wide arc around, so as not to leave any footprints for Niabi to see.

Damian tightened her fingers around the reins of the horse as the warriors with her readied their weapons.

It's time to put an end to this.

She raised the crystals to her mouth again.

"Now."

Niabi's ear twitched, but as arrows flew toward her from three directions, she growled and leaped back. One planted in her shoulder as she struggled to dodge and she let out a snarl, though only half of the arrowhead seemed to penetrate. Part of Damian couldn't help feeling ill as the second volley flew and the fox woman blindly retreated back, not having enough time to see the arrows before they converged on her.

"Go!" Damian commanded, both to the warriors beside her and through the crystals.

Raising their weapons, the Makils and Kathecs charged down the slope toward Niabi.

Niabi focused on the new threats as they passed out of the protection of the unseeing spell. A third volley of arrows fell before the charging warriors drew too close. Another arrow planted in Niabi's thigh, but aside from a brief stumble, she ignored the wound.

Damian held her breath as the charging warriors converged on Niabi, who watched them without moving. As they raised their weapons, Niabi nimbly leaped aside, darting beneath a swinging pike and spinning behind the wielder, dropping her with a hard kick. Niabi leaped over the fallen warrior as two others near her stumbled, their feet clearly stuck in place. Damian could see dried grass wrapping around a fourth as Niabi turned to face a charging eagle warrior. She twisted effortlessly out of the path of his blow and knocked him to the ground with a flat-handed blow to the back of his neck.

Then, the snow shifted around her feet and Niabi let out a cry, stumbling but not moving her feet. Damian could barely see the slabs of stone jutting out of the ground into Niabi's ankles, holding her in place. Damian couldn't help flinching at the sight, remembering Yanuk's mages casting the same spell against her during the Battle of Albrith. The light of small fires shone against the grass holding the other warriors to the ground.

Niabi's eyes darted around at the movement as the nearest eagle warrior regained his feet and charged toward her back.

With a wrenching of her leg, Niabi pulled one bloodied foot away and turned just as the eagle warrior swung. He aimed high, trying to smash his axe into her head, but she grasped his wrist before the blow could land and dragged him around in front of her. Wrapping her other hand around his throat, she effortlessly lifted him off the ground as the other warriors pulled themselves free of the constricting grass.

As Damian watched, the eagle warrior's arms and legs fell limp and his flesh desiccated, shrivelling back on his bones. His skin turned grey as his muscles wasted away. Niabi's golden fur, however, seemed to regain some of its lustre, and her back straightened.

Damian gasped, cupping a hand over her mouth, and beside her, Rhyslen swore.

Niabi carelessly tossed the body behind her and lifted her other foot free as if it was merely buried in snow.

"Don't let her touch you!" Damian cried as the rest of the warriors rose. Several seconds of frenetic activity passed before she realized the unseeing spell still covered her. The warriors engaged with Niabi couldn't hear her.

Niabi's eyes narrowed as she charged. The remaining warriors kept their distance, a spear-wielding Makil stabbing out while another danced back and threw small blades at the malakh. The Rturans beside Rhyslen, no longer trying to hit Niabi with arrows, hurried down the slope to join the others, along with the rest from Poppy's and Merle's forces.

"You coward," Niabi snarled as she danced around the stabbing blades, hardly reacting to the arrows and throwing knives that struck her. "I should expect no less from a cursed child than to strike against me from the shadows when I am alone."

Damian's grip tightened around the reins. From the corner of her eye, she saw Rhyslen clench his fingers around the ashen remains of the fennel in his hand.

"You have the audacity to try to take the high ground after the things you've done?" Damian snapped back. "Threatening to kill Garrick just so you can make Nephrita surrender? Stealing people's lives?"

Niabi growled.

"Destroying part of Albrith and murdering people who live

there?"

"I am bringing Light back to the world!" the fox woman roared.

"Light never left! But your gods care more about how many people worship them than taking care of their followers."

Dried grasses sprang out of the snow and wrapped around some warriors' legs while others were knocked down by protruding stones or pits opening up in the earth. Poppy and Merle edged partway down the hill as they focused on their spells, Ashik and Liam reaching the edge of the melee to cut free the ones who were bound. Rhyslen glanced at Damian and she nodded, and they proceeded partly down the rise.

"They are the True Gods!" Niabi shouted back. "You humans should be grateful for their favour!" Her movements grew jerky and sluggish and she struggled to defend herself against the attacks converging on all sides.

Damian fought to steady her voice. "Their 'favour' levelled a village that never did anything but worship them. At least the Gods of Time don't claim to be righteous when they only care about themselves. The Gods of Light are a poison, and you are the wound that lets it in. Show her the same mercy that she has shown her followers!"

The free warriors responded with a yell, some shouting for their country or fallen comrades. Blades glinted in the wan light as they charged Niabi as one from all sides.

Niabi's eyes flashed between the warriors as they bore down on her. She raised her arms and then swung them down. A ring of earth four paces wide around her abruptly dropped and then sprang back up, like a ripple from a stone dropped into still water. The ripple spread so quickly that Damian barely saw the warriors collapse before her horse stumbled and bucked. It whinnied when Damian lurched over and bounced off its neck. She crashed into the snow as the horse fell just behind her, Rhyslen yelping to her side.

The rumble of earth quickly faded away. Damian pushed her upper body up and looked out. She barely glimpsed the cluster of warriors just now rising before a flash of gold at the corner of her eye caught her attention.

Niabi was the wolf-sized fox, hurrying through the snow at the top of the rise to the west before disappearing over it.

Damian lunged to her feet and grabbed the reins of the horse, now scrambling to stand. Its nostrils flared and the whites of its eyes were showing. Damian shushed it and patted its neck as it got its hooves under it and rose. Hurriedly, she mounted and kicked the horse into a gallop, throwing her cloak off as it dragged the air. She soon reached the top of the rise to the west and saw Niabi a hundred paces ahead, snow flying up from her paws as she ran.

Damian urged the horse faster as she rode after the malakh, its hooves cutting through the snow far easier than the fox's paws. Then, movement to the side caught her eye. She had only a moment to look curiously at a trail running through the snow before Niabi moved strangely. By the time Damian faced her again, Niabi was two-legged once more, standing in the snow ahead.

Damian pulled the horse to a stop fifty paces away, readying herself for an attack. As the horse fell still, however, she could see Niabi lurching and swatting at what first appeared to be a strange mist swirling around her.

In between flutters of movement, Damian could make out a black cloak flowing around the figure, and a black blade slashing at Niabi.

Damian's breath caught as she watched Liam attack, Niabi blocking some of the blows with a small blade in her hand. The malakh's stunning robe tore and a few more bleeding cuts joined the wounds inflicted by Ashik's warriors. Niabi's attacks grew more aggressive, however, her long arm swinging in quick arcs through the air as she pushed toward the misty form of Liam.

As Damian watched, Liam's body increasingly appeared out of the mist, and he backed away as Niabi's small weapon bore down on him. The magic of his amulet was wearing off.

Kicking the horse's flanks, Damian approached again. Even moving faster than any normal person could, Liam could no longer attack with Niabi's savage slashes bearing down. Her lips curled back to show her gleaming fangs as her arm moved in a blur.

Damian lashed the reins as she came within twenty paces of the confrontation and she could see the last of his amulet's power disappear. She reached for Vashnir as she rode around Niabi's back. The fox woman was so focused on Liam that she didn't seem to notice Damian approaching.

Damian had just begun to draw the sword when Niabi feinted, moved inside Liam's reach, and drove her dagger hilt-deep into his chest.

All feeling seemed to flee Damian's body as he leaned over Niabi's arm, his face contorted in surprise and pain.

"*Liam!*"

Niabi yanked the blade free as she twisted around to sneer at Damian. With a flick of her free hand, a column of earth shot out of the ground and smashed into Damian. It knocked the horse over with a whinny and threw Damian over it, the hot sting of the blow quickly shifting to the frozen bite of snow as she fell.

Setting aside the ache in her head and all along her side, she pushed herself up. Over the horse, she saw Niabi leap to the side with her arms outstretched, shifting back into her four-legged form.

Cringing at the pain running through her body, Damian rose and focused on thoughts of chaos.

Niabi had taken barely three paces before the air flared with searing white light and a thump resounded in Damian's heart and through the earth. A crackle and rumble of thunder rolled into the distance, and Damian blinked to find Niabi halted before a patch of melted snow.

Damian moved around the horse, stumbling once more to its legs, as Niabi turned, towering over her again, to face her.

"Enough!" Damian shouted. "This malicious conquest of yours has taken too many lives already. It's time to put an end to what you started."

Niabi's muzzle wrinkled as her lips pulled back. "What I started? No, *this* is where it all began." She held up the dagger significantly, but Damian trembled with rage as she focused on the blood on the short blade.

"Your heretic gods made their intentions plain as day when they cast this into the home of the True Gods. *They* announced their intention to reignite the war. Those treacherous gods started all this again."

Damian wrapped her fingers around Vashnir's grip, the shape and weight now a familiar feeling. "Even if that were true, they're kinder to their own followers than you are." Drawing the sword with a clear, vibrant ring, Damian held it up high. "Gods of Time! If you truly are watching, then lend me your aid so I can cast down this blight upon Elderra!"

A rumble through the air was echoed by a grinding of stone to either side of Damian rushing toward her. She lowered her hand and reached for her power, but in that blink of an eye, she knew she was too late. As the stone shot out of the ground toward her, however, it cracked loudly and crumbled at Damian's sides.

A black mist swirled around Damian, crackling and electric with power.

Niabi sneered. A rustle of dried grass sprang up beneath Damian's feet. Tendrils of mist flowed out, stopping the grass before it reached Damian's boots. She stared at it for a second, entranced.

Then, Damian tightened her grip on Vashnir and narrowed her eyes at Niabi.

Niabi eyed the mist warily as Damian strode forward, brandishing her sword. The mist flowed after Damian, swirling and eddying over the snow. Damian still wasn't certain about using her power to unlock the energy in spell ingredients, but there was no guessing how a sword worked. And now, it felt reassuring in her hand as she approached Niabi.

Niabi lunged with a growl. Damian swiftly turned her sword up to parry the dagger, bracing her arms as the malakh struck hard. Her arms jarred from the impact and she took a shaky step back into the snow as Niabi pushed her dagger, and Vashnir, closer to Damian. Close up, Niabi loomed like a giant over Damian and she felt like a child in the shadow of the fox woman.

While their blades remained locked, Niabi swung her free arm down in a blur toward Damian's face, claws outstretched. Damian barely had time to see it, but a flare of energy crackled instinctively out of her. A flash of shadow snapped against Niabi's descending hand and she leaped back with a yelp.

As Damian's sword descended at her side, grass rustled through the snow and stuck the blade in place. Niabi jumped forward, swinging her dagger toward Damian. Damian let go of the sword with one hand and held it up toward Niabi. The falling dagger bounced and cracked off an invisible wall that flared blue before Damian's hand. While Niabi stumbled from the block, Damian pushed her thoughts down the blade of her sword. The grass burnt to ash and allowed her to pull her sword free.

Damian moved the sword in front of her again. Niabi half-crouched before her, but her eyes flitted to either side. Damian chanced a quick glance from the corner of her eyes. Her warriors surrounded them, watching intently with bows and throwing knives at the ready.

Niabi looked uncertain. Her ears twitched.

The icy air bit at Damian's face and lungs, her breath clouding on the air. The black mist swirled beside and behind her.

Damian sprang forward. Niabi swiftly brought her dagger up to stop Damian's sword. Niabi grabbed at Damian's shoulder, but she barely felt the claws dig into the layers of her clothes before the black mist sizzled. Niabi lurched back with a hiss.

Damian charged again, but Niabi kicked up, her furred foot slamming up underneath Damian's ribs. She coughed as she dropped to her knees, trying to focus on deflecting further attacks, but Niabi turned and retreated through the snow instead, straight toward one of the warriors.

Pushing aside the pain in her stomach to match the ache along her side and head, Damian straightened and threw a hand forward. As Niabi's legs sank into the snow, they stuck fast, and she let out a cry. Stumbling, she tried to pull her feet out of what had become solid ice.

Wincing, Damian raised Vashnir and raced after Niabi. The malakh struggled against the constricting ice as Damian lifted the sword to plunge into Niabi.

One step away, a stone jutted out of the ground in front of Damian and she tripped. She fell too quickly to correct her aim, so instead, she leaned all her weight on the sword as she drove it into Niabi's thigh. Niabi snarled as the sword stabbed in, Damian hanging off the hilt, but the blade only sank half a finger's length into her leg.

Before Damian could recover, Niabi's thick tail smacked her away, the sword pulling free as Damian tumbled to the side. By the time Damian regained her feet, Niabi had broken free of the ice and moved toward another of the warriors surrounding them, twisting away from the knives and arrows that flew toward her.

"No!" Damian shouted. A ring of flames shot up around her and Niabi. "You will face me."

Niabi turned to Damian with her ears flat back, great clouds of steaming breath hissing through her bared fangs.

"You wish me to kill you so badly?" she snarled, her voice barely human anymore. "So be it!"

She charged with a vicious swing of her dagger, too quick for Damian to meet it with her sword. A flash of blue flared in front of Damian, but the blade screeched off the energy barrier and continued, slicing with a hot bite across Damian's cheekbone and the top of her ear. She cried out as she finished raising her sword, trying to turn it to swipe Niabi with the blade. Before she could complete her swing, Niabi's head snapped down and her jaws clamped around Damian's wrist, sharp teeth digging through her thick glove and stabbing into her arm. Damian screamed again as Niabi's muzzle crackled and hissed from the black mist, but her fangs remained locked on, and her free hand reached toward Damian's throat.

Damian released the grip of her sword with her free hand and desperately smacked and pried at Niabi's muzzle, the pain in her wrist nearly blinding her. As it was, she couldn't make out what the warriors around her were shouting.

Then, Niabi's jaws ripped off of Damian's arm as she was thrown backward, stumbling for balance. Wincing, Damian dropped the sword as her arm fell. She gently clutched her bloodied wrist, trying to knit the wound together by focusing on thoughts of chaos and order, but pain continued searing through her arm.

A strangled noise before her drew her attention. The warriors had managed to lasso Niabi's arms, several on each side yanking at the ropes as another tightened around her throat from behind. Her fur looked ashen and brittle, her dark eyes going cloudy as she struggled against the bonds. Niabi let out choked cries as more arrows and knives lodged into her from all sides.

"Now, Damian!" Ashik cried, leaning his full weight against one of the ropes as they fought to hold her in place.

Maybe I can't make myself stronger, she thought, recalling some of the lessons the warriors had taught her, *but I know what can.*

Picking up the sword in her left hand, Damian charged toward Niabi. She focused her thoughts and energy on the blade of the sword and it began to glow red hot.

Vashnir, help me…

With a rabid howl, Niabi yanked her arms free, half a dozen warriors falling to the ground to either side of her. She swung again with the dagger, aiming toward Damian's face.

If I do not strike her down now, no one will…

Ducking beneath the short blade, Damian planted her feet in the ground and shoved up with the sword.

…let us break her!

She heard a crack as she stabbed the sword into Niabi's chest. The fox woman lurched, letting out a choked sound as her arm bounced off Damian's head, the dagger missing its mark. Gritting her teeth, Damian pushed harder, the sword sliding further in with a scraping sound as Niabi's knees buckled, her lithe body weighing heavily against Damian.

The warriors let out a whoop as Damian crouched with Vashnir impaled in the malakh's chest. Niabi's head tipped and Damian looked straight up to find a strange look in the black eyes.

Misery.

"Master…" Niabi uttered.

Then, her body fell limp. Damian struggled to tilt her sword to the side as Niabi's weight fell fully upon her, dropping the fox woman's body into the snow beside her. Damian watched, panting, as Niabi stopped breathing, muscles falling still and whiskers spreading out to a relaxed position.

A wave of revulsion spread through Damian as she stared down at the body of the malakh, servant of the gods, that she had killed. Blood stained her gloves, the wound on her cheek and ear and the one on her wrist stung fiercely, and she felt so exhausted she thought she would collapse in the snow beside Niabi.

Crunching footsteps through the snow tore her from her reverie. The warriors cheered her victory as they approached. They took her under the arms as she swayed, struggling to remain focused on her surroundings.

Dazed, Damian raised her head and turned. The black mist was gone. The only things around her were trodden snow, weary but elated warriors, the horse…

…and Rhyslen, kneeling beside a body in the snow twenty paces away.

CHAPTER 22
FALLEN

CHEST CONSTRICTING, DAMIAN pushed between the warriors and stumbled across the open space toward Rhyslen. The aches along her side, face, stomach, and wrist seemed like splinters to the deep, gaping pain in her heart.

Liam lay in the snow beside Rhyslen as she neared. In a glimpse, she saw Rhyslen's bag and the open pouches of spell ingredients beside him, and the stricken look on his face.

Damian slowed beside them, her entire body trembling. Liam lay almost peacefully in the snow, but for his brown hair splayed out around his head. Damian could barely see the gash in the dark leather of his breastplate.

She collapsed to her knees beside him. "Liam?" Her voice choked as she reached out to stroke his face. "Liam? Please…"

He stirred and moaned at her touch.

"Liam!"

Blinking blearily, he looked between her and Rhyslen before his blue eyes focused on her.

"Damian…" He raised a trembling hand to touch his glove gently below the wound on her face. The soft touch seemed to wipe away the pain. "You're hurt."

She sniffled. "It's fine. I did it. Niabi's dead."

The corner of his mouth turned up. "I knew you could. I should have given you my amulet. You would likely have had more success than me." He coughed and Damian could hear the gurgle in his breathing.

Movement from Rhyslen drew Damian's eye. He shook his head faintly. Damian trembled as she faced Liam again.

"Liam," she uttered. "Liam, hang in there." She placed her unhurt hand over the gash in his breastplate and shut her eyes, trying to reach her senses into the wound. *I fixed Ais Ainlan, I can fix this…*

Yet, in her pain and exhaustion, she couldn't sense the difference between order and disorder. Wincing from the effort, she focused harder.

Liam sucked in a pained breath, barely suppressing a moan.

Gasping, Damian pulled her hand back. "I'm sorry!"

He coughed, settling back in the snow. His face twitched slightly as he took in her expression.

"It is… worse than it feels, isn't it?"

She reached for her power once more, but she was exhausted and it wouldn't come. "Just hold on. Stay with me. Please."

His facade broke as he leaned his head back. "No, it's all right. I can't ruin anything else." He faced her again. For the first time since she had known him, a genuine smile lit up his face. It was radiant, completely transforming him and yet somehow making him look more natural, more like him, than she had ever seen.

"Damian… I love you."

Her entire body felt hollow. Hot tears flowed down her cheeks. She could barely hear her own voice reply.

"I love you, too."

His gloved fingers reached up toward the back of her neck and she leaned toward him with the weak tug. Her heart pounded even as it frayed apart. He lifted his head off the ground, trembling at the effort, as he drew her in close, and they kissed.

There was little strength behind it and his mouth felt chilled against her own, but the touch sent a thrill through her body at odds with the deep, aching sorrow. As much as she tried to focus on the sensation of his lips on hers, she couldn't help noticing the salty warmth of her tears sliding into their kiss.

His arm and body trembled from the effort of holding himself up and it wasn't long before he dropped back down with a wince. Damian swiftly caught him behind the neck and lowered him gently into the snow. Breathing hard from the effort, he turned to look at her, though his eyes were glassy and didn't focus quite properly. Despite that, his gaze upon her was intense.

"Damian," he said, his voice strained, "promise me one thing."

"Anything," she uttered, her own voice weak from pain.

"No matter what happens," he coughed out, his words halting, "don't lose sight of who you are."

"I won't."

He nodded faintly and his eyelids sagged. "Thank you, Damian."

His voice weakened. "You've made… my life… worth…"

His eyes shut.

"No… no! Liam!"

His breathing was thin and thready, his entire body limp as he lay in the snow.

"No!" She turned a hard look to Rhyslen. "Do something!"

"I can't," he answered firmly.

"He's still breathing! Don't just—"

"Damian!" he cut in. "The wound is too severe. I'm sorry. There's no fixing that. All I can do is mask the pain."

She fell against Liam's chest and sobbed. Snowflakes started falling and the cold seeped into her, so deeply she thought she would never be warm again.

Footsteps walked up behind her.

"I'm sorry, Damian."

Wiping at her nose, she glanced at Ashik. He stood a few paces away, holding her cloak and looking regretful. Her gaze drifted as she noticed the warriors behind him. Two sat in the snow, breathing heavily as Poppy kneeled before them, and another leaned against someone else for support, one leg bent.

Damian swallowed hard as she looked back at Liam.

"Go," she said huskily to Rhyslen. "Help the others. Do whatever you can."

Nodding, Rhyslen gathered his supplies and rose.

Damian said nothing as Ashik approached and held out her cloak. Taking it, she draped it over Liam.

She didn't know how long she knelt there, oblivious to the world around her as she stroked Liam's hair and face. It felt like hours, but the time seemed to drag interminable and it could have been mere minutes. She didn't even look at Ashik as he examined and tended to the wounds on her face and arm, and didn't mention the other lingering aches. She had eyes only for Liam.

He never woke up.

His breathing became so faint that it took Damian a moment before she realized when it stopped altogether. Tears welled up and she leaned over him, crying.

Gradually, the deep, aching pain subsided, leaving her feeling numb. Rising, she found the frigid air biting at her soaked trouser legs and torn glove and sleeve. She picked up her cloak and looked around.

While she had lain there, the warriors had retrieved and laid out the bodies of those killed in the battle. Injuries had been tended among the survivors, though one or two looked like they might succumb to their wounds as well.

Finding enough fuel for a pyre was a challenge, but with the mages' help, they managed to create a big enough fire for the warriors, and Liam. Damian fought back tears as the flames burned high and hot, quickly incinerating the remains. Ashik and a couple of the remaining warriors chanted over the fallen as others sang. Damian could see Rhyslen and Poppy looking uncomfortable at the ceremony and understood how they felt. What could one say to ease the departed when it felt wrong to pray to the Goddess of Life?

Fate, Damian thought as she watched the flames. *Fortune. Truth. Mystery. Change. All of them might watch over Liam and the others. Gods of Time, please guide their spirits along their next journey.*

Silence reigned for long minutes as the flames shrank. Ashik strode over to her as the embers illuminated shadowy shapes no longer identifiable as human.

"Niabi's body has faded. She is gone."

Damian nodded slowly. She knew she should be relieved at that news, but she couldn't muster the energy to care. She followed Ashik back to where the malakh had fallen. The indentation of her body remained in the snow, but all that lay within it was a withered willow branch, a severed foot from a red fox, and a shimmering emerald, now broken in half. Vashnir lay in the snow between the crystal pieces.

Part of her knew that the fist-sized, oval gem was worth a fortune. Expertly cut to reflect the pale winter sky, clear as glass, and a deep, verdant shade, even the fact that it was now broken likely did little to diminish the value of a stone worth probably as much as a small castle. However, as Damian stared at the emerald, all she could think was that it had been Niabi's heart.

Stepping over to where Niabi's arm had fallen, Damian picked up the dagger that had cut her face, still stained with Liam's blood and her own. Its style was old, but it was in impeccable condition, not unlike Nephrita's sword. Niabi's words about that dagger lodged in her mind, nearly breaking through her fog of numbness with discomfort.

Damian sighed, cleaning the dagger blade with snow and the corner of her cloak and slipping it into her belt before doing the same with Vashnir.

"Will you be heading back to the free lands?"

Ashik didn't answer immediately. Damian turned to him. He

shuffled his feet.

"I'm not so certain anymore." At her curious look, he added, "I'm beginning to feel like my place is with you. If you'll continue to have our company."

She glanced over the surviving free warriors. They returned the look with raised chins or deferential bows.

"Do they agree with you?"

Ashik met their eyes as well. "I believe they do." There was a solemnity in his voice she didn't quite understand, but didn't have the heart to ask about it.

She nodded once, surprised to find she was relieved not to have to leave the free warriors just yet. She glanced at each of her companions in turn, the group seeming so much smaller now. Her throat constricted as Liam's absence stood stark and conspicuous among the others still standing, but she pushed the pain to the back of her mind.

"Let's go."

EPILOGUE

IN THE WINTER, the landmarks leading to the underground home were easier to miss, but the trails through the snow in the gully made the door in the hill much more visible.

Damian went inside alone and found only Kina within. At Kina's request, Damian told her how she defeated Niabi.

"There was something else I wanted to ask you about," Damian said after she finished. "Niabi said that this was what started it all." She pulled the dagger from her belt and held it out.

Kina's eyes enlarged. "This is my knife."

Damian blinked. "Yours?"

"I lost it long ago." Reaching forward, she picked it up. "What did she say about it?"

"She said that the Gods of Time threw this into their home, as a challenge."

A look of horror crossed Kina's face. "Oh no…"

"What is it?"

"This knife was given to me by one of the Gods of Time. It was when I interrupted the Duke of Deverell's spell to summon Nephrita, at the doorway to the realm of the Gods of Light. I was facing the duke when this dagger accidentally went through the doorway."

Damian's surprise that Kina had met one of the old gods lasted only briefly. "You mean… this whole war was started because of a mistake?"

A worried frown crossed Kina's face. "I think there is more to it than that. But if this is what the Gods of Light truly believe…"

Damian leaned forward in her chair. "We have to do something."

Kina sighed. "It is too late. The Army of Light passes freely through Hesperia."

A chill stole over Damian. "What?"

"We received a letter from Lyle. The duke allowed the army to pass… and has joined his forces to it."

About the Author

After working for a number of evil empires, Catherine decided to forgo things like a salary and regular human interaction to start a business. She lives near Toronto, Ontario with her husband, daughter, and two crazy tabbies. Visit her website at thejinx.wordpress.com.

9 781928 011330